CHRONICLES OF Kith AND Kin

Carla,
To the connections that outlast time, memory, and distance.
Lauralee

Laura Lee Dooley

Of Kith and Kin
©Laura Lee Dooley

All rights reserved. This book or any portion thereof may not be reproduced or used in any manner whatsoever without the express written permission of the publisher except for the use of brief quotations in a book review.

Print ISBN: 979-8-31780-504-3
eBook ISBN: 979-8-31780-505-0

CONTENTS

1 "Hi, Sis" 1
2 Gathering 17
3 Tour 28
4 Questions 36
5 Comfortable 40
6 Beach 46
7 Dreams 54
8 Feast 59
9 Aura 63
10 Anniversary 67
11 Ache 71
12 Confession 76
13 Secret 85
14 Connection 94
15 Partners 100
16 Solution 113
17 Memory 118
18 Trance 126
19 Samsara 129
20 Resonance 142
21 Experiment 154
22 Nature 160
23 Connection 166
24 Spark 172
25 Conference 178
26 Uncertainty 183

27 Trust 190
28 History 197
29 Glow 214
30 Dissipation 219
31 Secrets 224
32 Threat 230
33 Bait 234
34 Guilt 239
35 Another 244
36 Investigation 253
37 Celebration 261
38 Revelry 269
39 Prelude 275
40 Sparkle 279
41 Morning 286
42 Emergence 291
43 Suspicion 299
44 Aware 304
45 Awakened 309
46 Manifestation 314
47 Flow 317
48 Turning 320
49 Changed 326
50 Enkidu 336
EPILOGUE 343

1
"HI, SIS"

(MAY 12, 2019)

The late afternoon sun beat down on Tae-hee Kim as she stood at the bus stop. While she waited, she cleared away the day's troubles with a silent calculation.

Fifty-five thousand five hundred and sixty-three days. Seven thousand nine hundred and thirty-seven weeks. One hundred fifty-two years. Thirty leap years.

The litany contained a secret she held more closely than any other.

She rolled her neck and shoulders, then stretched her arms. Tugging out the hair band, she ran her fingers through her long black hair, letting the strands brush against her back. A lifetime of stress and weariness had forged her muscles—a century of work as a nurse, fighting exhaustion, danger, and pain day after day. She wasn't famous like Eunice Coleman or the legendary Jang-geum, but her role at Community Care Hospital kept her busy. Fortunately, pain and fatigue vanished quickly.

A deep sigh escaped her lips as she closed her eyes. She drew strength from the cool breeze and the pulse of those around her. The quiet hum of groups was a balm, easing the strain from her work at the hospital.

When the bus arrived, she slipped into the waiting line, moving with the steady rhythm of habit. She scanned her pass and found an empty seat near the back. Dropping into it, she placed her worn backpack in the empty seat beside her and stared out the window, watching the people who passed on the street.

The bus merged into traffic, and the familiar bustle of Springfield filled her senses. She barely noticed the man making his way down the aisle—until he stopped beside her. Her gaze flicked toward him, then to the rest of the bus. Every other seat was full. Suppressing a sigh, she pulled her backpack onto her lap and returned her gaze to the window.

"Gamsahamnida," the man said, taking the now-empty seat beside her.

She would have ignored him had he not thanked her in Korean.

"I'm so glad I finally found you," the man continued, quiet but confident.

Tae-hee tightened her arms around her backpack and retreated into the corner of her seat as she shot him a wary glare.

"Hello, dongsaeng," the man continued. "Did you miss me?" His accent identified him as having originated outside the United States. He sounded British, yet he spoke perfect Korean.

The stranger offered a pleasant smile as Tae-hee scrutinized him.

"What do you mean 'dongsaeng'?" she asked. It was a Korean greeting that an older brother used to address a younger sibling. Although she was born just minutes after her twin brother, Tae-soo, he used the address as a teasing term of endearment when he spoke with her. It was rude for a stranger to call her so.

The man softened his voice and said, "We were born on the tenth day of the second month of the twenty-fourth year of the reign of King Gojong in the country known as Joseon."

Tae-hee's eyes widened.

"Tae-hee," the man said as he met her gaze. "I am Tae-soo, your older brother. Your older twin, to be exact."

Finding it difficult to breathe, Tae-hee put a hand to her chest.

"I know you don't recognize me, but I have an explanation. Please hear me out."

Tae-hee needed to escape. She reached up and pulled the stop-request cord repeatedly. When the bus slowed, she stood and forced the stranger to give way. She rushed to the back door, pushed it open, and leaped to the curb. She hurried down the sidewalk to put distance between herself and the bus.

"Tae-hee! Wait! Please!" the stranger called.

She spun around and held her hands up to the man who pursued her. "Stop!" she yelled. "Stay!"

When the man stopped, Tae-hee scanned her surroundings to get her bearings. Fortunately, she had drawn enough attention from the passersby that she felt safe. Because Springfield was a university town, many students, professors, and townies walked these streets.

She dropped her hands to her side and studied the man. There were two reasons this stranger could not be her twin brother. First, he looked nothing like Tae-soo. Second, her brother was dead. She had seen his battered, bloody, mangled corpse. She had washed him, wrapped him, and buried his ashes at Ganghwa Island, beside the grave of their mother.

Tae-soo's death was the most traumatic event in Tae-hee's life. When grief overwhelmed her, Tae-hee escaped to America. Although she maintained many Korean traditions, the many death anniversaries of her loved ones became a burden. The *jesa* ceremony for Tae-soo was the last one she relinquished, and sometimes she regretted it.

Despite the memories of the devastating loss of her twin, the stranger's self-assured attitude ignited a spark of hope within her. She stepped toward the man and stared into his dark brown eyes. Could these be Tae-soo's eyes? The shape of his face was different, and he was taller. His claim to be her brother seemed impossible. But the twins' very existence challenged impossibilities.

The man remained still and silent while Tae-hee studied him. She narrowed her eyes as she examined his features. Plastic surgery couldn't change someone that much, could it?

"Who are you?" she asked. Nobody knew about Tae-soo, not even Sameer Khan. Angry that a stranger used her dead brother's name to approach her, she growled, "Why are you doing this?"

"Tae-hee," the man said. "Really and truly, I am Tae-soo." Sincerity glistened in his eyes. "Give me time to explain."

She backed away from him. "No. That is impossible. Tae-soo is dead."

"Can we go somewhere to talk?" the man pleaded. He pointed to a cafe just steps behind her. "I'll buy you coffee."

"It's too late for coffee."

"Then tea, a sandwich, dessert—whatever you please."

She *was* hungry since she hadn't eaten lunch. But his offer to buy her a meal might make her beholden to him. Still, he didn't appear threatening, and his claims piqued her curiosity. She pointed at a sandwich shop with seating in front of a window.

The man nodded. "Okay, dongsaeng. We'll go there."

"Stop calling me that," Tae-hee muttered.

The man held the door for her and followed her to the sandwich counter. After Tae-hee ordered her standard tuna salad sandwich, the stranger leaned toward her and whispered, "Are you sure their tuna is *tuna?*"

"Stop," murmured Tae-hee. His comment generated a mixture of frustration and amusement. His sense of humor wasn't unlike her brother's.

The stranger leaned against the counter glass. "Do you have egg mayo?" he asked the sandwich maker. When met with confusion, he frowned. "I guess not. Then, I'll take a ham on wheat."

While Tae-hee's sandwich order was simple, the stranger took time to direct the makers of his meal. His posture was not unlike Tae-soo's. Even his gestures and tone were consistent with those of her twin. As she studied his familiar mannerisms, she began to wish what he said was true.

Another thought entered her mind. If the stranger's claim was true, a public conversation might also reveal her secrets. She didn't want any rumors to spread about her. She liked her life in Springfield.

She pulled out her phone and texted her best friend, Jong-hyun Park, to ask him to meet her at her apartment. When he replied he was on his way, Tae-hee relaxed. With Jong nearby, she could allow this man to present his case.

"Please make the sandwiches to go," she told the sandwich maker.

The stranger drew his brows together but didn't question Tae-hee. He paid for the sandwiches and collected the meals.

"Follow me," instructed Tae-hee.

"Where are we going?"

"Someplace where we can talk."

She led him out of the restaurant and down the sidewalk toward her apartment.

Halfway there, she asked, "How did you find me?"

"Social media. For obvious reasons, I had to meet you in person."

She drew in a sharp breath when she remembered deleting a social media post she wrote during one of the rare times she got drunk. Jong had taken her out to help her overcome a depressing work week at the hospital. By the time Jong dropped her home, she was sober, so she downed more beers. She poured out her loneliness to the ghosts of her family—her mother, father, twin brother, and her foster family. She was an unusual species, a being who remained young and healthy despite living far beyond the standard allotment of human years.

Tae-hee shook her head and frowned, angry at herself for being so careless about a past she kept hidden. She glanced at the stranger, wondering what other information he had found through her social profile posts.

They continued their journey in silence. When they reached Tae-hee's apartment building, Jong stood in the lobby, his shoulder-length hair gathered in a band at the back of his head. He walked toward them, appraising the man who stood beside her.

"Is everything okay?" Jong asked.

Tae-hee nodded, pulled him aside, and whispered, "Can you stay outside my apartment while we talk?"

"Sure."

Jong knew not to ask questions. She'd explain things to him after she learned more about the stranger.

When the elevator arrived, they entered, and Jong pressed the button for the seventh floor. He leaned forward and extended his hand to the stranger. "My name is Jong-hyun Park, but everyone calls me Jong. And you are?"

Taking the handshake, the man replied, "I'm Tae-hee's brother."

"Really?" Jong sought confirmation from Tae-hee.

"It's been a long time since we last met," the man said. "Tae-hee thought I died."

"Aha," said Jong.

Once again, he exchanged glances with Tae-hee, who tried not to cringe. The stranger announced their sibling-ship so easily, even though Tae-hee had yet to accept that characterization of their status. Unfortunately, she couldn't express her thoughts to Jong, and his shaman ancestry did not grant him the gift of telepathy. Besides, she never revealed her true nature to Jong. Only Sameer Khan understood who—and what—she was. Maybe she should have called him as well.

When the elevator doors opened, Tae-hee exited first, followed by the man, then Jong. They walked down the hall in a silent parade.

Tae-hee unlocked the door of her apartment and glanced at Jong again. His calm smile and nod confirmed that he would rescue her if necessary.

Inside the apartment, Tae-hee dropped her backpack on the floor as she stepped out of her shoes and put on her slippers. The stranger removed his sandals.

"I don't have any slippers that will fit you," she said. "Jong wears socks." She walked to the middle of the apartment.

"Is he your boyfriend?" the stranger asked. When Tae-hee didn't respond, the man nodded and said, "I guess I should tell you I go by the name of Kit now."

"Kit," Tae-hee repeated. It was a strange-sounding name for a man and not at all Korean. His carefully crafted identity had holes.

"Do you mind if I look around?" Kit asked.

Tae-hee placed her sandwich bag on the coffee table, shrugged, and folded her arms over her chest. In her attempt to keep her secret, she had invited a stranger into her home. Having Jong outside her door provided a certain level of comfort with that choice. She hoped it was the right one.

Kit placed his sandwich bag beside hers and then strolled through the apartment. He appeared more inquisitive than threatening and took a keen interest in mundane items: the potted plants on the window ledge, reminders left on the wall calendar, and the handwritten notes on the desk. He scanned the various volumes on her bookcase, the pictures on the wall, and the dishes and silverware in the kitchen. When he stopped by the small collection of horse figurines on a shelf, his expression turned pensive as he examined them more closely. He considered the commonplace things in her life with a sort of reverence.

Tae-hee judged Kit's design. He was classically handsome, with well-pronounced cheekbones and dark eyes like hers. Unlike her black hair, his hair was lighter, almost brown.

As she followed him around the apartment, Tae-hee was even more confident that Kit could not be her brother. Tae-soo had only been slightly taller whereas this person was noticeably so. For that reason alone, there was no way that this tall stranger named Kit could be Tae-soo.

Before she could stop him, Kit walked down the short hallway to her bedroom and blew a long whistle. Tae-hee ran down the hall after him.

"Qu'est-ce que c'est?" he murmured as he walked over to the corkboard hanging on the wall. Tae-hee moved in front of the board, trying to hide the notes, drawings, and miscellaneous scribblings. Since Kit was tall, he peered over her head at the Hangul letters.

"This is private," Tae-hee said as she spread her arms to block his view.

Unphased by her attempt to obstruct, Kit asked, "Did you do all this yourself, dongsaeng?"

"Stop calling me dongsaeng."

Focused on the mind map of information, he scratched his head and said, "Do you still think our father is alive?"

"If I am, then maybe . . ." Tae-hee drew in a startled breath and held it. How did this stranger know about her father?

"He abandoned us. Pure and simple," said Kit. His lips curved into a faint smile as he leaned forward, his face just inches away from Tae-hee's. "Breathe, sister."

Her annoyance, coupled with her anxiety, caused her to burst out, "Don't call me sister!"

Her words hung in the air, a dark, dismal cloud of disdain. Kit frowned, closed his eyes, and sighed. "You won't let me call you dongsaeng or sister. What am I supposed to call you?" When he opened his eyes, his gaze told her his teasing was over. "You are Kim Tae-hee, and I am Kim Tae-soo. You are my only family, and I found you."

As Tae-hee scanned Kit's dark brown eyes, she felt the urge to believe him. But facts were facts, and Tae-soo's lifeless body was an undeniable fact.

Unable to formulate an effective response, Tae-hee clenched her fists, released an angry groan, and stomped out of the room.

She plopped down in the armchair by the sofa, upset at her childish behavior, frustrated with Kit's unrelenting resolve. She closed her eyes, put her head in her hands, and gathered her thoughts. Kit couldn't be Tae-soo. Yet his words wore away at what she knew to be true.

When Tae-hee sat up and opened her eyes, Kit's face was inches in front of hers. She retreated into the throw pillows piled loosely on the chair. He smiled, then knelt beside her.

Taking her hands in his, Kit said, "Although I have changed, these facts remain the same: you are my twin sister, born moments after me. We were born in Joseon on the twenty-seventh day of March 1867. Our mother died in childbirth. We lived on Ganghwa Island with our father until he abandoned us in 1871. The Kim family took us to Gwangju, where they raised us, changed our surnames from Park to Kim, and added us to their family registry. In 1892, our foster brother Kim Joon-gi left us to live in Hanseong. Ahjusshi and Ahjumma died during the 1918 flu epidemic. A year later, we went to Hanseong, where you took up nursing at Severance Hospital, and I attended classes at Chosun Christian College."

Tae-hee's mouth hung loosely open as Kit laid out the details of their shared history. "We stopped aging in our twenties. We last met a century ago, before the March First Independence Movement. I introduced you to Lee Seung-gi. You liked him, and he liked you." He stroked the back of her hands with his thumbs and said, "He was a bright light during the Japanese occupation. I loved him. But they killed him." His eyes glistened from the mournful remembrance.

"Who are you?" Tae-hee whispered. She thought to pull away, but his sincerity and the warmth of his hands prevented it.

"I am your brother, Kim Tae-soo." Kit offered a half-smile as he clarified, "Or should I say your brother is me?"

"You can't be. My brother is dead. I saw his body."

"I'm sorry you had to see that. It must have been terrible," Kit frowned as he caressed the back of Tae-hee's hands. "It's true that I nearly died. But I revised my understanding of life and death that day." He released her hands, sat back on his heels, and breathed out a sigh. "Something happened to me, to Kim Tae-soo."

Tae-hee searched for deceit in his expression but only found earnestness. Kit wanted her to believe he was Kim Tae-soo. His knowledge of her life annoyed her as much as his persistence. She wanted to slap Kit and punish him for reminding her how much she missed her brother. What did Kit want? How did he know so much about Kim Tae-soo?

"I don't believe you," Tae-hee said.

Kit rose to sit on the corner of the sofa next to her. "After the Samil massacre," he said, "they put me in jail. When they released me, Kim Joon-gi sent me back to Ganghwa Island. He said it was to protect everyone I cared about. He registered me as Pāku Tesu, a Japanese version of my birth name, and removed me from the Kim family registry. Since you never aged, and he did, he listed you as his adopted daughter to protect you."

"Joon-gi said Tae-soo went to Japan."

"Joon-gi lied to you," said Kit, frustration coloring his tone. "He wanted to protect you. It's all my fault. After they killed Lee Seung-gi and his brother, I was grief-stricken, inconsolable, and furious. I could not think straight. I attacked the Japanese soldier who shot them." He clenched his fists and glared at the event, visible only in his mind. A moment later, he relaxed and continued.

"They imprisoned and tortured me. They thought I was part of the Independence Movement and tried to use me to get the names of others. I had no names to offer, so I remained silent even as they pushed me to the brink of death each day." Kit bit his lip and heaved a sad chuckle. "I confounded them because I returned each day healed, as if the prior day's abuse never happened. But I felt everything they did to me."

Tae-hee stared at Kit's expression, his face masked in pain, as he took a deep breath and continued. "After my release, the Japanese watched me. When Joon-gi died years later, I tried to find you. But the world was at war. A year after the war ended, I changed my name back to Kim Tae-soo and returned to Seoul to find you."

Everything Kit said rang true, but it was not enough to convince Tae-hee. This wasn't the brother she knew. He was a stranger, not the reflection of herself she expected. His words did not erase the fact that she mourned over Tae-soo's lifeless body sixty years ago.

Yet his narrative compelled her to learn more. She needed to hear his explanation for how Tae-soo could be dead and alive at the same time. "After the Second World War," she said, "the U.S. government set up nursing schools in Korea. I was part of that initiative. Then the Korean War began, and I worked in M.A.S.H. units."

"That *was* you. I was right," murmured Kit. He brightened as if he discovered something he'd lost. "You were in a M.A.S.H. unit near

Seokhyeon-dong Northern Hill, what the Americans called Pork Chop Hill. You took care of wounded Thai soldiers."

Tae-hee searched through her memories of the Korean War. "I suppose I did," she replied. "But how would you know that?"

"I was part of the Korean Service Corps," Kit replied. "In November 1952, I was at Seokhyeon-dong Northern Hill. That is where I met Lieutenant Chanchai Thanadorn Noratpattanasai. He was part of the Thai battalion defending the outpost. The Chinese attacked the night I arrived."

Weaving the fingers of his hands together, he paused as if unsure whether to continue. Shaking his head, he said, "If you saw my body, you saw what happened to me. Mortar fire blew off my legs. Chanchai tried to rescue me. The shocked look on his face confirmed what I already knew."

Kit paused again, his brows drawn tightly together. "You know how our bodies heal. This time, my wounds were too severe, too extensive. I was bleeding out. I knew I was dying. I felt myself draining away." Kit's gaze conveyed his earnest wish to be believed as he said, "I looked up at Chanchai and jumped."

"You . . . jumped?" repeated Tae-hee.

"Yes. I jumped into Chanchai. I was looking up at Chanchai, and then, suddenly, I was looking down at Tae-soo. Me. *Dead* me."

The surreal idea was unimaginable for Tae-hee. Yet, somewhere within the core of her being, she felt a flicker of hope. Could this person be telling the truth? Could she believe her twin brother existed within the body of this person named Chanchai, nicknamed Kit?

"If Tae-soo jumped into the body of Chanchai, what happened to the original Chanchai?" Tae-hee asked.

"He is still here with me." Kit's words were more measured, choosing each one carefully, as if afraid of how she might respond. "When I woke up in the M.A.S.H. unit, I was confused. Instead of losing my legs, I had a head wound. I clung to a metal tray, looking at my reflection, not recognizing my face. I was so disoriented. I couldn't recognize you as my sister.

I surprised you because I rapidly healed." He ran his fingers over a spot above his ear. "You removed the stitches from my head."

Tae-hee pulled her hands away as she searched her memories. She placed and removed stitches from many soldiers. Then she remembered the Thai soldier who asked her if she recognized him, the Thai soldier whose memories came and went, the Thai soldier who discussed the death of Tae-soo two days before she saw her brother's body. That Thai soldier clasped the metal tray to his chest. But shouldn't that man be in his eighties or nineties now?

Unless what Kit said was true.

Tae-hee nibbled on the tip of her thumbnail as she tried to navigate the information he shared with her. "So, when you say you 'jumped,' you mean you transmigrated?" she clarified. Sameer Khan had never told her of the possibility of transmigration.

"Yes. I don't understand how it happened. My guess is some compatibility between Chanchai and Tae-soo allowed it. Now I am like this. Chanchai and Tae-soo exist together in this one body. Our lives are separate but woven together. It's weird, but it works."

Tae-hee pushed the edge of the rug with her toe as she turned his words over in her mind. Kit remained still and silent.

"And that happened in the 1950s?" she asked.

"Yes. November 1952," continued Kit. "It took me years to understand. But now it makes sense. I am different, and I am okay with that. I want you to be okay with it, too. You are Kim Tae-soo's twin sister and the only family I have. I remember growing up with you in Joseon and Korea. I also remember Chanchai's life. We are separate but together," He paused and chuckled. "That's why we chose the name 'Kit.'"

"Explain. Why Kit?"

"Like a soldier's mess kit. Separate but one. Chanchai Tae-soo," he explained, folding his hands together. "It seemed appropriate since it happened on the battlefield."

Tae-hee tried to hide her mild amusement.

"After Seokhyeon-dong Northern Hill," continued Kit, "I was confused. Trying to sound lucid as I merged two lives together was difficult. Everyone thought I was crazy. No one wanted a crazy person in the military. They sent me to Thailand and put me in a psychiatric institution. It was the best choice. Even though I hated being confined and questioned by doctors, it forced me to focus on who I had become. When I figured things out, I continued my search for you. I never forgot you."

Kit leaned forward and held Tae-hee's hand again. "First, I lived as Chanchai in Thailand. After the tsunami in 2004, Tae-soo took us back to Korea. Unable to find you, I worried you were in the North. I was so happy when I discovered you were in America. I'm sorry I did not come to you until now."

"You said you found me on social media."

"At first, I hired a detective," said Kit grimly. "But they only searched for you in South Korea. As the internet grew, I found hints about you online. Then I found photos of you. I recognized you right away. But when I saw your recent post mentioning Tae-soo, it confirmed that you missed me as much as I missed you. I was so thankful. I summoned the courage to face you, even though I am like this." He waved his hands over his body.

Tae-hee took stock of the differences between Kit and Tae-soo. While Kit's face was more angular, she saw a bit of Tae-soo's softness in it. Both Tae-soo and Kit were good looking, but Kit appeared more mature. Realizing her gaze was fixed on him a bit too long, Tae-hee focused back on what Kit was saying.

"I still miss the face and body of Tae-soo," he said, "but I've come to terms with it, given the alternative. And Chanchai is a good man."

Tae-hee shook her head, unable to let go of her doubt. "You could have made all this up. You could have researched me."

"Sister, who else but Tae-soo knows and accepts that we've been alive for over a century and a half?"

Kit scanned the apartment, then stood and pulled Tae-hee with him into the bathroom. He turned on the light and placed her in front of him, facing the mirror. She was several inches shorter than Kit. For the first time, she compared their features. The color of her skin was a shade lighter than his and her face was rounder. His nose was narrower and more pronounced than hers. Even the shape of their eyes differed.

"What color are our eyes?" he asked.

At least they shared one physical characteristic. "Brown," she said.

"*Dark* brown," emphasized Kit. "Our eye color has always been dark brown, almost black, right?"

"I suppose. But why is that important?"

"Keep watching," said Kit. He closed his eyes for a long moment. When he opened them, his eyes were now a crystalline caramel color.

Startled, Tae-hee murmured, "How did you do that?"

"A moment ago, Tae-soo was the lead personality. Now, Chanchai is the lead. Strangely, it causes our eye color to change."

"So you are Chanchai now?"

"I am Kit. Both Tae-soo and Chanchai are who I am." Kit closed his eyes once again. When he opened them, his eyes returned to their dark brown color.

"This is too freaky." Tae-hee shook her head and strode out of the bathroom.

"I don't know how else to explain it to you," Kit said as he followed her. She slumped into the armchair while Kit continued to the sofa. "You are my sister and the only one who knows me. While I haven't disappeared, sometimes I feel invisible. That's why I needed to tell you the truth. I still heal, and this body hasn't aged since then. I don't know how or why this happened, but I've been able to live both as Tae-soo and Chanchai. Chanchai saved Tae-soo's life. And because of Chanchai, Tae-soo was never alone after that."

"I was alone," Tae-hee murmured.

"I am so sorry, Tae-hee," said Kit. "I always searched for you. I always kept you here." Kit put his hand to his chest. "Tae-hee. Dongsaeng. Sister. You could always tell when I was lying. Am I lying now?"

She narrowed her eyes as she assessed his sincerity. Beneath the power of her gaze, Kit shrunk back into the sofa and moved his thumbs in slow circular motions around each other as he waited for her response.

A slight but distinct vibration began within her core. She had noticed it before, as they stood on the street, but failed to recognize its significance. It was the same comforting resonance she had felt long ago with her twin brother. Sameer Khan called it an artifact connection—an energy link shared between them.

"What was our mother's name?" she asked.

"Lee Eun-sol," said Kit. "I visited her grave on Ganghwa Island on my way here." He sat up, straightening his posture, eager to answer her questions. "I was there on her death anniversary, our birthday. March twenty-seventh. It was strange. Someone left flowers. And there were steles erected for her and Kim Min-woo."

The mention of Kim Min-woo shook Tae-hee. Even their foster family talked little about Min-woo after his death. He was Joon-gi's uncle, who died around the time their father disappeared. Someone had erected steles for her mother and Kim Min-woo. She had not. She hadn't set foot on Ganghwa Island in decades.

Uneasy, she scanned the room until her gaze fell on a shelf. She pointed at it. "You paused at the horse figurines. Why?"

The corner of Kit's mouth turned upward in a sad smile of reflection. "That is one of my last memories of our father. We rode a horse like the brown one in the middle. It reminded me of our father's mare." Tae-hee stared at the figurine she had bought for that very reason.

"Do you remember him?"

"I can't remember what he looked like. He was a Joseon officer who abandoned us when we were very young." Kit's words overflowed with her brother's bitterness.

Tae-soo never forgave their father for leaving them.

Tae-hee searched for something else that only Tae-soo knew, something personal in their shared history. She remembered a conversation from long ago. "What's my favorite color?"

"Orange," Kit replied.

"Why?"

"Because it's delicious, like carrots and yams and hallabongs." He shook his head. "No, that's not right. We ate mandarins back then, but only on special occasions."

The soft vibration that circulated through Tae-hee's core grew more intense. She could no longer ignore its deep resonance. Her bottom lip quivered as tears welled up in her eyes.

She grabbed a throw pillow and leaped at Kit. "You were dead!" she yelled as she struck him with the pillow. "You came home in a box! Do you know how I felt when I saw your broken, bloody, pale, dead, mangled body?" She stopped beating him and slunk to the floor, sobbing. "Do you know how I felt as I wrapped your body and cremated you?"

Kit slid off the sofa and wrapped his arms around Tae-hee. "Mianhada, dongsaeng. I am so sorry, Tae-hee. I never wanted to leave you. I searched for you after Joon-gi died and even after I became Kit. I never stopped. Now I am here."

Tae-hee wrapped her arms around Kit as she let herself believe the unbelievable.

Her dead twin brother had returned to her.

Alive.

2
GATHERING

(MAY 18, 2019)

"Come to Saturday brunch with me," Tae-hee said days later. "I'll introduce you to everyone."

Less than a week had passed since Tae-soo reunited with Tae-hee in his new form as Kit. Acknowledged as her twin brother, Kit moved from the hotel to the sofa in her apartment. Since his only possessions were in his duffle bag and backpack, this arrangement was comfortable and cost-effective until he found a permanent place of his own.

By inviting Kit to meet her friends, Tae-hee confirmed her belief in who he was—at least in part. Kit had shared little information about Chanchai, whose physical form he shared. She did not know Chanchai was born in 1860, seven years before the twins. He hadn't mentioned that, like Tae-hee and Tae-soo, Chanchai possessed an unusual longevity, resilience, and youthful vitality. Nor had he shared Chanchai's encounters with glittering, translucent tendrils, experiences unknown to Tae-soo during his long life. Reuniting Tae-soo with Tae-hee was enough; Tae-hee didn't need to know the details of the origin of the body Tae-soo now shared.

Tae-hee's frequent mentions of her friends at "KSH House" put him on edge. These people were the most important to Tae-hee, possibly more so than Tae-soo. He needed to meet them if he wanted to reconnect with Tae-hee in a meaningful way. Kit had grown accustomed to keeping his distance from close, binding relationships. He worried about Tae-hee and her deep ties to the people at KSH House, knowing the nature of their existence. Her friendships there, precious as they were, could eventually break her heart when her youthful longevity forced her to move on.

As Tae-hee drove them to the brunch location, Kit grew apprehensive for a different reason. The only physical trait Kit had in common with Tae-hee was the color of their eyes. Even more concerning, the last memory she had of Tae-soo was his mangled corpse, shredded and bloody from the waist down. He hadn't forgotten her startled look when he revealed who he was.

"Tae-hee," said Kit. "Does what I look like now bother you?"

"It still surprises me," she replied. "But it has been less than a week since you returned."

Kit needed more specificity. "No. I mean, do I look strange to you? Will how I look make you uncomfortable in front of your friends?"

Tae-hee guffawed. "Are you kidding me?"

"I am serious, Tae-hee."

Tae-hee exited the highway and drove along a meandering, tree-lined road. She turned down an unmarked lane and pulled into a gravel parking lot that surrounded a large house. When she stopped the car and sat back in her seat, Kit nervously waited for her reply.

"I miss Tae-soo's face," she said. "We used to look alike. Now, you are different. But I recognize Tae-soo in you. Maybe it's because you talk to me comfortably. Or that you remember things I forgot. Or because something about you resonates with me. I will admit one thing, though. I always thought Tae-soo was nice-looking. But Kit is a step up on the handsome scale." With a note of sincerity, she added, "Sorry, Tae-soo."

Wait, what?

As Tae-hee stepped out of the car, Kit mulled over her words. Because Tae-soo existed in Chanchai's body, they were no longer *physically* siblings. He hadn't considered that she might find him attractive.

That would be awkward.

Seriously awkward.

Kit shook the thought out of his mind as Tae-hee walked around the car and knocked on his window. "Are you okay?"

"I am processing what you said."

"Honestly, Kit," Tae-hee said as she opened the car door. "Sometimes, you overthink things. Everyone here will love you because you are my brother."

Tae-hee's confident affirmation of their relationship eased Kit's mind. As his concerns faded, a new question surfaced—one that touched on a very different aspect of his life.

"Tae-hee," he began, "have you ever seen glittering tendrils?"

"Glittering tendrils?" Her puzzled look confirmed she had not.

"Never mind," replied Kit. Maybe he was the only one who encountered the glittering translucent tendrils that saved him in life-threatening situations. With a shake of his head, he pushed those thoughts aside.

"Remember," said Tae-hee. "Everyone thinks we were born in 1986. That makes us thirty-three years old."

"I haven't forgotten."

As they approached the back of the house, Kit noticed the modest signpost near the door that read "KSH House."

"What does KSH stand for? I assume it means something," he said.

"K, S, and H are the initials for the Hindi words for saffron, white, and green, the colors of the stripes on the Indian flag. Sameer Khan and his partners—the co-owners of KSH House and Trust—are Indian by birth, so it's a recognition of their heritage." A soft laugh escaped her lips. "Initially, I thought KSH somehow stood for Sikh, Muslim, and Hindu, representing Kiran, Sameer, and Abhimanyu. Sameer said the thought was endearing."

A cozy entryway at the back of KSH House led directly into the kitchen, where the rich aroma of coffee mingled with savory scents, creating a warm welcome amidst the lively buzz of activity. Standing just behind Tae-hee, Kit observed several people moving in sync around the room. He immediately recognized Jong-hyun Park, who preferred to be called Jong.

"Sorry, we're late, everyone!" The kitchen activity came to a halt as everyone turned to Tae-hee and Kit. "This is my brother, Kit."

Jong hurried over to Kit and offered his hand. "Nice to see you again, Kit," he said.

During their first meeting, Kit focused on Tae-hee. Now, he focused on Jong, who was his height, with pale skin, jet-black shoulder-length hair, and chestnut-brown eyes that bore into Kit. Something in Jong's expression and manner made Kit feel vulnerable.

How much does he know?

After Kit took the handshake, Jong pulled him further into the kitchen to introduce him to the others.

Jong put his hand on the head of a bronze-skinned boy with bright, amber eyes. "Short stuff here is Naeem. He's twelve. Jackson and Renuka are his parents." He nodded at the Black man with dreadlocks, who extended his large hand for a handshake.

"Jackson George Jones," the man said in a deep, comforting voice. While Kit was taller than most of his contemporaries, he felt small in Jackson's presence. The bear of a man released the handshake and put his arm around the shoulders of a South Asian woman. "This is my wife, Renuka Mukherjee Jones."

She smiled and offered a well-manicured hand to Kit, who shook it briefly.

Jong slung his arms over the shoulders of a dark-haired man in his forties and an older, gray-haired man. He nodded toward the older man and said, "This is Abhimanyu Khatri. He spends most of his time outside KSH House, meeting with sellers and clients." Jong tilted his head toward the other man with thick, black hair. "And this is Sameer Khan. He is a history professor at Sempiternity University. They are co-owners of KSH House. The third owner, Kiran Ahuja, is in India. He doesn't visit often."

Abhimanyu Khatri pressed his hands together and said, "Namaste."

Sameer extended his hand to Kit with a warm smile. "Welcome to KSH House." As they shook hands, Kit sensed Sameer's natural ease, a self-assured comfort that seemed to flow outward. Unlike Sameer's warm welcome, Abhimanyu remained reserved, nodding his welcome rather than extending a hand.

Jong moved around the table to put his arm around the shoulder of the woman who placed a large salad bowl on the table. "And this red-haired beauty is Emily."

"You're such a flirt, Jong," said Emily. "Don't mind him, Kit. Pick a place at the table. Brunch is ready."

"Where should I sit?"

Tae-hee sat down and motioned to the chair beside her. "Sit beside me," she said.

Jong chose a seat on the other side of the table. "We generally sit wherever we like. There are no assigned seats here—except for Naeem; he gets the highchair." As Naeem playfully punched Jong's arm, Kit wondered if Jong often made jokes at the expense of others.

"Watch out, Jong," Jackson said. "We'll force *you* to take a turn in the highchair."

"Okay, okay!" said Jong. "I'll take it back." He looked at Kit and said, "We picked up an old-fashioned baby highchair. It was a special request from one of our customers. Naeem tried climbing into it and got stuck, and we've been teasing him ever since."

Kit nodded when he realized it wasn't a mean-spirited comment but a lighthearted joke shared among friends.

Jong held a plate of fluffy pastries for Kit. "Jackson makes a killer cinnamon roll," he said. Kit placed a sweet roll on his plate. Other serving dishes loaded with sweet and savory foods were passed to him. Kit helped himself to the brunch fare as he observed the character and interactions of KSH House members.

Sameer, who sat at the head of the table, was the stalwart director who observed everything around him, only providing insight when he had something important to offer.

Jackson, Renuka, Naeem, and Jong sat on the other side of the table.

Jackson maintained physical contact with his wife, leaning against her, putting an arm along the back of her chair, or touching her hand. Renuka was calm and observant as she supervised her husband and son and interceded with a glance rather than a word. Naeem seemed to share this trait, although Jong and Tae-hee had a way of drawing him out.

On Kit's side of the table sat Emily, Abhimanyu and Tae-hee.

Emily's interactions with Sameer reflected a long-standing relationship. Abhimanyu Khatri was the thoughtful elder of the group with a voice that carried authoritative weight.

Jong captured most of Kit's attention. Charismatic and brimming with knowledge, Jong's easygoing banter should have put Kit at ease. Yet, his presence unsettled Kit—the comfortable connection he felt bordered on something more profound, almost seductive. No one had ever affected Chanchai or Tae-soo this way—not Archibald Andrews, not Perth, not the king or the princes, not even Lee Seung-gi.

Jong radiated the warmth and familiarity of someone Kit had known his whole life. Perhaps they'd met in a past life, for Kit knew they'd never crossed paths in either of his current ones. The strange pull Jong had over him was troubling.

"Okay, okay. Let me explain," Tae-hee said, raising her hands over her head to interrupt the conversation. "This is for your benefit, Kit."

Kit swallowed the bite of cinnamon roll and gave his full attention to Tae-hee.

"Jong, Emily, Jackson, Renuka, and I met at Sempiternity University," Tae-hee said. "Emily and Jackson were business majors. Renuka majored in education, and Jong was in the science department. I enrolled in pre-med. During our first year, we were in Sameer's introductory course on Asian history."

"South Asian history," corrected Sameer.

"Of course, India, Pakistan, Bangladesh, Sri Lanka. We read the 'Ramayana.' Anyway, Jackson and Renuka fell in love and married after graduation. Renuka works as an assistant teacher at an elementary school.

Emily and Jackson work at KSH House with Sameer. Renuka works as an assistant teacher at an elementary school. Jackson is passionate about cooking, so he prepares most KSH House meals."

"Basically, Jackson runs this place," Sameer chuckled. "And he is an excellent chef."

"I'm so glad you kept this kitchen," said Jackson. "Any other business might have just used it for storage."

"We need the kitchen for when we host our auctions. Plus, it's cost-effective to dedicate a common space for group meals."

"I keep telling Jackson he should write a cookbook," said Renuka. Her gaze displayed the deep affection and confidence she had for her husband.

Jackson shook his head. "My recipes are all up here," he said, tapping a finger to his temple. "It would take a lot of effort to turn what I know into a book." He crossed his arms and leaned on the table. "My mom and grandmom always cooked together. They filled the house with aromas that made your mouth water. They passed on their legacy to me, so cooking connects me with them. The ability to use ingredients to unlock the senses is a sublime gift. It's an art form that contributes to the health and well-being of my family and friends. The best part is that KSH House foots the bill."

Tae-hee's eyes lit up. "Jackson, Renuka, can I invite Kit?" she asked.

"Invite me where?"

Jackson and Renuka silently negotiated through subtle nods and glinting gazes.

"Absolutely," said Renuka. "We'd love to have Kit join us. We budgeted for eight."

"The more the merrier," said Jackson.

Kit looked from Renuka to Jackson to Tae-hee. "What just happened?" he asked.

"Our tenth anniversary is in June," said Renuka. "We've invited everyone from KSH House to join us to celebrate."

"And I get to prepare a seafood feast," replied Jackson as he leaned over to give Renuka a quick kiss.

"There they go again." Naeem pretended to be annoyed.

"Great," said Tae-hee. "He can take party pooper Abhimanyu's place."

"I am sorry to miss the celebration," said Abhimanyu, "but I always wish you the best."

Renuka smiled. "Thank you, Abhimanyu. We know Kiran is expecting you in India."

"Oh, I forgot to talk about Jong," said Tae-hee. "He just finished his Ph.D. in astrophysics."

"Now, I work as a lecturer at Sempi," explained Jong. "Not to brag, but students entering the physics and math departments benefit from my tutelage."

"It's because you are a nerd," said Naeem.

"Agreed," said Jong. "I get excited when a student understands and retains information. High school education focuses too much on memorization. Students should learn to comprehend and analyze, not just memorize. Anyway, lecturing provides a modest income, and I supplement it by working part-time for Sameer."

"Jong's a good teacher," said Naeem.

Tae-hee put her arm around Naeem. "Naeem, our superstar, entered middle school this year."

Naeem held his head high and grinned with pride.

"You can tell he's your son," Kit said, turning to Jackson and Renuka. "He looks just like you both."

"I know," said Naeem. "No one would know I'm adopted. Right?"

"You were adopted?"

Renuka placed her hand on Jackson's and smiled at Naeem. "Early in our marriage, Jackson and I discovered we couldn't have children," she said. "We fell in love with Naeem on sight. He was four years old. Destiny brought us together."

"My mom and dad are cool," murmured Naeem, a broad smile on his face.

Tae-hee raised her arms over her head as she continued her commentary. "This is the house that Emily's father built. In 2008, they sold it to KSH Trust, the parent company of KSH House." Drawing her hands to her chest, she said, "Sameer, is it true that Emily is going to move in here to help manage the business?"

Sameer laid his utensils on his plate, wiped his mouth with his napkin, and raised an eyebrow at Tae-hee. "As expected, word travels fast. The answer is yes. KSH House is too big for Jackson and me to manage. Plus, I plan to travel during my sabbatical. But, there is one stipulation.

"Emily and I discussed it, and we would feel more comfortable having another woman at KSH House. Customer misunderstandings could occur. So, we would like to extend an offer to you, Tae-hee. We'd like you to consider moving here as well. It's closer to the hospital, and you could keep Emily company. I'll offer you a reasonable rent. Though I intended to rent the upstairs rooms for Airbnb, it's not as economically sustainable or technically feasible as I hoped."

"I'd love to!" said Tae-hee without a moment's thought. "Oh, wait," she said as she raised a hand to her mouth and looked at Kit. "If I move, where will you stay?"

"I still haven't found someone to move into my loft apartment," said Emily. "Since it was a gift from my father, I don't want just anyone moving in there. And I don't want to sell it. Would you be interested, Kit?"

"I'm not sure how long I will stay in this area."

"We can work something out, perhaps a month-by-month lease. If you are available, I'd be happy to show you the apartment later this afternoon."

"That would be great," said Kit.

Tae-hee clapped her hands together and squealed happily.

Your sister is hilarious.

Yeah, she is pretty great.

"Then that's settled," said Sameer.

"When can you move in?" Emily asked Tae-hee.

"By the end of the month. My lease ends on the thirty-first, and I haven't signed a new contract yet."

"That's perfect," said Emily.

After lunch, Emily, Sameer, and Tae-hee cleaned up while Jackson, Renuka, and Naeem went to the main foyer. At KSH House, the custom was that other members washed dishes when the Jones family cooked. As it was his first time at KSH House, Emily and Tae-hee refused to let Kit help with the cleanup.

He wandered to the main foyer. The centerpiece was a recessed lobby with leather sofas arranged around a table. Jackson and Naeem sat together and inspected a collection of cards spread across the table.

"A scientist created the Pokémon Mewtwo through genetic manipulation," Jackson said as he held up a card. "He's got the same DNA as Mew, but he's not an evolution of Mew. He's his own guy and doesn't evolve. Actually, I call him a 'he,' but Mewtwo is genderless. They are a mean Pokémon, whose main purpose is to fight."

"Jackson is thirty-three years old," Renuka said as Kit sat on the sofa, "and he's still into Pokémon cards. Did you play?"

Kit shook his head.

"So, what do you do for a living, Kit?" she asked.

"This and that," said Kit. Realizing it wasn't a sufficient response, he added, "Most recently, I co-owned a bistro."

Jackson's attention turned to Kit. "Really? What dishes did you prepare?"

"Traditional Asian dishes updated for the palettes of international tourists."

"I'd love to learn more."

"I'm sorry," Kit said. "I owned the bistro. I didn't prepare the food."

"So, you are Tae-hee's brother," Renuka said, changing the subject. "You two look nothing alike."

"Are you two really siblings?" asked Jackson. "Or were you born from different families and adopted?"

"Fun fact, Renuka. Kittens from the same litter can have different fathers," said Jong, jumping over the sofa to sit beside Kit. "That's why kitten siblings can be different colors—tabby, calico, ginger, black. It's called superfecundation."

Kit looked at Jong, who met his gaze and held it. His dark eyebrows made Jong's brown eyes stand out even more. Kit tried to read Jong's expression until he realized he gazed at him for far too long.

Why is Jong looking at us?

Why are we staring at Jong?

Jong's calm smile made Kit grin, despite his self-consciousness. A moment later, his cheeks reddened, and his skin tingled. He stared down at his hands as sight and sound drifted away. A buzzing emerged in his head and vibrated down his neck into his chest as a wave of dizziness washed over him. He clenched his hands, closed his eyes, and took several deep breaths.

He was unaware of how much time had passed before Jong touched his shoulder, and Kit's dizziness subsided. Relieved, Kit raised his head.

"That's a great idea," Jong said. "You want to do it now, Kit?"

All eyes were on Kit as they awaited his response. Although he hadn't followed the conversation, somehow, he knew he could trust Jong. "Sure," he replied.

Jong jumped to his feet and waited for Kit to join him.

3
TOUR

(MAY 18, 2019)

Kit's nerves prickled as he followed Jong down the short hallway toward the kitchen. Just before they arrived, Jong paused and gestured to a spacious, glass-walled room to Kit's right. Inside, Sameer and Abhimanyu sat among desks, chairs, computers, printers, and shelves brimming with shipping boxes and office supplies. A row of potted plants lined the far wall of windows, adding a touch of greenery to the space.

"Next to the kitchen is the KSH House office," Jong explained. "Originally, the architect designed it as a greenhouse and sunroom. That's why we keep plants there. Plus, nature."

Kit relaxed when he realized Jong was giving him a tour of the KSH House. Maybe this was a good thing. Maybe more time with Jong would reduce Kit's unease around him.

"KSH House sells antiques and vintage artifacts from around the world. While we sell most merchandise online, we also take care of special orders, such as hard-to-find items or unique collections. Once a year, we host a charity auction. Of course, the business follows fair trade and source of origin laws."

"Downstairs are storage rooms where we organize and package all the items we buy and sell. Sameer keeps those rooms locked."

Jong's statement seemed more like a directive not to enter the basement. Kit surveyed the long metal stairs that descended steeply to a small platform. It turned at an angle and continued downward, out of sight.

As Kit surveyed the steps down to the deep basement cavern, his breathing became shallow, and the nerves in his palm began to tingle. It was the same feeling Chanchai experienced decades ago during the Korean War, before Tae-soo's transmigration. He felt it as an enemy combatant expired beneath the press of Chanchai's hand. Kit rubbed his thumb over his prickling palm.

"Jackson prepares the merchandise for mailing," Jong continued. "The basement has a high ceiling, like the main foyer. The storage room has a dumbwaiter that connects to the auction hall. Which is here."

Kit clasped his hands behind his back and followed Jong through the double doors across from the office. The large auction hall was bright, designed with light brown and burnt orange colored woodwork, the palette of nature. A large rug ran the length and breadth of the hall, decorated with intricate designs. "Sameer had this rug made in India," said Jong. "It cost him a fortune on shipping alone."

Large picture windows with window seats lined the outside wall. Solar shades muted the bright sunlight to allow a view of the forested landscape surrounding KSH House. Off-white drapes hung at intervals along the row of windows. The drapes provided privacy when closed, while clerestory windows preserved natural light. Three chandeliers hung from the high ceiling, their crystals catching the sunlight streaming through the windows. Sparkling reflections danced across the ceiling, casting bursts of light in every direction.

"Here's the stage," said Jong. "We store extra chairs beneath it. Once a year, we hold auctions here to raise funds for local charities. You just missed the last one in April. Sameer, Abhimanyu, and Kiran collect items that appeal to our wealthy clients. I can show you some of our auction catalogs." Jong crossed the room to another set of double doors at the back.

"Auctions are big deals around here. By the way, Sameer doesn't allow food or drink here. This is a hard and fast rule."

Jong is quite loquacious.

He's interesting.

Kit grinned and followed Jong through another set of double doors that lead from the auction hall to the main foyer, where Jackson, Renuka, Naeem, and Tae-hee sat.

"The main foyer is where we hang out during non-business hours. During business hours, we meet customers here. We don't get many in-person visitors, but we always keep the foyer clean and treat it with respect, just in case. It's the first room people see. It should be a welcoming space."

He led Kit past the sofas to a door near the staircase leading upstairs. With an air of mystery, he said, "Never go into this room."

"Why? Is it dangerous?"

Jong smiled. "It's Sameer's room and his private space. He's Muslim, so he uses his room for prayer. Coincidentally, the back of this house faces Mecca." He pointed at another door. "There is another large bedroom beside it. I think that will be Emily's room."

Jong crossed the foyer and opened another door. "This is the library," he said.

Kit inhaled a strong almond-vanilla aroma as they entered the room. The ample open space in front of the picture windows and window seats matched the configuration in the auction hall. A sofa, wing chair, and rectangular table with four chairs equipped the room for the casual reader or the dedicated student. Solar shades protected rows of tall, sturdy bookshelves from direct sunlight. The same off-white drapes as in the auction room lined these windows.

"Sameer has an impressive collection of classical literature from around the world in their original languages: English, French, Spanish, Thai, Chinese, Japanese. There's a Hindi section here." Jong pointed at the shelves. "And a Hangul section over there." Jong picked up a small basket of yellow cards. "If you borrow a book, leave one of those yellow cardboard markers with your name and the book title in its place on the shelf." He placed the basket on the shelf. "It's an excellent room if you need quiet. I practically lived here when I was working on my dissertation."

"Tae-hee said you studied astrophysics?"

"Yes. I finished my Ph.D. a year ago. There aren't many job opportunities for astrophysicists in Springfield outside of teaching. Adjunct professors don't earn much, so Sameer offered me a part-time job and a place to stay. I figured I'd use the time to figure out my next step. And here I am."

"Have you figured out your next step?"

"Right now, I'm happy with what I'm doing."

Jong crossed the hall and opened another door. A clean, fresh fragrance wafted out. "This is the laundry and storage room. We store bedding, towels, and furniture here. There's detergent and fabric softener. A fan at the back keeps this place free from mold and mildew." He shut the door and pointed to the end of the hall. "The first-floor bathroom is down there. Sameer uses it and keeps it spotless, just in case any clients come to visit."

Jong turned and walked back to the staircase. "That's it for the first floor, now for the second floor."

Jong led Kit upstairs. When they reached the second floor, he opened another door. "This is a guest room. It's the smallest room in the house. Abhimanyu stays here when he visits. Emily sleeps here when she works late at night. I guess she won't anymore since she'll have her own room."

"Are Emily and Sameer together?"

"That's a brilliant question." Jong leaned closer to Kit. In a low voice, he said, "I think they want to be together, but neither wants to make the first move. They've been friends for so long."

He closed the door. "Emily's father was an architect. He designed this house as a demonstration project, and it became their family home. Her parents lost their retirement savings in the 2008 recession. They sold the property to Sameer, who turned it into KSH House. When Emily's parents passed away, Sameer brought Emily on part-time to manage the property and help with the business."

"So, now Emily will work full-time?"

"It makes sense. Along with Kiran and Abhimanyu, she and Jackson helped Sameer build the business. It'll be good because Sameer teaches and travels a lot. He, Abhimanyu, and Kiran go to auctions, estate sales, and second-hand markets around the world. Sometimes Sameer finds something rare enough to offer to a museum, or we get a request from a restaurant."

"A restaurant?"

"Sometimes restaurants want nostalgic items such as old-fashioned toys or farm implements for their decor. When we get an order like that, we scour farm auctions, flea markets, or second-hand stores. Sameer treats it like an archeological dig." Jong peered over the railing at Jackson, Renuka, Naeem, and Tae-hee in the main foyer. "The second-floor landing is cool because it gives you a view of everything below."

"We can hear you, you know," said Jackson.

Jong chuckled and backed away from the railing to continue the tour. "Sameer planned to make these Airbnb rooms. But we're on the outskirts of town, and it's difficult to bring strangers into KSH House and make them follow the rules."

Kit wondered how Jong managed to thrive in such a rule-heavy household; he didn't seem like someone who'd be strict about regulations. There was an intriguing duality to Jong—a dedicated scholar with the personality of a playful puppy.

Jong opened one of the doors lining the landing. "Here's my room." Kit took stock of the tidy quarters. Two twin beds. A desk. A chair. A lamp. Jong pushed the drapes open, exposing an enormous picture window. "The room faces east, so I get the morning sun." He entered a doorway to another room. "The closet is my favorite part of the room."

Who likes a closet?

Jong switched on a light to display the neatly organized walk-in closet. A quick scan revealed Jong's preference for casual dress shirts, T-shirts, and jeans rather than suits. Several shelves held books and boxes.

It is a nice closet.

Jong flipped off the light and waited for Kit to follow him out of the room. "Sameer renovated the bathroom at the end of the hall, combining it with a storage room."

He turned on the light in the bathroom. In addition to the basic amenities, the spacious facility had a generous countertop, a closet full of toiletries and towels, and a large tub and shower stall at the far end.

"Now, for the best part." Jong led Kit up a narrow staircase to another large room. A sliding glass door led to a patio balcony overlooking a field and a forest. Two reclining wooden chairs and a table sat on the patio. "Sometimes, I'll bring up a sleeping bag and fall asleep under the stars."

Starry-eyed Jong.

"You're a romantic," said Kit matter-of-factly.

"I prefer nature-lover, but whatever floats your boat." Jong sat in a chair. "This is the perfect place to chill." He leaned his head back and closed his eyes.

Kit's gaze lingered on Jong as he contemplated the contrast between the serious studiousness of the astrophysicist and his warm and casual disposition. Jong's peculiar charisma must have drawn Tae-hee to him. Was Kit also affected by Jong?

Kit walked over to the railing and took a deep breath. Poor air quality alerts were common in his home countries, but this place had the fresh scent of clean air his body craved. As he scanned the landscape, he noted the shorn grass below. Although the field was wide, there was no garden or amber waves of grain, as mentioned in the American national anthem. The field could serve a greater purpose, such as growing food.

What a waste.

Naeem ran onto the field with his soccer ball and dribbled it back and forth. Kit grinned. The field served a greater purpose, after all.

"Do you play soccer?" Jong asked. "I mean, football. Do you want to join him?"

"I'd say yes, but Emily plans to show me her apartment."

"Well, Naeem dribbles the ball in that field whenever he's here," explained Jong, "So, you'll have lots of opportunities."

"It sounds like you expect me to spend my time at KSH House."

"Tae-hee spends most of her free time at KSH House. Now she will live here. Sameer seems to like you, and if Sameer likes you, he'll bring you to KSH House. Maybe he'll offer you a job."

"I have money." Given the trajectory of his life and no family to support, Kit had built a respectable financial foundation. He wasn't rich, but he was comfortable.

Jong walked over to the railing. "You're staying, right? I know she said month-to-month, but if you take Emily's loft apartment, you should consider staying a year, at least."

Things were moving faster than Kit expected. He hadn't intended to be tied down by a year-long lease—he needed flexibility. For the last six decades, he had avoided close ties to anyone. Now that he reconnected with Tae-hee, there were a myriad of ways he could maintain contact with her when he left. His life would become troublesome if others clung to him.

We can't be tied down.

But a year isn't that long, considering our longevity.

"I should find Emily," Kit said. He held a hand up in farewell, and headed downstairs.

* * * *

After Kit left, Jong leaned on the railing and watched Naeem dribble his soccer ball. But Jong's attention wasn't on Naeem. Instead, he analyzed his interactions with Kit. Jong could read the nature of people and he detected a dualism within Kit. One moment, he was friendly and accessible; the next, he was closed off and focused inward. Kit behaved like two different people. His aura shifted between indigo and purple, like the faceless man in Jong's recent dreams.

Whether concealed by ruse or deflection, Jong knew there was something unusual about Kit. A broad smile spread across his face as his fascination with Kit grew. He looked forward to learning more about Taehee's brother.

* * * *

Downstairs in the office, Sameer confirmed the latest shipment from India with Kiran Ahuja. When he ended the phone call, he announced that he and Abhimanyu would be in the basement, reviewing the inventory. Whenever Abhimanyu or Kiran came to KSH House, they would retreat to the basement with Sameer for hours. No one disturbed them, not even Jackson or Emily.

After descending the stairs to the basement, Sameer unlocked one of the storage room doors. He and Abhimanyu entered the small room, and paused, shaken by what they saw. A soft glow emanated from the rows of shelves lining the walls, illuminating the dark room.

For the first time in over 150 years, the thousands of small, oval threlphax vessels collected by Sameer, Abhimanyu, and Kiran—dubbed "aakash se aatmayen"—glowed.

4
QUESTIONS

(MAY 31, 2019)

Emily, Jong, and Kit assisted Tae-hee with packing and moving her things into KSH House. Tae-hee's move was straightforward: a box of knick-knacks, a few books, a dresser, and the contents of a small clothes closet. The rest of the furniture and kitchenware belonged to the apartment owners.

Kit's move was even more straightforward, with only a large duffle bag and backpack. Emily drove Kit to the loft apartment. Kit helped her load her remaining boxes into the car. She didn't need to take the furniture, so she left behind the sofa, several tables and chairs, a dining table, a few bookcases, a queen-size bed, a dresser, and a full-length mirror.

Since he was Tae-hee's brother, Emily decided on a modest monthly rent for Kit. She organized the paperwork and gave Kit a final tour, pointing out the idiosyncrasies of the loft apartment. When he excused himself to use the bathroom, Emily went to the kitchen. She pulled out a small watering can from beneath the sink, filled it, and crossed the room to water the spider plant hanging beside the bed.

On her way back to the kitchen, Emily noticed Kit's passport on the dresser. Despite knowing it was a breach of privacy, curiosity got the better of her. She put the watering can down and opened the passport. It was a passport from Thailand, which struck her as odd—Tae-hee's brother should have a South Korean passport. Beside his photo was the name "Chanchai

Thanadorn Noratpattanasai," along with an immigrant visa from Thailand. Kit didn't share Tae-hee's surname or national origin.

The official document made Emily question whether Kit was truly Tae-hee's brother. Tae-hee took everyone at face value. Could he be an imposter who deceived Tae-hee? But wouldn't Tae-hee recognize her own brother?

"You found my passport," said Kit. His voice was close behind her.

"Ah, yes." Emily turned to face him, trying to mask her nervous embarrassment at being caught examining something she shouldn't have. "I can be a bit too nosy sometimes."

"No harm was done." He pulled the passport from her hand. "You must wonder why I have a Thai passport when my sister came from South Korea."

"I was curious," she said, surprised he addressed her indiscretion so directly.

"Have you ever questioned why Tae-hee became an American citizen?"

"I assumed she had her reasons." She picked up the watering can.

"As did I when I became a Thai citizen," Kit said. "Do not let this passport confuse you. I am Tae-hee's brother."

"I'm sorry," said Emily. "Tae-hee is a good friend of mine. She's important to me."

"My sister is very important to me, too," replied Kit, his voice tense. "After Tae-hee and I separated, circumstances required me to change my name and nationality. I've explained everything to her."

Tae-hee was always tight-lipped about her family, so she never spoke of a brother. She must have omitted this to hide something in their shared history. Tae-hee was so happy when she introduced Kit to KSH House. Emily wanted to trust Kit.

"I'll need a photo of your passport to attach to the rental agreement," she said. Although the passport was required documentation, Emily also saw it as a layer of protection for Tae-hee.

"Of course," Kit replied.

Aware that she held the watering can like a shield in front of her, she raised it to draw Kit's attention. "Please water the fern by the bed once a week," she said as she pointed at the hanging planter. "Just stick your finger in the soil; if it's more than half an inch dry, water it."

Emily returned to the kitchen and placed the watering can in the cabinet under the sink. After a final look around, she exited the kitchen and went to the dining room table to pull her phone from her purse.

He opened the passport and placed it on the table so she could take a photo. When she nodded her satisfaction with the image, Kit closed the passport and put it in his pocket.

"Please don't let this cause you to question my relationship with Tae-hee," he said.

"I won't."

Emily pulled a pen from her purse and handed it to Kit, who paused a moment before he signed his name on the lease in Hangul, Thai, and English to the rental agreement. The English name was simply "Kit."

"Does that work?" he asked.

Although it was an odd way to sign, Emily had the photo of the passport, so she chose not to press the issue. She nodded and retrieved the key fob from her purse. She took Kit's hand and placed the fob in his palm. "I didn't mean to upset you. I can tell you care about Tae-hee. You don't need to worry." She hoped to put his mind at ease. "You have the door code, but if you forget it, you can use this. And please let me know if you change the code."

"I will," said Kit.

"Jong will pick you up around nine o'clock tomorrow morning for brunch. You can meet him downstairs. If you haven't figured it out, everyone at KSH House eats together as often as we can. That means weekend brunches and daily dinners. Sameer says it makes us family."

After Emily left, Kit drew the drapes to block the afternoon sunlight that streamed in through the balcony windows. He sat on the bed and rubbed his temples with his fingertips. Never in his long life had he ever experienced headaches before. Kit did his best to ignore the mild throbbing while Emily was there. Now that she was gone, he lay on the bed and willed himself to sleep.

5
COMFORTABLE

(JUNE 1, 2019)

"So, how was your first night?" Jong asked as they drove to KSH House.

"Restful," replied Kit.

Jong chuckled.

"Did I say something wrong?" Kit asked.

"No," said Jong with a shake of his head. "It's just that . . ." He trailed off, leaving the sentence unfinished.

"Just what?"

What does he know?

Did Tae-hee tell him about us?

Kit did his best to appear calm as he waited for Jong to gather his thoughts.

"Tae-hee is my best friend," Jong said. "But sometimes even I find her bubbly personality overwhelming. You're not like her. How did you survive growing up together?"

Kit grinned at the unexpected response. His thoughts drifted back to those early years when Tae-hee was just a child. After their biological father deserted them, Tae-hee became the anchor for her brother in ways their foster family never could. She cooked for him, mended his clothes, and shared conversations that truly mattered. But most of all, her unwavering cheerfulness eased the weight of Tae-soo's anger over being abandoned.

"Because of Tae-hee, Tae-soo survived."

Ignoring Jong's confused glance, Kit stared out the window for the rest of their trip to KSH House.

After brunch, Sameer, Jackson, and Abhimanyu pulled Kit into the office. Tae-hee prepared kimchi in the kitchen saying she wouldn't feel right visiting Kit in the loft apartment until she'd made him a housewarming gift. Jong leaned against the kitchen counter, watching her slice a head of cabbage into quarters.

"Your brother said something interesting this morning," Jong said. He tossed a small piece of cabbage into his mouth.

"Really? What?"

"He said Tae-soo survived because of you."

"Well, that was his given name."

"But he spoke in the third person."

"Sometimes he does that."

"Don't you think it's weird?"

Tae-hee rolled her eyes. "I think you're making a mountain out of a grain of sand."

"You mean I'm making a mountain out of a molehill."

"I've never seen a molehill. I only know sand."

Jong let out a quiet laugh as he reached for another piece of unsalted cabbage. Tae-hee slapped his hand away. "This is for Kit, not you," she said.

With a grunt, Jong pushed away from the counter. It would be ridiculous to admit he felt a bit jealous of the attention Tae-hee gave Kit. After all, he was her brother.

"Jong, take care of Kit," Tae-hee said.

"What's that supposed to mean?" said Jong.

"We're short-staffed at the hospital. I can't be around all the time to help Kit adjust. I just want Kit to feel welcome and to find friends."

"He's been here for three weeks."

"Yes, but when he's not here, he spends his time alone."

"Really? He seems charismatic enough to find friends," he said.

Tae-hee stopped her hands mid-motion between the cabbage leaves. "Kit? Charismatic? Are you kidding me?"

"You don't think so?"

She resumed salting the cabbage. "Well, I haven't seen him in a long time. I guess he is more outgoing than he was."

"How so?"

"Well, besides me, the only close friend he had . . ." Tae-hee gazed off as if retrieving a long-lost memory. After a moment, she gave Jong a tight-lipped smile. "You're the charismatic one, Jong." She placed the salted cabbage in a large bowl. "Everyone at KSH House likes you. You're nice, friendly, funny, and a good listener."

"You changed the topic from Kit to me," teased Jong. "It makes me wonder what secrets you two are hiding."

Tae-hee rolled her eyes and filled the cabbage-laden bowl with water. "Go," she said.

"Your wish is my command," Jong said with a very formal bow.

* * * *

On the patio balcony of KSH House, Kit sat in a chair, his eyes closed, his fingers pressed against his forehead. Sameer tried to engage him in conversation, but Kit had excused himself when the strange buzzing in his head became too distracting.

Footsteps crossed the deck, and Kit squinted against the sunlight as he opened his eyes. The pain in his temples from a few moments ago suddenly eased, and he stopped rubbing his head. Kit relaxed his gaze and studied Jong's shape, how he wore his jeans, the muscles that contracted in his upper arms as he leaned on the railing, and his shoulders slightly wider than his waist.

He is well-built.

"How is Emily's place?" said Jong.

"I thought it was my place," Kit replied. He followed the flippant answer with, "It's clean and comfortable."

Jong's smile confirmed he understood Kit's quip.

"Did Tae-hee send you up here?" Kit asked.

Jong nodded and raised a fist with his thumb up. "You are correct," He swung around to face Kit. "She thinks you need male companionship."

"You make it sound as if it's an obligation."

"It's not an obligation. Maybe because you are Tae-hee's brother, I feel comfortable around you. But I'm intrigued as to why your sister specifically asked me to extend a hand of friendship to you. What's up with you two?"

"We've been out of touch. I've changed."

Hahahaha.

He can't imagine how much.

Kit suppressed the smile prompted by his internal dialogue.

"How have you changed?"

The straightforward challenge to his casual remark made Kit uneasy. He wasn't sure how to respond. His story was anything but typical.

"I've just become more freestanding."

"Freestanding?" Jong sat in the chair beside Kit. "That's a strange description. Don't you mean independent?"

Not independent.

How does self-co-dependent sound?

He wouldn't understand.

We are still trying to understand.

When Kit didn't answer, Jong filled the void. "I've lived at KSH House for six years," he said as he leaned back in the chair. "Sameer gave me a place to stay and a part-time job while I was a post-graduate. I spent lots of nights out here studying the stars."

"The very definition of a stargazer."

Jong laughed softly as he raised his hand against the glaring sunlight. "So," he continued, "what do you look at when you think about the big picture?"

It was a strange concept. How did Jong define the big picture? The world constantly shifted and revised itself. People, cultures, and governments changed. Time transformed traditions.

Kit exhaled a soft sigh. "Now that I've found Tae-hee, I don't think about the big picture. I am satisfied with living day-by-day." Jong's gaze fixed on him, waiting for further explanation.

Say nothing more.

How could he explain his long history with its wars, political battles, and revolutions? In his long life, Chanchai was a fruit seller, student, monk, soldier, teacher, statesman, and small business owner. Tae-soo fought his own personal battles as Korea emerged from the hermit kingdom of Joseon. Now, as Kit, he understood the struggle to maintain identity in a world becoming more interconnected.

"Yeah," said Jong when Kit remained silent. "We each have our secrets."

What is that supposed to mean?

Does Jong know about us?

Did Tae-hee say something?

What does Jong know?

"I'm not sure what you mean by that," Kit said.

"I'm good at reading people," said Jong. "I can tell that you and Tae-hee are hiding something." He took a long look at Kit. It wasn't a judgmental stare but a sincere gaze. "You should know, Kit, KSH House is a safe place. No judgments."

Easy to say. Hard to deliver.

"Enough said," Jong declared as he stood and stretched. "I've known Tae-hee for over a decade. She's like a sister to me. I don't know what is going on between you two, but I think she's worried you'll leave her again. That may be why she wants us to become friends. More ties to bind you here."

Kit's brows drew together as he reacted to Jong's candid assessment.

Tae-hee is like a sister to Jong.

Are we jealous of their relationship?

"I really want to figure you out," Jong said.

Kit remained silent, even though he knew Jong might understand his silence as a tacit acceptance. With a single nod, Jong turned and headed into the house.

"Jong," called Kit.

Jong paused in the doorway.

"Thank you for being there for Tae-hee," Kit said.

Jong smiled, then dropped out of sight down the staircase.

6
BEACH

(JUNE 5, 2019)

Thanks to Emily's meticulous planning, the beach trip celebrating Jackson and Renuka's tenth anniversary was a well-orchestrated event with clear roles for everyone—including Kit. While Jackson, Renuka, Sameer, and Emily were set to arrive at the rented property early Friday afternoon, Jong, Tae-hee, Naeem, and Kit reached the sprawling beach house on Wednesday evening to prepare for the weekend ahead.

They explored the property as they unloaded their luggage and weekend supplies from the SUV. The beach house had two bathrooms and a utility wing housing the laundry and storage rooms. Three of the four bedrooms were furnished identically—two desks, chairs, beds, and wardrobes—while the fourth featured a queen bed, which Tae-hee designated for Jackson and Renuka. Each room had sliding glass doors that opened onto a covered stone patio stretching the length of the house and overlooking the beach.

At the heart of the house was a generous kitchen that opened to a spacious common area with several sofas. A wide hallway with built-in benches ended in glass doors that opened onto the patio, where two picnic tables offered the perfect spot to gather and enjoy the ocean breeze.

As they unpacked non-perishable food, Tae-hee stopped and leaned on the large kitchen island, staring at the ocean.

"I love KSH House," she mused, "but I wouldn't mind living here."

"We got enough stuff to live here," replied Jong, as he seemed to debate with himself over which cupboards to store the various kitchen tools and gadgets Jackson had packed.

Kit chuckled as he watched Jong struggle.

Frustrated but amused by the difficulty of the simple task, Jong held up handfuls of wooden crab mallets. "You wanna do this?"

Kit laughed and leaned back away from Jong. "No. I have my boxes to unload."

Tae-hee rolled her eyes and snatched the crab mallets from Jong's hands. "I'll handle it," she said, returning the mallets to their box before inspecting the cabinets. She rearranged the beach house kitchenware into two cabinets and organized Jackson's items into the remaining ones. Kit smirked as Jong stepped aside with a shrug. Once everything was sorted and stored, Tae-hee closed the cabinets with a satisfied nod, ensuring everything was exactly where it belonged.

Naeem rushed in from exploring the outside of the beach house. "What's for dinner?"

"Well, Jackson always cooks," said Jong as he rubbed the back of his neck. "We should get something he wouldn't make."

Kit raised an eyebrow. "What about Korean barbecue?"

"Oh, such a good idea!" squealed Tae-hee. Opening an app on her phone, she scrolled through a list of restaurants.

"What's Korean barbecue?" asked Naeem. "Is it spicy?"

"It depends. But it is delicious," said Jong. "My mom's barbecue was more sweet than spicy, although she always added plenty of garlic."

"That sounds great!" said Naeem.

"I found one," said Tae-hee in a sing-song voice as she held up her phone. "This place has excellent reviews! Let's go!" Before anyone could stop her, she grabbed her purse and headed to the front door.

The rich aroma of charcoal and grilled meat greeted the foursome as they entered the restaurant and took their seats. While Tae-hee and Jong placed their orders, Kit observed their easy dynamic. He couldn't help but envy Jong's affection for Tae-hee and their sibling-like closeness. It was a connection that felt stronger than his own with his twin sister.

Kit absently twirled the metal chopsticks in his hand as the server set marinated short ribs onto his plate. Rebuilding Tae-soo's relationship with Tae-hee wouldn't be easy. It would require patience and effort, one moment at a time.

"Kit," said Jong. "Are you okay?"

"Yes," replied Kit. He lifted the cover from his bowl of warm rice. "You know," he said, "Tae-hee makes a great tteok-galbi."

"What is that?" asked Naeem as he stuffed a slice of meat into his mouth.

"Mashed short ribs. Rice cake ribs. Short rib patties," explained Kit. "Tae-hee's marinade is what makes it so good."

"Why didn't I know that?" Jong asked Tae-hee.

Flustered, Tae-hee said, "It has been decades since I made tteok-galbi."

"Decades?" laughed Jong. "So, you mastered tteok-galbi when you were a kid?"

Tae-hee shot a nervous glance at Kit.

"Sure," Kit said. "Tae-hee started learning how to cook when she was very young. Of course, as we grew, our tastes changed. But Tae-hee's tteok-galbi was my favorite."

"Well, Tae-hee," said Jong. "Now that Kit is here, you should reprise your recipe."

As the four continued their meal, they discussed the weekend plans until they reached the level of satiation that prompted their departure from the restaurant.

The sun hung low in the sky when they returned to the beach house. They sat together on the beach, watching the sky's colors deepen as the sun dipped below the waves. The surf's rhythmic crashing and the salty tang of the sea infused the air. When night fell, the chill of the ocean breeze prompted them to retrieve sweatshirts, jackets, and blankets, determined to savor the evening on the beach. Jong was the last to rejoin them, having turned off the lights inside the beach house.

He laid a blanket and stretched himself out on it. "Look up," he said as he traced a finger across the star-filled sky. "You can see the center of the Milky Way."

Tae-hee settled onto the blanket beside Jong and stared up at the night sky. "I never appreciated how beautiful it is," she said.

"I wanna see," said Naeem. He squeezed his body onto the edge of the blanket.

"Fortunately, there isn't much light pollution out here," said Jong. "There are other places where you can get a better view, but this is decent."

Kit pulled his sweatshirt hood around his head and leaned back against the cool sand as he studied the hazy formation of stars that cut a path across the sky. During their time in Gwangju, Tae-soo and Tae-hee would stare at the night sky searching for falling stars. Yet, in all the years that Tae-soo and Chanchai looked up at the heavens, they had ever seen the sky quite like this.

Jong pointed upward, tracing a triangle with his finger. "That's the Summer Triangle—Vega, Deneb, and Altair," he said. "Astronomers think there's a black hole at the center of our galaxy, in one of those regions."

"There is," said Kit, although he could not recall how he knew.

"If we were here in November," continued Jong, "we'd see the Pleiades, the Seven Sisters constellation."

"I know a Buddhist folk tale about the Pleiades," said Kit.

"Tell us," urged Naeem.

Kit sat up and folded his legs beneath him. "Once upon a time, an elderly couple lived in the forest with a family of chickens—a mother hen and her six chicks—which the elderly couple raised. One day, an ascetic forest monk happened upon the couple's home. He asked for a place to sleep and a bowl of rice to eat in the morning. Delighted to have such a guest, they agreed. They didn't know that the monk was the deity Phra In, protector of the Lord Buddha.

"After the monk went to sleep, the couple discussed what they could offer the monk for his morning meal, for it was not enough to give their guest a simple bowl of rice. The wife suggested they kill the mother hen and make a curry. Even if the mother was sacrificed, they would still have six chicks. 'No!' replied the husband. 'We cannot take away the mother hen! What will the chicks do without her? I will not do it.' The wife replied, 'I will do it.'

"The couple's house sat on stilts to avoid flooding and wild animals. The mother hen wandered beneath the house, searching for grubs, and overheard the conversation. She gathered her six chicks together and told them, 'Tomorrow, I must leave you to become a meal for the monk. I am happy to repay the kindness of the elderly couple with my life. They fed and cared for us for so long. Take care of each other when I'm gone.' The six chicks wept and pleaded with the mother hen not to leave them, but she accepted her fate. Inconsolable, the chicks would rather die with her than live without her.

"The next morning, the elderly woman woke early. She lit a fire to boil a pot of water. The mother hen slept surrounded by her chicks when the woman took her, killed her, and plucked away her feathers. She put the chicken in the pot of water and began cooking the rice. The chicks, who awoke when the woman took the hen, watched these events. The chicks were unwilling to part from their beloved mother. They hurried onto the stove and jumped into the pot to die with the hen.

"The elderly woman prepared the curry and rice for Phra In, who expressed his appreciation. When he finished his meal, he rose into the sky—for, remember, he was a deity. Phra In remembered the sacrifice of the mother hen and the love of her chicks. The deity immortalized the seven chickens as the stars of the Pleiades."

When Kit finished the story, Tae-hee, Naeem, and Jong speechlessly stared at him in the darkness.

Jong broke the silence. "What the hell kind of story is that?"

"I didn't say it was a fairy tale."

"It started like one," retorted Jong. "You'll give Naeem nightmares."

"Cut it out," Naeem said as he gave Jong a playful shove.

"Kit," said Tae-hee. "Do you remember the story our father told us?"

Kit recalled the last story their father told before leaving them. The tone of his father's voice lingered in his memory, but the details of his face had faded long ago.

"I hope your story is better than Kit's," muttered Naeem.

"Let's see," Tae-hee said. "Once, there was a woodcutter whose axe fell into a lake. There was a spirit who lived in the lake. The woodcutter was very sad. The spirit arose from the water with a golden axe and asked the woodcutter, 'Is this your axe?'"

"No, that is not my axe," murmured Kit, repeating the exact words that the young Tae-soo and Tae-hee gave their father a century-and-a-half ago.

Tae-hee smiled. "The spirit showed the woodcutter a silver axe and asked him, 'Is this your ax?' The woodcutter said—"

"—no, that is not my axe," Kit replied.

"The spirit showed the woodcutter a rusty iron axe," Tae-hee continued. "He asked the woodcutter, 'Is this your axe?' The woodcutter said—"

"—yes, that is my axe."

"And what happened?"

"The immortal gave the woodcutter all three axes," said Kit.

"Oh, that's right. It was an immortal, not a spirit, that lived in the lake."

"Yes," said Kit. "It is important to be loyal." Their father had ended the story with the moral: *It is important to be honest*. In changing the statement, Kit voiced Tae-soo's resentment toward his father.

"Kit," said Tae-hee quietly.

"You never talked about your father," said Jong.

"That's because he abandoned us," replied Kit with the conviction of an undeniable fact.

"You don't know that," said Tae-hee. "Kim Joon-gi said they never found . . . never mind."

"Found what? Who is Kim Joon-gi?" Naeem asked.

"He was our foster brother," Tae-hee said.

"Was?"

Kit stood and brushed the sand off his pants. "I'm going to take a walk."

"Can I come?" asked Naeem.

"It's your choice," Kit said over his shoulder.

Kit's frustration softened with Naeem by his side. The boy projected a sense of innocence. He hadn't yet learned to view the world through the lens of bitterness.

Naeem darted toward the retreating waves, only to shriek and dash away as the water surged back up the shore. In a rare burst of playfulness, Kit hoisted Naeem onto his shoulders and charged toward the waves, pretending to toss him in. Naeem squirmed and cackled, his laughter doubling when Kit abruptly turned and fled from the oncoming surf.

Kit set Naeem down, and the two playfully pushed each other along the shoreline, dodging the waves as best they could. Naeem reminded Kit of the rambunctious temple boys Chanchai knew from his time as a monk at Doi Suthep. Their youth and innocence brightened the atmosphere at the Buddhist temple.

Kit and Naeem settled into a relaxed stroll, and their laughter faded into easy conversation. Despite their efforts to avoid the waves, their shoes and pants became wet and coated in sand.

When the shadow of the beach house appeared distant, Kit asked, "Shall we go back?"

"Sure." Naeem rubbed his arms as he shivered. Kit draped his arm around Naeem's shoulders, lending what warmth he could as they retraced their path along the water's edge.

When Naeem stopped shivering, he said, "I never want to meet my birth parents."

"Why would you say that?"

"They didn't want me."

"Maybe they did want you but couldn't keep you."

"I don't care about their story," Naeem said firmly. "I have parents—Jackson and Renuka. They wanted me, kept me, and treat me well." He spun around and walked backward in front of Kit as he continued. "I think other people gave birth to me because Jackson and Renuka couldn't have their own kids. I know Jackson and Renuka love me. It doesn't matter where I came from. I'm happy where I am now."

"Why are you telling me this?"

Naeem came to an abrupt stop, causing Kit to halt as well. "Because proper parents are those who love you. I don't know why your dad left you. But the story he told you and Tae-hee makes me feel like he wouldn't abandon his kids on purpose."

Kit exhaled a short laugh and shook his head. Naeem was right. Hidden beneath his anger, Tae-soo knew their father had loved them. The bitterness of abandonment masked the sweetness of that love. Tae-soo's wall of resentment had a chink in it. He draped his arm around Naeem's shoulder. "How did you get to be so smart?" he asked.

"I'm not a baby, you know."

"No, of course not. You're ten, right?" teased Kit.

"I'm twelve!" protested Naeem. "I'll be thirteen in February!"

When they returned to the beach house, everyone got ready for bed. Naeem chose the bedroom closest to the kitchen, Tae-hee took the one across the hall, and Jong moved his and Kit's belongings into the third room.

After a restful night and a simple breakfast of eggs and oatmeal, Jong and Naeem spent Thursday morning setting up the small pavilion beside the beach house where the couple would renew their vows. With Jackson's shopping list in hand, Tae-hee and Kit headed to the local market. Upon their return, Kit and Naeem unloaded the groceries while Jong and Tae-hee meticulously decorated the "anniversary bridal suite," adorning it with roses, champagne, and chocolates.

That evening, the four of them shared a late dinner and, worn out from the day's preparations, retired to their rooms for a well-earned rest.

7
DREAMS

(JUNE 7, 2019)

Jong lay in a field of tall grass near the ocean. His hand stretched upward to block the sun as he playfully filtered its rays through his fingers. Another hand joined his, mirroring the gesture, and he turned to see Kit lying beside him. Kit sat up and leaned over Jong, a soft smile on his face.

Kit's intimate proximity made Jong gasp, pulling him out of his dream. He opened his eyes to the morning sunlight that streamed through a gap in the window drapes, pulling him back to reality.

Jong calculated this was the seventh dream he'd had about Kit. The recurring visions, once hazy, had grown clearer since Kit's arrival. Thankfully, he always woke before the dreams ventured into something more erotic. Sitting up, Jong glanced at Kit, who slept soundly on the other bed, his face cast in shadow by the bedside table shielding him from the morning light.

It was unclear whether his dreams were a glimpse of the future or a reflection of a hidden desire. These feelings were far beyond Tae-hee's simple request that he and Kit become friends. Before Kit arrived at KSH House, Jong had dreamed of a faceless figure—someone whose presence he felt but whose identity remained unclear. When Tae-hee introduced her brother, Jong recognized him instantly.

Kit had a pull that Jong couldn't ignore, but he was uncertain whether it was the pull of friendship or something more profound. And if it was something more, how would Kit react?

Jong slipped out of bed and pulled back a corner of the drapes to gaze at the ocean. Though the day was still young, Tae-hee and Naeem were already on the beach, kicking a soccer ball back and forth.

The dream lingered in his mind, and Jong wanted to talk it through with Tae-hee. Over the years, their relationship had developed into one of deep trust. Countless heartfelt conversations and shared silences had forged a connection beyond mere friendship. Kit's arrival, however, had nudged Jong to reevaluate that bond, pushing him to take his relationship with Tae-hee to a new level of openness.

He changed into shorts and a T-shirt and hurried out the patio door to Tae-hee and Naeem.

"Hey, Jong!" called Naeem.

"Hey, Naeem," replied Jong. "I need to borrow Tae-hee for a minute."

Naeem clicked his tongue. "Go ahead," he said, disappointed.

Jong clapped Naeem on the shoulder. "Sorry, man. She'll return when we're done talking."

Naeem nodded, and Tae-hee followed Jong to a bench along the tree line. Jong stared at the surf while Tae-hee waited. When he summoned his courage, he blurted out, "So, what's the deal with your brother? Is he seeing anyone?"

"Why? Are you interested?" laughed Tae-hee.

"Maybe," Jong said. He let out a spirited laugh, hoping to mask the weight of his confession. "Do you think he'd be interested in someone like me?"

Tae-hee raised an eyebrow. "I said to be his friend, not his boyfriend."

Jong took a different tactic. "I told you I come from a long line of Korean shamans, right?"

"Of course, although you rarely talk about it."

"I never wanted this to define me or control my life. Actually, I lean more toward being a mystic than a traditional Korean shaman. I don't communicate with gods, demons, or the dead. Maybe it's because I'm half Korean, half Japanese, and my mom's really into Bible studies. I read auras, sense unseen emotional planes, and have prophetic dreams. Dreams are significant for a shaman, and sometimes mine are vivid enough to predict reality."

"What does this have to do with Kit?"

"Tae-hee, for months now, I've been dreaming about the same person."

Tae-hee's eyes widened as Jong's words sank in. "Are you saying the person in your dreams was Kit?"

Jong knew from experience that his dreams wouldn't stop until he acted on their message. Even to himself, it felt strange to be dreaming about Tae-hee's brother. He paused to reorganize his thoughts before attempting to explain.

Unwilling to wait, Tae-hee asked, "What happened in the dreams?"

The question unsettled Jong, pushing him into unfamiliar, profoundly personal territory. He had never discussed his sexuality with Tae-hee, and she had never brought it up.

Before he could formulate a response, Tae-hee suddenly gasped. "Oh my gosh," she said. "Have you been having sex dreams about Kit?"

Tae-hee was on the right track, but Jong didn't want her to get the wrong idea. "It wasn't just those kinds of dreams," he explained. "I dreamed about being with him—spending time together, like you and me. I know I haven't known Kit for long, but the moment you introduced us, I knew he was the man from my visions."

"I'm not sure how to respond to that," Tae-hee said. "I mean, sex dreams about Kit. Really?"

"You're focused on the wrong thing," Jong said. "The point is, I feel a strong connection with Kit. Like fate or destiny demands it. Like an invisible string connects us."

"Jong!" said Tae-hee. "That's my brother you're talking about."

"That's why I'm asking for permission."

"Permission?"

"Permission." Jong grew solemn. "If he's interested, can I pursue your brother?"

"You are serious."

"I am serious."

Jong relaxed into his sincerity as Tae-hee scanned his expression. His confession was less important than his need to know their friendship would remain intact. If Tae-hee was uncomfortable with his interest in Kit, he would stop here.

She laughed lightly. "You are serious," she repeated. "I didn't even know you were gay. I mean, I guess I wondered. I just thought you were too busy to date anyone."

"I was. I am. But I wouldn't have told you if I wasn't confident. It's not just about the dreams. When I'm around Kit, things that didn't make sense suddenly do. Whether it's chemistry or something deeper, he draws me in. I need to know if he feels the same way I do—if I have a chance with him."

As he spoke, Tae-hee dug the tips of her sneakers into the sand. "I don't know if Kit is ready for a relationship," she said. "I can't say whether he'd be receptive to you. But there was that one time . . ."

Her voice faded under the weight of her memories. She raised her eyebrows and said, "If he is interested, I'm okay with you dating him. But if you hurt Kit, I'll never forgive you." She punctuated the threat with furrowed brows and a finger pointed at Jong.

She dropped her hand and looked toward the ocean. "Kit's been through a lot in his life," she said. "He's felt abandoned many times. He's lost important people in his life, and he's been a casualty of war. I know you might not see it, but he's guarded. He's dealing with things nobody can understand. Not even me."

"You make it sound as if Kit's crazy."

"He's not crazy," said Tae-hee. "After all he's been through, he's the most stable person I know. He's just different."

She widened the hole she dug with the toe of her shoe. Ever since Kit arrived, Jong knew both Kit and Tae-hee harbored secrets. Kit's painful past clearly weighed heavily on her.

Jong shifted his focus, attuning himself to her aura. The peaceful aqua energy he typically associated with Tae-hee had shifted to a deep violet hue. She was navigating through troublesome waters.

"Tae-hee, are you okay with Kit being here?"

"Oh, yes!" Tae-hee's smile reinforced her words, though her eyes betrayed lingering sadness. "You have no idea what it means to me to know he's alive and well. I truly thought I'd lost him forever. I want to hold on to him, but sometimes, it feels like he might slip away again. And that terrifies me."

"I figured as much," said Jong. There were many things Jong needed to learn about Kit. "You said Kit was a casualty of war. Was he in the military?"

"Something like that." Tae-hee's violet aura darkened, a clear reflection of her sorrow. It briefly brightened as an unspoken memory made her grin, but the smile faded as her expression turned pensive. Tae-hee's brother stirred a storm of emotions within her. "Kit doesn't need another reason to mistrust people," she said softly. "Don't play with him. Don't break his heart."

"Tae-hee, it's me, Jong-hyun Park," Jong said, his voice steady with sincerity. He hoped she could hear the honesty in his words. When she nodded, he asked, "So, do I have your permission?"

"It's not really my permission you need, is it?"

"No, but I didn't want to do anything that might make you uncomfortable." Jong took a deep breath and rose to his feet. "Thanks," he added, winking at Tae-hee as he extended a hand to her.

Tae-hee brushed the sand with her feet before accepting his hand. Together, they strolled across the beach to rejoin Naeem.

8
FEAST

(JUNE 7, 2019)

Kit woke to the sound of distant laughter. Seeing that Jong was absent from the other bed, he sat up and checked the time on his phone. He hadn't intended to sleep so late.

He slipped on his jeans and T-shirt and wandered down the hall toward the kitchen, where Tae-hee, Jong, and Naeem were preparing breakfast.

"Good morning," said Tae-hee. "Did you sleep well?"

Kit nodded and joined the others for the breakfast of eggs, ham, and rice with kimchi. Afterward, they finished arranging the patio in preparation for Jackson's seafood feast that evening.

When the other members of KSH House arrived in the afternoon, they brought several coolers that Jackson had packed with a bounty of shellfish from a local seafood market.

Jackson orchestrated the meal preparation by demonstrating the proper cleaning technique for each type of shellfish. Kit was the most accomplished since he had experience with seafood preparation. Recognizing Kit's skills, Jackson asked him to supervise those less talented in shellfish cleaning.

The oven, stovetop, and grill were ready an hour before mealtime. Jackson, Renuka, and Kit oversaw the final preparations and cooking. When dinner was ready, they brought trays, bowls, and plates full of fresh, grilled, baked, and steamed mussels, shrimp, clams, crab claws, scallops, and oysters, along with corn-on-the-cob and grilled vegetables.

"I don't know where to start," Emily said. Her eyes widened as she scanned the feast.

"Start with the oysters," suggested Renuka.

"Raw oysters?"

"Gotta have the raw oysters," explained Jackson. Taking an oyster shell, he freed the bivalve from the shell, poured the meat and liquor into his mouth, took a few bites, and then swallowed.

Following his lead, everyone tried the oysters. Some liked the salty taste more than others. Kit and Jong were each on their fourth oyster when Tae-hee announced. "I heard oysters are an aphrodisiac."

Jackson reached for another oyster shell. "Oysters are rich in zinc and boost testosterone and dopamine levels. So, yeah," he said. He ate the oyster, then smiled at Renuka and kissed her.

"It is good that you are sleeping in Sameer's room tonight, Naeem," said Jong.

Oblivious to the subtle inference, Naeem said, "I'm really glad we are sharing a room. I wanted to ask for help on a history paper for the summer session."

"What's the prompt?" asked Sameer.

"Write five pages outlining the history of an ancient city or civilization. Everyone else took the good ones: the Incas, the Mayans, Ancient Greece, Rome, Pompeii. It's due in a week, and I still haven't picked a civilization."

"What about Mohenjo Daro? Or Uruk?"

"Uruk?"

"Sure. Uruk was the world's largest city over four millennia ago. It is an ancient city in modern-day Iraq. The 'Epic of Gilgamesh' and the Book of Genesis mention Uruk. In fact—"

"—Sameer," interrupted Emily. "We're here to celebrate Jackson and Renuka's anniversary, not have a history lesson."

Sameer winked at Naeem. "We'll talk later."

"Many couples get married in June," mused Tae-hee to Jackson and Renuka, "but your June wedding was the most memorable."

"Was there a reason you picked a June wedding?" Kit asked.

Renuka leaned forward, her excitement evident in her features. "We both thought June was the month to get married because it showcased our values. June has World Environment Day, Pride Month, and Juneteenth. India celebrates Vat Purnima Vrat, a traditional Indian festival where wives fast and pray for their husband's long life and good health. We even picked the date, June 8, for the wedding at the ocean because it was World Ocean Day. It was a Monday, but we made it work. June is this amazing month where the world is a better place."

The thoughtful explanation intrigued Kit. "So, it was love at first sight when you met in Sameer's class?" he asked.

Jackson and Renuka grinned at Sameer, who chuckled and replied, "I take no responsibility for matchmaking."

"We sat beside each other the first day," said Renuka. "I liked how he looked with his short, sexy dreadlocks."

"I liked her looks and her accent, but what sealed the deal for me was her confidence," said Jackson. He put his arm around Renuka as the couple gazed at each other. "I still love that about her."

"The five of us sat together," Jong said. "It was Tae-hee, me, Renuka, Jackson, and Emily. We were the only non-history majors and ended up in the same study group."

"Ended up?" chided Sameer. "You chose your groups."

"The class was Intro to South Asian History," said Emily. "The first exercise was to shift our seats to demonstrate Partition."

"Wait a minute," Jackson said to Sameer. "You never told us whether we moved to India or Pakistan."

Sameer chuckled. "I think you created your own country."

"Aww," gushed Renuka, "that's so sweet, Sameer. We created our own country."

Kit cracked open a crab leg as he reflected on Sameer's statement. KSH House was indeed its own country that Sameer led. Emily managed it. Jackson, Renuka, and Naeem provided public services, and Tae-hee offered health services.

Jong.

What did Jong bring to this KSH House country?

Heart.

Jong captured Kit's attention. He reminded Kit of a British friend he had known more than a century ago, the boisterous Archibald Andrews, who led Chanchai on strange adventures. Both men were honest, Archibald dangerously so. Fortunately, Jong was more analytical. Maybe that was why Jong held his attention. Yet, even Tae-soo's first love, Lee Seung-gi, didn't produce the response generated in him. Jong beguiled, confused, and captivated Kit.

A sharp poke in Kit's side caused him to turn to Tae-hee, who sat beside him.

"Kit," Tae-hee murmured, her voice muffled into the cup she held up to her mouth. "You were staring at Jong."

As if he heard Tae-hee's quiet admonition, Jong smiled at Kit.

Rising to his feet, Kit picked up his plate. "I'll start cleaning up," he said as he escaped to the kitchen.

9
AURA

(JUNE 8, 2019)

Kit had been awake long enough to shower and dress.

Jong was still asleep, lying on his side, his blanket arranged haphazardly over half his body. One knee hung out over the edge of the bed, and his arm hung over the side, hugging a second pillow to his chest. Even in sleep, Jong was uninhibited. Kit coughed out a quiet laugh.

"What are you laughing at?" Jong's voice was low and deep with sleep. He squinted an open eye at Kit.

"I never saw anyone sleep that way before," said Kit.

Jong rolled onto his back and stretched, pushing the blanket off his chest and pulling the pillow to his side. "I have to hug something when I sleep, and I'm too old for stuffed animals." He closed his eyes and seemed to drift back to sleep.

Kit stared at Jong's exposed body, taking in his well-formed torso and the armband tattoo on his left bicep.

"See something you like?" said Jong, his eyes wide open, directed at Kit.

He noticed.

Embarrassing.

"I was just wondering when you were going to get up," Kit explained, relieved that he offered a reasonable response.

"What time is it?"

"A little before seven."

Jong pulled the pillow to his chest, rolled onto his side, and pulled the blanket around his shoulders. "I'm going to stay here a while," he said.

An inviting aroma drifted from the kitchen, signaling to Kit that others were awake. "I'll go and see if there's something to eat," murmured Kit. He headed for the door.

"Can't you smell it? Jackson is already making breakfast," murmured Jong. "Give him a half hour."

"But isn't he supposed to be spending time with Renuka, getting ready for the ceremony?"

"You still don't get Jackson, do you?" said Jong. "When he's around, if he's not cooking it, you're not eating it."

Kit bypassed the kitchen and took a solitary walk by the ocean. He relished the feel of the sand on his feet, the breeze on his skin, and the smell of the sea, which reminded Chanchai of Thailand. Tae-soo recalled his life on Ganghwa Island and the salty scent of the sea. Decades later, he stood as Kit on the beaches of Phuket.

Chanchai's education in England connected Kit to the world beyond Thailand. His continued studies, the internet, and interactions with foreign tourists educated him on American culture, making him comfortable in the United States. Kit regretted that he had waited so long to return Tae-soo to Tae-hee. She lived so long with only the memory of her twin brother's corpse.

He watched a group of birds rush the shoreline as the waves receded. They poked their heads into the sand, searching for food, before running from the waves that washed to shore. As he approached, the flock chirped and hurried away down the shoreline, where they returned to their frenzied foraging. Kit stopped and watched the undulating ocean. Above the horizon hung great puffy clouds of various hues of white, a sharp contrast to the brilliant blue sky and the dark waters below. Kit looked at his feet, partially buried in the sand from the backwash of the waves that crashed against him. An intense emotion forced tears to well in his eyes.

Joy.

Kit laughed at himself. So few times had he experienced the innocence and mind-boggling feeling of pure joy. He had spent most of his life hiding who he was. Reuniting with Tae-hee gave him the freedom to live unrestrained. A mixture of love, grief, and euphoria overwhelmed him and nearly brought him to his knees. As the moment passed, the crushing feeling inside his chest washed away as the surf receded into the ocean.

What is happening to us?

Kit stood a few minutes longer until he was ankle-deep in the sand. He took a deep breath, pulled his feet from the water-logged depression, and walked back the way he came. As he approached the beach house, he saw Jong sitting cross-legged in the sand, just out of reach of the waves washing up on the shore. Jong's eyes were closed, his back straight, his wrists resting on his knees. His pose showed he was in deep meditation.

Sitting a few feet from Jong, Kit hugged his knees to his chest and viewed the undulating ocean. Chanchai spent years of his life in meditation. With Tae-soo, he experienced a broader world.

The wind danced through Jong's shoulder-length dark hair and tightened his red T-shirt against his chest. The forceful movement of the wind contrasted with the stillness of Jong's meditation. Once again, Kit found himself in a conundrum, unsure whether to describe Jong as handsome or beautiful. He was both.

A warrior prince.

It was a strange thought. Jong was not like the patriots and princes Kit had known. Yet something about Jong resonated with Kit.

Jong raised his hands, took a deep breath, and exhaled through his mouth. He opened his eyes and turned to Kit.

Does Jong know we've been watching him?

Why do we keep watching him?

"I'm sorry," said Kit. "Did I disturb you?"

Jong shook his head. His silent smile broadened until Kit became uncomfortable. Kit dropped his knees, crossed his legs, and gazed at the ocean. As Jong continued to watch him, Kit drew figures in the sand with his fingers and tried to appear casual.

"Do you know you have a pink aura?" said Jong after a long pause.

Kit raised an eyebrow at Jong. "I don't know what that means."

He's so cryptic.

He's interesting.

"A pink aura means you are a faithful and loyal romantic," he explained. "People with pink auras are natural healers with strong psychic abilities. They're strong-willed creatives who hate injustice, poverty, and conflict. They want to make the world a better place."

Flustered by the generous description, Kit asked, "What's the downside of having a pink aura?"

"Why does there have to be a downside?"

"Nobody is perfect."

"Did I make you sound perfect?" replied Jong.

Kit felt his face become flushed. He turned his attention to the sand as he scooped up a handful and let it flow between his fingers.

"You're a strange person, Jong," said Kit.

"You're not the first to tell me that," Jong said. He stood up, brushed the sand off his backside, and held his hand out to Kit. "Let's go in for breakfast," he said. Kit grabbed his hand in a wrestler's grip and stood. As they headed to the beach house in silence, Jong's hand brushed against his.

During breakfast, Jong sat at one end of the table while Kit sat at the other. Jong was more reserved than usual. Kit feared he had invaded Jong's private space by sitting with him during his meditation.

At the other end of the table, Jong tried to tamp down the incredible bundle of positive energy derived from his morning meditation, his brief conversation with Kit, and the casual touch of their hands as they walked back to the beach house.

10
ANNIVERSARY

(JUNE 8, 2019)

Several hours later, Kit stood outside the pavilion where Jackson and Renuka would renew their vows. He ran his hand over the front of his Sharkskin suit.

Sameer wore an embroidered kurta and dhoti. Jackson arrived in a maroon suit with a maroon and silver-checked vest. Naeem wore a suit that matched his father's, though he removed the suit coat.

"Where's Jong?" asked Jackson. They looked at Kit.

"I . . . I don't know," Kit stammered. Since they shared a room, he realized everyone might expect him to know where Jong was.

"There he is," said Naeem, nodding to the figure jogging over to them.

"Sorry I'm late," said Jong. Kit parsed through his reactions to Jong's rose-pink skinny suit and vest. Kit wondered whether the pink aura Jong saw around him was the same shade. "Are we all set?" Jong asked, rubbing his hands together.

"You remember to bring it?"

"Of course," said Jong, patting the breast pocket of his suit jacket. "I wouldn't want to mess up your big day when you worked so hard to get your dreadlocks redone."

"Yeah. It took all day Thursday to make me look this pretty," Jackson said with a broad smile. "Let's go."

Jackson and Naeem stood at the front of the pavilion on the platform decorated with flowers and ribbons. The others found their seats with cards bearing their names; Sameer and Jong sat on one side, and Tae-hee and Kit sat on the other. They exchanged glances as they heard Renuka and Emily approaching. Renuka smiled when she saw Jackson and Naeem. She joined Jackson on the riser.

Renuka wore a strapless ivory satin dress embellished with tiny maroon flowers and leaves covering the bodice. The flowers cascaded down the ivory tulle skirt, gathering in a decorative design of flowers along the hem of the skirt and train. This was not a typical wedding dress, but it was not *unlike* a wedding dress. Its design matched Jackson's suit.

Jackson and Renuka grinned broadly as they admired each other. Emily pressed the record button on the camera to capture the event. She gave a thumbs-up and sat in the empty seat between Sameer and Jong. After a brief silent exchange with Emily, Sameer rose and took his place between Jackson and Renuka. He placed a folder on the lectern, opened it, and took a breath.

"I have the honor of leading this celebratory event," he said, "not because of my gifted speechmaking talent, but because these two blame me for bringing them together."

The group chuckled.

Sameer continued, reflecting on Jackson and Renuka's marriage and how they made a family with Naeem. Although Kit heard the words, he focused on the couple as they gazed at each other.

Is this what love looks like?

Sameer asked others to share their reflections. One by one, each stood to give their fond impressions of the couple.

Kit was an outside observer, watching the lives of others. He captured details of the people in his memory, like snapshots in an album: the compassion of Prisana, the support of the Chinese fruit seller, the strength of King Chulalongkorn, the directness of Prince Vajirañāṇa, the mischief of Archibald Andrews, the regret of Kim Joon-gi, the love of Lee Seung-gi, the steadfastness of Pridi, the understanding of Mae Noi, the friendship of Perth. They had passed through his life like loose change in an arcade coin pusher while he had remained young and healthy.

Kit's melancholy forged by his long life made him understand why Tae-hee treasured these KSH House friends. It also made him wonder what meaning his presence brought to this occasion. Maybe it was to learn more about the intertwined lives of these people. He considered how these relationships were formed and nurtured. What about this group united them, bound them, brought them here, to this place, to this modest celebration?

Is this really family for Tae-hee?

After the others spoke, Kit asked, "Would it be okay if I said something?"

Jackson and Renuka nodded.

Kit rose and said, "Tae-hee and I lost our parents when we were very young. Good people raised us, and we were filial to the end. But we . . . I . . . never felt like they were family. Even less so when circumstances forced my separation from Tae-hee. Though I haven't known you long, seeing you together makes me understand what a proper family is. Naeem is fortunate to have you as his parents. Thank you for showing me that."

Kit did not seek a response as he sat and stared at his hands. He only hoped he had said the right thing. Tae-hee put a hand on his and leaned her head on his shoulder. At least she understood.

"Now, let's give Renuka and Jackson a chance to speak," said Sameer as he stepped off the riser and sat beside Emily.

Renuka and Jackson held hands and faced each other.

"I'm going to go first," said Renuka. "Otherwise, I won't be able to remember what I wanted to say," She composed herself before continuing. "Jackson, you are my inspiration and my soul's fire. You bring magic to my days. You make me laugh. You teach me about love. Your love is my shelter. You free me to be myself. You fill my life with meaning. Thank you for taking me as I am, loving me, welcoming me into your heart, and building a family with me. I promise to love you, respect you, and be faithful to you forever." Her voice tight, she forced out a quiet, "I love you" before she hugged Jackson.

When she regained her composure, it was Jackson's turn. He held Renuka's hands, gazed into her eyes, and took a deep breath. "Renuka, my lovely wife," he began, "with you, I am whole and full. You are kind and thoughtful. You bring me joy. When I'm sad, you let me weep. You are my breath and my every heartbeat. I am proud to be your faithful husband. I love you when the sun shines, when the rain falls, in sickness, and in health. Forever." He motioned to Jong, who placed something in Jackson's extended palm.

"What's that?" asked Renuka.

"When I married you, Renuka, you always commented on the unusual shape of your wedding ring and how much you liked it. I never told you, but I only gave you half of the ring. I held on to the other half. But it wasn't because I only gave you half of my love. I kept it because I wanted to show you I have more love to give you. Today, I give you the other half of the ring, along with the promise of more love." He slipped the ring on her finger and interlocked it with the wedding band Renuka wore, making it complete. "When you look at this ring, always remember I've got more love to give you."

"Jackson!" said teary-eyed Renuka as everyone clapped.

As the applause subsided, Sameer stood and said, "American journalist and author Mignon McLaughlin is attributed with the statement, 'A successful marriage requires falling in love many times, always with the same person.' I think Jackson and Renuka exemplify a successful marriage. Jackson, it's time to kiss your bride."

Everyone stood and clapped as Renuka smiled and wiped away her tears before Jackson leaned in and kissed his wife.

11
ACHE

(JUNE 8, 2019)

The group ate an early dinner at a local restaurant selected by Jackson. Renuka wanted an expensive, relaxing meal, while Jackson wanted to check out the menu. Kit revised Jong's early morning declaration: Jackson only ate what passed his strict approval process.

The group spent time looking at photos taken that afternoon. There were photos of both Jackson and Renuka with the ocean backdrop, group photos of the Jones family, and photos of all the KSH House members gathered around the couple. In several of the photos, Kit stood beside Tae-hee. It was another reminder of how different they looked from one another.

Later that evening, after they had returned to the beach house, Kit excused himself. The onset of another buzzing ache in his head made him moody. He didn't want his unusual symptom to be found out. It would upset Tae-hee. He walked alone down the beach to the boardwalk, where he sat down, closed his eyes, and focused on the rhythmic sound of the ocean.

The painful buzzing in his head began after his first visit to KSH House, but he couldn't attribute it solely to the building's environment. The irritation also occurred once when he was in the loft apartment. Fortunately, the ache would fade with time and rest.

He surmised that his chronological age was likely catching up with him. He had lived for more than a century and a half. All this time, his body remained healthy. Tae-hee was the same, but there was one significant difference. Kit was both Chanchai and Tae-soo. Maybe it was too much for his body to handle.

The back-and-forth movement of his hand across his forehead offered a modicum of relief.

He contemplated seeing a physician, but how could he explain himself to them? If anyone learned of his composition, he would become an object of interest, an aberration that needed scientific study, a prisoner of a series of unending tests. His British friend Archibald Andrews warned him of that possibility, and his time at the Somdet Chaopraya Institute of Psychiatry confirmed it.

The ocean calmed Kit and relieved the dull pain that had started in his head and now spread throughout his body. Underlying it all was the "something" that scratched at his mind, nagging at him, causing the full-body ache. Kit closed his eyes and massaged his temples with the tips of his fingers. He wished it would all stop.

Over the decades, as others aged while he did not, Kit had become more isolated. Friendship found him, but he never went in search of it. Chanchai was charismatic, while Tae-soo was more reserved. It was Chanchai's charisma that naturally drew people to Kit, but Kit often disappointed them because Tae-soo kept his guard up as he struggled with the tragedies that had shaped his life.

Tae-soo had endured the loss of his family, survived torture, and faced death itself—but none of it compared to the lingering pain of losing Lee Seung-gi, a wound from which he never healed. Decades later, when Perth confessed his feelings, Kit turned him down and left Phuket forever. He would not let himself love someone so deeply again. Painful memories could never be erased.

The unique bond forced Chanchai and Tae-soo to learn about and from each other. In its own way, it was perfect. Chanchai offered a calming influence for Tae-soo, and Tae-soo grounded Chanchai. As Kit, they could live alongside Tae-hee until it became necessary to move on. In an unending future, this would be their life.

The pain of Kit's headache subsided just as someone approached and stood beside him. Jong leaned against the wooden railing, holding a soda bottle.

Now, he is someone with charisma.

Kit looked back at the ocean. Their conversation would be brief. If he was terse, Jong would go away. Keeping his distance was easier than enduring another deep friendship.

"Tae-hee told me you got injured in the military," said Jong.

"Mmhm," grunted Kit.

Civilian and military.

But, yeah, we got injured.

One of us fatally.

"Which military?"

Thai Military. The Little Tigers.

Korean Service Corps.

1952.

Seokhyeon-dong Northern Hill.

South Korea.

Before you were born.

Maybe before your father was born.

Kit's silence prompted Jong to ask, "Did it hurt?"

"It hurt." Tae-soo remembered the terror as he clung to Chanchai and felt his life drain away.

It killed me.

I am here. You are safe.

"It doesn't matter," continued Kit. "You follow orders and hope you don't get injured or killed."

Or you have your legs blown off, and you become someone else.

"Did you gain something from the military?" asked Jong. "I mean, was it worth it? Did it make you a better person? My high school friends joined and seemed to think so. They think it's important. Something every man should do. That it's important to serve your country."

We fought for our future.

We felt there was no choice.

"My grandfather served in the Korean War," continued Jong. "He said serving in the military makes you more of a man."

Sometimes.

"I don't know," Kit said. "People have different reasons to join. It's good for some, maybe not so good for others. Soldiers can save people, but there are also soldiers who kill people. Soldiers attack and get attacked. Some soldiers never have to fight. I learned much from the military. But if I had to relive what I went through . . ." Kit let his words float away as he shook his head.

We'd do it again.

Jong slowly swirled the soda in his bottle, watching the bubbles rise and fade.

"Do you think people who didn't serve are lesser men?" he asked.

"I don't think you're a lesser man."

Jong took a long drink of his soda, then released a quiet burp. Kit hid his amusement.

"So, I guess you experienced what they mean when they say, 'war is hell,' huh?"

"Something like that."

Jong straightened, finished the remaining soda, and dropped the bottle in the recycling bin. He leaned against the railing. Hanging his head, he frowned. "Do I make you uncomfortable, Kit?"

Yes.

The direct question caught Kit like a rat in a maze of his own making. Kit's blunt responses had annoyed Jong. He felt apologetic.

We like you.

We like you too much.

"I'm not sure," muttered Kit.

"I'll back off if you want me to," Jong offered.

Kit's mind raced.

What to say?

What to do?

He thinks we're angry.

He doesn't know anything about us.

What if he finds out?

We can't be friends for long.

We should push him away.

That's the safest decision.

Jong tapped the rail with his palms. "I'll leave you alone, then."

Kit heard the disappointment in Jong's footsteps as he walked away.

But that's not what we want.

Kit's body tensed. "Jong," he called.

Jong stopped, turned, and waited.

Jong has become important to us.

"There are things . . . about me . . . I cannot explain . . . that you wouldn't understand. I don't know how to act around you."

"Just be yourself," replied Jong. "I think Kit is pretty cool."

"I'm not good at friendships," Kit admitted. "Please be patient with me."

Jong smiled. "That's enough to give me hope."

Hope.

Kit relaxed as he watched Jong descend the boardwalk onto the sandy beach. Without revealing too much, they had shared an understanding. But was it the same understanding? As he listened to the crashing waves and bursts of sea foam, Kit wondered what Jong hoped.

12
CONFESSION

(JUNE 9, 2019)

After Sunday's breakfast, everyone packed up. Kit went with Sameer, Jackson, Renuka, and Naeem to check out the antique shops. Sameer showed Kit the most popular and worthwhile items for KSH House resale.

Everyone spent the afternoon at the beach. Large puffy clouds kept the water warm and the sun's rays at bay. Jong, Naeem, Sameer, and Jackson wore swim trunks; Kit opted for longer board trunks. They stood together at the edge of the water.

In one-piece swimsuits, Tae-hee, Renuka, and Emily sat near the shade along the tree line.

Tae-hee giggled as they watched the men.

"Why are you laughing?" asked Renuka.

"They are such eye candy," said Emily.

"The heavens have blessed us," said Tae-hee as she raised her hands to the sky.

Kit and Jong picked up Naeem and carried him, kicking and screeching, into the water. They submerged, then jumped out of the water to splash one another. Sameer and Jackson ran to join the battle.

Renuka handed Emily the sunscreen. "You're getting red."

"The sun always burns me regardless of how much sunscreen I slather on," said Emily. She opened the tube and spread lotion on her skin. "Red hair, fair skin. The sun and I are mortal enemies."

"Slather," repeated Renuka. "That's such a sexy English word. 'I want to slather it all over Jackson.'"

Emily and Tae-hee shrieked with laughter. Renuka remained calm, smiling to herself.

"Did any of them put on sunscreen?" Emily asked.

Tae-hee drew in her breath. "I don't know whether Jong or Kit did."

"I made sure Naeem did," said Renuka. "And I always use it as just a chance to massage Jackson." She moved her hands to pantomime the massage. "Slathered it all over him . . ."

"I can't believe you two have been married ten years," said Emily. "You still act like newlyweds."

"When you find your soulmate, you find your happiness."

"Have you made any progress with your family?"

Renuka sighed. "A little. I expect in another thirty years, they may invite Jackson over for a meal." Despite providing ten years of proof that Jackson and Renuka were perfect for each other—not to mention that they were raising a child together—the conservative Mukherjee family voiced their disappointment that Renuka did not marry a nice Hindu, preferably Brahmin, Indian boy. Renuka navigated the waters of her family's resentment and her husband's concern with amazing grace.

Renuka looked at Emily. "What about Sameer? Has he made any moves now that you live at KSH House?"

"No." Emily dug her hand into the sand. "Though he's progressive, he's old school with relationships. Plus, he's Muslim, and I'm Christian. I think he doesn't want to expose me to the prejudice he's experienced."

"Does he still go to the mosque?"

Emily nodded. "He still goes to pray every Friday he can."

Renuka put her arm around Emily's shoulder. "I know he cares for you. I've seen the way he watches you."

"Ditto," said Tae-hee.

"If we're talking about who's watching who," said Emily, trying to change the topic, "what's going on between Jong and Kit? They're like peanut butter and jelly."

Renuka and Tae-hee laughed. "Which one is which?" asked Renuka.

"Who cares," said Emily. "They just stick together all the time."

"Can I tell you a secret?" said Tae-hee.

"What?" asked Renuka and Emily as they leaned closer to Tae-hee.

"Jong says he likes Kit."

"What?" asked Renuka. "You mean he *like* likes Kit?"

"Whatever form that takes, whether friendship or something more, Jong likes Kit. A lot."

"Tae-hee," said Emily, her tone taking a serious note. "I need to tell you something. When I helped Kit settle into the loft apartment, I came across his passport. It was Kit's picture, but I saw the name in the passport was 'Chanchai Thanadorn' something."

Tae-hee pursed her lips. How was she to explain what happened to Tae-soo? She couldn't imagine the repercussions of telling the truth. For now, she would confirm that Kit was her brother and put Emily's concerns to rest. "He had a life-changing experience. When he left Korea, he changed his name and nationality."

"That's what he said," replied Emily. "I know you said he experienced something devastating, but I didn't know it was that tragic. He appears to be fine now."

"I'm glad that Jong has taken an interest in him. Whether as a friend or lover, Kit could use someone like Jong in his life."

They nodded their understanding, then turned their attention to other matters.

"So, how do you like living at KSH House?" asked Renuka.

Tae-hee and Emily exchanged broad smiles.

"It's great," said Tae-hee. "I'm closer to the hospital. The downside is that there isn't a lot of public transportation near KSH House, so I have to drive."

"For me, it feels like home," said Emily. "It would be perfect if you lived there, too. Jackson practically lives there anyway."

"Ah, that's sweet," said Renuka. "I'll consider it should we ever need to escape for a day or two. I love the children I teach, but it gets harder every year." She picked up her smartphone. "I have to compete with this for the student's attention."

"Do you ever think about giving up teaching?" asked Tae-hee.

Renuka shook her head. "No. I find value in teaching. Although the landscape of education is changing, I feel like I'm paying it forward to the next generation. Quitting would mean depriving the children of a pretty good teacher."

Renuka's confident smile made Emily and Tae-hee grin. They turned their attention back to the ocean, letting the sound of the crashing waves wash over them.

Sameer and Jackson swam with Naeem near the shoreline while Jong and Kit bodysurfed. It was still high tide, so they rode larger waves longer. Since they swam out deeper than everyone else, they were cautious to avoid the occasional jellyfish scattered here and there on the ocean surface. They stopped swimming to tread water, bobbing with the ocean swells, watching for the next tall wave.

"So, where'd you learn to bodysurf?" asked Jong.

"Thailand. There are great beaches there. You?"

"We used to live in southern California."

"Did you ever surf with a board?"

"I did. But I needed to focus on school, so I gave up surfing."

"You are driven to succeed."

"My parents wanted me to succeed," said Jong. "I wanted to make them happy. Right now, I'm helping others succeed by lecturing. That makes me happy. When I'm happy, my parents are happy."

Kit wondered how it felt to have the pride of one's parents. Chanchai had no memory of his parents, and Tae-soo had only a fleeting recollection of the father who abandoned them. The family who raised Tae-hee and Tae-soo were kind but not loving.

"How long did you live in Thailand?" asked Jong.

"Long enough," Kit replied when he saw the next wave. He and Jong positioned themselves and swam with the wave, letting it carry them inland.

After an hour, Kit and Jong stepped out of the water. On their way to the beach towels, they stopped to admire the sandcastle Naeem and Tae-hee tried to protect from the pounding waves. They smirked when they saw Jackson sharing Renuka's towel and Sameer lying on the towel beside Emily. As Jong approached, he shook the water out of his shoulder-length hair at the group, who pulled back, laughing and fussing at him.

Sameer did not move. "I curse you," he said in a quiet but firm voice. Emily patted Sameer's arm.

Tae-hee ran over and took her place on her towel. Kit sat on the towel next to Tae-hee, and Jong spread his towel next to Kit. Tae-hee picked up the tube of sunscreen and held it out to Jong and Kit. "Did either of you put on sunscreen?" she asked. She pointed to her shoulders. "You two are looking red."

Jong took the tube and squirted sunscreen onto his hand. He rubbed it around his chest, neck, and shoulders but struggled to distribute it to his back.

Kit reached over, took the tube, squirted lotion onto his hand, and motioned for Jong to turn around. Every nerve in Jong's body buzzed as Kit's hands splayed over him, spreading the lotion across his back. When Kit finished, he handed the tube to Jong and grunted, encouraging him to do the same for Kit. Jong's body still tingled as he applied lotion to Kit's back. He handed the tube back to Kit, and as he watched him apply the lotion to his chest and stomach, he felt heat rising within him.

"Can I get anyone anything to drink?" Jong said, jumping up and wrapping his beach towel around his waist.

"Why don't you get water for everyone," said Sameer, reaching for his wallet.

"It's okay, I got this," said Jong as he slipped on his zoris and headed to the boardwalk.

"I'll come with you," said Kit, jumping up and sliding his feet into his sandals. He hurried to catch up to Jong.

"See?" said Emily, leaning over to Renuka and Tae-hee. "What did I tell you?"

"What are you talking about?" asked Jackson.

"Emily is shipping Kit and Jong."

"Yeah, so?" said Jackson. "I thought everyone noticed they are like peanut butter and jelly."

Emily and Tae-hee giggled.

"Wait, are you shipping them, too?" Renuka asked Jackson, surprised.

"Who needs to ship them? They're shipping themselves."

When Kit and Jong returned, the group discussed the plan for their return to KSH House.

"You are such a killjoy, Sameer," said Tae-hee.

"I'm just keeping us focused," Sameer replied.

Jong and Kit handed out the water, distributing the ice-cold bottles. Their task complete, they lay down on their towels. They both placed their right hand behind their heads and closed their eyes. Tae-hee noticed their matching poses and quietly motioned for Renuka and Emily to take note. Tae-hee surreptitiously snapped a photo.

"Hey, Tae-hee," said Kit. "Hand me my sunglasses, please." Tae-hee dug them out of her backpack, along with Jong's sunglasses. She handed both pairs to Kit. He thanked her, compared them, and gave one pair to Jong. "Here are your sunglasses."

Shielding his eyes from the sun's glare, Jong took the glasses Kit held out to him and put them on.

* * * *

At some point, the roar of the ocean lulled Kit to sleep. When he woke, he sat up and scanned the horizon where a sailboat passed a container ship.

Nearer to the shore, a motorboat sped by. Down the beach, on the right, a group of children tossed popcorn into the air for the shrieking seagulls to gobble up.

He looked down at Jong, who adjusted his position on the towel, making the elaborate tattoo that encircled his bicep more noticeable. Kit lay back on his towel. "So, Jong," he said, "what's the significance of that tattoo?"

Jong looked at the tattoo encircling his left upper arm.

"Ah, yes," said Jong, treating it almost as a forgotten item. "I got it my senior year of high school. My family on my mother's side comes from a long line of Korean shamans. The tattoo is a reminder of my heritage. I inked it to prepare for my move from the safety of home to the big-bad world of Sempiternity University."

"Are you a shaman?"

That explains why he said we had a pink aura.

"Would it be weird to say I am?"

Kit offered no response.

Jong continued, "Actually, I am more of a mystic. Mysticism is more internally focused. Shamanism is more externally focused. Up until high school, I studied shamanism, but I practiced mysticism."

"Did your parents support you?"

"They couldn't. My parents didn't have the resources to support either shamanism or mysticism. It was just part of my genetic history."

"Are you still interested? In shamanism, I mean."

"I've always been interested. I was into it in high school. In secret, of course. It was mostly research that I found in books and online. My interest in shamanism is why I chose to study astrophysics. Science answers *how*, while spiritual practices answer *why*. Pythagoras understood the world through numbers. But that's just one way to perceive the world. There's an entire universe that we have yet to understand. It's ridiculous to think that we are anywhere near comprehending its complexity."

"As a shaman, do you believe in spirits?"

Jong chuckled. "What I believe," he began before he rolled on his side to prop himself up on his elbow.

"Everything comes from the same source—whether you call it nature, energy, or stardust—and everything is connected. I believe life is a journey of knowledge and experience. Birth, life, death, and the great beyond are steps along that journey."

Kit gazed up at Jong. Intrigued by Jong's view of the world, he became more comfortable with how he felt about the man.

We like what Jong says.

Would he understand us?

We don't understand ourself.

Don't spoil the conversation.

Naeem ran up to Renuka and Tae-hee. "Why aren't you going in the water?" He pulled on their arms. "Come on, Mom! Come on, Tae-hee! Get with the program!"

Against modest protestations, Jackson helped Renuka up, and she ordered Tae-hee and Emily to come, too. Jackson and Sameer followed. Once they reached the surf, Naeem splashed Tae-hee and Renuka until everyone was waist-deep in the water, joyfully playing in the ocean.

Jong sat up and watched them while Kit watched Jong. Although he was tired now, he liked bodysurfing with Jong. He liked talking with Jong. He liked . . .

"Do you miss home?" Jong asked as he lay back on the towel.

Which home?

Thailand or Korea?

"Sometimes," said Kit. "But being here with Tae-hee is more important."

"No special someone waiting for you?"

It might confuse Jong to confirm that Chanchai played that role for Tae-soo—and vice versa. To avoid future complications, Kit stretched another truth. "I am in a long-term relationship."

"Really?" Jong seemed surprised. "Tae-hee didn't mention that."

"Tae-hee doesn't know much about this person." That much was true. For now, Tae-soo was the dominant personality in Kit, so Tae-hee knew very little about Chanchai. It was best to maintain a simple life, so he doubled down on a simple answer. "We've been together for many years."

"Do you think that person and Tae-hee wouldn't get along?"

"I want to focus on Tae-hee."

I need to be Tae-soo for her.

"Doesn't this other person feel neglected?"

"It's complicated."

"Is it a guy?"

Kit gave no response. Jong's questions were digging into the core of who Kit was. How could he explain his life as both Tae-soo and Chanchai? While Tae-hee accepted it, she was his sister, who drew on their shared history to confirm who Kit was. He hoped his silence ended Jong's questions. In the quiet, the sound of the waves lulled him into a sleepy, meditative state.

Jong's voice broke through Kit's reverie. "For what it's worth, I like you, Kit."

As the resonance of the words vibrated through him, Kit became wide awake.

13
SECRET

(JUNE 9, 2019)

Kit was quiet during the ride home from the beach. Tae-hee drove while Jong entertained her with animated conversation since Naeem was riding home with his parents.

After they dropped Kit off at the loft apartment, Tae-hee and Jong silently returned to KSH House. Sameer and Emily helped them unpack the car before retiring for the night.

Jong had just removed his shoes when his phone rang. Surprised by the caller, he chose not to answer. Instead, he stepped out of his room and knocked on Tae-hee's door. He would speak with her face-to-face.

Tae-hee opened the door, her phone still pressed against her ear. She smiled and disconnected the call as she hurried Jong into the room and sat him down on the edge of the bed.

"Did you tell Kit what you told me?" she asked as she hovered over him.

Jong frowned. "Kit says he's in a long-term relationship."

"He did?" Tae-hee paused, working through Kit's words. "Well, it's complicated."

"That's what Kit said. Tae-hee, if you knew he was with someone, why didn't you tell me?"

"It's because he's different," she muttered. "We're different."

"What does that mean?"

Tae-hee huffed and paced across the room.

"What aren't you telling me, Tae-hee?"

Tae-hee sat down beside Jong and gently took his hand between hers. She bit her lip and narrowed her eyes as she said, "You told me that as an astrophysicist, you believed that alien life forms exist, right?"

"Are you saying you and Kit are aliens?" Jong chuckled.

"Not exactly," said Tae-hee. "But not exactly not." Tae-hee scrunched her face in thought, then shook her head, only to nod with newfound determination. She ran to the landing and leaned over the railing. "Sameer! Can you come upstairs?"

Sameer came out of the office and looked up at her, "What's wrong?"

"I need you to come upstairs, now," pleaded Tae-hee. She returned to her room and settled beside Jong. "Sameer will explain," she assured him, as she nervously played with her fingers.

"I will explain what?" Sameer asked. His breath was deep and fast, his eyes wide. He had rushed up the staircase. "Is everyone okay?"

"We're okay. But Jong likes Kit and Kit . . . Maybe it's time to tell Jong about us."

Sameer raised a characteristic eyebrow and relaxed into a defiant pose with his arms crossed over his chest.

Tae-hee shrugged at Sameer. "Can you explain it to Jong? Please?"

Sameer clenched his jaw, then shifted his focus to Jong. He sighed and tilted his head back as he said, "Tae-hee, you know this isn't something to share with just anyone."

"But it's Jong." Tae-hee's voice was nearly a squeak. She extended her arms around Jong as if to put him on display. "It's Jong," she echoed.

Jong was uneasy with the exchange between Tae-hee and Sameer. "Okay, you are making me nervous. What's going on, Sameer?"

Sameer closed his eyes and let out a sigh of resignation. "Come to the washroom," he said. Tae-hee tugged at Jong's arm to encourage him to follow Sameer.

After the three of them entered the bathroom, Sameer shut the door and leaned on the edge of the countertop. "Now, Jong, you cannot share what you are about to witness with anyone else," he said. "This could create significant problems if people learned of it."

"Okay," Jong said.

Sameer pulled out his pocketknife and opened the blade. He held it above his open palm and leaned toward Jong with a concerned look. "You don't faint at the sight of blood, do you?" he asked.

"N . . . no," replied Jong.

"Good," said Sameer. He glanced at Tae-hee, then pressed his lips together as he drew the blade over his palm, cutting into the flesh. His soft exhalations of pain echoed against the tiled room as blood seeped out of his wound into the sink.

"Sameer!" yelled Jong as he grabbed a towel to stop the flow of blood. Sameer pushed Jong away with his elbow.

"Watch my hand," said Sameer.

Glistening specks flickered along the wound until the bleeding stopped, and the deep cut in his flesh disappeared. Sameer wiped away the residual blood with his thumb to expose his intact palm.

Jong's forehead creased in disbelief. He dropped the towel and grabbed Sameer's hand to examine it.

"Is this a magic trick?" he asked, probing Sameer's palm with his thumbs.

"No. I cut myself," replied Sameer. He held out the knife handle toward Jong. Small droplets of blood remained on the blade. "Do you want to try cutting me?"

Jong shook his head and retreated a step. "Of course not!" he said. "But you need to explain it to me," he said.

Sameer rinsed the blood from the sink as Jong gave a sharp glance at Tae-hee, who remained unruffled. Sameer dried his hand and knife, closed the knife, and put it in his back pocket. He folded his arms across his chest and leaned against the edge of the countertop as he focused on Jong.

"Tae-hee and I—"

"—and Kit—" added Tae-hee.

"—and Kit," continued Sameer, "heal rapidly from any wound or physical ailment. Our genes have been modified. Errors in our genetic code have been corrected. Healthy cells replace damaged cells at a super-human rate."

"How were your genes modified? By medicine? By scientists? By doctors?"

"Not exactly," said Tae-hee. "But not exactly not."

"Get to the point," groused Jong. "What makes you different from me?"

"We host extraterrestrial life forms," said Sameer.

Jong took a step backward, away from Sameer and Tae-hee. "You're not pod people, are you?"

"Pod people?"

"Parasites who want to colonize our planet." As the words came out of his mouth, Jong worried he had said too much. If Sameer and Tae-hee were pod people, what would they do to him? Jong mentally shook the question out of his head. He needed to hear them out before he impugned their intentions.

"No," said Sameer. "Although their origin is beyond our planet. The threlphax—"

"—that's the alien life form—" added Tae-hee helpfully.

"—are not parasitic organisms. They don't feed on us or make us conform to their will. They are something akin to what we might call spiritual companions. On the physical side, they keep us healthy and extend our lives. They are observers, but when we merge, their life experience becomes part of our life experience, and our life experience becomes part of theirs. Of course, because the threlphax have existed far longer than we can imagine, we can only access a portion of their thoughts, as necessary. We don't know everything they know. According to my threlphax, that would be too much for any human to handle."

Jong sat down on the toilet lid as he tried to make sense of Sameer's words in the reality he knew.

Tae-hee continued the explanation. "Sameer's off-world threlphax arrived during a Geminids meteor shower. I'm not sure how Kit's and my threlphax happened."

"So, these threlphax aren't parasites?" said Jong.

"No," said Sameer. "They're companions. They care for us, but they're not controlling us."

"You said the threlphax modified your genes."

"Yes."

"And they extend your lives?"

"Yes."

"So, how old are you?"

Jong's desire to understand overwhelmed Sameer's reluctance to respond. "I was born on April 22, 1822, in Shimla, India," Sameer confessed. "I was already an anomaly when the threlphax fell, having lived forty-two years at a time when the average life expectancy was twenty-five years."

"Kit and I were born on March 27, 1867, in Joseon," said Tae-hee, "on Ganghwa Island in modern-day South Korea."

Jong clicked his tongue as he scanned the faces of Sameer and Tae-hee. "This is hard to believe. Why do you look so young?"

"Once our brains fully develop, the threlphax halt the aging process," explained Tae-hee. "So, after we reach twenty-five years of age or so. Of course, if we've already passed that age at the time of the merge, like Abhimanyu or Sameer, then the threlphax will maintain that older age."

Sameer raised an eyebrow in response.

"Well, you merged with a threlphax when you were older, Sameer. I was born with my threlphax."

Jong held up his hands. "Okay. Let's say this is true. What about Kit?"

"Kit doesn't know."

"What do you mean he doesn't know?"

"Kit is unique," said Tae-hee. "There are other things that Kit is dealing with that I can't discuss."

"There's more?" asked Jong.

"Something happened to Kit that explains the relationship he talked about," said Tae-hee. "I can't give details. It's something I don't even understand. However, things might make more sense once he knows this part, the threlphax part."

"You think *this* makes sense?"

"Jong," said Tae-hee, taking Jong's hands. "We trust you. We wouldn't have told you if we didn't trust you. Can you trust that we're being honest with you? That we're telling you the truth?"

Jong looked from Tae-hee to Sameer. Tae-hee was his best friend, and Sameer was a man he respected. As a doctor of philosophy in astrophysics, Jong studied exoplanets and contributed to the ongoing research efforts to discover extraterrestrial life. It would be hypocritical for him *not* to believe them. Besides, Sameer had just sliced open his hand and bled so that Jong might understand. He should trust them. What they shared was huge. What if his colleagues in astrophysics knew? What if NASA knew? What if the world knew?

All the plots of every sci-fi movie he had ever watched came into focus. New species led to curiosity. Curiosity led to experimentation. Experimentation led to . . .

"Ah, man," said Jong as he realized the huge responsibility Sameer and Tae-hee had placed on him. "Do you really trust me, Sameer?" he asked.

"I wouldn't have told you if I didn't. But you cannot tell anyone. Not even Kit. I will talk to him first."

Jong felt confused. "Are you saying that no one else knows?"

"That's right."

"Why *did* you tell me?"

"Because Tae-hee would have bugged me until I did," said Sameer under his breath.

"Because something is going on between you and Kit," clarified Tae-hee. "Even though he says he can't open up to anyone, he has opened up to you. When Kit is around you, he's different. Because of our connection, I am aware of what he feels. I don't want what is different about us to get in the way. Besides, you're my best friend. I've been dying to tell you."

Sameer grinned and put his hand on Jong's shoulder. "Are you okay with this, Jong?"

"I'm not freaking out if that's what you mean."

"Good," Sameer replied.

"When will you tell Kit?"

"I'd like to give him a little more time," said Tae-hee.

Sameer frowned. "I haven't told Kit because you asked me not to, Tae-hee. When I return from my business trip, I hope you will have changed your mind. Knowing about the threlphax would allow Kit to come to terms with who he is."

"I know," Tae-hee agreed. "I'm just trying to protect him."

While Jong was in no position to dictate when and how Kit should be told, he disagreed with Tae-hee's decision. "Tae-hee," he said, "there is a difference between protecting someone and withholding information from them."

Tae-hee sighed, then nodded her agreement.

"I'm glad we all agree," said Sameer. Turning to Jong, he added, "No doubt you will have more questions, but this is all I can tell you for now." He waggled a finger at him. "And don't try to use this information against us. You never know what we'll do when forced to defend ourselves with our superhuman powers."

"Sameer!" squawked Tae-hee, lightly slapping his arm. She turned to Jong. "Don't believe him. We're totally normal."

* * * *

Over in the loft apartment, Kit wandered back and forth as he mindlessly emptied his duffle bag. He returned from the beach trip bewildered. Jong clearly said he liked Kit, but what did that mean exactly? Was it a confession? How should he respond to Jong? Should he respond? Midway through his unpacking, he stopped to focus on his internal dialogue.

Does Jong like Kit as a friend?

Are we reading too much into this?

What are you frightened of, Tae-soo?

I have you. I don't need anyone else.

You know we both need more.

When Jong knows about us, he will abandon us.

If he likes us, he won't.

We can't ruin Tae-hee's friendship.

Kit tossed the toiletries in the hamper and his beach clothes in the sink. How did Jong get so deep into his headspace? He sat on the bed briefly, then wandered across the apartment to the balcony. He stared at the large grassy field behind the parking lot. He imagined Jong standing there, smiling at him. He smiled back.

Jong.

The resonant sound of his name.

Jong.

He shook off the vision and returned to the apartment. What was wrong with him?

Calm down.

He plopped face down across the bed. Maybe he needed to sleep. But he wasn't tired. He was what? Anxious? Nervous? Irritated? Excited?

Kit's phone buzzed. He pulled it from his pocket and checked his notifications. There was a new text message associated with an unfamiliar phone number.

Tae-hee gave me your number. I had fun this weekend. Hope you did, too. Jong.

Sitting up on the edge of the bed, Kit saved the number under his contacts, then began composing a response. He worked on it for several minutes, trying different combinations of words, wanting to say something meaningful and not stupid. Backspacing over several drafts, he finally typed in a satisfactory response and pressed send.

* * * *

Back at KSH House, Jong watched the three dots flash on his cell phone screen for an excessive amount of time. He chewed on his thumbnail while his leg bounced up and down as he waited for the response.

"What is Kit writing," he muttered to himself, "a novel?"

Finally, a short reply popped up.

Kit: Yes

Jong ran his thumb over the message, wanting to continue the conversation. Before he could organize a response, another message came through.

Kit: I enjoyed our time together

A grin spread across his lips as Jong read the words. Repeatedly.

14
CONNECTION

(JULY 1, 2019)

After the beach trip, everyone settled back into their day-to-day routines. Tae-hee and Jong introduced Kit to the attractions Springfield had to offer. Renuka took Naeem to soccer camp, and Emily and Jackson managed KSH House while Sameer prepared to travel to India to meet with KSH House partners Abhimanyu and Kiran Ahuja.

During June, Abhimanyu and Kiran had traveled throughout Asia scouring estate sales, second-hand shops, and antique stores for merchandise to add to the KSH House inventory.

When Sameer arrived in Delhi, the three partners photographed and completed detailed descriptions for each item. They packed merchandise and completed the paperwork to ship the items to the United States.

When they finished in India, the three men traveled to their small warehouse in South Korea. Among the items that Abhimanyu and Kiran collected was a Joseon-period sitting desk. They insisted that Sameer meet the desk's former owner, a man they deemed a meaningful new connection for KSH House and Trust.

As he waited in the hotel suite, Sameer occupied his thoughts by reviewing the shipment inventory. He felt uneasy and wanted to return to KSH House. He trusted Jong, but he wondered what questions went unanswered. Jong dove headfirst into new knowledge, but Tae-hee might not answer all of Jong's questions. Her understanding of the threlphax was limited. He frowned and sipped his bubble tea.

A knock at the hotel suite door drew his attention. Abhimanyu smiled at Sameer and Kiran and then went to the entryway to answer the door. He greeted their guest, who responded with a polite but good-natured greeting. Abhimanyu returned, accompanied by a well-dressed Korean man.

"You know Kiran Ahuja, of course," Abhimanyu said. The man bowed to Kiran. Abhimanyu directed his attention toward Sameer. "And this is Sameer Khan." The man bowed again. "This is Dr. Seung-do Lee," explained Abhimanyu. "He's a medical doctor and a businessman from Seoul."

Sameer stood and offered his hand. The doctor accepted the handshake, meeting his eyes with an amicable smile. Sameer couldn't shake the uncanny feeling that he met him somewhere before.

"Mr. Khan, it is a pleasure to meet you at last," Seung-do Lee said. He paused, then added. "Mr. Khatri and Mr. Ahuja introduced me to the work of KSH House and Trust. I hope that our discussion will be beneficial to us both."

Sameer squinted at the doctor. "I'm willing to listen," he said. Even if Abhimanyu and Kiran trusted this man, Sameer needed time to evaluate him.

Abhimanyu directed the men to the table near the kitchenette. "Before we begin," he said, "we should explain how Kiran and I met Dr. Lee. On one of our excursions, when Kiran and I traveled to Indonesia, we visited the Hindu temples at Gedong Songo. There, we met Dr. Lee, and we struck up a conversation."

The doctor held up a hand and said, "Please, call me Seung-do."

Abhimanyu nodded. "We continued our conversation with Seung-do over dinner. Our discussion wandered onto various subjects, and soon, Kiran mentioned the Geminids meteor shower of 1864, of which, you know, we have very little documentation. While we were talking, Mr. Lee produced an item of interest. It was at this point that we discovered our connection."

"What item?" asked Sameer with a raised eyebrow.

Seung-do tightened his jaw, then leaned on the table, weaving his fingers together. "I have carried this item with me for a very long time," he said. "It is important to me. I do not plan on parting with it. Ever." He stared at Sameer as he paused and allowed his silence to emphasize his words. Though his eyes sparkled, his tone sounded threatening.

Intrigued, Sameer forced a grin. "I'm sorry for making you uncomfortable. But what business do we have if you refuse to part with the item?" They held eye contact longer than necessary. Despite the tension between them, Sameer couldn't shake the strange camaraderie he felt with this man. The doctor not only felt comfortable challenging Sameer, but he also clearly enjoyed it.

"I sense hostility," Seung-do said. "May I remind you that your colleagues asked me here to show you this item? If you aren't interested, I can leave."

Abhimanyu jumped into the conversation. "As promised, I haven't told Sameer about the item," he said. When he received no response, he added, "Let us understand one another."

Unwilling to let the men continue their silent altercation, Kiran slammed his palms on the table, breaking the stalemate. He grabbed four shot glasses, a bottle of soju, and a bottle of sparkling water from the kitchenette. The clink of the glasses, the sound of the bottle lids, and the *glub-glub-glub* of the beverages punctuated the interim armistice.

Kiran slid soju shot glasses to Seung-do and Abhimanyu, a sparkling water glass to Sameer, and then held up his own glass.

"I propose a toast . . ."

The men stared at the interloper.

"To . . . a . . . to . . ." Kiran stammered. "To old friendships across the universe."

Sameer tilted his head at Kiran, who responded with a suspect smile. Abhimanyu's eyes glistened with amusement as he tossed back his soju while Seung-do offered a smirk before finishing his glass in one gulp.

Sameer leaned back in the chair as memories from a different past emerged and changed his focus.

He is a threlphax host.

"What is the object?" Sameer asked.

"Now you care?" said Seung-do. His smirk changed to a full-toothed grin. He was a predator who was about to capture his prey.

Sameer grimaced. Unwilling to be cowed, he asked. "What is your name?"

"Lee Seung-do."

"No. Your threlphax name."

The doctor's eyes danced with delight. "I'll tell you mine if you tell me yours." He grabbed the soju bottle and poured himself another shot.

As the Korean lifted the glass to his lips, Sameer leaned forward and, in a deep voice, said, "Mussick."

Seung-do nearly spat out the liquor as he laughed. He slammed the glass on the table and said, "No wonder you were so hostile. Mussick always had trust issues."

Sameer's eyes widened with recognition. "Taedlum?"

Seung-do's broad smile confirmed the identity of the threlphax he hosted. Together with their tribe, they traveled the universe seeking knowledge through first-hand experiences. Along with Mussick, Taedlum was one of the inner circle of advisors to Trax, the leader of the threlphax tribe. After falling to Earth more than 150 years ago, Denyal and Phemeos—the threlphax who had merged with Abhimanyu and Kiran—had finally reunited Mussick and Taedlum.

Laughing, Sameer and Seung-do rose to their feet. They hugged and clapped each other on the back, like old friends.

"Mussick should have recognized you, but for these vessels . . ." Sameer waggled his finger at the three men. "You tricksters," he said with a big grin. "You set me up, didn't you?"

"Well . . ." said Abhimanyu.

"Exactly," added Kiran gleefully.

"When they confessed they were threlphax hosts of Trax's tribe, I couldn't believe it." He poured another shot, then raised his glass. "To old friends and new friends together!"

With his arm draped around Seung-do's shoulders, Sameer picked up his glass and said, "To old friendships across the universe!" The four men downed their drinks.

"It took you long enough to figure it out," said Seung-do.

"Mussick was remiss in not sensing Taedlum immediately," Sameer replied. "It has been a long time since Mussick read the energy of another merged member of our tribe."

"Ah well, Taedlum tends to be reticent," said Seung-do. "Threlphax energy runs through me, yet my life has turned Taedlum into a recluse. We are delighted to meet friends from both sides of the universe."

"So, what item did you show Abhimanyu and Kiran?" Sameer needed to close the loop regarding their earlier conversation.

Seung-do opened his leather bag and retrieved a small iron box inlaid with intricate silver designs. He adjusted the sides of the small iron box and removed the lid. He unfolded the fabric that surrounded a small, ornate, oval-shaped object. Its soft glow indicated a threlphax was inside the vessel.

"Who is that?" asked Sameer.

"It's Tamar," replied Seung-do.

"Tamar didn't merge with anyone?"

"Soon after Taedlum merged with me, Tamar merged with Lee Eun-sol, the woman I married," Seung-do paused. Sameer waited for Seung-do to prepare the next part of his explanation. "Lee Eun-sol died in childbirth. She lost too much blood, and Tamar couldn't stop the bleeding or replenish her blood. When Lee Eun-sol died, Tamar returned to her vessel."

The four men stared at the glowing threlphax vessel.

After several minutes, Sameer said. "Your child. Where is it now?"

"I don't know. Fate separated us when they were four years of age. I never saw them again."

"They?"

"Lee Eun-sol gave birth to twins. A boy and a girl."

Together, Sameer, Abhimanyu, and Kiran plopped down in their seats. Seung-do had suffered great loss in his long life.

"What were their names?" Sameer asked.

"Tae-hee and Tae-soo. Park Tae-hee and Park Tae-soo."

"But your surname is 'Lee,'" said Kiran.

"Yes, well, that is another story."

15
PARTNERS

(JULY 2, 2019)

The four men talked late into the night, sharing experiences from their long lives. Abhimanyu and Kiran drifted off to sleep while Sameer and Seung-do sat together on the floor in front of the sofas. Several spent soju and sparkling water bottles sat on the coffee table. Lee Seung-do's flushed cheeks gave him the look of someone who'd spent hours in the sun—even though his threlphax self worked to offset the effects of the liquor.

"We just shipped off some items, including the Joseon-era desk you sold to us. Too bad you weren't here to give us a detailed description."

"The desk was a gift to me from Lee Eun-sol. But it had become a burden to carry."

"You said you were a soldier?"

"Yes, long ago. I rode a horse and swung a sword. There's not much call for those skills anymore. The world was very different 150 years ago. The arrow of time constantly urges us on."

"India was still under the thumb of the British," said Sameer. "Where did you learn English? You sound like an American."

"American missionaries taught me. Then, I worked with the Americans during the Korean War. Looking back, it seems so strange. Earlier in my life, I fought against the Americans. Less than a century later, they became our allies." Time changed everything in dramatic ways. As long-lived threlphax hosts, they experienced these changes first-hand. "So, you are a history professor and an antique dealer?"

"We purchase items from estate sales and resell them. Sometimes, we come across misappropriated items. We find the rightful owners and return their property to them. Abhimanyu and Kiran established a global network of contacts, suppliers, and grateful owners.

"But the main purpose behind KSH House is to collect and nourish threlphax vessels. We have intact vessels for thousands of members of our tribe. As a history professor, it is my responsibility to learn all I can about the history of this world. Mussick has a voracious appetite for knowledge, and we feed what we learn to the threlphax vessels through meditation and the energy of thought."

"Is caring for the threlphax tribe a burden?"

"It is a hope for the future." Sameer refilled Seung-do's glass with soju. "Tell me about your merge," he said.

Seung-do turned his glass with his fingertips. "In 1864, when Korea was still the hermit kingdom called Joseon, I followed Tonghak rebels into the forest. Alone. They ambushed and critically wounded me. Three arrows."

Seung-do touched his right shoulder, left shoulder, and the side of his belly where arrows had pierced him. "My horse carried me to a village and a fig tree in a courtyard belonging to Lee Eun-sol. She was a young widow. She and her household tended to my wounds. They did everything they could to bring me back to health. But it wasn't enough. I was dying when Taedlum merged with me. Because of my life-threatening injuries, the merge was fast and deep. My wounds completely disappeared within days, though I required additional time to heal from the sepsis."

"Taedlum saved you."

"I think we saved one another." Seung-do tossed back another shot of soju. "But when Lee Eun-sol died, the emotional toll was immense. Seeing Tamar forced to abandon . . ."

His voice wavered, and he took a calming breath. "It was the first death Taedlum observed through human emotions. I shut down. I don't even remember burying her. I thought Tamar would help Lee Eun-sol survive. Both Taedlum and I fell into a pit of mourning. Fortunately, I had people who waited for me. They took care of the twins. When I recovered, my children gave me a reason to exist."

He poured another glass of soju, which he readily consumed. Sliding the empty glass onto the table, he said, "The Western Disturbance came four years later. Heungseon Daewongun demanded we push back the American invasion or face execution as traitors. We lost. So many countrymen died that day. Because of that battle, I lost my children, my livelihood, and almost my life. I lived quietly with no support network. Except for one person. He was a threlphax host who saved my life—twice."

"You met another threlphax host?"

"Yes. He taught me about the threlphax. But we parted ways long ago."

"Experiences are embedded in threlphax energy. It must have been difficult for you."

"The pain is still raw."

Sameer tipped the soju bottle to refill Seung-do's glass. "Did Tamar merge when Taedlum did?" he asked.

"No. A few months after Taedlum merged with me, Lee Eun-sol contracted scarlet fever. She was very ill. I was desperate to save her. We didn't have the medical knowledge that we do now. That was when Tamar merged with Lee Eun-sol and healed her."

"You said your children's names were Tae-hee and Tae-soo?"

"Yes. Twins."

"Interesting. I know someone named Tae-hee—"

"—I have met people named Tae-hee or Tae-soo more times than I care to remember."

"The Tae-hee I know is a good friend. She's a threlphax host, but she didn't know it until I told her. The resonance of her energy signature feels different. I just learned a few weeks ago that she has an older brother. It's difficult to read his energy signature. His name is Kit."

"Kit?" repeated Seung-do. "A nickname, I suppose."

"Yes. He left Korea for Thailand. Kit changed his name and nationality."

"Kit," echoed Seung-do. It was a short word composed of plosive consonants that lent strength to the name. Seung-do tried to imagine the design of someone named Kit. Unable to conjure an outward appearance in his imagination, he shook his head. It didn't matter since Kit had nothing to do with him.

"When did Mussick merge?" he asked.

"Probably the same time as Taedlum since the tribe followed the path of Mroniea and Trax. Denyal, Phemeos, and Mussick were fortunate to fall near us. It was December in Shimla, so we built a fire to warm ourselves. When the threlphax fell, an explosion sent us flying. A sharp tree limb pierced my body. As I hung there, Mussick hovered over me, and I agreed to the merge." Sameer grinned at the memory. "When we first merged, I hated it. Mussick's thoughts were too noisy."

"They say opposites attract," Seung-do chuckled. When Sameer raised an eyebrow, he explained, "Abhimanyu and Kiran described you as stoic."

"I should have a word with them."

Seung-do grinned. "They seem like good men. I'm sure they meant it as a compliment."

"They adapted faster than I did," said Sameer. "Mussick caused my head to spin. Memories, thoughts, conversations—they flooded my mind beyond its capacity. But I eventually adjusted to Mussick. It helped that Abhimanyu and Kiran experienced something similar with Denyal and Phemeos. The threlphax saved our lives many times. Mussick tells me he observed human courage and strength after merging with me. It is humbling."

"Fortune smiles on you. Sometimes I've forgotten that I am a threlphax host. Then I look in the mirror. I haven't changed in a century and a half. Taedlum's presence is . . ." Seung-do stared at the ceiling and shook his head as he searched for the words that eluded him. "Sometimes, I worry that the tragedies in my life burden Taedlum, who often remains silent. But I know Taedlum is here."

He held his hand out, and translucent glittering tendrils emerged across his palm.

"That's a neat trick," said Sameer.

"That's all it is . . . a trick." The tendrils receded as he folded his fingers into his palm and dropped his hand. "Taedlum and I are like oil and water; we don't always mix unless agitated. But on rare occasions, I speak words and think thoughts that aren't mine. Like now, with you. Some words are mine, while others pour out as liquid through a sieve. It is a strange existence."

"As a doctor, haven't you tried to understand the threlphax-human merge?"

"Of course," said Seung-do. "But I have only had myself as a subject. I can't imagine what I could learn by associating with you three."

The two men fell silent as the late-night and comfortable conversation eased their minds. Though he was a threlphax host, Seung-do nonetheless felt the influence of the alcohol. He wouldn't be drunk for long, and he wouldn't experience a hangover. Fortunately, soju wasn't that potent of a potable, to begin with.

"Do you think the threlphax knew it would be this way?" asked Seung-do.

"They escape from one unpleasant experience to another," replied Sameer. "There are sayings for this. My favorite is 'jumping out of the frying pan into the fire.'" He nodded as he appreciated the sad humor in that phrase. "Humanity can be brutal."

"Yes, but humans can be kind, also," said Seung-do. "Did you know that in Korean, the words for person, life, and love sound very similar? Saram, salm, sarang. Perhaps our ancient Korean ancestors wanted us to understand the connection among these three things." He downed another shot glass of soju before proclaiming, "Sarang. To live a full salm, saramdeul need sarang."

"Pyaar," sighed Sameer. The two men nodded.

"It is a shame that we did not meet earlier," Sameer said. "It must have been a lonely existence for you."

Seung-do put his head back and breathed a sigh. "After Taedlum merged, we were happy for a while. Then, I lost my wife, my children, and my good friends. Even before the threlphax fell, my life seemed to bring ill fate to those close to me." He looked at Abhimanyu and Kiran, draped across the sofas. "You are fortunate. You kept your friends over the years. Both there and here," he said as he tapped his chest with his fist.

"Despite the turmoil and our differences, the three . . . " began Sameer before he corrected himself. "No, the six of us have maintained a close friendship. We trust each other. We have saved each other's lives."

Seung-do scrunched up his face. "What of Mussick's twin, Mroniea?"

Sameer scowled. "That threlphax merged with a blue-eyed, blonde-haired Englishman during the British Raj."

Seung-do chuckled and released a brief snort.

"It's not funny."

Sameer's response made Seung-do laugh even harder. When Abhimanyu and Kiran stirred, Seung-do tried to muffle his laughter.

"As you said earlier, Mussick and Mroniea have trust issues," said Sameer under his breath.

"I'm sorry. I'm sorry," said Seung-do, trying to ease his laughter. He tittered a few more times before calming himself. "But of all the vessels to choose—"

"—that vessel was on the verge of ending his life when Mroniea fell," said Sameer. "Mroniea is the dominant energy signature. He calls himself 'Mroniea Hadwyn Clarke.'" He pursed his lips and sighed. "Even though Mroniea is a strong threlphax, Mussick pities him."

"Because of what happened to Mroniea before the threlphax fell?"

Sameer nodded. "Our unique twinship, born at the intersection of two universes, made us strong but not invincible. Because Mroniea was born from an antimatter universe into ours, he has always been a pariah.

Then he experienced the dissipation of his whole threlphax tribe." He ran his fingers over a spot at his temple. "It agonized me to experience it through our artifact connection. It must have been excruciating for Mroniea. Then, to face the torment of restoration. Mussick understands why Mroniea lashed out at Trax. Even now, I can sense Mroniea's struggle. Mussick's twin is strong to have survived."

Sameer's mention of Trax, Mroniea, and the artifact connection caused Seung-do's threlphax energy to stir. Artifacts were small implants of energy shared between threlphax. Too many artifacts could slow threlphax energy flows, so threlphax shared these artifacts selectively. Trax, the threlphax leader, shared an energy artifact with each tribe member, which kept the tribe connected. Taedlum's close relationship with Tamar enabled them to share an artifact connection. The artifact connection between Mroniea and Mussick forced them to experience each other's existence.

"How are you able to endure your connection?"

"Mussick doesn't have a choice. They are two sides of the same coin, as they say," quipped Sameer. "These vessels buffer threlphax energy signatures so we can meet face-to-face. But it has been years. Mroniea last came to us before Partition. He warned us it would be brutal. We didn't believe him. We were wrong."

Seung-do sobered at the mention of the event that laid bare deep religious and cultural divisions when India and Pakistan emerged from the British Raj's controlling influence. "The three of you remained together despite everything."

Sameer looked at the two men sprawled on the sofa. "Mroniea offered to take us to England, but we stayed in India. When the killing began, Kiran and Abhimanyu protected me. Kiran even stabbed me so others would not." Sameer ran his palm over his shoulder. "He can be a terrifying individual."

"It must have been difficult." Although his words were sincere, they failed to convey his true thoughts. He had experienced violent events in his country as well.

Sameer wobbled his head. "Everyone in India felt the pain of Partition. After things settled down, we reimagined our relationship and our future. That's when we formed an official partnership, KSH Trust. Because it is a formal organization, it opens doors for us to search for threlphax vessels. We've gathered many, but not all."

"And you haven't seen Mroniea since 1947?"

"No. But I sense instability." Sameer frowned and shook his head. "Mroniea is in danger . . . and is dangerous."

Seung-do poured himself another glass of soju. "What about Trax?"

"No sign of Trax, and I don't think Mroniea found him."

This world was wide. There were billions of people, millions of hectares of land, and hundreds of millions of kilometers of ocean. Seung-do hoped that Trax was somewhere safe.

"Do you sense the artifact?" said Seung-do. "Taedlum cannot sense Trax's energy."

"Trax's energy artifact has not dissipated. I have felt its resonance a few times over the years."

The confirmation put Seung-do's mind at ease. Early in his life as a threlphax host, worries about Trax filled his mind. But that changed after Lee Eun-sol's death. After he lost his children, he became disinterested in and disconnected from the world. Maybe Taedlum's dormant artifact connection to Trax exacerbated that feeling. Sameer confirmed that the leader of the threlphax tribe still existed somewhere in this world. Regardless, it was unusual for Trax to remain dormant for so long.

"No one has heard a word about Trax since the threlphax fell," continued Sameer. "There are three possibilities." He held up his hand and ticked off his points with his fingers. "One: Trax's vessel is buried. Two: Trax's vessel broke in a place devoid of a willing host."

Seung-do shivered at the thought of the leader of the threlphax tribe dissipating into nothingness for lack of finding a host. In one quick movement, he drained his glass and asked, "And the third possibility?"

Sameer held up a third finger. "Trax is living within a host but is hiding. He could manipulate the tribe's artifacts to prevent detection."

"Hiding? That doesn't sound like Trax. Trax thirsts for discovery. That's part of what makes Trax such a great leader," Seung-do said.

"What if the damage Mroniea did to Trax was more severe than anyone thought?" said Sameer. "Maybe Trax needs time for restoration. Mroniea ripped away a significant amount of energy. It seems like a long time by human standards, but for threlphax—"

"—not that much time has passed," nodded Seung-do. "What about a fourth possibility? The energy Mroniea stole compromised Trax's artifact with the tribe. If Trax needs time to gather and transform energy for restoration, it would be negligent to rely on human energy alone. Both threlphax and host would dissipate. What if Trax found a host but never merged? Trax could gain experience from the host while gathering supplemental energy, all the while remaining separate from the threlphax community and Mroniea."

"Is that even possible?"

"For a threlphax leader, anything is possible." Seung-do ran his thumb along the edge of his soju glass. "When we find Trax—"

"—Trax will leave with the tribe," said Sameer. He grunted as he reached for the sparkling water bottle across the table and filled his glass. Tilting his head at Seung-do, he raised the soju bottle in silent inquiry, but Seung-do raised his hand and shook his head. He was done. Sameer set the bottle on the table, leaned back, and turned his small glass between his fingertips.

"The problem is," Sameer said, "Mussick does not want to leave. We have made many human and threlphax host connections here. Granted, it is challenging to manage IDs and paperwork, given our true chronological ages. The reason I left India to become a U.S. citizen was to create a different paper trail."

"You are an American citizen?"

"Yes." Sameer hung his head and laughed once. "But I have not given up my birthright. I keep the status of Overseas Citizenship of India. But when the paperwork requires renewal, I may need to look elsewhere."

Circumstances required Seung-do to forge his own paperwork on a frequent basis. It was so much easier when he could fabricate official documents. Now, computers digitized and stored everything.

"Taedlum has observed enough and is ready to leave," said Seung-do.

"Did your threlphax tell you that in those words?"

"No, but we were never a good match."

Sameer drew his eyebrows together, troubled by Seung-do's definitive disclosure. "You know what unmerging from Taedlum means, do you not?" he replied.

"I know," said Seung-do. Experience demonstrated that the separation of threlphax and human would lead to the death of the host soon after. "Aside from the brief time with my wife and children, I have lived a long, lonely life. I should let Taedlum move on with the threlphax tribe and accept my human mortality."

"Your life would become part of the collective observations of the threlphax," Sameer said. "Maybe together we can find Trax. In the interim, I look forward to learning more about Dr. Seung-do Lee before he accepts his human mortality."

Seung-do released a sad laugh and shook his head. He was tired. He leaned back into the sofa, closed his eyes, and gave himself over to the comfort of rest.

* * * *

Early in the morning, Kiran awoke to the pain of a hangover. Muslim, Hindu, and Sikh scriptures forbade the consumption of alcohol. While Sameer held steadfast to this rule, Abhimanyu imbibed, but he was discreet in the amount of alcohol he consumed to avoid intoxication. Once Kiran understood the capabilities of the threlphax within him, he would enjoy a spirited beverage if the occasion called for it. He was confident his threlphax could return his body to its pure state after intoxication. However, this belief did not play out. Whenever Kiran drank, he paid for his transgression.

Most threlphax could help their hosts remove the adverse effects of alcohol within hours. Not so with Kiran's threlphax, Phemeos. Kiran experienced hangover headaches after a night of drinking because his threlphax couldn't offset the consequence of his intoxication.

Sameer stepped out to find a cure for Kiran's rare but potent hangover. When he returned to the hotel room, Abhimanyu and Seung-do were deep in debate. Kiran lay on the sofa, his head buried in pillows.

"You know that, as hosts, we share a co-evolutionary relationship," said Abhimanyu.

Seung-do shook his head. "That is a hypothesis. There is nothing to prove it."

"But the relationship causes us to evolve from one form of human into another," countered Abhimanyu.

"We regenerate, yes, and co-exist. But no one has proven that we are co-evolving," argued Seung-do.

Abhimanyu shifted in his chair to engage more directly in the debate. "That is because we cannot measure the co-evolution of the physical with the metaphysical. We cannot undergo a standard physical, and because the metaphysical is still not an accepted branch of practice, research methods aren't available to analyze and measure co-evolutionary changes in our energy signatures."

"My point exactly!" said Seung-do as he leaned forward. "You cannot reach a conclusion without scientific analysis. Since no scientific method exists to measure our threlphax-host relationship, co-evolution is a hypothetical theory, open to doubt."

"But it's the best theory we have!" answered Abhimanyu, his face inches from Seung-do's.

Sameer slammed the bag of hangover remedies on the table. His stern frown forced Abhimanyu and Seung-do into silence, and they retreated from their lively debate.

"Take your medicine, Kiran," Sameer instructed.

Kiran floundered up from among the sofa cushions, stumbled toward the table and bellowed, "THANK YOU!" The vibration of his voice in his head made him wince but didn't pause his momentum as he staggered to the table. He gave Abhimanyu and Seung-do a harsh look as he grabbed the bag and pulled out the aspirin bottle. He struggled to open the lid, poked a hole through the safety seal, pulled out the cotton filling, and upended the bottle toward his mouth. His unsteadiness caused most of the aspirin to spill to the floor, but several fell into his mouth. He crunched on the bitter pills as he glowered at Sameer, Abhimanyu, and Seung-do.

Sameer unscrewed the lid of the hangover drink and handed it to Kiran, who grabbed it and gulped it down. He dropped the bottle, swung around, and launched himself away from the table.

"Shower!" he declared as he flung his arm out and staggered toward the bathroom.

"I thought Sikhs didn't drink alcohol," said Seung-do.

"They don't," said Sameer. "But after Kiran became a threlphax host, he survived many injustices. We all did. Outwardly, Kiran seems like a stable and happy person, but his memories haunt him. His human self wishes to forget, but his threlphax self remembers every detail. Even though it is temporary, alcohol dulls the mind and offers relief. When he overindulges, his threlphax drags him through brutal hangovers to remind him who he is."

"It is unfortunate that both Kiran and Phemeos suffer," added Abhimanyu.

Sameer took a seat across from Seung-do and opened a box. "I brought rice omelets," he said.

As Abhimanyu and Seung-do helped themselves to the food, Sameer drummed his fingers on the table and scrutinized the Korean. He leaned back in his chair and announced, "I have decided." He raised his index finger and aimed it at Seung-do. "You are coming with me."

"Where?"

Sameer's eyes sparkled as he dropped his hand to the table. "To America."

16
SOLUTION

(JULY 7, 2019)

Mroniea Hadwyn Clarke drew .05 milliliters of the liquid into the syringe, ensuring no air bubbles. It was a minuscule dose of the chemical compound. This was the latest in a series of tests he'd performed on himself. While self-experimentation presented ethical issues, he was confident this small dose wouldn't cause disastrous effects. It had to work.

Over eighty years had passed since he began his study of applied chemistry in human cellular and molecular biology. Decades of research experience had allowed him to test different combinations of chemicals to gain firsthand experience with biochemical reactions.

The safe separation of threlphax and human energy was a unique problem that went beyond the physical to the metaphysical. The threlphax could impede matter, but targeting energy pathways within the human biophysical landscape required a nuance of narcotics. Any sudden, drastic changes to their merged energy could have harmful impacts, leading to dire consequences for both threlphax and human vessels.

His human self, Hadwyn Clarke, withstood these tests because the ambition of the threlphax, Mroniea, was to extract energy from hosts without harming them. His merged selves hoped he had created a substance to achieve this goal.

Hadwyn felt a twinge of guilt for the negative thoughts he acted upon that fateful evening in December 1864. His overbearing and controlling father had announced at a dinner party in Dorset that Hadwyn was to be shipped off to India. The announcement was a surprise to Hadwyn, who was unaware of his father's machinations. Angry and inebriated, he rode out to Old Harry's Rocks and nearly threw his life away for petty reasons.

When the threlphax Mroniea fell, the impact threw Hadwyn's body up in the air and turned him around. When he landed, a snap at the back of his neck preceded intense pain and his inability to move. His neck was broken. As he lay helpless, a cloud of glittering translucent tendrils enveloped him. The threlphax became Hadwyn's healer and liberator, offering him a new life.

After the merge, the threlphax Mroniea transformed a portion of Hadwyn Clarke's energy into threlphax energy. Hadwyn grew foggy-headed and lackadaisical in spirit, but he didn't mind. Despite the negative impact, the threlphax was essential to who Hadwyn Clarke was, leading him to appreciate the life he once disdained. But Hadwyn was equally essential to the threlphax, so Mroniea sought alternative methods to address its slowly dissipating membrane.

He positioned the needle above his upper arm. The dendritic cells of his muscle would distribute the chemical throughout his host body, touching the merged threlphax-human energy that circulated through this vessel and gave it life. He slid the needle into his arm and pushed down the plunger. The sharp pinch and rush of chemicals were nothing compared to the violence he visited upon threlphax hosts to get grafts of energy to patch his own.

The injection complete, he withdrew the needle and placed the syringe in the tray on the nightstand.

He reclined on the bed and waited for a reaction. The room spun, and the muscles in his throat trembled. Sucking in a deep breath, he tried to relax. Tiny pinpricks of pain circulated throughout his body.

Sadness.

Fear.

The merge of his human and threlphax selves was coming undone. His vision blurred, and his mind became disoriented.

Tiny bursts of energy preceded the translucent tendrils that emerged from his human self as the threlphax Mroniea surfaced. The being of energy climbed out of Hadwyn Clarke, and sprawled over him. Its many coiled tendrils swayed haphazardly around them, afflicted by slow dissipation.

As Hadwyn Clarke regained his vision and comprehension, he lifted his head to survey his companion and savior. Hadwyn reached up to brush his hands through Mroniea's tendrils, feeling them tingle against his human flesh.

Turning his head, Hadwyn Clarke looked in the mirror above the dresser and surveyed the gray areas around what he perceived as Mroniea's tiny glowing threlphax core.

You must be suffering, he thought.

"Mroniea," Hadwyn Clarke whispered, calling the threlphax name out loud before his body shut down, forcing him into a deep sleep. Mroniea slipped back into Hadwyn Clarke to merge their energy signatures and return his host to health.

When Mroniea Hadwyn Clarke opened his eyes, he looked at his watch. Seven hours had passed since he injected the chemical compound, and he felt the merged threlphax-human energy signatures flowing through him as if they had never separated.

"It worked." Mroniea grinned as he jumped up and crossed the room to stop the video recording. "It worked," he laughed.

After he confirmed the recording on the computer, he clicked on the icon to rename the file. He paused as he contemplated what had necessitated the development of the chemical compound.

Everything turned wrong because of Mroniea's incompetent threlphax leader, Chymza. As the threlphax tribe approached the center of the galaxy, Mroniea warned of the energy fluctuation. Instead of heeding Mroniea's warning, the leader continued to guide the threlphax tribe too close to the supermassive black hole.

Mroniea would never understand why the leader ignored the warning. Perhaps it was the tribe leader's prejudice toward Mroniea, an Anti, or anger about having its leadership challenged. Mroniea was used to threlphax resentment for existing in the wrong universe. Nevertheless, the leader was wrong to ignore Mroniea's warning.

He tightly pursed his lips as the threlphax remembered nearly dissipating when the leader's energy artifact forced dark energy into Mroniea's signature. Mroniea hung back, away from the tribe, as they entered the event horizon. The threlphax remained alone, unable to protect anyone but itself.

When something shifted in his threlphax membrane, he realized Chymza's artifact had not dissipated. Instead, the connection had become a curse as it began the slow dissipation of Mroniea's energy signature. In a moment of panic, Mroniea unblocked the energy artifact shared with its threlphax twin, Mussick.

Mroniea and Mussick were born when two universes collided. Mussick's core was matter, belonging to this universe. With its core of antimatter, Mroniea belonged to another universe. The twin threlphax emerged just as one universe crashed into the other. Their energy resonance was identical, but they had core differences. Mroniea learned that antimatter was antithetical to this universe.

Despite the threat they posed to each other should their cores become exposed, Mroniea felt a true kinship with Mussick through the energy artifacts they shared. While they traveled in different tribes, their threlphax vessels allowed them to share their thoughts across massive distances through their shared energy artifacts.

Unblocking the artifact was both a cry of fear and a warning. Mroniea's twin should not approach this region of the cosmos. If Mroniea's antimatter core became exposed, the energies of both Mussick and Mroniea would dissipate.

As energy drained from its tendrils, bit by bit, Mroniea had worried it would lose threlphax memories along with the tribe. As long as

Mroniea remained beyond the pull of the black hole, maybe the omniscient Conveyance would rescue it.

Instead of Conveyance, Mussick's tribe arrived to find Mroniea in a terrible state. The tribe leader, Trax, tried to restore Mroniea's damaged energy signature, a torturous ordeal for the wounded threlphax. Whether it was cowardice or fear, Mroniea could not withstand the torment of restoration. Mroniea ripped energy from Trax to graft to his own and escaped on a passing asteroid. Trax and his tribe pursued Mroniea, where they fell into the gravitational pull of this place its inhabitants called "Earth."

One hundred and fifty years on Earth was a blip in the timeline of Mroniea's existence. After the weakened threlphax merged with Hadwyn Clarke, it became keenly aware of the press of time. Mroniea lived in fear that its energy signature would grow so thin that its antimatter core would become exposed, causing its annihilation and that of its threlphax twin, now merged with Sameer Khan. For now, this human vessel and energy signature served as an adequate buffer to protect them both.

All this was because of Mroniea's incompetent threlphax leader, Chymza.

"Chymza, you idiot," he murmured as he typed "Chymzafyde test 217" into the title field of the video file. "I will never forget nor forgive you."

17
MEMORY

(JULY 26, 2019)

Kiran Ahuja and Abhimanyu Khatri returned to India, while Sameer Khan stayed in South Korea. Lee Seung-do introduced Sameer to places from his past—Gwangju, Ganghwa Island, and sites around Seoul—while the government processed the paperwork for travel to the United States. When Seung-do's visa came through, Sameer arranged their flight to America.

Upon their arrival in the United States, Seung-do passed through airport customs without a hitch. Customs agents spent more time checking Sameer's luggage and asking him questions, even pulling him aside for added scrutiny and a pat-down. Once cleared for entry, he repacked the contents of his backpack, scattered on a table for inspection.

"Do you always go through that?" asked Seung-do when Sameer joined him.

"The way I look has a disadvantage. Kiran stopped traveling to the States because of misunderstandings."

After stopping in the restroom, they found their way to the baggage claim and collected their luggage from the carousel. Sameer checked his phone for messages.

"Emily has arrived to pick us up," he told Seung-do, slipping his phone back into his pocket.

"So, she's the one?" During their trip to America, Sameer's interest in Emily Scott became a significant topic of discussion.

"Because she's not threlphax, I haven't pursued the relationship. But, yes, she's the one."

"I count myself fortunate to have married Lee Eun-sol. Even though we were together for a short time, we were happy. If you love Emily, tell her how you feel."

"It's complicated."

"People say that to avoid reality."

"I thought you were a medical doctor, not a psychologist," said Sameer. He led them to the bench at the bottom of the escalator.

"I trained in both," said Seung-do.

Sameer nodded toward the escalators. "There she is now," he said. "The redhead."

Seung-do slipped his passport and visa into his backpack and zipped it shut. He looked up as Emily stepped off the escalator and walked toward Sameer.

"Emily Scott," said Sameer, offering a formal introduction. "This is Dr. Seung-do Lee."

Emily stopped and stared wide-eyed at Seung-do. "Park Bong-soo," she gasped. Her breath caught, and her body became limp. Sameer and Seung-do caught her as she collapsed.

"What's wrong?" Sameer asked as he cradled her shoulders and brushed his fingers against her face and hair.

Seung-do checked her pulse. Her palms were damp, and her heart rate was fast. Using his watch, he estimated 145 beats per minute.

"I'm not sure why she fainted," Seung-do said. "But her pulse is racing."

Airport patrons looked on, curious about the two men hovering over an unconscious woman. When security personnel arrived, Sameer grew concerned.

"I'm a doctor," Seung-do said. He pulled his Seoul hospital name badge from the pocket of his leather bag and handed it to security to verify his credentials. They nodded, handed the badge back to Seung-do, and encouraged the crowd to disburse.

Seung-do returned to Emily's side. Emily moved, but kept her eyes closed.

"Sameer," she muttered. "Take me home."

Sameer reached for the keys still clasped in her hand. "I'll go get the car," he said. "Seung-do will stay here with you. He's a doctor and a friend. You'll be safe."

Emily nodded, but did not open her eyes. Sameer ran up the escalator, leaving Seung-do alone with Emily.

"I'm going to move you," Seung-do said. He lifted her in his arms and carried her to the bench along the wall. He laid her down, took off his jacket, draped it over her, then rechecked her pulse. Her pulse had slowed to 110 beats per minute.

It was rare, but extreme anxiety could cause humans to pass out. Usually, such a reaction suggested some other underlying condition. While this concerned him, what occupied Seung-do's mind was what Emily said before she blacked out. She looked directly at him and called the name *Park Bong-soo*. It was his birth name. He hadn't used that name in over a century. He hadn't even told Sameer that name. How did Emily know it?

Sameer said Emily was not a threlphax host. She looked to be in her early thirties, so she couldn't have lived before 1919. She wouldn't have known that Park Bong-soo adopted the identity of Lee Seung-do. She wouldn't have known that on his deathbed, the original Lee Seung-do asked his doppelgänger and friend, Park Bong-soo, to take his place and protect his family. Emily wouldn't have known any of that.

So, how did she know his original name?

He unzipped the pocket of his backpack and retrieved the ornate iron box that carried the threlphax vessel with Tamar. However unlikely it was, he had to test his hypothesis.

Seung-do opened the box and pulled back the muslin lining. The faint glow of the threlphax vessel intensified as tendrils snaked out toward Emily.

"No!" he whispered harshly.

The tendrils receded, and he hurriedly draped the muslin over the vessel and closed the box. Seung-do sat back on the floor and stared at Emily. It couldn't be possible, could it? Did Tamar's instant reaction indicate recognition of the energy signature of its former host? Could Emily be the reincarnation of Lee Eun-sol, his wife? Maybe he misunderstood Tamar's reaction. Perhaps the threlphax sought Emily because it sensed her suffering.

But Emily clearly said *Park Bong-soo*. She called him by a name he no longer used. She knew who he had been. He stared at the box he cradled in his hands. What would happen if Tamar merged with Emily? Would Lee Eun-sol's memories become hers? Would she rekindle her relationship with him?

What could he say to Sameer?

He watched the escalator, wondering how long before Sameer returned. Though he and Sameer had just met, their threlphax knew each other well. They were companions who long ago pledged to support Trax, the leader of their threlphax tribe. The merge of the threlphax with these two men extended their strong bond of friendship to their human hosts.

But now, there was a wrinkle. The threlphax Taedlum and Tamar had always been together. Though threlphax did not mate, they did form bonds. The bond between Taedlum and Tamar was more akin to lovers—even more so given the relationship of their human hosts—while Taedlum and Mussick enjoyed a close brotherhood. Seung-do put his head back and sighed.

How was he going to tell Sameer?

Did Emily love Sameer? If so, would that change Tamar's relationship with Taedlum? Threlphax were observers, beholden to the whims of their hosts. Apart from a few who became primary energy signatures within a host, they allowed their hosts to make their own choices, provided those choices didn't cause harm to the host or the threlphax. Seung-do wished he could hear Taedlum's thoughts and counsel him on what to do, but his threlphax offered no guidance.

Seung-do put the iron box in his jacket pocket and checked Emily's pulse. It was now down to 100 beats per minute. He held her hand, still cold and clammy but not as damp as before. Her recuperation was slow but steady.

"Seung-do!" Sameer called to him from further down the lobby. As he approached, Seung-do stood. "I've pulled the car up outside. I'll help Emily. Can you bring the luggage?"

Before Seung-do could respond, Sameer was at Emily's side. He spoke to her briefly, then helped her stand and walked with her through the lobby and out the sliding doors to the car parked by the curb. Seung-do followed with their luggage.

Emily lay down in the back seat, and Sameer adjusted Seung-do's coat over her. Seung-do placed the luggage in the trunk.

"Should we take Emily to the hospital?" asked Sameer as he and Seung-do climbed into the car.

Seung-do shook his head. "Her pulse is returning to normal. She should be okay with rest." If his assumption was correct, no hospital could cure what ailed Emily.

Sameer started the car and navigated out of the airport. As they drove to KSH House, the two men remained silent, shaken by Emily's collapse. Seung-do was sure his presence had caused it, and he worried about the implications for Emily, Sameer, and himself. Beneath his pang of guilt for Emily's state, he felt a sliver of hope.

When they arrived at KSH House, Sameer helped Emily to her room. Seung-do followed and pulled back the bedcovers so they could settle her in bed.

Seung-do checked Emily's pulse, then nodded at Sameer, who sat on the other side of the bed. As he held Emily's hand in his and watched her, his forehead creased with concern.

"Stay with me," said Emily. "Until I'm asleep."

He sat with her as her breaths slowed, and she fell asleep. Sameer relaxed.

"Sameer," said Seung-do quietly. "Before Emily fainted, she called me *Park Bong-soo*."

"Really? Maybe you reminded her of someone."

"Sameer, my original name was Park Bong-soo. I changed it to Lee Seung-do in 1919."

"So, what are you saying?"

"No one alive today would associate the name Park Bong-soo with me."

If Emily was Lee Eun-sol reincarnated, he and Sameer needed to come to terms with that to address the underlying cause of her reaction. Avoiding the truth would cause pain for everyone. "You must know what I'm thinking," Seung-do said.

"Explain it to me," said Sameer.

"Tamar reacted to Emily." Seung-do's statement tore away any prevarication, exposing the painful truth. It was like ripping away a bandage stuck to a scab. His words wounded them both, although he wasn't sure whether he or Sameer suffered the greater injury.

Sameer's expression turned somber. It was difficult to tell whether he was angry or hurt. But he didn't seem surprised.

"Are you suggesting that Emily is a reincarnation of someone who knew you?" Sameer exhaled a sad laugh. "Are you saying she was your wife?"

"I don't know, Sameer. I'm just trying to understand the facts as they present themselves. What happened isn't a figment of my imagination. We have to consider the possibility that Emily is Lee Eun-sol reincarnated."

Sameer ran his thumbs over Emily's hand and shook his head. "Maybe you were right. Maybe I ruined my chance because I hesitated."

"Sameer, who she may have been, is not who she is now."

Jong and Kit appeared in the doorway. "Is Emily okay?" Jong asked as Tae-hee squeezed past them to enter the room. Outside, Jackson, Renuka, and Naeem gathered.

"She needs rest," replied Seung-do.

"And you are . . . ?" Jong asked.

"He is Dr. Lee Seung-do," said Sameer, "a colleague from South Korea. He will be staying at KSH House."

"Cool," Jong replied. With a broad smile, he stepped forward and offered his hand to Seung-do. "My name is Jong-hyun Park, but you can call me Jong." This man was the gregarious Jong whom Sameer described. Although he wasn't a threlphax host, he drew Sameer's attention.

Jong continued the introductions. He nodded at the woman at Emily's side. "That's Tae-hee Kim." She bowed her head in greeting to Seung-do.

Jong motioned toward the man who leaned against the door frame. "His name is Kit. Just Kit."

Kit bowed his head slightly to Seung-do. This was Tae-hee's older brother. Seung-do glanced from Kit to Tae-hee and back again. They didn't look like siblings.

"Outside is the Jones family, Jackson, Renuka, and their son, Naeem."

Seung-do bowed to the group. "I'll be in your care."

"What happened to Emily?" asked Renuka.

"She fainted," replied Seung-do. It was the best answer Seung-do could offer the group. He wanted to be sure of his reincarnation theory before he shared it further. Sameer would agree.

"Is there anything we can do?"

"She just needs some rest," Seung-do replied.

Renuka nodded. "Take good care of Emily." She, Jackson, and Naeem retreated from the room.

"If only we could mind-meld with Emily," Tae-hee said. "Maybe we'd know why she fainted." Her eyes brightened, and she ran over to Jong and took him by the wrists. "You are a shaman. Can you help her?"

Jong pulled away from Tae-hee and folded his arms across his chest. "Tae-hee, there's no ritual for this. A shaman might help if we needed to exorcise a demon or a grudge. But there's nothing for someone who fainted." He nodded at Seung-do. "She needs a doctor. Besides, it's been over ten years since I've practiced."

"A grudge, you said?" asked Seung-do.

"The Jindo Ssitgimgut is used to cleanse grudges of the dead. But Emily's not dead, and I don't think she's holding any grudges."

"What if she is the reincarnation of someone who died burdened with deep sorrow?"

18
TRANCE

(JULY 26, 2019)

"Seung-do," warned Sameer. He tightened his grip around Emily's hand and shot a warning glance at Jong. It was an obvious threat that told Jong not to be rash. Seung-do and Sameer understood something concerning Emily. But neither revealed what they were thinking.

"Reincarnation is an interesting idea," said Jong, "but exploring that is way beyond my capabilities." He adjusted his vision to examine Emily's faint aura, which shifted between green and red. "I could try to read her emotional state." Jong judged Sameer might be okay with that much.

"Do you need any special equipment?" Tae-hee asked.

"No," chuckled Jong. He pulled out his phone and scrolled through the apps. "The right music can help me focus." He brought up a video and read the description.

"Okay," Jong said as the sound of drumming and a voice singing in Korean streamed through his phone. "This is a ritual by shaman Park Byung-Chun. He introduced the Ssitkimkut ritual of the dead to America back in the 1990s."

Jong's enthusiasm was met with baffled expressions. "I admire his work," he sighed. "But since we're in America and I'm not a bona fide shaman, I'll pick something natural."

Jong quickly searched, pressed play, adjusted the volume, and put the phone on the nightstand. Instead of a shaman ritual, birdsong, rustling leaves, and a peaceful running stream filled the room. Jong sat on the floor, cross-legged, and assumed a comfortable posture as the forest litany washed over him.

He closed his eyes and relaxed his consciousness until it flowed with the sounds of nature. As he slowed his breathing, his arms and legs became heavy, and he drifted free from his physical moorings. He focused first on Emily before letting his comprehension freely flow around the room. He recognized the aqua-colored aura of Tae-hee and the silver aura of Sameer. A second silver aura radiated from Seung-do. Sparkling translucent clouds surrounded the two men.

These are threlphax, he thought. Until now, he had never understood this about Sameer and Tae-hee's auras. The threlphax presence was strongest in Sameer and Seung-do and weaker in Tae-hee. He sensed no such presence in or around Emily.

Jong's breathing slowed further, and the floating sensation intensified.

This, he thought as he basked in the familiar state of flow, freedom from the physical. Space and time fell away, and Jong sensed light and dark, love and remorse, healing and pain. He followed the energy current in the room. It pulled and stretched his consciousness in multiple directions, connecting him to the emotions of those around him.

As he floated amidst the sensations, he felt the streams of regret and sorrow streaming from Sameer and Seung-do toward Emily. The streams tugged at Jong and he relaxed further, allowing himself to be pulled into the current. Settled in the emotional flow, he felt the soft reverberation of an indistinct voice that swirled around Emily and ebbed toward Seung-do.

In this mournful flow, Jong's calm became agitated. He drew away from Emily and found a direct line of compassion that drew him toward Tae-hee. As he drifted toward her, a new presence appeared. The complexity of this entity bent his awareness in a new direction.

Kit, thought Jong. He sensed the threlphax within Kit, surrounded by a unique dualism different from the other threlphax hosts in the room. A dark stream of emotion flowed from Kit toward Seung-do. While this fascinated Jong, he was more intrigued by the bright glow of something greater concealed within Kit. Jong pushed his mind forward, seeking to experience this unique energy.

The music stopped.

The sound of breathing and shuffling bodies pulled Jong's energy flow back to his body. Moments later, he took a deep breath and exhaled. He opened his eyes and scanned the room. His gaze stopped on Seung-do.

"Emily's condition is associated with you," Jong explained. He searched for the right words to describe his experience. "The emotions carry an aura of extreme heartache. She blocked access to these emotions. That means that she's blocked off access to healing. She's a wreck. If I was in her emotional state, I'd prefer to remain unconscious."

When Sameer and Seung-do exchanged glances, Jong realized his exploration confirmed their shared understanding. They had caused Emily's unstable emotional state. Sameer and Emily cared for each other, so Jong doubted the issue was between them. Seung-do was the wild card. Yet, Jong sensed no animosity between Sameer and Seung-do.

Jong frowned and rose to his feet. "You need to resolve the issues among you three. Otherwise, her emotional state will continue to eat away at her physical self."

Sameer nodded. "Could everyone give us time alone? Seung-do, please stay."

Kit, Jong, and Tae-hee exited the room, closing the door behind them.

19
SAMSARA

(JULY 26, 2019)

Jong's words confirmed Seung-do's conclusion. When Emily came face-to-face with Seung-do, she shut down, overwhelmed by the clash between two versions of herself. Lee Eun-sol's Joseon husband, Park Bong-soo, stood before her, turning Emily into an anachronism as her modern self unraveled under the weight of memories from her former life.

Although his presence caused her current state, Seung-do possessed a solution. "If Tamar can provide healing, we should encourage Emily to accept the merge," he offered.

"When we met, you said you would never part with Tamar," said Sameer.

"I admit my statement was flawed. I did not foresee this situation."

Sameer hung his head. Seung-do's proposed course of action had ramifications. As observers of the universe, threlphax carried the memories of the beings with which they merged. If they merged Tamar with Emily, those memories might change Emily. Seung-do saw that the thought weighed heavily on Sameer.

"Tamar may help bridge the gap between Emily's old self and her new self," said Seung-do. "Isn't this why you asked me to stay back, Sameer? This situation is painful and awkward for everyone. If she was Lee Eun-sol—"

"—*if*," emphasized Sameer.

"Jong confirmed that I'm responsible for Emily's condition. If seeing me unlocked memories of her past life, why is she only experiencing heartache? Lee Eun-sol and I loved each other. Heartache came at the very end when Lee Eun-sol died. Maybe Tamar can restore the happy memories of her life as Lee Eun-sol. Then Emily can move on. If you care for her, you should at least ask her."

Sameer clenched his jaw as he tightened and loosened his grip on Emily's hand in a fretful massage.

Seung-do pressed the issue. "Sameer, I'm not saying this for my personal gain. I'm saying this for Emily's sake. If fragmentary memories of her past caused her to pass out, then she must embrace her complete memories and, by embracing them, find healing."

"I know!" spat Sameer.

Seung-do pulled the small iron box from his jacket pocket and laid it on the nightstand. "I told you I would never part with Tamar," he said. "But I have changed my mind. I trust you'll do what is in Emily's best interest." Seung-do headed for the door.

"Do you hope to reunite with your wife?" Sameer asked.

Seung-do paused with his hand on the doorknob. "I cannot deny I wonder whether Tamar's merge with Emily could bring back the person I knew as Lee Eun-sol. And I know you're concerned because of Taedlum and Tamar. They were close companions for as long as they can remember. As Taedlum's host, I have carried Tamar in her threlphax vessel with me all these years. But does any of that matter now? If you love Emily, you'll do whatever it takes to help her."

Seung-do left the room. As he closed the door, Tae-hee rose from the sofa and gave him a nervous smile.

"It's okay," said Seung-do. "Emily will be fine."

Tae-hee nodded.

Seung-do stepped outside KSH House to walk off his anxiety. What would Emily remember if Tamar merged with her? Would the restored memories make her fall in love with him again? What of his newfound friendship with Sameer? Though he had only known Sameer for a short time, they had a rapport he hadn't experienced in decades. Could he have both relationships?

He stopped in the shade of a thicket of branches. His thoughts were getting ahead of reality. He needed to be pragmatic. The first step was to heal Emily. The merge with Tamar could stabilize her. There might be an emotional minefield afterward. But he had endured turmoil in the past.

A powerful gust of wind announced an approaching storm. Leaves rustled around Seung-do, and a branch laden with figs danced in the breeze.

A fig tree.

Finding himself surrounded by the sprawling branches of a fig tree may have been a coincidence, but Seung-do interpreted it as a positive sign. Throughout their romance and marriage, fig trees had held special meaning for Lee Eun-sol and Park Bong-soo. He laughed to himself as he wondered what he would say to Emily. The Park Bong-soo she knew and loved had changed. He would have to explain why he had cut his hair and changed his name and profession after she died.

He shook his head at his shallow thoughts.

Lee Eun-sol was more changed than he was.

* * * *

Inside Emily's room, Sameer struggled between anger and reason. His threlphax self, Mussick, mused at how strange it was to see Taedlum's host, Seung-do, display so many of the same personality traits as the threlphax. Taedlum was always logical and even-tempered, while Mussick acted without weighing the repercussions. For that reason, Mussick always followed Taedlum's lead.

In his heart, Sameer knew Seung-do proposed the best course of action. However, once Tamar merged with Emily, the memories of Lee Eun-sol might change her into someone different. If she changed, would Sameer feel the same way about her? He cared for the woman Emily was, and he regretted that he had never confessed his feelings to her. Now, it might be too late.

Stupid. That's not what is important.

"Quiet," he told Mussick. He brushed stray hairs from Emily's forehead. Emily's red hair, pale skin, and light freckles attracted his attention the first time they met. But when her green eyes focused on him, he nearly forgot to breathe. He chuckled to himself. He was smitten with her from the beginning. Faced with a choice that could help Emily, he should not be selfish. Whether for friendship or love, he had to do the necessary.

He sighed and pulled out his phone, scrolled through his contacts, and pressed the call button.

"It took you long enough," answered Seung-do.

"Be quiet and get back here. I'm not doing this by myself."

Tae-hee was already in the room when Seung-do arrived. She was a threlphax host, a nurse, and Emily's friend. Her presence made Sameer feel more secure.

Seung-do took his place in the corner, out of Emily's line of sight. If Emily saw him, their task might be more difficult.

"Emily," Sameer called. "Can you hear me?"

Emily raised her hands and opened her eyes.

"Tae-hee is here as well," added Sameer.

Emily shifted her focus to Tae-hee, who consoled her with a smile. Emily looked back at Sameer.

"Do you remember who you saw at the airport?" said Sameer. He tried to sound calm.

"You . . . and my husband, Park Bong-soo." Emily's eyes darted back and forth as her forehead wrinkled under her confusion. "No . . . that can't be right . . . I'm not married."

"It's okay," said Sameer. "We believe the person you saw may have caused you to recall memories of a previous life."

"You mean reincarnation?"

"Possibly," said Sameer. "We have a way to tell whether it is true. You said that you trust me."

Emily gave a slight nod in confirmation.

"We need you to accept something that will help you. It is called a threlphax." Sameer felt his voice strain as he revealed what he had kept hidden from her. "It will become part of you, as it has become part of me and Tae-hee."

Emily searched Sameer's eyes before whispering, "Will it hurt?"

"No," smiled Sameer. "There is nothing to fear, Emily. I know who you are and what you believe. I would never ask you to do something that could cause you harm. You know I care about you, right?"

Emily relaxed into a gentle smile. "I do."

Sameer kissed her hand, then held it against his cheek.

"Are you worried?" Emily asked.

"A little," said Sameer. He glanced at Seung-do and then replied, "It may change how you think about the people around you."

"Will I forget you?"

"No."

"Will it change how you treat me?"

Sameer shook his head. "You will always be my dear friend. But you may experience memories you didn't know you had."

"Then, I will accept it."

Sameer sighed and released her hand. "Now, close your eyes."

Emily followed Sameer's instructions. Sameer nodded to Seung-do, who crossed the room and opened the small iron box on the nightstand. After he unfolded the muslin and exposed Tamar's brightly glowing vessel, Seung-do stepped back. Glittering translucent tendrils snaked out from the vessel and moved toward Emily.

Tae-hee nervously approached Seung-do and whispered, "Is that what it's supposed to do?"

"Yes," Seung-do said. "Tamar recognizes its host. This should be a smooth merge."

The glittering, translucent tendrils wrapped around Emily's body, encasing her in a luminous, glittering cocoon. As the threlphax merged into her, the tendrils faded. Seung-do retreated against the wall while Tae-hee sat down in the chair next to the bed as they waited for Emily's response.

Sameer held Emily's hand and stroked her hair. Silent seconds turned into minutes. Seung-do crossed his arms and shifted his posture.

"Tell me about your wife, Seung-do," said Sameer. "Tell me about Lee Eun-sol."

Seung-do stared at the ceiling momentarily, exhaled, and lowered his head to gaze at Emily.

"I met Lee Eun-sol when she was a young widow," he said. "She was petite, but she wasn't weak. As a widow in Joseon, she was a target. Despite being mistreated, she cared about others: those cast aside, the wounded, and those who needed a helping hand. This is where she found her joy, and her smile was lovely. She was lovely."

Seung-do closed his eyes. "Tamar saved Lee Eun-sol from scarlet fever. A short time after Tamar merged with Lee Eun-sol, I returned to duty, leaving her behind. The separation was difficult. Thoughts of her filled my mind, pulled both by my human desire and my yearning for threlphax companionship.

"Months later, I returned and asked her to marry me. We moved to Ganghwa Island, where we lived with my friend Kim Min-woo and his brother's family. It was an opportunity for Lee Eun-sol to have a fresh start. When she became pregnant, I worried because we were threlphax hosts. But she was confident. She was stronger than I was. During her pregnancy, word spread that she was a widow remarried. Joseon society frowned upon such a thing. I don't know whether she ignored the whispers and critical glances or just didn't see them. But she never complained."

He smiled as another recollection came to mind. "There was a fig tree in the yard with a bench beneath it. We sat and talked together there. We watched the fruit grow and ripen. She even fed figs to my mare."

On the bed, Emily murmured. "I remember." She stirred, opened her eyes, and searched the room. Still holding her hand, Sameer waited until she focused on him.

"Emily," said Sameer. "How are you feeling?"

"I'm fine, Sameer. Where is Park Bong-soo?"

Sameer and Tae-hee looked at Seung-do. He stepped away from the wall so she could see him. "I am called Lee Seung-do now." When she smiled, he moved to the side of her bed, across from Sameer.

"Lee Seung-do," repeated Emily. "Yes, I remember." She lifted her hand and urged him to sit on the bed. Tae-hee shifted in her chair to make room for Seung-do.

"I dreamed I stood on a grass-covered hill." Her hand moved in gentle strokes through the air. "I felt the thick, plump foxtail plumes. On the plain below me stood a man in an officer's robe, his sword drawn. His back was to me as he faced seven men wearing black who surrounded him. When he turned, I saw it was you. The men disappeared, but you remained. You looked so sad, even though you smiled at me."

Seung-do lifted Emily's hand and kissed it.

"Thank you for carrying Tamar all these years," she said. "Tamar helped me remember our life. I was so sorry that I could not continue with you." She glanced at Tae-hee, then looked back at Seung-do. "What happened to the twins? Did they survive?"

"The twins lived," said Seung-do.

"What did you name them?" asked Emily.

"Park Tae-soo and Park Tae-hee," replied Seung-do.

When Tae-hee gasped, Emily smiled at her before looking back at Seung-do.

"Are they still alive? Can I see them?"

"You need to rest," he explained, deflecting the question. Emily nodded, and he adjusted the comforter as she sank into sleep. Emily had confirmed what Seung-do believed, and Sameer had to accept. As the reincarnation of Seung-do's Joseon wife, Lee Eun-sol, her destiny was with Seung-do. But as Emily, she was with Sameer.

Feeling the interloper, Seung-do said, "I'll give you some time."

As Seung-do stood to leave the room, Tae-hee appeared anxious. She wrung her hands as she looked from Emily to Seung-do and back again. As a doctor, he saw many caregivers worry until they became physically ill. However, she seemed unduly perturbed. "Emily will need to sleep during this first phase of the merge," he explained.

Tae-hee followed him out of the room and closed the door behind them.

"How is Emily?" asked Jong, who sat in the foyer.

"After some more rest, she should be fine. Sameer will stay with her."

Tae-hee grabbed Seung-do's wrist. "I need to talk to you," she said. Her eyes were wide, her expression filled with anxiety.

Seung-do bowed to the group as Tae-hee led him into the library. Once inside, she pulled out a chair for him. "I think you will want to sit for this, Dr. Lee," she said.

"You may call me Seung-do," he said as he took the proffered seat. "Was this your first time seeing a threlphax?"

Tae-hee paced back and forth in front of him, wringing her hands while she organized her thoughts.

"You can speak openly," said Seung-do. "You won't offend me."

"Okay, okay," Tae-hee spun around, turning her back to him. She took a deep breath, then blurted out, "I was born in 1867 on Ganghwa Island. My mother died giving birth to my twin brother and me. We lived with our father until he disappeared in 1871. After he disappeared, friends of our father took us to the Joseon peninsula. We never saw our father again. I've lived this long because I'm a threlphax host." She rocked back and forth as she fiddled with her fingers. "Do you understand what I'm saying?"

Seung-do grunted. What she was implying was incomprehensible to him.

Tae-hee nodded once, then turned to face him as she continued in a matter-of-fact tone. "Kim is the name of our foster parents. Our biological father's name was Park Bong-soo. When our father disappeared, the Kim family added Tae-soo and me to their family registry."

Seung-do searched Tae-hee for traces of the little girl he cradled, told stories to, and loved. He saw his daughter's likeness in her dark eyes, the shape of her face, her bright smile. Had his little girl grown into this woman who stood before him? Why was his daughter here, where he would never have looked? Remorse washed over him. Should he have done more to find his children? Why didn't he know she was still alive?

Tae-hee sat down in the chair beside him and wrapped her hands around his. "Appa, what happened to you?"

Seung-do struggled to find the right words. Though he mourned the loss of his family, he never imagined the conversation if they reunited. How could he explain himself? What should he say?

Tae-soo squeezed his hands and repeated, "What happened to you, Appa?"

He forced out words despite his shock. "That year, the Americans attacked Ganghwa Island. A rifleman shot me, but I recovered. I went to find you, but you were gone. Everyone was gone. I was too late. I waited for you at our hanok. For four years. After a century of wondering, I thought you died." He drew a hand over his face to hide the sadness and regret that surged through him.

"Appa," said Tae-hee as she squeezed his hand. "Appa, you found us."

"How are you here?" he choked out. "How are you a threlphax host?"

"When we were growing up, we noticed that we never got sick and rapidly healed. We stopped aging in our twenties. We always knew we were unusual. Our foster family knew it, too. Because we were born super healthy, we thought our ancestors looked after us."

She paused and chuckled. "Sameer is the one who explained it to me. He sensed the threlphax in me."

Her calm smile soothed Seung-do's fluctuating energy. He held up his hand and released a small portion of his threlphax energy. Tiny, glittering translucent tendrils spread across his palm.

Smiling, Tae-hee drew her fingers across the tendrils. "Sameer never showed the threlphax to me like this."

He gasped as his energy fluctuated, quickly crescendoed, then settled into a soft hum. Their connection was unmistakable.

"My threlphax is called Taedlum," he said. Seung-do had never spoken about the threlphax with his young children.

Tae-hee laid her palm against his and closed her eyes. He wrapped her small hand in his, thankful for this miracle of fate. The hum within him became a reassuring resonance. Its flavor differed from Tamar's energy, but it wasn't unfamiliar. He scanned Tae-hee's features, comparing them to the daughter he raised and the design of her mother. Hers was the same smile that had brightened his heart over a century-and-a-half ago.

Opening her eyes, Tae-hee asked, "Appa, how did we become this way? Did you put threlphax in us as you did with Emily?"

Seung-do withdrew his threlphax, released her hand, and shook his head. "No, nothing like that, Tae-hee." His eyes moved back and forth as he sought an explanation. "Your mother and I were both threlphax hosts when we conceived you. We must have passed threlphax energy to you through our genes. You must have been born with your threlphax. I never knew that could happen. Not until today. Not until now."

"An Earthborn threlphax," said Tae-hee. "That explains why we never knew." She smiled at Seung-do. Then, Appa, it's really you, right?"

This was the woman his daughter had become—a kind, honest person who cared for others. He stood and swept her into his arms. "Oh yes, Tae-hee. I am your Abeoji. I am so sorry I lost you. Mianhada. I am so, so sorry." He hugged her and continued whispering affirmations and apologies until words no longer mattered. After more than a century of searching, he had found his daughter. "Did you grow up well? Were you happy? Were you treated with respect? Did you ever marry?"

"I grew up well and happy. I didn't marry."

"What about Tae-soo?" he asked. "Does he still live?" His experience proved that having a threlphax didn't always secure a long life. There were exceptions.

"It's complicated." Tae-hee leaned back and looked up at Seung-do. "You need to sit for this."

After they settled in their seats, Tae-hee collected her thoughts. "I lost contact with Tae-soo right before the March First Independence Movement. Things happened to him." As she calmly spoke, she watched his expression. "Because of the political upheaval, Kim Joon-gi sent Tae-soo away. Kim Joon-gi changed the family registry to name me as his adopted daughter and took care of me until his death in 1946."

"There was no record of Kim Joon-gi having a daughter. I checked the registries when I searched for some clue about you."

"That may have been my fault. After Kim Joon-gi died, I removed my name. The less paperwork circulating about me, the better. The next time I learned of Tae-soo was when I claimed his body in November 1952."

Seung-do's heart sank as he translated her meaning. His son, Tae-soo, died during the Korean War.

Tae-hee shook her head and waved her hands. "But he wasn't dead. I thought he was, but he wasn't. He was wounded and knew he was dying, so he jumped into a Thai soldier's body."

"He jumped? You mean he transmigrated?"

"That's what he told me. But he didn't take over the Thai soldier's body. He cohabitates in it. Both Tae-soo and Chanchai are living together in one body. I guess it has something to do with Tae-soo's threlphax."

Seung-do raised a hand to pause her account as he absorbed this latest information. "So, Tae-soo exists in another person's body?" he clarified.

"Yes."

"You are sure of it?"

"Yes. He knows and does things that only Tae-soo would know and do. Sameer taught me that threlphax twins share an artifact connection.

And I feel our connection. I love him and talk with him as I loved and talked with Tae-soo. And he's a good man."

"Where is he? Can I see him?"

"You have seen him, Appa. Tae-soo is Kit."

Seung-do searched his memory for his direct interactions with Kit so far. Apart from Jong's introduction, there were none. As he sifted through the details Tae-hee related, he made a connection with his past.

"Severance Hospital," said Seung-do. "1919. Did you study at Severance Hospital?"

"How did you—?"

"—I met Kim Tae-soo in 1919. But I didn't realize who he was. His sister worked at Severance Hospital. He lost someone dear to him. We both lost people dear to us."

When Seung-do started for the door, Tae-hee leaped in front of him and blocked his way. "I'm not done yet," she said forcefully. "There's more you need to know. Sit down."

Seung-do reluctantly complied.

Tae-soo . . . Kit . . . doesn't know about the threlphax," she said. "So, you mustn't run out and tell Kit that you're Tae-soo's father. He is dealing with a number of issues. Tae-soo has just come back to me as Kit. He's navigating a new country and new friends. And he's got something going on with Jong."

"Is he in a relationship with Jong?"

"No, not yet. But Kit is in love, even though he hasn't admitted it. And so is Jong. That's a fact. Jong told me how he felt. Kit doesn't need another distraction."

"A distraction," Seung-do sighed.

"Did I just minimize you?" Tae-hee asked.

Seung-do pinched his finger and thumb together. "A little. But I understand. You know Kit better than I do. I won't tell him. Besides, we've got to get Emily back on her feet."

"That's another thing," said Tae-hee. She tossed so much information at him that he worried about what would come next. "I understand what Emily means to you. And I know what this means for Tae-soo and me. In her former life, she was the one who gave birth to us. The two of you are the reasons Tae-soo and I exist. But Emily and Sameer are sort of a couple, right?"

"Don't worry, Tae-hee," said Seung-do. "Sameer said as much."

"Really? Seriously? That's so awesome! He never said it to us, but everyone knows."

"Based on what my threlphax conveys of his threlphax, I'm not surprised that Sameer doesn't speak of his personal life."

"Are you saying that your threlphax knew Sameer's threlphax before it merged with him? I bet you have stories."

"Honestly, my threlphax energy isn't completely harmonious with my human energy, so I'm not sure—"

I have stories.

A rush of images and thoughts flowed into Seung-do's mind. Unable to interpret their meanings, he gave up and encouraged his threlphax Taedlum to take control of the conversation.

Seung-do laughed under his breath. "Taedlum has a few relevant memories," he said.

Over the next hour, they filled the library with hushed tones and quiet laughter.

20
RESONANCE

(JULY 27, 2019)

The following day, Emily continued resting in her room as she merged with the threlphax, Tamar. After brunch, Tae-hee brought a tray of food to her. After she placed the tray on the nightstand, she gently woke Emily from her slumber.

"You should eat something," said Tae-hee.

Emily sighed and pushed herself up to sit on the edge of the bed. Tae-hee moved the tray onto her lap to make it easier to reach.

"Tae-hee," said Emily. "I have memories—"

"—of your past life," said Tae-hee as she peeled a clementine. "Here, eat this. Vitamin C will make you feel better."

Emily took the fruit and pulled apart the carpels, eating each one slowly as she savored the sweetness of each segment. "That's good," she said. She placed the half-finished clementine on the tray and wiped the juice from her fingers with the napkin.

"I don't understand any of this," she said. "I am to believe that in my past life, I was married to Park Bong-soo, who is now called Lee Seung-do."

"Yes."

"And I gave birth to two children."

"That's right."

"And you are one of them?"

Tae-hee smiled and nodded.

"And Tamar is a being of energy called threlphax. Tamar exists in me and carries memories of my past life. And you have a threlphax that kept you alive—and young—for over a century and a half?"

"Yes," said Tae-hee. "But I host an Earthborn threlphax, while Tamar is an off-world threlphax."

"Are they different?"

"I've only known what it's like to be an Earthborn threlphax."

"I see." Emily twisted the edge of the napkin between her fingers. Emily's furrowed brow revealed her mental struggle as fragmented facts coalesced into understanding. "But Tae-hee, I can't be your mother," she said. "We're friends."

Emily needed assurance. "Emily," said Tae-hee, "I don't expect you to be my mother. Just be yourself. Your understanding of our relationship may have changed, but our friendship hasn't." Despite Tae-hee's desire to learn more about her birth mother, there would be time for Emily to share memories of her former life once she was comfortable.

"What do we tell Renuka?"

"I told Renuka that you just wore yourself out with the move to KSH House and the added responsibilities while Sameer was away. It happens to everyone. Well, not everyone. Threlphax hosts don't really wear themselves out."

"Kit is not just your brother. He's your twin, isn't he?"

Emily's ease in unraveling Tae-hee's secrets shouldn't have been unexpected. Still, her candidness surprised Tae-hee.

"Yes," said Tae-hee.

"What do we tell him?"

"Nothing." Tae-hee stared blankly ahead as she contemplated the dilemma. Her thoughts wandered to Seung-do, equally entangled in the situation.

When she became aware of Emily's confused stare, she added, "I mean that when it's time, Sameer and Seung-do should be the ones to tell him. Kit doesn't know about the threlphax. It might be easier for them to explain everything all at once. I am not a threlphax expert and you're new to all of this."

Tae-hee kept things simple by not mentioning Kit's unique composition.

Emily nodded, then pursed her lips and frowned. "About Seung-do... it's difficult to ignore Lee Eun-sol's memories."

"Just because you have Lee Eun-sol's memories doesn't mean you must live her life. You are Emily Scott, and this is *your* life." Though Tae-hee couldn't fully understand Emily's struggle, she understood Emily's heart. She handed Emily the remaining clementine. "Now, Emily Scott, eat your food."

Emily smiled and wrapped her arms around Tae-hee. "Thank you, Tae-hee. Thank you so much."

* * * *

In the basement, Seung-do waited while Sameer unlocked a door, flicked on a light switch, and stepped inside. When Seung-do followed him into the nearly empty room, giddiness consumed him. Blanketed by an exhilarating resonance, Seung-do closed his eyes and took a deep breath to steady himself.

"What is this feeling?" he murmured.

Sameer closed the door and walked to the far side of the room. "Your threlphax senses the energies of the rest of the tribe. They flood the room with their resonance." He stood beside a series of shelves containing wooden bins lined with soft padding. In each of the bins lay threlphax vessels, each elongated sphere the size of a small egg. There were hundreds of them.

Seung-do exhaled a light laugh and crossed the room. The vessels brightened a bit as he ran his hand over the shelves. He admired the rows upon rows of living vessels, each with a unique design, each containing a threlphax being.

"Is this the whole threlphax tribe?" he said.

"I'm not sure," said Sameer. "We don't know how many vessels survived or how many threlphax merged." He retrieved a basket of fractured vessels. "We collected the fragments of vessels, but we don't know how to repair them. And we don't know what happened to the threlphax inside. We can only hope they found other vessels."

"This is amazing, Sameer. Who else knows about this?"

"Abhimanyu and Kiran. They helped collect all these. But I haven't let Tae-hee down here. I don't know how her threlphax would react. Aside from Abhimanyu, Kiran, and me, no one comes to the basement except Jackson and Jong. As non-hosts, they aren't susceptible to threlphax energy; however, I have instructed them never to enter this room. Fortunately, they have never questioned me."

Seung-do felt familiar wisps of energy flow to his hand as he held it over a group of vessels. Translucent, glittering tendrils surfaced in the center of his palm. Similar tendrils emerged from the threlphax vessels to reach across his palm and around his host body. Until now, he didn't know how deeply his threlphax longed to share this communion with the rest of the tribe. The energy within him surged, and he sighed in the abundant joy the connections produced.

Sameer placed his hand over Seung-do's palm, ending the threlphax interlude. "You will have time to connect with the tribe later," he said. "Right now, everyone is waiting for us." Sameer took a few steps toward the door.

"Sameer," said Seung-do. "Why did you ask me to come to KSH House?"

"It seemed the right thing to do."

"Did you know?"

Sameer exhaled and scratched his temple as he strolled back to Seung-do. "Are you talking about you and Tae-hee?"

"Taedlum can't read energy signatures like Mussick or Trax can." Seung-do turned toward Sameer and gave him a hard stare. "Why didn't you tell me?"

"I am sorry. I was going to, but then Emily fainted, and, you know." Sameer paused to prepare a more thoughtful response. "When I first met Tae-hee, she was a student in my class. It surprised me when I felt her threlphax energy. Your energy has a similar resonance, and when you mentioned the name Tae-hee, I wondered if it was possible that you could be her biological father. Still, I wasn't certain." He leaned against the wall, crossed his arms, and tilted his head. "Are you angry with me?" he said with a raised brow.

Seung-do exhaled a deep sigh. "No. The person I am most angry with is myself. I never considered that I passed threlphax energy to my offspring. They are Earthborn threlphax hosts. I should be thankful that Tae-hee and Kit ended up here with you."

He shook his head as he surveyed the threlphax vessels. "It devastated me when I lost my wife and the twins. I am relieved that my children are alive. But now I regret the years of separation even more. I wonder what claim I have on them. Though Tae-hee has accepted me, I am not sure Kit will." He coughed out an exclamatory laugh. "Tae-hee told me not to approach Kit because he knows nothing."

"I had planned on telling Kit about the threlphax when I returned." Sameer straightened as he struggled with a thought.

"What is it?"

"Seung-do, are you sure Kit is your son?"

"Tae-hee believes it. What do you read of his threlphax energy signature?"

"Its resonance is similar to yours and Tae-hee's energy signatures, yet it feels strange."

"How so?"

Sameer wobbled his head. "Kit has a duality that goes beyond the threlphax-human merge. It is difficult to decipher."

"I agree that there is something unique about Kit. In 1919, I met Tae-soo in Hanseong . . . Seoul. I didn't recognize him as my son, and he didn't recognize me as his father. But that's not the most important thing."

"What is?"

"Kit is not the man I met."

"Kit isn't Tae-hee's brother?"

"I didn't say that. Are you aware of Tae-soo's transmigration?" Seung-do stepped closer to Sameer and lowered his voice. "Tae-hee told me that Tae-soo was wounded during the Korean War. Apparently, it was a fatal wound. She said he transmigrated into a Thai soldier. That Thai soldier is Kit." He raised his eyebrows. "Is transmigration even possible?"

Sameer shrugged. "Transmigration would explain why Tae-hee always calls Kit her older brother, not her twin. It explains the personal circumstances that led Tae-soo to leave Korea and become a Thai citizen. Maybe Earthborn threlphax merge in such a way that allows them to transmigrate the energy signatures of their original human hosts. Earthborn threlphax could be a different species from off-world threlphax. That would explain the difference in the resonance of Tae-hee and Kit's threlphax. Kit seems to have more secrets than I knew."

Not wanting his words to trouble Seung-do, Sameer added. "Kit is a good person. Whatever secrets he may have, I am sure he told Tae-hee. She accepts him as her brother and asks us to be patient." Offering a confident grin, he added, "Mussick's experience as Mroniea's twin leads me to believe that she recognizes the resonance of his energy signature better than we ever could."

This confirmation calmed Seung-do's worries about Tae-hee as his daughter and Kit as his son. His thoughts shifted to Lee Eun-sol, the remaining member of his family.

"Sameer. About Emily—"

"—it's not your fault."

"I know I've put you in an uncomfortable situation. Things will return to what they were when I return to Korea."

"Return? I hoped that you'd stay and spend time with your family."

"I feel like an intruder. I am happy enough to know my family lives."

Sameer put a hand on Seung-do's shoulder. "For the longest time, the only other off-world threlphax hosts I've known were Kiran, Abhimanyu, and Mroniea. Maybe it's just the threlphax, but I feel a kinship with you. So do the threlphax, as they've just demonstrated."

"I don't want to get in the way."

"In the way of what? I understand what your wife meant to you. I can't say that finding out Emily is the reincarnation of Lee Eun-sol doesn't concern me. But it's up to Emily to decide her future. I am happy that she and I are good friends. Whatever the future holds for us, I am satisfied with friendship."

"Thank you, Sameer," said Seung-do. "Thank you for finding me and bringing me to KSH House."

"You know," replied Sameer in a humorous tone. "I didn't bring you here only to reunite you with your family. I want your appraisal of that Joseon sitting desk you sold to Abhimanyu. Everyone is waiting in the auction hall to hear the expert."

Seung-do hung his head and chuckled. "I can't believe you ended up with my desk." His meeting with Abhimanyu and Kiran was the impetus to sell what had become a sentimental burden.

Sameer patted him on the shoulder as they left the room. After he locked the door, they proceeded upstairs to the auction hall. Halfway up, Sameer stopped Seung-do and whispered, "By the way, although Jong isn't a threlphax host, he knows about us."

Seung-do's mouth fell open for a second before he asked, "Is there anything else you need to tell me?"

"The Jones family knows nothing of us," smiled Sameer. "They see me as a friend and mentor. Regardless, they are an important part of KSH House."

When Sameer and Seung-do arrived in the auction hall, Tae-hee, Jong, Jackson, Renuka, and Naeem sat around a small table in a semicircle. Seung-do's sitting desk sat on the floor beside it. Emily was absent from the group, but she would know the details of the Joseon desk through her gradual merge with the threlphax Tamar. Kit leaned against the wall, his hands stuffed into his pockets.

"Apologies for our tardiness," began Sameer. "Besides being an eminent physician, Seung-do has an extensive understanding of Korean history. He's here to educate us about the Joseon desk we obtained during our recent trip."

"What's a Joseon desk?" asked Jackson.

"Let's start with a history lesson," Sameer explained, lifting the sitting desk onto the table. "Korea was called Goryeo from 918 to 1392, then Joseon until 1910." Sameer stepped back and motioned for Seung-do to continue.

"Before chairs came into widespread use in the east," Seung-do explained, "we sat on the floor. So, we had sitting desks. A sitting desk was an important piece of furniture that reflected one's stature. It demonstrates craftsmanship that you rarely see today."

Seung-do ran his fingers over the surface of the desk, tracing the familiar designs of the wood pattern and the inkstone stains. Over a century ago, Lee Eun-sol had gifted him the desk. What a strange twist of fate to find his past at KSH House, with his wife reincarnated as someone who could no longer call him husband.

Looks of anticipation alerted Seung-do that his musings had stymied his discourse. He continued, "Joseon carpenters focused on the natural patterns of the wood grain. No artificial ornaments or colors could exceed the beauty of nature. For that reason, craftsmen didn't use metal nails because they could damage or interfere with the artistry of the wood. They didn't use lacquer or painted finishes. Instead, they applied seed oils. It was a natural glaze that polished the surface, protected it, and accentuated the wood grain. It achieved a beautiful sheen."

"If they didn't use nails, how did the desks stay together?" asked Naeem.

"Through durable joineries, such as a mortise and tenon joint." He paused, taking in the blank stares around the table. He pulled a notebook and pen from his jacket pocket and drew a diagram of the joint, then continued, "Carefully designed grooves and holes. The ultimate goal was to build a functional, lasting desk that would bring the beauty of nature to Joseon studies." Everyone leaned forward to compare the drawing to the Joseon desk on the table.

Seung-do looked up at Kit, who expressed no interest in the conversation. He stared back with a deep frown on his face. Did this person host his son's energy signature? Did he recognize Seung-do from their meeting in 1919? While Tae-soo and he had experienced the same bitter events, why did Kit direct his anger at Seung-do?

Kit pushed away from the wall and left the room.

* * * *

Later that evening, after dinner, Tae-hee found Kit in the library. When she approached him, he closed the book he was reading to give her his attention.

"Why do I feel like you've got something on your mind?" he asked with a raised eyebrow.

"Because I do," she said.

"What did I do now?"

"I'm just curious," said Tae-hee. "Why are you so rude to Seung-do?"

"I'm not trying to be rude. He just reminds me of things I don't want to remember."

Tae-hee bit her bottom lip to avoid blurting out Seung-do's true identity. There was so much Kit didn't know. Kit had been forthcoming with her from the beginning, while Tae-hee maintained secrets. How was she going to unravel everything?

She sat on the window seat beside Kit and put her head on his shoulder. "Kit, you know I love you, right?"

Kit nodded.

"There are things I need to tell you."

"Like why we are the way we are?" he said. "Do you know?"

"I'm sorry. I promise to tell you everything. But I want to give you time to settle into life here first."

"Tae-hee, you are making me nervous."

"Please trust me. Also, I need you to be nice to Seung-do. He is very important to me."

Kit leaned away from Tae-hee and wrinkled his brow. "Are you romantically interested in him?"

"Oh my god, *NO!*" said Tae-hee as she sat upright, her eyes wide.

Kit and Tae-hee shared a moment of confusion as they stared at each other and tried to decipher the underlying meanings their reactions conveyed.

The library door opened. Naeem hurried in, followed by Renuka and Jackson.

"Oh, sorry," said Jackson. "Are we bothering you?"

"No," replied Kit and Tae-hee at the same time. Kit shifted away from Tae-hee as she folded her hands and scowled at him.

"We're looking for something for Naeem to read," said Renuka. "Any recommendations?"

Kit handed Renuka the book he had been reading. "This is an interesting story. I just finished reading it." Renuka turned the book over in her hand.

"Oh, yeah. I've heard of that book," said Naeem. "It's a story of a kid surviving in the wild." Naeem grinned at Renuka and Jackson. "Mom. Dad. Can I go camping?"

"What? Why camping?" replied Jackson.

"My friends have gone camping."

"You can't miss school to go camping," said Renuka. "Are you okay with missing soccer?"

Naeem tilted his head in thought, then said, "Coach lets us miss two games or practices, and I haven't missed any yet."

Renuka turned to Jackson, who raised his hands in defense. "Don't look at me. I've never gone camping."

"I *love* camping!" said Tae-hee, jumping up from the window seat. "I can take you. I'm sure I could borrow tents and sleeping bags from someone."

"Seriously? Can I go, Dad?"

"I don't think you should go alone with Tae-hee," said Renuka.

"Jong and Kit can come along, too!" said Tae-hee with her usual confidence.

Kit grimaced at Tae-hee and Naeem, but their enthusiasm doused his dissent. He nodded.

"I'll go tell Jong!" said Tae-hee as she hurried out of the library.

In the kitchen, Jong loaded the dishwasher while Seung-do wiped down the table.

"Jong, my love," Tae-hee sing-songed as she pranced over to him, her hands clasped behind her.

"Now, this is the tone Tae-hee takes when she wants something," said Jong. He continued to rinse and load dishes into the dishwasher.

Tae-hee hugged Jong from behind and said, "Come camping with Naeem and me."

"Why camping?"

"Because Naeem wants to go camping." She smiled and winked at Seung-do. "I've invited Kit to come, too."

Jong became more attentive. "Kit's going to go? Then I'm in."

Tae-hee giggled. "I'll start making a list of the equipment we'll need." She left Jong and Seung-do with grins as she skipped out of the kitchen.

Seung-do finished wiping the table and folded the washcloth. "So, I understand you're involved with Kit," he said.

"Not yet," said Jong. "But I'm working on it."

"How much do you know about him?"

"A little more than he knows himself, I think."

"Such as . . ."

"I'm not really comfortable talking about it."

"Does it change how you feel about him?"

"What are you, his father?" joked Jong.

Seung-do masked his reaction with a calm demeanor. "I'm just curious."

"Well, he's hot. I mean, he's the standard tall, dark, and handsome. His eyes draw me in. You know, the eyes are the windows to the soul. When I look into Kit's eyes, I see something I can't walk away from."

"That's very specific," said Seung-do.

Jong shuddered. "Yeah, sometimes I'm like that."

"Has Kit reciprocated your feelings?"

"I think he's being cautious. He's in a new country, reconnecting with Tae-hee, trying to find his purpose here. Sameer offered him a part-time job." Jong turned off the water and dried his hands on a towel as he leaned against the counter. "Why are you so interested in Kit?"

"Oh," said Seung-do. "I'm interested in everyone. I have spent little time with Kit. He doesn't appear to care for me that much."

"Yeah, I'm not sure why. Kit gets along with everyone. I guess he just hasn't warmed up to you yet." Jong closed the dishwasher and turned it on. "Seung-do, I believe you're a good man. Sameer wouldn't have brought you here if you weren't. If Kit has an issue with you, I hope it gets resolved quickly. Until then, my loyalty belongs to Kit."

"Don't worry," replied Seung-do with an understanding grin. "I'm sure everything will work out."

21
EXPERIMENT

(AUGUST 5, 2019)

Although the monsoon rains offered some relief, Delhi in August was oppressive, so Kiran Ahuja was glad that Abhimanyu Khatri had decided they should return to Shimla. The abundant trees, green pastures, and snow-capped peaks contributed to an abundance of fresh air. Kiran hoped the burgeoning population and climate change would not bring drastic change to Shimla in the future.

Shimla's architecture reflected the British Raj. Foreign tourists came to witness history and engage with the local population. Kiran used humor and his good looks to entertain these foreigners, share a meal, and invite them to visit the prestigious KSH showroom. Though these relationships were always short-lived, they brought him a sense of normalcy and a steady income for KSH House and Trust.

Kiran had been a threlphax host for over a century and a half. Long-term relationships were unrealistic, and marriage was inconceivable. Despite wishing for more, he consoled himself by pursuing women he knew wanted a short-term, casual relationship. One day, the world would accept the Sikh turban he wore, and he would leave India to travel with Sameer and Abhimanyu. They would live somewhere with a cooler climate, like Canada or one of the Nordic countries, such as Denmark or Finland.

Kiran wiped the sweat from his face with the cloth draped around his neck as he passed the various shops along Mall Road. Although the weekend was a peak time for tourist traffic, he saw few foreign tourists among the many nationals who traversed the road. He stopped at his favorite spot overlooking the hills. White homes and buildings with green and orange roofs peeked out between the greenery of the forest.

As he continued on his way, he saw two stray dogs resting along the side of the thoroughfare. They were recent additions to The Ridge and recognized Kiran as he approached. He pulled out the foil-wrapped food scraps he had saved from the previous night's dinner. He unwrapped the foil package and placed it on the ground for the mongrels. An older woman who passed by clicked her tongue in disapproval and glared at him. Kiran stroked the animals' necks and backs, baffled that anyone could be against caring for them.

When the dogs finished the scraps, Kiran scooped up the foil and tossed it into a nearby bin. He crossed The Ridge, looking for the person who had called him. A few meters away, a dusty-blonde Englishman sat alone on a bench. Hunched over, he held his chest and stared at the ground. Kiran rushed over to Mroniea Hadwyn Clarke.

"Are you okay?" he asked.

Mroniea struggled to sit upright. "I have a favor to ask," he muttered.

"How can I help?" said Kiran.

"I have a room at Willow Banks. Let's talk there," said Mroniea.

Kiran helped Mroniea to stand. Taking a deep breath, Mroniea nodded his readiness, and the two men proceeded toward Willow Banks Hotel. Although Kiran knew Mroniea through his threlphax twinship with Sameer Khan, it was unusual for him to contact Kiran directly. He wondered whether he should have mentioned their meeting to Abhimanyu Khatri.

Ten minutes later, they reached the hotel and Mroniea's room. Mroniea turned on the fan and excused himself to disappear into the bathroom. Kiran inspected the room. He picked up a promotional brochure from the desk and read the overview.

Established in 1871, the landmark Willow Banks estate marks history by exemplifying an era of gracious living. Originally owned by the "Architect and Builder of Shimla" Arthur James Craddok, Willow Banks is a fitting tribute to his memory. The building was redesigned into a hotel, endowed with all modern amenities and comforts. It effortlessly blends into the surrounding pine trees and landscapes, enhancing its beauty.

Mroniea had chosen one of the priciest hotels. Kiran wondered if Mroniea stayed here or had rented the room only for their meeting. The only sign of habitation was a bottle of McDowell's No.1 beside the glassware on the desk.

Sunlight streamed through the windows as the fan circulated air, enveloping Kiran in cool comfort. Kiran sat on the side of the bed, testing its softness. Falling backward, he spread his arms across the mattress and closed his eyes, enjoying the gentle breeze.

Mroniea exited the bathroom and lurched toward the desk. Kiran sat up as Mroniea extracted two vials from a small, zippered leather bag. He placed the vials and a small syringe on the desk before zipping the bag shut and placing it in the desk drawer.

Opening the bottle of McDowell's, Mroniea poured two glasses and handed one to Kiran. He sat in the desk chair, took a sip of whisky, and then focused on Kiran.

"Thank you for meeting me," Mroniea began. "I didn't expect to find you back in Shimla. I have a place in Mumbai. Bandstand Apartments. Do you know the place?"

"Mumbai is too crowded," explained Kiran. "I prefer Shimla."

Kiran wanted him to move beyond small talk to the purpose of their meeting.

"You know, Phemeos," Mroniea said, addressing Kiran's threlphax self. "I haven't been right after my tribe encountered that black hole."

So, this is it. Mroniea never recovered.

"As you know, the event disrupted my energy signature," continued Mroniea. "I know the tribe tried to restore me, but it was just too painful to bear. I was in agony. I tried to endure for Mussick's sake, but . . ." Mroniea shook his head. "Maybe I made the wrong decision to run from Trax then. But here we are."

Bracing for what Mroniea was about to say, Kiran took another sip of whisky.

"I've done things I'm not proud of just to protect my energy signature," Mroniea continued. "They were necessary evils. Because I am an Anti, you understand what would happen if my core became exposed." Mroniea stared at Kiran with a desperately exhausted look in his eyes.

Mussick would dissipate.

Sameer's life would end.

Matter and antimatter should not exist together.

For Sameer to live, Mroniea must live.

Kiran took a longer sip from his glass. He pitied Mroniea. It was unfortunate that the threlphax had been born into a universe that was antithetical to its existence. Even more tragic was that Mroniea knew its fate once its threlphax core became exposed. Kiran and his threlphax would ensure Sameer and his threlphax continued to exist. That meant preventing Mroniea from dissipating.

Mroniea fidgeted in his chair and swished the whisky around in his glass. He placed it on the desk and leaned forward. "You know, after all these years, my antimatter core hasn't been able to restore my degrading energy signature. My membrane is being eaten away. It is a slow dissipation. I have survived by obtaining threlphax energy from other hosts. To expose donor threlphax energy, I have done unspeakable things. It's becoming more difficult to find willing donors."

Kiran took another sip. His threlphax self wondered if Mroniea used physical violence to separate threlphax and human energy signatures.

A distant memory rose to the surface. Over a century ago, after Kiran was falsely accused of exploiting a young woman, her brothers beat and cut him with machetes. As he lay crushed and bleeding, his threlphax, Phemeos, tore away from their full merge to repair the near-fatal wounds of its vessel. The fragile Kiran faced the pain of his wounds, along with the agony of his threlphax abandoning him. Kiran found relief when he succumbed to unconsciousness. Distressed by the recollection, Kiran's energy oscillated uneasily.

"So," Kiran said. "You want Phemeos' energy? You want to rip it away like you ripped away part of Trax's energy?"

"No!" Mroniea cried out. He squeezed his eyes shut and hung his head.

Kiran's comment was too harsh. Even though Mroniea's actions badly injured Trax, not even his twin reminded Mroniea of the tragic event. "Forgive me, Mroniea," he said. "I'm just trying to understand. How much of Phemeos do you need?"

Mroniea drew a hand over his face and sighed. "Just enough to patch my energy signature and prevent further thinning of my energy membrane."

Kiran took another sip of whisky. "We are merged." The voice was Kiran's, but the words belonged to Phemeos. While threlphax merged with different species they encountered across the universe, the merge with human hosts was substantial. The threlphax wasn't sure how to donate energy without ripping apart the merge. "Will it harm this host?"

Mroniea lifted a vial between his finger and thumb. "I have become a biochemist," he said. "I believe I can extract energy painlessly." He focused on the vial. "I tested this on myself. It's a non-invasive way to weaken the merge of the threlphax and host. I can then remove a portion of threlphax energy without harming the vessel. Your recovery will take several hours while Phemeos reconstitutes the extracted energy and returns the integrity of the merge with you."

After taking another sip of whisky, Kiran walked over to the bay of windows. He didn't notice the people circumventing the street or the lush green landscape of the Shimla forests. He focused internally as he negotiated with his threlphax self to reach a decision.

"I'm the first one you're trying it with?" Kiran asked.

"Besides myself, yes," replied Mroniea.

Kiran questioned whether the chemical would have the same effect on him as on Mroniea. Mroniea was an Anti. Would their divergent energies respond to the chemical the same way?

"What if you use too much?"

"I'll be honest. I don't know. Too much might dissipate you. But Sameer would hate me if I harmed you. I will give you the dose I gave myself."

Kiran trusted and pitied Mroniea. He didn't want Sameer to punish the Anti if anything went wrong. While merged with Kiran, Phemeos observed hard lessons about prejudice, injustice, and equity. Mroniea was only doing the needful. He admitted his wrongdoings and tried to set things right. However, Kiran couldn't deny that he was nervous about being Mroniea's test subject. "I must call Abhimanyu first," he said.

"Yes, yes," said Mroniea. "I want you to be comfortable."

Kiran pulled out his phone and pressed the button to call his friend and partner. After several rings, the call went to voicemail. Kiran waited for Abhimanyu's introductory message to finish, then spoke. "Abhi, this is Kiran. I am at Willow Banks Hotel with Mroniea. He asked for my help, and I agreed. When you receive this message, come find us." Kiran pressed the end call button and stared at the phone screen. Was he doing the right thing? Would he come to regret this decision? Yet, if Mroniea's core ever became exposed . . .

After taking another sip of whisky, he turned to Mroniea. "Okay," he said. "Tell me what I need to do."

22
NATURE

(AUGUST 10, 2019)

Tae-hee organized the gear and logistics for the camping trip. Jackson and Renuka handled menus and food preparation. Early Saturday morning, Tae-hee, Naeem, Jong, and Kit set off for the two-hour drive to the campsite. Since it was Naeem's first time camping, Renuka insisted they make it an overnight stay.

The campground lay deep within a forested area, and their chosen spot featured a fire circle carefully cleared of debris. While drought conditions persisted in some states, no campfire restrictions existed where they were.

After they set up their tents, Tae-hee announced, "Naeem is going to go exploring with me."

"How long will you be gone?"

"An hour or two."

Jong smiled. "Are you going on a snipe hunt?"

"Snipes?" asked Naeem, concerned. "What's a snipe?"

Tae-hee pushed Naeem forward. "Jong's just joking with you. There are no snipes around here."

Tae-hee glared at Jong as she muttered something about Jong being inappropriate. She grabbed two water bottles and escorted Naeem to a nearby footpath.

"What should we do while they're gone?" Jong asked Kit.

"On the way in, I saw a stream. Why don't we hike there? Maybe we will see snipes."

"You know that was a joke, Kit, don't you? Snipe hunting is a search for a non-existent animal. Going on a snipe hunt is a rite of passage."

"But snipe birds exist, don't they?"

Jong clapped his hand on Kit's shoulder. "You have much to learn about our ways," he said with a broad grin.

The two men followed a series of signposts that directed them to the stream. The crunch of their footsteps on the dry soil mixed with the birdsong and buzz of insects, creating a comfortable rhythm.

"You enjoy teasing Naeem," said Kit.

"I treat him like a little brother."

"The teasing doesn't bother him?"

"Does it bother you?"

"I'm not sure," said Kit. "I'm not used to it."

"Naeem was four years old when Jackson and Renuka adopted him. But he didn't talk. They were worried. Tae-hee and I tried to help him come out of his shell. When I joked with him, he responded. That's how our friendship developed."

When Kit nodded, Jong hoped he understood.

"Have you been camping before?" Kit asked.

"When I was in scouts. My mom's church sponsored the pack."

"Is your family religious?"

"You could say that. My mom is Methodist, and my dad is Shinto. I'm more spiritual than religious. I don't claim any religion for myself."

"What are your parents like?"

Jong smiled. "They're the best in the world."

"You talk like Naeem."

"I wasn't a simple kid to raise," chuckled Jong. Seeking to change the topic, he said, "So, I understand you are a Thai citizen now. What made you change your nationality?"

"It just happened that way."

It was a non-answer. Four months into knowing him, Kit still maintained secrets. It shouldn't have bothered Jong, but it did.

They walked along quietly for a distance until Kit's occasional glances made Jong speak up. "Is there something on your mind?" he asked.

Kit nodded. "I've wanted to ask you about Emily," he said. "What did you do that day?"

Two weeks had passed since Emily suffered her collapse. In all that time, Kit never spoke about the incident. Jong wondered what prompted his sudden interest.

"Oh, that," said Jong. "It was a deep meditation. Just one of my many mad skills."

"You said that Emily was a mess."

"Yeah, she suffered from intense emotions. She was afraid to experience them."

"How could you tell?"

Kit's non-judgemental tone conveyed genuine interest and made Jong want to open up completely. "Sometimes, when I'm meditating," he said, "I feel an altered state of consciousness, where I detach from my body and float free. When I reach this state, I understand emotions as tangible things I experience with my senses. Which is weird because you'd think my senses would stay connected to my body instead of my mind."

Kit nodded but offered no response as they walked onto a wooden pier that overhung the stream. Their percussive footfalls on the neatly arranged planks fractured the natural calm around them. They leaned on the wooden railing beneath the shade of the tall trees that branched out to block the sun's rays. Below them, small shadows moved around stones submerged in the rippling water.

"Do you meditate?" Jong asked.

"I used to meditate a lot. Not so much recently."

"Why did you stop?"

"My lifestyle changed."

The smirk on Kit's face reflected an untold truth, one that Jong wanted to know.

"Want to try it now?" Jong asked.

"You mean to meditate here?"

Kit's raised eyebrows were a prompt to retreat from the idea. But Jong pressed on. "Sure," he replied as he sat cross-legged on the pier. "The sound of the water is enough to center us. It's the music of nature."

Jong laid his hands on his knees, palms up.

"You're not planning to read me the way you did Emily . . . right?"

The pink aura around Kit had turned gray. Although Jong knew Kit had secrets, Kit didn't want Jong to trespass on them.

"No," Jong said. "You can trust me."

After a momentary pause, Kit sat across from him. Jong raised his hands, offering them. Kit rubbed his palms on his pant legs, then laid his hands, palms down, on Jong's.

Jong smiled and said, "Close your eyes."

"You don't need to narrate," murmured Kit.

The serious tone in which Kit delivered the statement caused bubbles of laughter to dance in Jong's chest. He took a deep breath to scatter them, then relaxed and focused on the air as it slowly passed in and out of his lungs.

Cascading water murmured a gentle melody, harmonized by the whine of cicadas, rhythmic bird calls, and the soft rustle of leaves. Drawn by nature's symphony, Jong's thoughts drifted effortlessly on its resonance, allowing the serenity to calm and nourish him. His thoughts floated along with nature's energy and drew him further into his meditation.

He let his mind wander, exploring his connection with Kit. During his meditation with Emily, he had already seen a unique dualism and bright glow that existed within Kit. If those facets of Kit were so easily available to Jong, perhaps he could incorporate them into the meditation. He focused his meditation on the subtle shifts of their joined hands, influenced by the slight motions in their fingers and knees, their breaths, and the steady rhythm of their hearts.

Colors bloomed in the darkness, flowing seamlessly through the spectrum. They twisted and merged into intricate patterns, forming an ever-evolving kaleidoscope. As the vibrant display quickened its pace, Jong responded by slowing his breath.

A sharp explosion pierced his mind, forcing him to jerk away from Kit. Shock ricocheted through him and his breath hitched in rapid, uneven gasps. His palms buzzed with an unsettling tingle, and he rubbed them frantically, trying to quell the itch crawling beneath his skin.

Kit stared wide-eyed at him. "Are you alright?" he asked.

Jong calmed his breathing. "It's as if I got stung," he said.

"Did I do something wrong?"

"No," said Jong. "I guess your threlphax felt threatened." Jong shook his hands in the air to release the energy from the experience.. "Are *you* alright?" Jong asked.

"What did you say?" Kit asked.

Jong closed his eyes and sighed. Sameer had warned him not to reveal their secret. He hadn't meant to mention the threlphax; it just slipped out. Sameer and Tae-hee would surely understand.

Jong grimaced and said, "Sameer and Tae-hee told me about you."

"What? What did they tell you?" Kit leaned forward, his forehead creased with concern.

Jong wanted Kit to trust him. Honesty was the best way to earn trust. "They told me you've lived a long time, and you heal rapidly," he said. In deference to Sameer's wishes, he chose not to elaborate.

"So, you three talked about me?"

"Blame Tae-hee. She told Sameer to tell me."

"Doesn't what they said bother you?"

"Not really."

It wasn't Jong's mention of the threlphax that bothered Kit. What disturbed him were the conversations behind his back.

There were too many secrets swirling around Kit and Tae-hee.

23
CONNECTION

(AUGUST 10, 2019)

By late afternoon, everyone was back at the campsite. Naeem and Tae-hee shared stories about their hike, while Jong and Kit talked about the view from the pier.

"I'll start the grill for dinner," Jong said when the conversation ebbed. "Does anyone want to help?"

Naeem jumped up, "I'll help! Then I won't have to clean up afterward." He smiled at Tae-hee. KSH House rules extended to the campsite.

Kit sat at a picnic table ten yards away and watched Jong and Naeem as they worked together. Tae-hee retrieved something from her tent and donned a strange smile as she walked over to Kit.

"Jong said you and Sameer talked about me," said Kit.

"Jong likes you, you know."

"He likes everyone," retorted Kit. Tae-hee's grin broadened. "Why are you smiling?"

"I'm a nurse. So, I have something for you," Tae-hee said, holding out a small brown bag.

Kit hesitated before taking it. He opened the bag and pulled out a plastic bottle and a square box. His eyes widened. Kit shoved the lubricant and condoms back in the bag. "Are you crazy?" he whispered.

Tae-hee sat on the bench beside him. "Look, Kit. The way you and Jong are going, it's inevitable."

"But this? Aren't you being pushy? I'm not even sure how I feel about him."

"I see how you are with Jong. You light up when he enters the room. He lights up when you walk into the room. He agreed to come on this trip because I told him you were coming. Do you remember what Tae-soo told me before introducing me to Lee Seung-gi?"

"I said, 'I want to be beside him.'"

"You remember. So, I ask you, do you want to stay by Jong's side?"

Kit answered with a grin. "Are you trying to live vicariously through me?"

"Well, you are my brother, so your happiness is my happiness."

He watched Jong and Naeem laugh as they hovered over the charcoal grill. Kit's insides felt scrambled. He hadn't wanted to admit his feelings to anyone—even himself.

We enjoy our time with Jong.

He's a nice man, a good person.

We want to trust him.

Can we be together?

Tae-hee tilted her head and asked, "Why are you holding back?"

"You told him about me, didn't you? About my longevity and healing."

Tae-hee's bright smile turned apologetic. "Well," she said. "I knew you'd use that as an excuse not to get close to him."

"He'll never understand me."

Kit shifted on the bench to face Tae-hee. He still had secrets he needed to tell her. Perhaps she had answers.

A large flock of blackbirds flew overhead, a timely precursor to what he was about to share. "Tae-hee," he said. "Have you ever found yourself surrounded by black orbs about the size of a sparrow's egg?" The question sounded strange, even to his ears.

Tae-hee frowned in her confusion and shook her head. "But since you are asking me, it seems like it happened to you."

Kit bit his lip as the flock of birds flew out of view beyond the trees. "Yes."

"When? Where?"

"In 2004. In the ocean."

"What were they?"

"I don't know," Kit sighed. "Whatever they were, I thought they saved my life. But now, I wonder. It was probably just a school of fish."

"Why did you bring this up?"

"You seem to know more about us than I do. There are things I don't understand about my life."

"You can't understand what it is to be me, either." She took Kit's hand in hers. "Don't avoid your feelings for Jong—"

"—you are obsessed with Jong and me—"

"—I just care about both of you—"

"—caring isn't pushing—"

"—I know I'm not an expert in romantic relationships—"

"—yet this seems to be your constant topic of discussion—"

"—but I understand what it's like to love someone else from the heart. I know you do, too."

"The only person I've ever been intimate with was Lee Seung-gi."

"Seriously? No one else?"

"No one. After Lee Seung-gi died and I separated from you, I lived alone on Ganghwa Island, faced war, and then transmigrated into Chanchai. I never forgot what happened to Lee Seung-gi. I still haven't. I never want to feel that pain of loss again. Does that make me strange? I know I'm strange because of who I am now."

"You aren't strange."

"Not to you." Kit frowned and refolded the top of the small paper bag. "I'm not sure what liking Jong means. I don't know whether I can love someone again."

Tae-hee bit her lip, then said. "Of course you can. I saw Tae-soo when he was with Lee Seung-gi. Tae-soo is part of who you are. For whatever reason, you and Jong have connected."

Kit looked at the brown paper bag clutched in his hand, clicked his tongue, and shook his head. "I'm not sure if I should thank you for this. But, thanks."

"Good luck. If you have questions, the Internet can help with the technical part." She winked and hurried over to Jong and Naeem.

Kit wasn't sure he could stay long in this place. He was a nomad who had traveled between Thailand and South Korea and ended up in the United States as he searched for his sister. Now that Kit had found her, a dark cloud of aimlessness hung over him. War, revolutions, natural disasters, and life as a monk were the experiences he knew. Pursuing a romantic relationship with Jong seemed unrealistic.

Kit walked over to his tent and shoved the bag deep into the side pocket of his backpack. When he stood up, Jong was watching him.

Did he notice the bag?

Does he know what's in it?

He couldn't have seen it.

It doesn't look like he saw it.

Everything is okay.

Kit offered a tight-lipped grin, and Jong replied with a broad smile as he waved the tongs and spatula over his head. Kit wondered what it would be like to have Jong as a partner. Tae-soo's romantic experience with Lee Seung-gi was the only thing he could draw on. His lover had lived his life with passion and purpose, qualities that led to his untimely death. Like Lee Seung-gi, Jong spoke his mind with unfiltered honesty.

Yet, Jong was not Lee Seung-gi. He lived in a very different time in a vastly different country. The corners of Kit's lips turned ever-so-slightly upward as he remembered Jong sitting on the beach, his shirt and hair blowing in the breeze.

A warrior prince.

A day later, Kit prompted physical contact when he spread sunscreen on Jong and encouraged Jong to reciprocate. Kit's grin widened as he recalled the feel of bare hands upon bare skin.

Why did we do that?

Maybe we wanted Jong to touch us.

Maybe we wanted to touch Jong.

Are we getting stiff just thinking about this?

We are getting ahead of ourself.

Jong gave him a puzzled look. Kit's face grew warm, and he wandered away across the field. Pulling out his phone and earbuds, Kit opened a music app and selected a song. His throat tightened and his eyes moistened as emotions swelled within him. When the song ended, he muttered, "How do you know, Tae-hee?"

* * * *

Jong and Naeem prepared a feast of grilled mushroom kabobs, barbecued cauliflower steak burgers, and a pesto pasta salad. Kit remained introspective during their meal. His silence didn't matter since Jong, Tae-hee, and Naeem chattered among themselves.

After dinner, Kit collected wood for the evening's campfire. Since they ate dinner late in the day, it was already dusk. After gathering logs from the campground woodpile, he picked up the empty water bucket and headed into the woods to collect kindling.

Naeem followed him and helped gather dry sticks from the ground. "What did you do all day? You were quiet during dinner."

"Read, listened to music, hiked with Jong, talked with Tae-hee. What's that American word? Chillaxed? I chillaxed." He used a word he had heard from tourists in Thailand.

"No one says 'chillax' anymore," said Naeem.

"I say it."

Naeem laughed. He jumped over a moss-covered log to pick up a fallen branch. After breaking it into smaller pieces to stuff in the bucket, he said, "Can I ask you a question?"

Kit leaned over to collect pieces of brittle bark and dry leaves. "Yes."

"What do you think about Jong?"

Kit dropped the tinder in the bucket, shrugged, and said, "He's okay."

"I mean, do you *like* him?"

"Did Tae-hee tell you to ask me that?"

"No. It just seems like you like him."

"Well, I like you, and I like Tae-hee, too."

"You know that's not what I mean."

"This isn't a conversation for a ten-year-old."

"I'm twelve," corrected Naeem. "Why does everyone bring age into it?" he muttered as he stomped through the underbrush.

Kit raised an eyebrow, indicating that the talk about Jong was over. Naeem kicked the ground, gathered a handful of sticks, and spoke about less significant matters.

24
SPARK

(AUGUST 10, 2019)

An hour later, as the evening darkened the landscape, Naeem gloated over the campfire he had helped build. Kit, Tae-hee, and Jong made sure he stayed outside the fire ring, beyond the reach of the flames, as the four of them roasted marshmallows and made s'mores.

"Why do they call them 's'mores?'" asked Naeem as he stuffed a third marshmallow onto his long roasting stick.

As the self-appointed s'mores guru, Tae-hee giggled, "Because you always want *some more!*"

She showed Kit how to pull the sticky cooked marshmallow off his stick onto the graham cracker and chocolate sandwich. Kit surveyed the melting confection and took a bite. Liquid chocolate, glutinous sugar, and crumbling crackers spilled onto his lips and hands. The treat was palatable, but sloppy.

"You don't like it?" asked Tae-hee.

"It's messy," Kit said. Using his tongue and fingers, he removed bits of the snack that clung to the corners of his mouth.

"I can't believe you haven't had s'mores before," Jong said.

"They're not a popular food in Asia," said Kit. "I'm used to mung bean candy, ice cream rolls, sticky rice—sweets you can buy from a store or a street vendor. These s'mores feel too artificial. They can't be good for you."

Tae-hee held up her hands. "Roasting marshmallows over an open fire is an art form."

"What do you mean?" said Jong. "You just stick it in until it catches fire. Marshmallow flambé!"

"Some people brown their marshmallow by rotating it above the flame."

Jong guffawed. "That's a waste of time."

Naeem stuck his marshmallow-laden stick into the fire and watched as the three stacked marshmallows ignited. "Who wants a marshmallow?" he asked, holding out the flaming stick. The fire turned from white to blue to orange, making the stacked clumps of whipped sugar and gelatin bubble and blacken.

"Aren't you going to eat those?" asked Jong.

"No, I'm just making them."

"No way! You make your own!"

"You want them?" he asked as he swung around and held the charred marshmallows out to Kit. The sudden movement made the gooey lumps slip. Kit jumped away as the marshmallows sagged and plummeted to the ground.

Naeem stared at the marshmallow clump in the dirt.

"Oops," he said.

After the group finished their snacks, cleaned up, and packed away the s'more ingredients, Kit pulled out a guitar. The others listened as he tuned and strummed the instrument.

"When did you get the guitar?" asked Jong.

"Sameer let me borrow this. He picked it up from an estate sale. I mentioned I played and he let me borrow it. He wanted my opinion on its quality."

"My brother is amazing," said Tae-hee.

Kit couldn't hold back his broad smile.

"Do you sing, too?" asked Jong.

Kit scoured his memory for a song he knew well enough to play. "Okay, here's one. But I can't guarantee my singing will be good."

The song he chose was a gentle tune that featured both Korean and English lyrics. As he sang, Naeem leaned his head on Tae-hee's shoulder and stared into the fire. When the song ended, Naeem said, "That sounds like a Christmas song. What does it mean?"

"The song is by a Korean group," said Jong, smiling in admiration at Kit's performance.

"It's a song about love," said Tae-hee.

Naeem nodded, then yawned.

"Well, that's enough for us. It's time for bed," Tae-hee announced. "Come on, Naeem, let's go to our tents." She helped Naeem stand, waved goodbye to Kit and Jong, and led Naeem away from the campfire toward the warmth and comfort of their tents.

For the next hour, Kit played various songs while Jong stared into the fire, listening to the impromptu concert. After a while, Kit stopped and leaned back in his chair.

"That's all for tonight's repertoire," said Kit.

"I enjoy listening to you. It's comforting."

Kit strummed a few chords. "Do you need to be comforted?"

Jong tilted his head as he looked at Kit. "I think I do."

An invitation?

What does he want?

Kit felt his heart race as Jong gazed at him. Jong leaned closer to him until the guitar became a clumsy obstacle. He retreated, leaning back in his chair. Kit relaxed, released his breath, and turned his gaze to the campfire. The flames had retreated to the heart of the meticulously arranged logs, concealing its waning strength among the blackened wood.

Why are we nervous?

I should be clear with Jong.

Kit worked out a litany of responses, none of which sounded suitable. He decided on his standard refrain. "Jong, you don't know me."

"Yeah. You said that before," replied Jong. He took a stick and poked at the campfire, sending sparks into the air. "It sounds like an excuse to keep me at arm's length."

Kit should have expected such an honest reply. Still, Jong's words hurt. Kit had trouble explaining who he was, why he was different, and why Jong shouldn't pursue him. Frustrated, Kit glared at the night sky. He hated that Jong's candor cornered him. "Do you remember I said I was in a long-term relationship?" he asked.

"Yes."

"That person is the reason I can play the guitar."

The statement was punctuated by the crackling fire and chirping of crickets.

We'll deflect Jong's interest.

Why does that make us sad?

Kit laid the guitar on his lap and ran his fingers along the fretboard. He liked Jong, but he couldn't *like* Jong. When Jong learned who Kit was, he would see him in a different light. It was best not to give Jong any reason to pursue him.

The guitar shifted in Kit's lap. Jong lifted it away and placed it in the empty camp chair beside him. He took Kit's hand and ran his thumb back and forth over his palm. Kit watched the gentle movement, an erotic touch that unnerved him, making his heart beat faster and his skin warm. What was Jong doing? What gave him such confidence?

Kit pulled his hand away and rubbed his palm against his jeans. "I told you I'm in a relationship, Jong."

"I'm not interested in stealing you from anyone," Jong said. "But the thing is, Kit, I've known you for three months. You've never spoken the name of this person. You've never shown us a photo."

Surprised by Jong's confrontational tone, Kit could prove nothing. How could he explain the relationship between Chanchai and Tae-soo?

Our heart is beating faster.

"Right now, right here, it's just you and me," Jong continued. He touched Kit's knee with the tip of his finger and leaned forward. Kit froze as Jong's gaze shifted from Kit's eyes to his lips and back again. Everything Jong did was seductive. Kit knew he should stop Jong, but he wasn't sure he wanted to. Jong continued, "We are sitting here in the dark, next to a warm, romantic campfire." His rich, musky scent mingled with the aroma of the burning wood.

Come closer.

Kit's impatience surprised him.

Jong smiled as if he read Kit's unspoken thoughts. "This may be my only chance to kiss you." The light from the campfire cast a warm orange glow on Jong's perfect skin. He was close enough that Kit could feel his breath as he whispered, "May I kiss you?"

Kit froze. His skin warmed as Jong stared at his lips and leaned toward him. As he moved in, his gaze searched for any sign he should stop. Kit closed his eyes.

Jong pressed his lips to Kit's. With barely a touch, the soft connection created a whirlwind deep within Kit's chest, drawing his breath away. The intensity of this response confused him, yet he desired to withstand it, explore it, and experience it fully. His heart beat loudly in his ears as he parted his lips, giving way to the feel of Jong's mouth, the brush of his breath, and the sound of his tender movements.

This.

Jong ended the kiss and leaned away. Kit remained still, not retreating, not advancing. Every sense stirred emotions he had put aside long ago.

Again.

Please.

As if in response, Jong leaned forward and performed a more thorough exploration of his lips. Kit relaxed into the kiss, deepening the intimate connection. With each gentle movement of their lips, he lost himself in the touch of their flesh, the taste of Jong's mouth, and the slip of their tongues.

Jong ran his hands around the sides of Kit's head, and Kit grabbed handfuls of Jong's shirt. As he immersed himself in the kiss, the whirlwind within Kit settled into a tingle of energy that flowed through his core. He recognized this feeling. Tae-soo had experienced a similar response to Lee Seung-gi a century ago. However, this time, the intensity of the feeling overpowered him. Was this Tae-soo? Chanchai? Both?

As the kiss deepened, heat flowed through him, and Kit released a soft moan. Jong ended the kiss, leaving Kit intoxicated by the moment. When he opened his eyes, Jong softly smiled as he studied him.

"The fire is making your eyes glow," Jong said.

Jong's eyes didn't glow. Kit tilted his head away from Jong and the campfire light.

What do we do now?

Run.

25
CONFERENCE

(AUGUST 13, 2019)

Dr. Mroniea Hadwyn Clarke sat at the back of the dimly lit conference hall, scanning the sparsely populated room where researchers, nurses, biostatisticians, and medical informaticians were scattered, attentive to the presenter who droned on about their latest research.

The Conference on Medical Informatics had drawn experts from across the globe to Rome, Italy, to explore the latest breakthroughs in biomedical technology. It was the second day of presentations around cutting-edge technologies, and Mroniea struggled to focus. His mind kept drifting back to Shimla—to Kiran Ahuja and the uncertainty of his fate.

Kiran had trusted him, and Mroniea had failed.

The memory clawed at him relentlessly. He had spent years developing Chymzafyde—a chemical compound designed to weaken the merged energies between threlphax and host—to allow the extraction of enough energy from the threlphax without harming the human vessel.

In the past, he could only access the threlphax energy after he critically injured the host and weakened the merge. Such violence was not in Mroniea's nature nor Hadwyn Clarke's. He sought a way to weaken the threlphax-human merge without violence. The chemical agent would facilitate the removal of threlphax energy from the human hosts to repair his own.

Theoretically, it should have worked. The merge should have unraveled smoothly, granting the host temporary independence. But that wasn't what happened.

Despite administering such a small dose, Kiran had a virulent reaction. As the signs of the threlphax dissipation became apparent, Mroniea panicked while Kiran accepted his fate.

Mroniea repeatedly asked himself the same questions: Was it something in the chemical catalysts? Did the compound compromise the catabolic system? He rubbed his forehead as he struggled to decipher why the compound caused the dissipation of Kiran's threlphax, Phemeos.

When Kiran's adverse reaction began, he told Mroniea to leave. There was no ill will in Kiran's urging; to the contrary, Kiran encouraged Mroniea to do whatever it took to maintain his existence. They both understood the devastating repercussions if Mroniea's core became exposed. He left Kiran behind, hoping that Abhimanyu Khatri—or fate—would intervene where science had failed.

Now, thousands of miles away in Rome, surrounded by some of the world's brightest minds, Mroniea felt more alone and powerless than ever.

A quiet voice broke through his preoccupation.

"May I join you?"

Mroniea turned to find a distinguished man in his forties, sharp-eyed and composed, extending a hand. "Dr. Richard Carver. NeuBio Research."

Mroniea hesitated before shaking his hand. "Dr. Mroniea Hadwyn Clarke."

Carver smiled, settling into the seat beside him. "These conferences are so boring, but my company keeps sending me. Who sent you?"

"I sent myself," replied Mroniea.

"I see," said Carver. "What is your interest in informatics?"

"I'm on the cusp of a breakthrough, but I've had a setback. I thought I might find some answers here."

A woman sitting three rows in front of them turned and put a finger to her lips.

Carver chuckled silently, then leaned toward Mroniea and asked, "Have you found your answers?"

"Unfortunately, no."

"I'm not surprised. Some innovation proceeds at a snail's pace." Carver's gaze turned toward the stage, where the panelists continued their discussion. "I read your 2016 paper in *The Journal of Biochemistry*."

Dr. Richard Carver knew who Mroniea was. He was familiar with Mroniea's work. He approached him with an agenda.

"I'm surprised anyone read it," whispered Mroniea. He had submitted the manuscript to maintain his research credentials and to benefit from input from peer reviewers. The final product discussed the potential for modifying the human genetic code without revealing much.

"Actually, I was one of the peer reviewers," Carver said.

The woman three rows ahead of them stood and glared at the two men before she moved to a seat closer to the stage.

"Our work requires us to keep track of esoteric research like yours. At NeuBio Research, we've been exploring a path that doesn't merely interact with biological processes, but enhances them."

Mroniea raised an eyebrow. "Enhances them how?"

"Through artificial intelligence." Carver leaned in slightly, his voice lowering. "We've developed AI models capable of decoding and manipulating adenosine triphosphate—the energy that fuels life itself." He paused, studying Mroniea's response. "With precise control over ATP production and turnover, we can revitalize cellular structures, accelerate healing, even slow the aging process."

Mroniea frowned. "You're talking about artificial regulation of metabolic energy?"

"In a way, yes. But it's more than that," Carver said. "We've been able to recognize, sample, and harness a new form of energy that sustains biological function. In time, we will reverse cellular degradation altogether."

Over his long lifetime, Mroniea had studied a multitude of alternative energy sources, seeking to find one compatible with his own and that of his human host. Had he been successful, he would have been able to restore his membrane. If he had discovered an alternative energy to prevent his slow dissipation, he would not have compromised Phemeos and Kiran Ahuja's existence.

Mroniea exhaled slowly, the implications settling over him like a storm cloud. "What do you call this new form of energy?"

"That's proprietary information," said Carver.

"Of course." Mroniea frowned.

"But I can tell you that NeuBio Research is on the cusp of subliminal human evolution. Your research contributed to that."

Mroniea's energy fluctuated at Richard Carver's assertion. "How so?" he asked. What information had NeuBio Research found useful in that insignificant submission to that niche journal?

Richard Carver folded his arms across his chest. He leaned closer to Mroniea and looked him in the eye. "Your paper guided NeuBio's AI model in a new direction, breaking a three-year impasse."

With a smile, he arched his eyebrows and smiled at Mroniea before turning his attention to the question and answer session that had begun.

Richard Carver's choice to reveal this information made Mroniea uncomfortable. He shifted in his chair, unsure whether he should stay or leave.

After several minutes, he sighed and asked, "What do you want?"

"Would you be interested in furthering your research at NeuBio?" asked Richard Carver.

This is why Richard Carver approached him.

"I have my own research to pursue," Mroniea replied.

Richard Carver was unyielding. "As a consultant, we could provide you with resources that would be difficult to access as an individual researcher."

"I need independence."

"We could arrange a position at a university. NeuBio Research has agreements with several research departments in universities. Emerald Crest, Carter James, Sempiternity, Hawthorne, Jordan Ellis—"

"—Sempiternity University, you say?" It was the university where Sameer Khan had been a history professor for over a decade.

"Yes. In fact, there is an opening in the College of Science. One of their professors suffered a medical emergency."

That's too convenient, thought Mroniea. "What's the catch?" he asked.

"No catch. We just want your help testing our AI model and reviewing our research findings—like an in-house peer-reviewer."

"And the compensation? Adjunct professors aren't highly paid."

"As an adjunct professor, you could have access to a lab and research facilities. We could offer a generous stipend to help you get settled. It is a very favorable offer for a young, talented, and ambitious biochemist like yourself."

Mroniea withheld his laughter. Richard Carver had no idea who he was dealing with. "To seek new friends and stranger companies," he muttered.

"Pardon me?" asked Richard Carver.

"Nothing," Mroniea replied with a slight grin. "Shall we discuss the details over dinner?"

26
UNCERTAINTY

(AUGUST 15, 2019)

Tae-hee exited the hospital and headed toward the parking lot. Summers in Springfield were getting warmer, and while she enjoyed the late-day sunshine, she would be happier if it was more temperate. During her life in Korea, summers were warm but never this hot and humid.

She paused when she saw someone leaning against her car, staring at their phone.

"Jong?" she called as she approached the car.

Jong straightened and put away his phone. "Hi, Tae-hee."

"What are you doing here?"

"I had a departmental meeting."

Confused, Tae-hee scanned the parking lot. "Where's your car?"

"Ah . . . yeah. I left it by the science building. I thought you could drive me back."

"You walked here?"

Jong rubbed the back of his neck. "Yeah."

"The science building is on the other side of the university campus."

"I needed time to think."

"What's wrong?"

Jong sighed and shook his head. "Have you heard from Kit?"

"No. Not since the weekend. He told Sameer he was busy."

"Yeah, about that, I think he's avoiding me. I've been trying to reach him since the camping trip, but he's not answering his phone. He's not even replying to my texts."

"Why would he avoid you?"

Jong shifted and rubbed the back of his neck. "Because," he said. "I kissed Kit."

"Really? When?"

"At the campfire. I started it, but I know Kit kissed me back. I'm sure of it."

"Did he reject you?"

Jong's forehead creased as he worked through the answer. He shook his head. "Not exactly," he said. "He's just not responding. Maybe I pushed him too hard. I think I messed things up."

"Do you want me to talk to him?"

"No. I don't know. Look, Tae-hee, I'm trying to give Kit space. I don't want to make him uncomfortable. I'm just worried."

She leaned against the car and sighed. "Actually, I'm thankful."

"Why?"

"You've been honest with Kit. I've been keeping secrets from him."

"You mean about the threlphax?"

"That and other things. It's time to tell Kit everything." She smiled at Jong, then motioned to the car. "Get in. I'll take you to your car."

"I'm sorry, Tae-hee. I didn't mean to scare Kit."

"Don't worry. He's my brother. I know how to handle him."

* * * *

A half-hour later, Tae-hee typed the passcode into the loft apartment keypad. When she entered, she found Kit standing by the bed, his oversized duffle bag stuffed full of clothes. The dresser drawers were open and empty.

"What are you doing, Kit?"

"What does it look like?" Kit said. "I'm packing."

"Why?"

"Why do you think?"

"Wait," said Tae-hee, her voice hard, her eyes dark with anger. "Were you just going to abandon me?"

Kit hung his head and slumped down on the bed.

"You promised me you would never leave me again," said Tae-hee. She worried he was about to break that promise. "I want you to stay. Jong wants you to stay."

"Jong kissed me, Tae-hee. I just can't." Kit toyed with the clothes in his hands. He sighed and laid them on top of the duffle bag. "And there is something else. If I tell you, promise me you will not get upset."

"I'm already upset. What more can you scare me with?"

Kit folded his hands together and frowned at Tae-hee. "Our injuries heal quickly, and we've never been ill, right?"

"Yes," replied Tae-hee, drawing out her anxious answer.

Kit scanned Tae-hee's expression. He sighed again and hung his head. "I've been having headaches."

Tae-hee's eyes widened. The idea that Kit experienced cephalalgia frightened her. "Are you sure they are headaches?"

Kit lifted his hand and spun it in a circular motion beside his head. "It's a throbbing pain in my head. That's a headache, right? But there's more to it. Often, it feels like a buzzing inside my head."

"Buzzing? Like bees?"

"Yes. No. Maybe. It feels like there's meaning in the buzzing, as if it's the resonance of voices or music. But when I focus on deciphering it, the pain begins. Has this ever happened to you?"

"No. Not at all." Tae-hee put her palms on either side of his head, turning his face up so she could look into his eyes. "When did this start?"

"After I went to KSH House. But if you never experienced it, I guess that's just a coincidence."

"Maybe Seung-do should examine you. After all, he is a doctor."

"You're a nurse. If you don't know what's happening, what makes you think he would?" said Kit. "I'm okay. They don't last long. They go away when my attention turns elsewhere."

Tae-hee put her fingers along Kit's temples and asked, "Do you feel anything now?"

"No. I had my last headache during the beach trip."

"When, exactly?"

"Saturday night, after dinner. That's the reason I went off by myself. When Jong came to talk to me, it went away. He changed my focus."

Tae-hee grinned as she remembered the reason for her visit. "Tell me the truth. Have I been wrong about you and Jong?"

"Tae-hee, Jong is normal. I'm not."

"Normal," repeated Tae-hee. "What is normal?"

"Come on, Tae-hee," grumbled Kit. "You and I are different from Jong. And I have to ask—are you really the close friends you think you are? Jong said you told him about us, but I know you didn't tell him everything."

"Everyone has secrets. Even though you loved Lee Seung-gi, you didn't tell him everything, did you?"

"The relationship between Tae-soo and Seung-gi was different," countered Kit.

"How?"

"It just was."

Tae-hee gave him a feigned look of awe. "That sounds just like Tae-soo. He always said nonsense when he couldn't make a solid argument."

"At least you know."

"Admit it. You're using what happened to Lee Seung-gi as an excuse to avoid new relationships."

"That's not fair, Tae-hee. You don't know all the pain I've lived through."

"Okay. Let's talk about our painful pasts. You don't know the pain I felt when Tae-soo left me without a word. Kim Joon-gi protected me, but he never cared for me. I was okay because I knew you were alive and we would find each other again.

"Then you returned to me in a box. You don't know how hard I cried. When I saw your broken body, my heart really hurt. It was hard to keep breathing. I felt lost and excruciatingly alone. No matter how many times I cried, it never helped. I hid who I was from everyone, and I left Korea because I could no longer live in a country that reminded me of you.

"When I came to America, I tried to live my life for the both of us. I wanted to believe you were watching me from heaven. I would spend hours in my room talking to you, telling you about my day, looking for clues about how we came to be like this. You were gone, but I never let you go. Not really." Tae-hee wiped at the tears that flowed freely down her cheeks and sniffed. "Then you came back to me in such an unusual way. But you came back. You can't leave me again just because Jong kissed you. You can't disappear because you're unsure of your feelings. You just can't."

"I.m sorry, Tae-hee," said Kit as he pulled her into a hug, his head against her stomach. "I am so sorry. Things were difficult for both of us. I promise to take better care of you."

Tae-hee draped her arms over Kit's shoulders. "And I promise to take care of you, but only if you stay with me and everyone at KSH House."

Kit sighed, but kept his hold on Tae-hee. "I know you care about everyone at KSH House, but I don't see them the same way. I only care about you. I can only confide in you. Only you know who I really am. How can I open up to someone else? After the Korean War, I was no longer just Tae-soo, and I couldn't pretend to be the same Chanchai. It took me a long time to become whole and live this life as my two selves."

Kit looked up at Tae-hee, who sniffed and drew her fingers under her eyes. It would be unconscionable to leave her and add to her bitter memories.

His expression suddenly changed. With a smirk and glint in his eye, he added, "Anyway, who are you to give advice on relationships? Have you dated anyone? Ever?"

Tae-hee tightened her lips and clapped Kit on the back. "Don't change the subject," she chided.

"You haven't!" laughed Kit. "My sister is a gold miss!"

Tae-hee reached over to pull items from Kit's duffle bag. "Don't make fun of me!" she said as she tossed clothes hand over hand at him. Kit laughed and shrank from the onslaught.

"Okay! Okay!" yelled Kit. "I call a truce!"

Tae-hee stopped lobbing clothes at Kit and sat on the bed. Like Kit, she had many reasons not to get entangled with anyone. She viewed the passionate intrigue of flirtation from a distance. Apart from her friends at KSH House, she did not attach herself to anyone but her twin brother.

But Kit wouldn't leave the topic alone. "So, tell me, sister of mine," he prodded, "why haven't you ever had a romantic relationship? Even when we lived in Joseon, you said you would never marry. Why?"

"I have my reasons."

Kit stared at her, waiting for further clarification.

Tae-hee clicked her tongue. "Fine. At first, it was because I didn't want to leave you. I knew you struggled after we lost Abeoji, and when Kim Joon-gi left us, you were even more depressed. After you left me and Kim Joon-gi became my guardian, I tried to hide from the Japanese. I didn't want to be another Korean woman taken by them. Then there were wars, then Kim Joon-gi died, then you died. I didn't want to weep over another grave. I didn't want to have children who blamed me for passing whatever we are onto them. I didn't want to force someone else to live as I did. And now, even if I change my mind, it's too late. I've stopped menstruating. I've lived for so long that I've run out of eggs. Women are born with a certain number of eggs."

"That's it?" asked Kit. "Those are your reasons?"

Tae-hee tilted her head and shrugged her shoulders.

"You have too many worries in your life," Kit replied after a long pause. "But the eggs? Really?"

"Children are important," said Tae-hee, her voice small. "Besides, losing Tae-soo destroyed me. I can't imagine what it would be like to lose a child."

Remorse forced Kit to look away. He hung his head, unable to offer any words that could soothe the years of pain caused by the physical death of Tae-soo.

"But this isn't about me," said Tae-hee, brightening up. "We were talking about you. Even if you can define what normal is, being 'normal' has no influence on how you and Jong feel about each other. You are who you are. You feel what you feel. Like is like. Love is love. What do you feel?"

"I don't know," replied Kit. "It is just too much, too soon."

"Too soon?" Tae-hee crossed her arms. "Tae-soo fell for Lee Seung-gi in less time. I guess it shouldn't surprise me. This is just like Tae-soo. You never liked change."

"Tae-hee, it's not that I don't like change. It's that I don't like change thrust upon me. I mean, look at me. I've experienced enormous change. But I never asked for it." Kit picked up the clothes that fell on the floor and tossed them on the bed. "I don't want to run away. I just don't know how to stay."

Tae-hee wrapped her arms around Kit. "How about you flip it? Instead of what you want to run away *from*, focus on what you want to run *to*."

27
TRUST

(AUGUST 15, 2019)

The sound of the keypad and the loud click as the loft apartment door unlocked interrupted their sibling moment. Seung-do and Sameer entered, removed their shoes, and crossed to the dining table.

"Annyeonghaseyo," said Seung-do as he smiled and bowed.

Sameer put his palms together and grinned. "Namaste," he said.

Troubled by the twosome's unanticipated invasion, Kit pushed Tae-hee away and silently asked her for an explanation.

"Before I arrived, I invited them to talk to you," said Tae-hee. "Do you remember I said there were things I needed to tell you? Some of those things go beyond my expertise, so I've asked them to tell you instead. You'll understand once you hear them out. Listen to them, Kit. Talk with them." She gave Kit a quick hug, then gave Sameer and Seung-do a knowing glance before hurrying out of the apartment.

What did Tae-hee tell Sameer and Seung-do?

Seung-do put six packs of beer and soda on the table, took a seat, and waited for Kit to join him. Kit took note of their attire, looking for potential clues about their agenda. Sameer wore his standard button-up shirt and jeans, while the Korean doctor embraced a more contemporary fashion. Kit gained no new information from this cursory examination.

Sameer propped himself against the wall, his arms folded across his chest—the standard Sameer stance. Was what they said about body language true? Was Sameer on the defensive? Or was it just his most comfortable pose?

Kit imagined this is what it felt like to be called into an elementary school principal's office. Although the thought amused Kit, to be fair, he had never experienced a modern primary school education. When he felt the beginnings of a wry grin, he pursed his lips to hide his mirth.

What is Seung-do's relationship with Sameer?

What united them? Was it just because Sameer and Seung-do were contemporaries? Men with advanced education? Guys with exceptional people skills?

Feeling awkward and defensive, Kit wasn't sure he wanted to talk with them. However, Kit would hear them out in deference to Tae-hee's wishes. Sameer was a trusted friend and mentor to Tae-hee, and she had some sort of affinity for Seung-do. Was it because he was a doctor and she was a nurse? Would he know the cause of their unique physiology?

Kit kept Seung-do at a distance because they had a brief encounter in 1919. Seung-do had been an active part of one of the most devastating events in Tae-soo's life. Did Tae-hee know?

No.

Tae-soo hadn't shared that level of detail with her. She never met Seung-do before, though they could have met at Severance Hospital.

No.

If Tae-hee had met the doctor in 1919, she would have recognized Seung-do and told Kit. Besides, the staff at Severance Hospital knew him as Park Bong-soo. It was after the original Lee Seung-do died that Park Bong-soo embraced his name and life, especially since the Japanese were on high alert after Samil.

Seung-do slid a beer toward Kit, who warily walked over to sit at the table. Seung-do handed a soda to Sameer. He took a beer for himself. The three men opened their beverages and quietly drank.

Kit's patience ran out first. "What did Tae-hee tell you?"

"She told us that you were in the Korean War," explained Seung-do.

"That you changed," added Sameer, raising an eyebrow.

"And you believe her?" said Kit. He took a sip of beer. "Do I look old enough to have been in the Korean War? You should know how popular plastic surgery is for Koreans."

"Can plastic surgeons change your height, too?" asked Sameer. He pushed off the wall and sat in the chair opposite Kit. "We know you and Tae-hee are different."

"Different?"

"Both of you are older than you look," explained Seung-do. "Much, much older. And when you are sick or wounded, you heal faster than most."

"Good genes."

"There are other things," suggested Sameer.

"Such as?"

"Transmigration."

Kit felt his muscles tense. Tae-hee had told them about Tae-soo's transmigration into Chanchai's body. Kit expected a reaction to the idea, yet the two men continued sipping their beverages as if transmigration was commonplace. Who were they?

Relax.

Can we trust them?

Tae-hee trusts them.

She trusts everyone.

Tae-hee would never betray us.

"I've been wondering about you two," Kit said, trying to divert attention away from himself. "What is your relationship? There's an unspoken tension between you two."

Sameer grimaced. "We are friends, but circumstances separated us. Only recently did we discover each other."

Kit took another sip of beer while he considered Sameer's deliberate choice of words.

"Discovered," not "found."

Offering a good-natured grin, Seung-do said, "Let me be straightforward. We need to know the details of your transmigration during the Korean War."

Why do they need to know?

Kit put his beer on the table. "Tell me the truth. Who are you two?"

Seung-do leaned forward, his hands clasped together, fingers entwined. "You, Sameer, and I are more alike than you know. You can trust us."

Kit could see no ill intent in Seung-do. Though Seung-do brought up terrible memories for Tae-soo, he seemed like a good and honorable man. He gave up his life as he knew it to protect the Lee family. Tae-soo nearly destroyed himself when Lee Seung-gi died.

Kit shifted in his seat to scrutinize Sameer.

They know we are different.

But they are sincere.

They want to understand us.

Tae-hee told them of Tae-soo's transmigration.

But why? Why?

Frustrated at feeling cornered, Kit pushed away from the table and crossed the room. After briefly pacing in front of the sofa, he said, "Did Tae-hee tell you I have trust issues?"

Seung-do shot a glance at Sameer, who smiled, leaned on the table, and said, "Believe me, I understand trust issues. It is up to you whether you will trust us. But you should know that we are the ones most likely to understand you and keep you safe. You may not know it now, but we consider you a part of our family."

"Family? Like a cult?" Kit sat down on the sofa, thankful for the distance he had put between them.

"No," said Seung-do, rising from the chair. "We're not a cult." He furrowed his brow and shook his head. "It would be easier if you told us your story. Then we can explain."

"You want me to trust you before you trust me?"

Kit's words silenced them all.

Were we too mean? Will they give up on us?

No. They need to prove we can trust them.

Seung-do broke the silence. "Do you believe extraterrestrial beings exist?" he asked. Sameer clicked his tongue and gave Seung-do an uneasy glance.

Kit cocked his head, then burst out in laughter. "You're suggesting space aliens?"

Sameer raised an eyebrow as he and Seung-do stared at Kit. Their humorless expressions caused Kit to withdraw his laughter.

They are serious.

Are they crazy?

They seem trustworthy.

But are they crazy?

"Okay. Space aliens," confirmed Kit. "Is that supposed to scare me?"

"Have we given you cause to be scared?" asked Sameer.

Kit narrowed his eyes and pursed his lips. "Are you saying that you are aliens?" It was a cringeworthy question.

"Not exactly," replied Sameer. "The best way to explain it is that we have dual consciousnesses. One human, one alien."

Kit froze.

Two in one.

Like us.

Like us.

They would understand us.

But we are not aliens.

Does that matter?

Does it not matter?

Kit became dizzy. His internal conversation transformed from a stream of thoughts into a flood of emotions, creating a ringing that roared in his ears. It had been decades since he had felt this out of control. A tingling sensation spread through his body, like something was waking up from a long sleep. He was falling apart. He curled up on the sofa.

Seung-do's hand on his back brought him to his senses. Kit unfolded himself and sat up, straightening into a meditative posture to calm his breathing and emotions.

"I think we touched a nerve," Seung-do said, his voice cracking. The situation was affecting him as well.

Why?

As Seung-do rubbed Kit's back, the three men remained quiet. Only their breaths and movements broke the silence.

After several minutes, Kit composed himself. "I'm sorry," he said. "Excuse me." He pushed himself up from the sofa and escaped into the bathroom. Once inside, with the door shut behind him, he stood before the mirror and studied his reflection.

Why are we so overwhelmed?

He turned on the faucet and splashed water on his face.

I am uneasy, Chanchai.

So am I. But we are together.

I can't breathe.

Breathe, Tae-soo.

Kit leaned on the countertop, grabbed his chest, and took several slow, deep, even breaths. He jumped when someone knocked on the bathroom door. The muffled voice of Seung-do asked if he was okay.

"I'll be out in a minute," Kit replied. He patted his face dry, then opened the bathroom door.

When Kit emerged, Sameer and Seung-do stood by the sofa.

"I'm all right," Kit said. He sat on the sofa and waited for Sameer and Seung-do to take their places. Seung-do chose the other end of the sofa while Sameer sat in the armchair. Kit folded his hands together and began his story.

"In 1952, Tae-soo delivered supplies to Seokhyeon-dong Northern Hill as part of the Korean Service Corps." Kit chose to narrate his story as if he were a bystander rather than the subject of the event. "A Thai battalion protected the hill. Besides delivering supplies, the KSC rebuilt bunkers and performed other necessary tasks. Tae-soo met Lieutenant Chanchai Thanadorn Noratpattanasai on the hill. We had an instant connection.

"Since it was getting dark by the time we finished the work, our superiors ordered us to stay put. That night, the PVA attacked the hill. Chanchai asked Tae-soo to take ammo to the soldiers in the foxholes. Tae-soo took four rounds and delivered two to the machine gunners. As he crawled toward another foxhole, a mortar exploded nearby. It tore Tae-soo apart from the waist down. He felt his life draining away. Chanchai hovered over him, and the look on his face confirmed it. But Tae-soo wasn't ready to die. He still needed to find Tae-hee. That's when it happened."

"That's when Tae-soo transmigrated into Chanchai," said Seung-do.

Kit nodded. "It was strange to see Tae-soo's bloody and broken body. I don't think anyone could have survived losing half their body. Tae-hee saw the dead Tae-soo like that. She said it was horrific."

"And how are you now?" prompted Sameer.

"It took years for us to translate our memories. Once we figured things out, Chanchai and Tae-soo became friends, confidantes, soulmates," Kit said, blushing when he realized he had over-shared.

Seung-do and Sameer chuckled.

"I've said too much," said Kit.

"No," said Sameer. "We understand."

"So, I've told you my story," said Kit. "Now it's your turn to tell me yours."

28
HISTORY

(AUGUST 15, 2019)

Sameer and Seung-do took the next half hour to share their experiences as threlphax hosts.

Sameer explained how he, Abhimanyu Khatri, and Kiran Ahuja merged with threlphax the night the stars fell in 1864. He showed the threlphax healing power as he had to Jong by slicing his palm and watching it heal.

Seung-do explained that threlphax merge more quickly and deeply when the host's life is in danger from illness or injury. However, even the threlphax had limitations. His wife, Lee Eun-sol, died from blood loss after giving birth to twins in 1867. Unbeknownst to him, the children hosted Earthborn threlphax. Four years later, Seung-do was wounded in battle. When he recovered, he returned home to discover the twins had disappeared.

"So," said Kit when they finished their explanations, "you host the extraterrestrial life forms called threlphax that fell to Earth in 1864. Tae-hee and I host second-generation, Earthborn threlphax. You believe this alien life form is the reason for our health and longevity."

Sameer and Seung-do nodded.

"And you think the threlphax enabled Tae-soo's transmigration into Chanchai's body?"

Sameer and Seung-do nodded again.

Until now, there had been no rational explanation for Kit's unusual life. Sameer and Seung-do proposed a logical theory, though it failed to fully account for Chanchai's existence. Still, Kit found it difficult to accept that Tae-soo hosted the offspring of an alien life form.

"Does Tae-hee know all this?"

"Yes," Sameer replied. "I told her shortly after we met."

As he evaluated the information, he shifted his gaze to Seung-do.

This is Tae-soo's father?

Tae-hee knew.

This is why she said Seung-do was important to her.

It was a surreal moment for Tae-soo. Maybe the father, who he thought abandoned them, hadn't.

He is a good man.

"You were originally called Park Bong-soo."

"Yes."

Kit shook his head. "Tae-soo clung to a misinformed belief that prevented him from recognizing you." While he acknowledged who Seung-do was, he wasn't ready to call him father.

"Tae-hee recognized me the day I arrived at KSH House."

"She didn't tell me," Kit scoffed.

Sameer stood up. "I'll get some snacks. It'll be a long night." He left Kit and Seung-do alone in the loft apartment.

After a long silence, Seung-do said, "So, your host body's name is Chanchai." It was an awkward way to restart the conversation.

"Yes. Chanchai Thanadorn Noratpattanasai."

Seung-do nodded. "Chanchai, thank you for saving my son." The sincerity with which he offered those words caused Kit's emotional stability to fluctuate. He didn't deserve any praise since the act that saved Tae-soo occurred without forethought.

Narrowing his eyes at Seung-do, Kit redirected the conversation. "So, how old are you, exactly?"

"Hard to say," said Seung-do. "Do you want it in human years or threlphax years?"

"When was Park Bong-soo born?"

"April 19, 1832, the thirteenth year of King Sunjo's reign," replied Seung-do. He leaned forward and began a litany of dates to confirm his identity. "I was thirty-two years old when the threlphax vessels fell. I married Lee Eun-sol, your mother, in May 1866. Tae-soo and Tae-hee were born the following year, on March 27, 1867. In June 1871, circumstances separated us."

Kit exhaled a single laugh as he stared at his hands. "We always thought you abandoned us," he muttered. "I hated you for it."

"I never abandoned you," replied Seung-do, becoming more animated. "We were separated when the Americans invaded Ganghwa Island. My duty was to prevent the Shinmi Yang-gyo, but it wasn't even a battle of attrition, It was a slaughter. An explosion collapsed the wall of Gwangseonbo, and I fell down the cliff face, along with an American soldier. As I struggled with the soldier, a rifleman shot me. I knew I was dying. But because of the threlphax, I survived. When I returned to our hanok, everyone was gone. I didn't know where you went. For over four years, I waited for your return or at least an indication of where you were. I hoped the Kim family protected you, but I didn't know."

"You kept your promise," murmured Kit under his breath. It puzzled him that his father hadn't come for Tae-soo and Tae-hee in Gwangju. "Kim Joon-gi said they left a note for you that explained where we went," he said.

"A note? I never found a note."

Kit saw no deception in Seung-do's expression, only confusion mixed with concern. So that was it. Fate mocked them in an appalling way. He never found the item that linked Park Bong-soo to his children. Was it the wind, rain, or a curious creature that stole the note and separated their family? Tae-soo had resented a man whom he should have loved or at least pitied.

"We never held a memorial for you," Kit said bitterly. "They knew you were alive. They never told us the truth. Not once." Kit's brows drew together as he assembled what little he had learned about his father over the years.

The letter.

He jumped up and strode across the room to dig out a wooden box from his duffle bag. After opening the antique box, he pulled out a yellowed, mud-stained envelope. With feelings of dread and reverence, he carried it over to Seung-do and held it out to him. Nervously, he waited for Seung-do's reaction.

With much care, Seung-do took the envelope, opened it, and upended it to pour out the enclosed paper. He carefully unfolded the yellowed, brittle letter and read the message.

Do not return to Gwangseonbo. Be filial to your parents. Take care of Tae-soo and Tae-hee. If possible, I will reunite with them. Park Bong-soo.

Seung-do ran his fingers carefully over the Hangul script. "It is strange to see my handwriting like this. Did Kim Joon-gi give this to you?" he asked, carefully setting the brittle paper down on the table.

"Yes. It was the last thing Joon-gi gave me."

"I am surprised that he kept this. I was glad when Tae-hee told me he survived. Did he tell you why I gave this to him?"

"He said you saved his life."

"Kim Joon-gi was only fourteen," said Seung-do. "The regent, Heungseon Daewongun, ordered us to repel the American invasion. If we lost to the Americans, we would be traitors, and our lives would be forfeit. Kim Joon-gi's parents had only one son, and he insisted on joining the battle. His uncle, Kim Min-woo, and I were soldiers, so we were prepared to give our lives to protect Joseon. We couldn't let Kim Joon-gi sacrifice himself. His parents, Kim Min-seo and Kim Sook-ja, did so much for our family. His life was the last gift I could give them. I sent him away, asking him to remain filial and live with dignity."

"I think Kim Joon-gi resented us because of it. And I resented you because you never returned."

"Do you still resent me?"

Kit felt uncomfortable with the direct question. As he let his answer percolate in his mind, he folded the paper and placed it back in the envelope. He returned the envelope to the wooden box, closed it, and tenderly ran his fingers over the lid. After a moment of deliberation, he placed the box on the dresser.

"You are a stranger I met twice and respected," Kit said.

"I should have recognized Tae-soo when we met in Hanseong," said Seung-do.

Kit remembered the night in late February 1919 when Park Bong-soo, the original Lee Seung-do, his younger brother Lee Seung-gi, and Kim Tae-soo hid from the Japanese soldiers. They talked and smoked and shared secrets. When morning came, they walked home. Their misfortune came when they crossed paths with the Japanese soldier who would take the lives of both the Lee brothers. Their deaths and the violence that followed were the reason Park Bong-soo took the name and identity of Lee Seung-do. Before Tae-soo and his father might recognize each other, the Koreans rose to declare their independence. The turmoil of that day separated them.

"I know I can never make up for the past," said Seung-do, "but I hope I can be part of your future."

Kit wasn't sure what that meant. What would their future together look like? Would they be friends? Father and son? Would Kit have to be filial to this man? Could he make a place for this man in his life? Did he want to?

He stuffed his hands into his pockets and walked to the middle of the room. Chanchai helped Tae-soo parse through dozens of questions in his muddled thoughts. He settled on a simple question that he hoped would produce a simple response. "Why didn't you say anything when we met in Hanseong, before the real Lee Seung-do died?"

Kit waited for Seung-do's answer to the ill-formed question. But he was impatient. "Why didn't you recognize who Kim Tae-soo was?" Kit clarified.

"When you mentioned your twin sister, Tae-hee, I wondered." Seung-do carefully selected the words in his reply. "But I wasn't confident. You said your parents died in the flu pandemic, and you had another family member. How could I even ask you? Lee Seung-do knew nothing of my distant past, and you seemed uncomfortable talking about yourself. "

"I was."

"In the end, I was too afraid to hope, too afraid to ask. Besides, I was looking for a man in his fifties. At the time, I didn't know that Earthborn threlphax were possible. Even if my threlphax tried to tell me, I didn't listen. After years of waiting and searching, I believed you were no more. But what about you? Did Tae-soo not know the name of his birth father?"

Tae-soo grunted at the ridiculous nature of their relationship. "Tae-soo was very young when you abandoned . . . separated from us. Our foster parents didn't speak of you. Maybe they were trying to protect us. Only after the Independence Movement did Kim Joon-gi confirm our father's name. Even though you had the same name, I had stopped hoping for the father who had abandoned us. I was so young when you left and so many years had passed that I could no longer remember your face. Or maybe I didn't want to." Kit hung his head and sighed as he walked toward the balcony.

Would anything have changed if he had asked?

We understood nothing.

Sliding open the balcony door, Kit went outside and leaned on the railing. He watched the families play together in the park behind the apartments while Tae-soo sifted through the memories from when he was a young boy. His father's face remained obscured for most of Tae-soo's life. When it came into focus with Seung-do's face, complex feelings of relief and regret coursed through him.

So many years lost.

When he heard Seung-do approaching, Kit tried to calm his emotions. He looked away when Seung-do rested his hand on Kit's shoulder.

"I am truly sorry. I failed you both as a father and a friend," said Seung-do. His voice was deep and solemn.

He is hurting, too.

"I need time to adjust," said Kit.

Seung-do removed his hand and leaned on the railing, "I understand."

Tae-soo and Chanchai weren't the only ones who lived through world-changing events and life-changing losses. Seung-do also had experienced nearly two centuries of personal and political turmoil. After losing his wife and two children, how had he survived his long, lonely life?

"How did you meet Lee Eun-sol," Kit asked, "back when you were called Park Bong-soo?"

Seung-do smiled at the question. "There were a few rebellions after King Gojong took the Joseon throne. I pursued a Tonghak rebel into the forest. They ambushed me and struck me with three very painful arrows. I got back on my horse, but I passed out. My mare carried me to Lee Eun-sol's courtyard. It was probably the aroma of the fig tree that drew her attention. Miniso was fond of fig tree fruit, leaves, and bark.

'Lee Eun-sol was a young widow. She and her household nursed me back to health despite knowing the village would gossip. It was a brave decision on her part. But despite her best efforts, it wasn't enough to heal me.

"I was near death the night two threlphax fell through the roof of the hanok. Taedlum's threlphax vessel shattered. I was nearby, so Taedlum merged with me, saving us both. My injuries had been severe. Despite the skills of the threlphax, I needed time to heal, so I stayed with Lee Eun-sol. Later, when she got scarlet fever, the second threlphax—Tamar—merged and healed her.

"During that period, I fell in love with Lee Eun-sol, but she rejected me. She was always on my mind, even after I returned to duty. Months later, I returned to discover that, despite her rejection, she loved me as well. We married. A year later, you two were born."

"She died giving birth to us."

Seung-do straightened to look Kit in the eye. "Lee Eun-sol died from postpartum hemorrhage. Threlphax cannot replenish plasma, cells, and platelets fast enough when faced with major blood loss. And our knowledge of medicine wasn't what it is now. But, Tae-soo, you and your sister are not responsible for her death. She was happy to give you life, and I was happy to be your father."

"Tae-soo always blamed himself for the deaths of both of his parents," murmured Kit. He never admitted this truth to anyone, not even Tae-hee.

"Tae-soo, you mustn't blame yourself."

Kit clenched his jaw to hold back the emotions that roiled inside him each time this man, his birth father, spoke directly to Tae-soo.

"You are innocent," continued Seung-do. "As far as my fate, well, battlefields are covered in blood. I survived because of my threlphax. Fortunately, the threlphax genes we passed on also saved you. Although your threlphax saved you in quite a unique way."

"So, you believe the threlphax caused Tae-soo to transmigrate?"

"It's not a common human ability. If it were, humans would transmigrate all the time. Hospitals would no longer be places of healing but marketplaces for healthy human bodies."

The morbid idea amused Kit, coming from Seung-do, who was rational, compassionate, and affable—good qualities for a doctor.

"I visited Eomeoni's tomb on her death anniversary," said Kit. "It was the first time in over fifty years. It surprised me to find fresh flowers there."

Seung-do let out a light laugh. "I wonder how often our paths have crossed without recognizing each other. I've visited her tomb many times over the years. I even erected steles to ensure their burial mounds remained undisturbed. When I bought the Kim property, I turned it over to the historical society to maintain, though I planned to reclaim it in the future. Demolishing that place would have torn me to pieces."

"Now that you know what happened, do you hate the Kims for taking us away?"

"Ganghwa Island was a dangerous place—first the French, then the Americans. The Kims protected you by taking you away. I could never hate them. I only resent myself for losing you."

Even if Tae-soo accepted that Seung-do was his biological father, could he embrace the future Seung-do was so eager to share? Fortunately, both Tae-soo and Chanchai liked this man's honest demeanor.

"What made you decide to become a doctor?" Kit asked.

"I think the seed was planted because of Eun-sol's death," explained Seung-do. "I never felt so helpless. I realized that even the threlphax had limitations."

"You gave up your name and profession for Lee Seung-do and his family."

"When my friend Lee Seung-do died, everyone feared what would happen if the Japanese discovered he supported Korean Independence. As he lay dying, Lee Seung-do asked me to take his place. He thought it was the only way to keep his family safe. But he was wrong. Losing their two sons broke the Lee family. Both parents died within two years."

Tae-soo's memories transported Kit to 1919 and the room where the original Lee Seung-do lay bleeding, the result of a rifle shot by a Japanese soldier who crossed their path. Park Bong-soo, then a fledgling doctor, did his best to remove the bullet and tend to Lee Seung-do's wound. Tae-soo never considered how Park Bong-soo felt as his close friend lay dying. Park Bong-soo fulfilled Lee Seung-do's last wish because he could do nothing else.

"They left everything they had to me as Rii Shiungudo," Seung-do continued. "I felt guilty when I received the inheritance. I reclaimed Lee Seung-do's Korean name in 1945. It was the least I could do to honor him and his family. I wanted their faith and investment in me to have meaning. I used the inheritance to further my medical education. But they had more wealth than I'd imagined. I've invested in real estate and the market so the funds can finance my future self."

"Money laundering? You became a smurf?"

"Not purposefully. Since the funds were clean, I didn't need to launder them. However, my longevity requires me to manage my money and investments innovatively." Seung-do chuckled to himself. "I guess that some may question my methods. But I've gone unchallenged so far."

The two men allowed memories from their pasts to flood over them. Kit conceded that getting to know this man first as Park Bong-soo, allowed him to feel more at ease with him as Seung-do Lee. It saddened him that it took a century to meet again.

Seung-do asked, "What happened to you after Lee Seung-gi died?"

Kit clenched his jaw. Lee Seung-do's younger brother, whom Tae-soo loved, stepped into his sibling's shoes. The tragedy of that choice was that Lee Seung-gi's life ended shortly after his brother's and in similar circumstances. Kit's mind filled with the image of Lee Seung-gi lying dead on the Lee's kitchen table, his body bloodied from bullet wounds. Lee Seung-gi had been shot in the stomach, and Tae-soo carried him home, unaware that a second bullet claimed Lee Seung-gi's life. The two Lee brothers—Seung-do and Seung-gi—died within days of each other.

The man who stood beside him as the avatar of Lee Seung-gi's brother understood the tragedy of those deaths. Tae-soo never healed from the loss of Lee Seung-gi. As the man who witnessed it stood beside him, the memories tore through Tae-soo's wounded heart.

Kit took a deep breath. "Lee Seung-gi was more than a friend. He was Tae-soo's first love."

Seung-do's silent nod confirmed he knew of their relationship.

"After Tae-soo left the Lee home that night, " continued Kit, "he went to beat the hell out of the Japanese who shot Lee Seung-gi. Tae-soo had the Japanese soldier pinned to the ground, his face bloodied, before they dragged Tae-soo to prison. After losing Lee Seung-gi, Tae-soo didn't mind dying. Who would want to live in an unjust world? But the Japanese didn't kill Tae-soo. They just tortured him."

Kit acknowledged Seung-do's concerned expression with a bitter chuckle. "The Japanese thought Tae-soo was part of the March First Movement. They wanted him to give them names," he said. "I now know that the threlphax kept healing him each night. Tae-soo frightened the guards because his healing was unnatural."

"I'm sorry," muttered Seung-do. "I'm so, so sorry."

"I accepted everything. Tae-soo considered it punishment for not protecting Lee Seung-gi," said Kit. He remembered something Kim Joon-gi had told him. "Did you know that his father, Mr. Lee Byeong-ho, knew Tae-soo ended up in prison? He used his business connections with the Japanese to get Tae-soo released."

"Kim Joon-gi was in Hanseong?" Seung-do's baffled look took Kit by surprise.

Tae-soo lived with the dark cloud of abandonment over him for over a century and a half. When he met Park Bong-soo in 1919, they separated again after both Lee brothers died. Their stories wove together in an odd tapestry of tragedy and misfortune.

"Oh, right," Seung-do muttered. "That explains why Tae-soo said there was another family member. Mr. Lee rarely spoke with me after the March First Movement. I became Lee Seung-do, but they never mistook me for their son."

Despite his youthful appearance, Seung-do was an old soul who tried to hide the torment of his long past. The upheavals of Kit's life seemed insignificant compared to the pain and regret now painted on Seung-do's countenance.

I've shared too much.

He is struggling.

Kit tried to lighten the conversation. "What's with you and Sameer?"

"Oh," said Seung-do, shaking off his distress. "I guess you could say that our threlphax were friends before Sameer and I met. When we met, all the questions about who, what, why I was—everything—fell into place. I've known Sameer for less than a month, but I trust him with my life."

"Yet you sometimes seem at odds."

"It's complicated." Seung-do straightened and held out his right hand, palm up. "I know Sameer showed you in his own way, but just in case you still have trouble believing it . . ." He shifted his gaze to his hand, where tiny glittering translucent tendrils emerged and wafted across his palm. Kit leaned in for a closer look, moved by the beauty of the wisps as they swayed gently across Seung-do's skin.

"What is that?" Kit asked.

"This is my threlphax," explained Seung-do. "This being of energy runs throughout my entire body. Though it's merged with me, it remains a separate living being. It's ancient by human standards and tells me its name is Taedlum. Threlphax are genderless, neither male nor female. They adopt the gender qualities of their host."

"May I touch it?"

"You may."

As Kit drew his finger across the tendrils, a soft tingling reverberated through his being, conjuring emotions nearly too powerful to restrain. He pulled his hand away and took a calming breath.

"Better yet," said Seung-do, "try exposing your threlphax."

Surprised by the suggestion, Kit lifted his right hand and stared at his palm. "I'm not sure how."

"Imagine your energy flowing toward your hand. Not to be crude, but the energy flow is not unlike what you feel before sexual climax. Of course, the release feels different."

"I lack experience in that."

"It's been a while for me, but it's a convenient way to describe the energy flow in human terms. Once you become more practiced, such comparisons won't be necessary."

Kit closed his eyes and concentrated on the air flowing in and out of his lungs and the pulse of his blood. A tingling warmth crept across his back. He allowed himself to marinate in this feeling, this strange comfort, before focusing on his open palm. A moment of intense energy softened, and Kit opened his eyes. Tiny translucent tendrils moved across his palm in concert with the flow of his breath and the beat of his heart.

"I believe your threlphax energy resonates with mine." Seung-do stepped forward and placed his palm over Kit's, interlocking their thumbs. It was not a handshake or a simple handhold, but a personal gesture of connection. The cluster of Seung-do's threlphax energy soothed Kit with its strange familiarity.

Kit closed his eyes as his mind filled with scenes of Ganghwa Island. But these were not his memories. These were the memories of Seung-do that his threlphax shared with Kit. Scenes of Tae-hee and Tae-soo as toddlers danced in his mind. They rode a horse, learned the meaning of their names, and slept side-by-side. The children played with members of the Kim family. Kim Joon-gi, who would become his foster brother, carried Tae-soo on his shoulders. He was a teenager, full of laughter and a bright future, so different from the man Kim Joon-gi became.

The theme of the visions changed to Hanseong. He saw a secret kiss in a dark alleyway, running from Japanese soldiers, talking and laughing and learning to smoke in a dark room, and events leading up to the deaths of the Lee brothers.

When the vision changed to Lee Seung-gi lying dead on the kitchen table, Kit jerked his hand away from Seung-do, "That's enough! I get it!" His response was too abrupt, so he added in a more measured tone, "Thank you. Thank you for being there. I know you did what you could." He turned his back to Seung-do. "Can you give me a few minutes to organize my thoughts?"

"Take whatever time you need," Seung-do replied. He returned to the loft apartment, leaving Kit alone. With his mindset changed from that of a few hours ago, Kit wrestled with new thoughts. He had spent most of his life resenting his father for leaving them, while his father had suffered the loss of the children he loved. With Tae-soo reunited with his twin sister and father, what would Kit do now?

* * * *

When Sameer returned to the loft apartment, Kit and Seung-do sat together on the sofa. Sameer deposited a pizza box on the coffee table and retrieved the remaining drinks.

"All good?" asked Sameer.

Kit and Seung-do raised their beer cans, confirming the success of the conversation.

There was one question no one had asked, to which Kit needed an answer. "Chanchai was born in Siam in 1860." He waited for the information to register with the two men, then added, "Do you think Chanchai is also a threlphax host?"

Sameer tightened his brow as he focused on Kit. He exhaled and shook his head. "It would seem so if Chanchai lived a century before the transmigration. But I sense only one threlphax energy signature within you. To Mussick's knowledge, only one threlphax can exist in one vessel. But, again, two human energy signatures exist in your one body. Your situation is quite unusual."

Two threlphax?

"I'm sure you have many questions, Kit," added Seung-do. "I know I did. We can help you find the answers."

This was why Tae-hee sent Sameer and Seung-do to Kit. He could no longer say he was alone. In Seung-do, he found the long-lost father who understood his history. In Sameer, he saw a man who understood his design. Tae-hee wasn't the only one with the power to keep him here.

Where else can we go?

Kit pinched his bottom lip as he weighed the virtues of staying with Tae-hee and Seung-do.

Isn't this what we always wanted?

"There's one other thing that Tae-hee wanted us to tell you," said Sameer. "It's about Emily." He glanced at Seung-do, who visibly sank at the mention of Emily's name.

"Yes, well," said Seung-do. "The reason for Emily's illness was because she remembered her previous life." He paused and looked to Sameer to continue.

"We've confirmed it," Sameer said. "Emily is the reincarnation of Lee Eun-sol, Park Bong-soo's wife and your mother."

Although he should have been surprised, Kit couldn't prevent his soft laughter. "That explains why you two are sometimes at odds," said Kit. "You're pursuing the same woman."

Seung-do smirked while Sameer looked surprised.

"Oh, come on Sameer," said Kit. "Everyone knows about you and Emily. Even I recognized how you felt the first time I came to KSH House."

Sameer wobbled his head. "Fair enough."

These two men had revealed so much, yet Kit still had questions. "Sameer, is everyone at KSH House a threlphax host?"

Sameer sighed and shook his head. "No," he replied. "And at some point, we must leave KSH House when the others begin questioning us. Such is the life of a threlphax host. I'm sure you are already aware of that."

Jong is not a threlphax host.

A tightness in Kit's chest followed the reminder that Tae-hee, too, would leave the people she loved. Would they just abandon Jong, or would they leave gradually? Jong was strong. He could survive the loss of friends. That was part of being human. But the sudden sting Kit felt at the idea of leaving Jong behind caught him off guard.

Choosing to leave Jong feels very different from being forced to leave him. Why does the idea of leaving Jong bother us so much?

Kit had not yet responded to Jong's kiss at the campfire. Knowing what made him different made a relationship with Jong seem more difficult.

As Kit worked through his thoughts, Sameer added, "Even though not everyone at KSH House is a threlphax host, they are all good people. They are trustworthy, honest, and good friends to us."

Kit nodded.

"And about Jong," continued Sameer, "maybe it's because of his Korean shamanic heritage, but my threlphax self feels something is unique about his human energy signature."

Jong is ours.

Kit exhaled a short laugh at his jealous reaction in response to Sameer's words. To mask his reaction, Kit grabbed another can of beer, popped the lid, and took a big gulp of the bitter brew.

"I have something important to say," he announced, turning to Seung-do. "How would you feel if I came out? You wouldn't disown me, would you?"

"You and Jong, right?"

"Is it that obvious?"

"You smile like idiots when you see each other," said Sameer. "You can call it whatever you want to, but at its core, it's love."

"Besides," added Seung-do. "I saw Tae-soo with Lee Seung-gi, so I know your orientation."

"Uh. Right," acknowledged Kit. "I saw it in your memories. You witnessed the love affair that shook Tae-soo's world." He finished his beer and reached for another.

"Slow down, Kit," urged Seung-do.

Is this how a father advises a son?

Kit put the beer on the coffee table and shifted in his seat. "Would either of you have accepted my orientation back in 1864?"

"In 1864," replied Sameer, "the British considered homosexuality against the order of nature. They even wrote a law prohibiting it—section 377 of the Indian Penal Code."

"Confucian scholars in the Joseon period would not have approved," said Seung-do, "but unions between dragon and sun weren't infrequent. To tell you the truth, I may not have accepted it then, but as the world changes, I change with it."

"But now that I know what I am, I am uncertain what to do about Jong. He is just human. I am not." Kit's heart sank.

We like Jong.

"Kit, we can't control who we fall in love with," said Sameer. He glanced at Seung-do before he continued. "Jong is always sincere. You can trust him. Maybe you should let human nature take its course. See what happens. Don't let the future ruin the present."

"Don't overthink it," added Seung-do. "I wouldn't have married Lee Eun-sol and brought Tae-soo and Tae-hee into this world if I ignored my human feelings. Life is a journey, not a destination. We're fortunate to have lived long enough to see people at their best and worst. I've observed that people are at their best when free to give and receive love in whatever form it takes."

"Life is a journey, not a destination," echoed Kit. "Jong said the same thing. It sounds so cliché. My journey is more unique than I knew. Two men and a threlphax." Kit picked up his beer and lifted it in a solo toast before taking another gulp.

29
GLOW

(AUGUST 16, 2019)

Tae-hee encouraged Jong to meet Kit face-to-face. She told him that Sameer and Seung-do had spent the evening with Kit to help him overcome his reticence.

Jong stood in front of the loft apartment door and worked out his apology for making Kit uncomfortable. His finger hovered over the doorbell. What if Kit didn't answer? Jong knew the passcode, but what if Kit had changed it? He rubbed his damp hands on his jeans and muttered to himself as he tried to rebuild his fading confidence.

Kit must have seen him on the video monitor. A loud click announced that Kit had opened the door.

Surprised, Jong hesitated a moment before he entered. He closed the door, removed his shoes, and lined them up along the baseboard.

Kit stood in the foyer, his head tilted as he watched Jong, who gave a mild grin and raised his hand in a clumsy greeting.

"What do you want, Jong?" Kit delivered the prompt with a raised eyebrow.

"Kit," said Jong, hesitant and awkward. "I didn't mean to . . . well . . . I mean . . . I meant to . . . but I don't want it to be awkward between us. I like you. But I don't want you to feel uncomfortable."

"Is that what you came here to say?" Kit's voice was deep, but the glint in his eyes showed he wasn't angry. As he stepped forward, Jong backed away until Kit's advance pressed him against the unyielding wall. Kit splayed one hand against the wall and leaned in, a soft smile on his lips. "Tell me."

The deep brown irises appeared to have a lighter caramel color near the pupils that focused on him. Jong closed his eyes and breathed in his sandalwood scent. Caught between his anxiety and Kit's seduction, his nerves tingled. Jong wasn't used to this side of Kit.

He met Kit's gaze. "What do *you* want, Kit?"

Ever since he met Kit, Jong had been the pursuer. Now, he feigned confidence in the face of this reversal of roles. The change in dynamic made Jong vulnerable and insecure. In the interminable silence, Jong could not withstand Kit's stare. He pushed Kit away. "What are you doing?" he asked, irritated.

"Did you mean it?" Kit said. "Were you sincere at the campfire? Or was it just a romantic moment?"

Their kiss at the campfire had been on Jong's mind all week. What did Kit need from him to prove he was sincere? "I'm not messing with you, Kit," he growled. "So don't mess with me."

Kit brought his face next to Jong's ear and took a deep breath, just inches from him, causing heat to rise in Jong. "How are you doing this to me? Why am I so attracted to you?" Jong stiffened at the resonance of Kit's voice and the brush of his breath.

"Jong."

Jong swallowed and pushed Kit away again. "Stop playing with me, Kit!" he fumed as he bent to retrieve his shoes.

"Tell me what I should do."

"Just be yourself, Kit. That's who I like. That's who I'm attracted to."

"Be myself," repeated Kit. His smile faded as he spoke, and he backed away. "Jong." His voice was strained. "Sameer and Seung-do visited me last night. I am still trying to wrap my mind around the things they told me. What they said was freeing but also frightening. If I am acting differently, I'm sorry."

If Kit learned of the threlphax last night, he needed time to adjust, thought Jong. Nodding his understanding, Jong put down his shoes and turned to Kit. "You probably need some time."

Kit's eyes widened. "Jong, that's not it."

"Then what is it?"

"I'm trying to tell you how I feel . . . " Kit's voice trailed off as he struggled for words.

"You can't say anything." Kit's mixed signals frustrated Jong, yet he wanted to console him. "That's okay. I won't force you. I'll come back when you're ready to talk."

"No, Jong, no," Kit said. "I want to give you my answer. May I?"

Before he could respond, Kit ran his hand around the back of Jong's neck and pulled him forward into a kiss. When he ended the kiss and leaned back, his expression pleaded for understanding.

Jong touched his forehead to Kit's. "It's okay, Kit. Don't force yourself."

"No," said Kit. "You don't understand." Kit leaned forward and pressed his lips more urgently against Jong's. This time, the slow, thorough movement of his lips poured out his desire, desperation, and determination.

Kit's intensity convinced Jong they wouldn't stop. His heart pounded as he held onto Kit, answering his kiss with equal enthusiasm. Pulling at Kit's shirt, the two separated just long enough so Kit could pull his shirt off over his head and toss it aside. Kit wrapped his arms around Jong, continuing the kiss, pressing himself against him. He smiled when Jong stepped back and unbuttoned his shirt. A moment later, he threw it aside and yanked Kit into an embrace.

Aroused by the stroke of skin upon skin, they moved toward the bed and tumbled together onto the mattress, Kit on top. Jong put his head back as Kit ran his fingers and mouth over his chest and pressed himself against the rigidness between his legs.

Kit pushed up and said, "Do you understand what I want?"

With a broad grin, Jong said, "I'm not sure. Explain it to me some more."

Kit's next kiss was more intentional; he carefully explored the soft flesh of Jong's mouth. Jong closed his eyes and moved against Kit, grinding their hips together, increasing his arousal. Kit extracted soft moans as his hands and mouth explored Jong's bare skin. They slowly rolled together, lost in the pleasure of each other's touch, until they reached the edge of the mattress. Jong fell onto the hardwood floor with a thud, with Kit falling on top of him.

"Ow!" said Jong as he rubbed the back of his head. Kit lifted himself off of Jong to assess the damage.

"Are you okay?" Kit asked.

Jong inhaled a sharp breath when he looked into Kit's eyes. The light from the campfire hadn't caused the glow. It was Kit.

"Oh, wow," said Jong. He moved his hand from behind his head to brush away disheveled strands of hair from Kit's face. "Your eyes—"

"—What's wrong with my eyes?" Kit pushed away from Jong.

"They're glowing."

Kit glanced at the full-length mirror near the bed. Averting his gaze, he pushed away from Jong, wrapped his arms around his knees, and buried his face behind them.

The childlike, panicked pose amused Jong, but he knew he shouldn't laugh. Holding back his smile, he put his hand on Kit's arm. "Your eyes are sexy," he said.

Kit grabbed Jong's wrist and shoved it away.

"Hey. Look at me, Kit," coaxed Jong.

Kit shook his head. "You should go, Jong."

"No, Kit," Jong wrapped his arms around Kit and kissed the top of his head. When Kit lifted his gaze, Jong brushed the hair away from his face. "I've decided," said Jong. "You're mine. Sexy glowing eyes and all."

"I'm a freak, Jong."

"You're *my* freak, Kit."

"I don't know how. I don't know why. I can't control it."

Jong kissed Kit's forehead, trying to ease Kit's confusion and contempt for himself. He studied his eyes. "The glow is nearly gone," he said. "Maybe it happens when you're aroused?"

Kit pushed Jong away.

Jong laughed and, with a devilish smile, asked, "Do you wanna test my theory?"

Kit kicked at Jong, embarrassed.

"Hold on, Kit," Jong said between kicks. "Let's talk."

Kit sighed and unfolded his arms and legs. "Jong, I can't do this," he said. "There are things you don't know. Things even I don't understand. This is just the latest thing."

Jong placed his hand on Kit's leg, seeking to comfort him. "Kit," Jong said. "I'm not scared. I like you too much. Nothing about you will frighten me away." He stared into Kit's eyes, hoping he understood the sincerity of his words.

"Can we just take it slow, then?" Kit asked in a thin voice.

Jong smiled. "Yes. We can do that."

30
DISSIPATION

(AUGUST 17, 2019)

The following day at KSH House, Kit was quieter than usual. After brunch, Jong pulled Sameer and Tae-hee aside. "I need to talk to you," he said, ushering them into the library.

"Something happened with Kit last night," he explained as they sat at the table. "His eyes glowed."

"Like the X-Men?" Tae-hee asked, her eyes wide with interest.

"No, not like that," explained Jong, trying to curb their imaginations. "They didn't shoot out light. They just glowed. It was like a light turned on inside his head."

"What was he doing when this happened?" asked Sameer.

Jong felt the blood rush to his cheeks as he realized he was uncomfortable dissecting the passionate moment he and Kit shared. However, he needed to know if something was wrong. Since they were threlphax hosts, they could explain it. "We were . . . kissing . . ."

Sameer raised an eyebrow while Tae-hee barely hid her glee.

"Are you saying Kit was aroused at the time?" asked Tae-hee.

Jong neither confirmed nor denied. "Is that normal?" he asked.

"Normal?" Sameer said.

"I'm not sure," Tae-hee said. Her voice trailed off as she stared up at the ceiling.

Jong turned to Sameer. "I mean, have you with Emily?"

"Emily and I haven't—"

"Really?" said Jong and Tae-hee.

Sameer raised his eyebrow. "Was there anything else besides glowing eyes?"

"Nothing beyond the typical reaction . . . to stimulation . . . you know."

"What did Kit think?" asked Tae-hee.

"He freaked out," muttered Jong.

Someone knocked and opened the library door. Abhimanyu Khatri leaned inside and said, "Sameer. I need to speak with you."

Sameer nodded. He drew his brows together and rose from the table.

"Is something wrong?" asked Tae-hee.

"I didn't expect Abhimanyu to arrive today." He relaxed and shook his head. "Jong, talk to Seung-do about your issue."

"Is it okay for me to tell him I know he's a threlphax host?"

"How did you know?" asked Sameer.

"I sensed everyone in the room when I read Emily," Jong sheepishly replied. "The four of you had similar auras."

"Yet you said nothing. Our trust in you was well-placed," replied Sameer. "Seung-do may know more than we do."

"That's true," added Tae-hee. "As a nurse, I only work with humans, not threlphax hosts. Seung-do is older and may know more about threlphax-host physiology."

Before he exited the library, Sameer grinned at Jong. "By the way, Abhimanyu Khatri and Kiran Ahuja are also hosts."

* * * *

Abhimanyu paced the main foyer. When he saw Sameer, the elder Indian stopped and said, "I have news of Kiran Ahuja." He followed Sameer, who crossed the main foyer and knocked on the office window, motioning for Seung-do to join them.

The presence of Sameer's colleague surprised Seung-do. Abhimanyu said he would not return until year's end. He bowed his head to Jackson, then joined Sameer and Abhimanyu in the auction hall. "I just finished reviewing the listing for the sitting desk with Jackson."

"That's good," replied Sameer. He pulled out three chairs and motioned for Seung-do and Abhimanyu to join him. Once seated, Sameer crossed his arms and said, "So, Abhimanyu, tell us the news."

Abhimanyu shook his head, hesitant to disclose what he came to say.

"Abhi," urged Sameer.

"The thing is," said Abhimanyu, "Kiran is no more."

Sameer tilted his head and drew his brows together. "How do you mean?"

Abhimanyu's distressed expression reflected his words. "Our friend Kiran Ahuja is gone. He is dead"

Sameer uncrossed his arms and leaned forward. "Dead?" he repeated. His tone reflected his distaste for the word. "How? When? What happened to Phemeos?"

"The connection between Phemeos and Kiran weakened so much that Kiran could not survive. Kiran's energy signature expired when Phemeos dissipated. By the time I reached Kiran, it was too late. I could do nothing."

"Kiran. My friend," whispered Sameer as he slumped in the chair.

"How is that possible?" Seung-do murmured.

The three men sat silent, trying to comprehend the unimaginable.

"Kiran isn't the only host to die this way," said Abhimanyu. "I found several incidents in subsequent days." He put his hand on Sameer's shoulder. "Kiran died at Willow Banks Hotel in Shimla. Sameer, Mroniea was involved."

Sameer's breath caught. He stood and walked away from Abhimanyu and Seung-do. "That's not possible . . . maybe it's a mistake . . . maybe he didn't mean to . . . he couldn't have meant to destroy them."

"Before we blame Mroniea," said Seung-do, "we need more details regarding what happened to Kiran. It's not natural for a threlphax host to die, but it can happen under extreme circumstances."

"Kiran had called me that day. He said he was at Willow Banks with Mroniea." Abhimanyu reached into his jacket pocket and pulled out a small vial containing a clear liquid. Handing it to Seung-do, he said. "I believe this was what caused Kiran's death. I had a lab examine it." He pulled out a slip of paper from his pocket, unfolded it, and handed it to Seung-do. "The chemical makeup is complex. My guess is it targets threlphax energy signatures."

"How do you know?" Seung-do asked as he examined the vial labeled "Chymzafyde 2019-07-31.008" and the accompanying chemical analysis printout.

"I have reliable connections," Abhimanyu explained. "I hid the vial and convinced the authorities that it wasn't a crime. They attributed Kiran's death to heart failure. But I felt it."

"You felt it?"

"After I sniffed the vial's contents, my merge with Denyal weakened. It was frightening. I felt like Denyal would dissipate."

Abhimanyu's tone changed as he addressed the threlphax in Sameer and Seung-do. "After Kiran died, we learned of a handful of deaths with similarities to Kiran's symptoms. A vial of Chymzafyde was near each. The first victim was in Italy a week after Kiran died. Cases moved across the globe from east to west. The most recent cases are in the U.S. The dates and locations form a path that is approaching this location."

"I don't want to believe it's Mroniea," murmured Sameer. He focused inward for a moment. "But right now, he is blocking our artifact connection."

"One more thing," said Abhimanyu. "All of this started after Kit arrived at KSH House."

"Wait," said Seung-do. "Are you connecting this with Kit?"

"We've collected thousands of threlphax vessels over the years. The day Kit came to KSH House, the threlphax vessels glowed. The last time they glowed like that was over a century ago. We assume his unique energy configuration caught their attention. If someone is targeting threlphax hosts with Chymzafyde, they must have a threlphax connection. Maybe they sensed the threlphax vessels. If it was Mroniea, maybe Kiran's death was an act of desperation. Perhaps in dissipating threlphax, Mroniea wants to get Trax's attention."

"There is no reason to connect Kit with Trax," replied Seung-do. "Kit just learned that he is an Earthborn threlphax host."

"Besides, Mroniea doesn't want to see Trax," muttered Sameer as he returned to his chair. "He would choose to dissipate before undergoing restoration. Trax tried to restore Mroniea once already. That is the reason the threlphax tribe fell."

"I'm sorry, Sameer, but these are the facts I've gathered so far," replied Abhimanyu. "Given our connection with Mroniea, I fear KSH House, and maybe even Kit, could be a target."

The auction room doors opened. "What do you mean, 'target?'" asked Kit.

31
SECRETS

(AUGUST 17, 2019)

"Who is targeting me?"

Sameer, Abhimanyu, and Seung-do stared at Kit. Jong and Tae-hee emerged from the library and joined him beside the auction room doors.

"What's going on?" Jong asked.

Kit closed his eyes, unable to respond, unable to move.

Jong will know.

Jong put his hand on Kit's shoulder. "What's happening, Kit?"

No.

Kit looked to Sameer, his eyes wide and his lips parted.

"It is okay, Kit. Jong is aware of the threlphax," said Sameer. "Tae-hee and I told him several weeks ago. We asked him not to mention it until we told you. He has accepted the facts. He was an important part of our lives at KSH House even before he knew about the threlphax. Now, he's also become an important part of your life."

Kit's forehead tightened as his insides churned, making him dizzy. "Jong, you knew?" he asked, his voice hollow. "Did you know last night?"

Jong nodded once. He was not frightened. Instead, he wore a peaceful expression.

How can he look so calm?
Is he okay with this?
How much does he know?

Seung-do set up three more chairs for Kit, Jong, and Tae-hee. "Let's talk," he said.

Why didn't Jong tell us?

Jong guided Kit into the auction hall, settled him into a seat, and then sat in the chair beside him. Tae-hee closed the auction hall doors and sat on his other side. She took Kit's hand and tried to comfort him with a calm grin.

"Am I the last to know?" Kit asked.

"Sameer told me when I was a student," Tae-hee explained. "Although I just learned about the Earthborn part."

Kit quickly turned to Jong.

"Sameer and Tae-hee told me after we returned from the beach," Jong said.

They knew but kept it secret.

Kit stared at the floor, unsure whether he should be angry, sad, or confused. They had hidden something existentially important from him. His thoughts became muddled, and his breaths became rapid and shallow.

Jong squeezed his hand. "Look at me, Kit." Kit complied, but it did little to calm his emotional turmoil. "This changes nothing," Jong said. "Remember, on the camping trip, I said that Sameer and Tae-hee told me about you, right?"

Kit sifted through his conversations with Jong. He paused when he remembered Jong said the word "threlphax" when their meditation abruptly ended. Both had glossed over the reference. Now he realized Jong had slipped.

Jong knew.

Even then.

And he still wanted us.

Kit searched for any sign of betrayal in Jong's eyes. The only thing he saw was acceptance. He calmed himself and said, "Sameer, tell us everything."

"I'll start from the beginning," Sameer said as he relaxed into his explanation. "In 1864, a Geminids meteor shower passed by Earth. A passing asteroid caused it. Debris showered the Earth, primarily over India and East Asia, but most of it burned up in the atmosphere. What survived the fall to Earth wasn't meteorites. They were vessels. Alien vessels."

Sameer paced around the room. "These alien vessels were small. They could fit in your palm," he explained as he held out his hand. "They adapted to the environment, camouflaged in their surroundings. Every vessel hosted a being of energy, an alien life-form we call 'threlphax.' The vessels maintained the threlphax energy signature. When a vessel broke, the threlphax within required a compatible vessel to survive."

Kit felt his jaw tighten as nervous energy flowed along his spine.

Sameer stopped pacing. "Are you okay, Kit?"

Kit nodded but focused on Jong's reaction to Sameer's narrative. Jong remained still, his expression calm.

Have you been listening?

Did you hear the word "alien?"

Do you understand?

Jong squeezed Kit's hand and smiled. Kit looked at their intertwined fingers. Would Jong hold on to him after Sameer finished?

Jong is braver than I am.

Sameer thrust his hands in his pockets and resumed his slow pace around the room. "While a majority of the vessels that fell to Earth remained intact, some broke upon impact. The threlphax that found compatible new hosts survived. Humans were the most compatible species. The threlphax merged while maintaining autonomy, providing the host with companionship and a healthy, long life."

"The threlphax energy signature can manage its host's cellular and genetic structure," said Seung-do. "Technically, they manage the production and turnover of adenosine triphosphate, or ATP. ATP is the energy currency of life because it is the universal energy source for all living cells. Through the threlphax-human merge, the threlphax learns the nature of the host's anatomy and physiology. This merge deepens more quickly in a critically injured host. The threlphax revitalizes the cellular structure and decelerates the aging process."

"Energy is not matter," said Jong. "Can we see threlphax with the human eye?"

"Yes, they can manifest. They appear as translucent glittering tendrils because of the manipulation of cellular matter. Also . . ." Seung-do paused as he glanced at Kit and Tae-hee. "I've only recently learned that two threlphax hosts that mate can pass the genetic signature of the threlphax to their offspring. My wife and I passed threlphax DNA on to Tae-hee and Tae-soo."

"Wait," said Jong. "Are you saying you are—"

"—Seung-do is our biological father," Tae-hee confirmed.

Jong turned to Kit, his tense brow twisted in confusion. "You said your father abandoned you."

"I was wrong."

"I was wounded in a battle," said Seung-do. "The family we lived with took the twins to a safer place. By the time I recovered and returned home, they were gone."

"We left a note," Kit added, "but he never found it."

"Incredible," said Jong. "Not only have you found your family, but you also kept an extraterrestrial species alive and reproduced it."

"Jong, how can you react that way?" Kit said. "Doesn't this frighten you?"

"Well, I guess it might if I felt threatened by any of you. Which I don't," Jong replied. "Besides, the scientific community accepts that life forms exist beyond what we know. If you think about it, you are pioneers in human-alien relations. It's somewhat exciting."

"I like him," said Seung-do.

Kit stood and pointed at Seung-do. "What about him being Tae-soo's biological father? Isn't that weird to you? I mean, we look practically the same age."

"I think I look more mature," murmured Seung-do.

"Okay. Yes. That is truly weird," said Jong. "And since Seung-do isn't denying it, I'm guessing it's true." Jong frowned. "And while we're talking about weird things, it has always bugged me that you and Tae-hee don't look alike. Can you explain that?"

Here it comes.

Jong was too clever to accept all the discrepancies. Would Kit have to explain Tae-soo's transmigration? Would Jong believe him? Kit sighed and returned to his seat.

How can we accept him if we don't trust him?

Let everything go.

"Tae-soo and Tae-hee are twins," Kit said. "In 1919, circumstances forced Tae-soo to leave Tae-hee's side. Thirty years later, Tae-soo was mortally wounded during the Korean War."

Jong's ashen face caused Kit to speed up his explanation. "A Thai soldier named Chanchai tried to help, and I didn't want to die." Kit looked to Seung-do for support. "So, I jumped."

Jong said nothing.

"I transmigrated from Tae-soo's body into Chanchai's body. Now that I know about the threlphax, I understand how it happened. The body known as Tae-soo died, and we became Kit. Both Tae-soo and Chanchai exist within this one body. It belongs to both of us. I'm still Tae-soo, and I'm still Chanchai. I'm both of us."

Jong pulled his hand away and leaned forward, resting his elbows on his knees. His hair covered his face, so Kit could not see his expression. "You almost died?"

Why is he focused on that part of the story?

"But I *didn't* die," replied Kit. "Because I am Tae-soo and Chanchai and, I guess, my threlphax. We're separate yet merged entities. When it first happened, I didn't understand why or how. It took me years to adjust, but I did."

Jong sniffed and drew a hand across his face. He sat up and gave Kit a tight smile, then took his hand and nodded his understanding.

"Can I ask another question?" said Jong. He hesitated and creased his forehead in thought. "Sometimes I've seen Kit's eyes glow. Is that normal?"

Kit's eyes widened when he realized Jong was delving into their deeply personal affairs.

Seung-do exhaled a laugh, then turned somber. "What were you doing when this happened?"

Kissing, holding, touching.

Kit worried about what Jong might say. "Just second base," explained Jong, "though we were approaching third base."

Sameer leaned over and whispered in Seung-do's ear. The Korean's eyes gleamed as he lifted his hand over his mouth to hide his reaction.

"So, it's normal," said Jong. "For a threlphax host, I mean. It's the threlphax, right?"

Seung-do dropped his hand and cleared his throat. "There is evidence to support that," he said.

32
THREAT

(AUGUST 17, 2019)

Abhimanyu took control of the conversation. "Against this backdrop, I have unfortunate news. Kiran Ahuja, the third partner of KSH, has died."

"How is that possible?" said Tae-hee. "Isn't he a threlphax host?"

"He *was* a threlphax host," corrected Abhimanyu. "In the room where he died, I found a substance labeled Chymzafyde. Though I can't confirm who administered it to him, the last message he left me was that he was meeting with Mroniea."

Mroniea.

The name was familiar to Kit. The Chinese fruit seller who raised Chanchai uttered it before he died. Kit recalled the fruit seller's last words.

"Remember that Mroniea did this."

"He took a piece of us, of our energy."

"He is thinning."

"Trax is the only one who can save him."

What was Mroniea's connection to them? Did Mroniea cause the fruit seller's death? Who was Trax?

"After Kit came to KSH House, something changed. You must feel it, Sameer—even I feel it. If Mroniea is involved, perhaps he felt the change through your artifact connection."

Sameer cut Abhimanyu off with a piercing glance. "We don't know how or whether Mroniea is involved."

"And that doesn't account for the Chymzafyde," added Seung-do.

"Apart from infrequent artifact energy surges, Mroniea has been silent since before Partition," said Sameer. "Why would he approach us now?"

"I think Mroniea killed someone I knew," said Kit. His abrupt accusation of a man he didn't know was inconsistent with his nature. Then again, Tae-soo accused Seung-do of abandoning them when, in reality, they abandoned him.

"Someone attacked the fruit seller I knew," he continued, recalling the events around the mysterious death of the man who raised Chanchai. "I carried him home. Though I saw blood on his clothes, he had no wound. He said Mroniea was responsible, that he was thinning. He sent me to fetch some sticky rice for him. When I returned, he had died. Now that I know of the threlphax, I believe he was a host."

"If he was a host, he shouldn't have died," said Sameer.

"No, he shouldn't have." Seung-do said. "But if Mroniea's membrane continues to thin, it makes sense that he attacked threlphax hosts to weaken their merge. Maybe his energy membrane is so damaged that he asked Kiran for a transplant. Maybe Chymzafyde weakens the merge without violence. Kiran's death could have been a miscalculation."

"That doesn't account for the other deaths tied to Chymzafyde," Abhimanyu argued. "Whoever is using Chymzafyde is approaching our doorstep."

"Over the years, Mroniea has occasionally blocked our artifact connection," said Sameer, who had been pensive after Kit mentioned his connection to Mroniea. "Perhaps it was to hide his activities. Even now, our artifact connection is blocked."

Abhimanyu frowned. "We aren't the only ones who have been following Chymzafyde-related deaths. After the most recent death, the police have identified Mroniea Hadwyn Clarke as a suspect."

"This can't be happening," said Sameer.

"I know Detective Marcus Smith, who is leading the investigation of a recent incident. Like most others, the death was attributed to heart failure. But Marcus is focused on the Chymzafyde ampoule left at the scene. I can't be sure since I'm not great at reading energy signatures, but there is something different about him."

"Do you think he's a threlphax host?" asked Seung-do.

"Maybe. The little I can read of his energy feels similar to Tae-hee's," said Abhimanyu. "But before Marcus connects the dots and turns this into an international investigation, I must reveal details about the threlphax. Fortunately, like Jong, I believe we can trust him." He sighed and shook his head. "Regardless of who the culprit is, I can't help but think that Kit is a target. Even I can sense Kit's unique energy signature. He's good bait."

Unique energy.

Good bait?

"Wait a minute," Jong said. "What do you mean by 'bait?' What is this Chymzafyde? Are you saying that something is coming that could hurt Kit?"

Jong is defending us.

No, he's fighting for us.

"Kill him, you mean," clarified Abhimanyu. "Chymzafyde weakens the threlphax, killing the host. Kit's peculiar makeup is a unique beacon of energy that has drawn the attention of the purveyor of Chymzafyde. If Kit is not careful, he could end up dead."

Unique beacon of life-force energy.

Huh.

"Purveyor of Chymzafyde?" snarled Jong, jumping up from his chair. "I'd prefer it if you didn't treat threats to Kit's life so lightly."

Kit worried that Jong might punch Abhimanyu. "It's okay, Jong," he said in a soothing tone. "Let's hear them out." He pulled Jong back to his seat.

"I'm sorry for being so blunt," replied Abhimanyu. "It's just that I came here after our good friend Kiran Ahuja died. Sameer, Kiran, and I were friends before we became hosts together. Our threlphax were close companions. Both threlphax and humans feel the loss of Kiran deeply. I came to warn you and find a resolution to this threat. The situation is dire, so we don't have time to mince words."

Jong frowned but nodded his acceptance of Abhimanyu's assessment. "I'm truly sorry about Kiran. I know he was a good man and a good friend. But don't call Kit bait."

"No one wants Kit to get hurt," confirmed Sameer.

While there were so many unknowns about the situation, one thing stood out. Kit was involved. "What should I do?" he asked.

"Why don't you move into KSH House until we know more?"

"Do you have room?"

"If Jong doesn't mind sharing."

Jong's smile broadened into a full-faced grin. "I don't mind sharing."

33
BAIT

(AUGUST 17, 2019)

With the secrets and threats revealed, Jong drove Kit back to the loft apartment to pack clothes and personal items for his stay at KSH House. Although Jong was quiet during the short trip, his demeanor was bright. Was Jong genuinely okay with all this?

"So, I know your birth name is not Kit," said Jong, breaking the silence after he and Kit exited the elevator outside the loft apartment. Jong played with the car keys, swinging the keyring on his forefinger. He caught it in his palm, then smiled at Kit.

Kit typed in the passcode, and the two men entered the loft apartment and removed their shoes. "The birth name of Seung-do or, rather, Park Bong-soo's son was Park Tae-soo. 'Tae' means 'great' in Korean. Father named me Tae-soo, for 'great leader,' and my sister Tae-hee, for 'great joy.' Another meaning for Tae-soo is 'viceroy' in Korean. Did you know the viceroy butterfly looks like the monarch butterfly? But it's smaller, does not migrate, and has a defined line along its back wings. It's often mistaken for the monarch butterfly as if it's pretending to be something it's not."

"You're not pretending to be something you're not," said Jong.

Kit went to the kitchen, opened the refrigerator, and pulled out the water jug. "The Thai soldier's name is Chanchai Thanadorn Noratpattanasai. The entire name together means 'skilled winner of everlasting merit-making.'"

"Your parents must have had high hopes for you." Jong grinned and pulled two glasses out of the kitchen cabinet.

"I can't say."

Chanchai had no memory of his parents. One day, Kit might explain how King Chulalongkorn, the ruler of Siam, gave Chanchai his name.

"Do you know the meaning of your name?" he asked Jong.

Jong set the glasses on the countertop and nodded. "My parents told me Jong-hyun means 'profound knowledge,' but when I was going through teenage angst, I discovered it could also mean 'time to cry.'"

Kit tilted his head as he poured water into the two glasses. "None of this bothers you?" he asked.

"I'm enlightened enough to know we're not alone in the universe."

"What about my dualism?" Tae-soo, not Chanchai, mattered to those at KSH House. Although everything had been revealed, Jong had yet to comment on Kit's unique composition.

"I just want to clarify something," Jong said. "Do both Tae-soo and Chanchai like me? I mean, one of you isn't why you gave me the cold shoulder, are they?"

"No. If either Tae-soo or Chanchai didn't care for you, we wouldn't be here. What you've learned about my constitution should explain my hesitancy."

"That's true." Jong ran his finger over the marble countertop, following the patterns in the stone. "I have something to confess. I knew there was something unusual about you a while ago. When I evaluated Emily, I sensed your dualism."

Jong had proven he was a man Kit could trust with secrets. Moreover, he didn't judge Kit, even knowing he was different. Such acceptance was unexpected. Kit shook his head. "How can you be so calm? I think you should have some emotional response."

"Like what?"

"Shock, fear, or anger."

"Well, if you turned into a creepy bug, maybe I'd rethink my paradigms." He took a sip of water, then, with a playful smirk, asked, "Should I not have mentioned how your eyes glow whenever you're emotionally overwhelmed?"

"It's not just when I'm aroused?"

"Your eyes glowed today when you were worried. They weren't as bright as last night, but they glowed."

"You are the first person to tell me my eyes glow." Kit leaned against the kitchen counter and crossed his arms over his chest. He drew in a deep breath and shared another secret with Jong. "Becoming Kit changed my eyes."

"Of course."

"No, Jong." Placing his hands on Jong's arms, Kit moved him so they stood face-to-face. "Look at my eyes. What color are they?"

Jong leaned forward. "They are dark brown. The same as Taehee's eyes."

Kit closed his eyes and focused on Chanchai, pulling him forward to control who he was. When he opened his eyes, Jong raised his brows as the corners of his mouth curved upward.

"Your eye color changed," said Jong. "They're light brown, like crystalline caramel. They're beautiful."

"For most of the time you've known me, Kim Tae-soo was the dominant personality in Kit. Right now, Chanchai is the dominant personality. Our eye color changes depending on who is dominant."

"Where does the subordinate personality go? Does it sleep?"

"No. Tae-soo's still active, offering advice, commentary, and guidance as Chanchai takes the lead. I guess it's like driving a car. Only one person can be at the wheel at a time, even if multiple people are in the car. Right now, Chanchai is driving while Tae-soo is in the passenger seat, and, I guess, Tae-soo's Earthborn threlphax is in the backseat, or maybe the boot."

"So that explains it," Jong said. "I've seen a subtle change in your eyes before. I thought it was a trick of the light. Does it hurt? To shift like that, I mean."

Kit shook his head. "No." It was absurd for Jong to worry about Kit's state when his two selves shifted. Jong didn't react as one might expect. Kit closed his eyes to allow Chanchai and Tae-soo to return to their roles as Tae-hee's twin brother. When Kit opened his eyes, Jong didn't hide his amusement that his eye color was the same dark brown associated with Tae-soo and Tae-hee.

"Amazing."

"You are the one who amazes me. I didn't know of the threlphax until two days ago. I didn't expect you to be so calm when Sameer, Seung-do, and Abhimanyu explained things. When I showed Tae-hee how my eyes changed, she said it was freaky." Frowning, he murmured, "Nothing we said today bothers you?"

"That's not true," Jong replied. "It bothered me when Abhimanyu described you as bait. When I hear that, I cringe. My father took me fishing when I was a kid. I remember what we'd do to bait." Jong shuddered and took another sip of water. He placed the glass on the counter and stared at the floor.

Kit found the facts of his life incomprehensible. Jong's composure humbled Kit.

Kit put the water jug back in the refrigerator, which was barren of food. He closed it, muttering, "I hate to cook, anyway."

As Kit moved to exit the kitchen, Jong blocked his way. He rocked on his heels, took Kit's hand, and ran his thumbs over it. "I don't want you to be bait," he said. "What scares me more is that what I want doesn't matter. You are part of something I'm not part of, and that something might hurt you. *That* freaks me out."

Jong's eyes shimmered as he let his raw feelings surface. Kit had worried Jong would reject him. Instead, he wanted to protect Kit.

Less than an hour ago, Kit's insides churned as Jong learned of his secrets. Now, they churned because of Kit's deep fondness for Jong, who steadfastly stood beside him. He remembered Tae-hee's words of advice: *"Instead of what you want to run away from, focus on what you want to run to."*

Kit found his focus. He wrapped his arms around Jong.

"It's okay, Jong." It was all Kit could say. Anything else would have been smothered in a throat tight with emotion.

34
GUILT

(AUGUST 18, 2019)

Mroniea Hadwyn Clarke woke from his slumber. A male flight attendant hovered over him, too close for Mroniea's comfort. He leaned away from the man.

"Care for a warm towel?" the flight attendant asked.

Mroniea checked his watch. Six fifteen in the morning.

The flight attendant held the small steaming towel between tongs. "A warm towel might refresh you." Another flight attendant stood behind them in the dimly lit aisle, holding a tray full of rolled white towels.

Mroniea accepted the warm towel and ran it over his face and down the back of his neck. Steamy warmth seeped into his skin, purging the lingering weight of his guilt. The same dream sequence, in a variety of formats, shook him: Kiran reaching for Mroniea as he dissipated, carried away by the wind. His disintegration began with a finger, eye, knee, or line across his waist. As he begged for help, Mroniea watched, unable to move. The dreams presented a horrid reenactment of what happened, when the threlphax Phemeos began to dissipate before his eyes, leading to the sure death of its human host, Kiran Ahuja. The accident was real, but his host's imagination twisted the scenario into a ghastly nightmare.

Mroniea accepted these horrid night visions as a just punishment. In trying to save himself, he had harmed the dear companion of his threlphax twin Mussick, merged in the vessel known as Sameer Khan. It was a misfortune, an accident of fate, another blemish on his existence.

Even though Kiran Ahuja sent him away, saying he held no resentment, guilt tormented Mroniea. He had failed Kiran, running away before the end, leaving him alone. Now, he was a fugitive from the tragic accident he had caused.

After his conversation with Dr. Richard Carver, Mroniea agreed to pursue the research grant at Sempiternity University in the United States. It was a chance to atone for his error. Once he established proximity to Sameer Khan, he would unblock their artifact connection. Only then could he seek something he rarely pursued: forgiveness and understanding.

Mroniea dropped the damp towel into the plastic bag held open by the flight attendant, then put his head back and stared at the darkened seatbelt light above him. If he returned to sleep, his host might dream up another horrible scenario. Though the threlphax Mroniea was the dominant energy in the human vessel born as Hadwyn Clarke, dreams were a human experience unknown to threlphax. As observers of the universe, threlphax kept memories intact, storing them for integration into Conveyance. After Conveyance collected his memories, would it punish Mroniea for what he did to Kiran?

Mroniea retrieved his computer from its case in the empty seat beside him. He clicked on the overhead light and brought up his notes on Chymzafyde. After struggling with hypothesis after hypothesis for several minutes, Mroniea stopped. He was not in the right mind to solve the problem. The uneasiness of his human host interfered with his focus. He opened an internet search engine, typed "Dr. Sameer Khan AND history," and pressed return. Clicking on one result, the photo of his threlphax twin, Mussick's human host, appeared on the page.

He had learned in his long life that human vessels provided a decent buffer for threlphax energy signatures. This allowed Mroniea, with his core of antimatter, and his twin Mussick, with his matter core, to meet face-to-face. Mroniea and Sameer had met twice and survived.

Mroniea closed the laptop and leaned back in his seat. One of the many things he wished he'd done differently was not to leave the room so quickly. Kiran's slow dissipation so startled Mroniea that he left without the remaining Chymzafyde. He comforted himself, knowing that the chemical compound didn't target human energy. It would be difficult for any non-threlphax to discern its significance. If Abhimanyu arrived before the authorities found Kiran, he hoped he didn't mishandle the Chymzafyde.

He put a fist to his chest as his compromised energy shifted uncomfortably through his threlphax membrane. Mroniea found it more challenging to maintain the integrity of his energy flows. Two weeks had gone by, and he remained fixated on the loss of Kiran, leaving him no closer to finding a suitable threlphax host from whom he could steal a graft of energy. He needed to find another threlphax host, and soon.

Closing his eyes, he slowed his breathing to sense the human vessels around him and the energy that circulated through the cabin. It surprised him that most humans could not conceive of the dynamic energy that flowed within and around them. Their vibrant energy invigorated almost as much as threlphax energy. However, his experience with his human host proved that transforming such energy was potentially deadly for the donor.

One energy signature caught his interest. Mroniea focused on the woman who sat three rows up on the left. Mature but not old, the woman leaned over to stare at him. She offered an inviting smile and stood, then walked toward the galley. He leaned into the aisle and watched her, judged her, weighed her worth. Mroniea chuckled at the way she moved, like a cat, inviting trouble. Threlphax-human energy flowed through her—animating her movements and creating her thoughts—and it tantalized him.

She opened one of the bathroom doors and peeked around it at Mroniea before she entered the small plastic cubicle. He tucked his computer into the bag, hurriedly undid his seatbelt, and walked down the dimly lit aisle toward the bathrooms. He stopped outside the cubicle the woman had entered and tapped his knuckle on the door. The door opened, and she pulled him inside.

"Are we acquainted?" Mroniea asked with a raised eyebrow. He knew the answer, but she inspired him to play dumb.

"Ah, you are British." The woman smiled and shook her head. "This is such a long trip. I can't sleep, and I'm so bored. Maybe we could help each other relax." She slid a finger behind his belt buckle, inside his pants, and tugged at his waistband. Her twisted smile conveyed her lechery as she breathed, "You've got pretty eyes."

Mroniea glanced in the mirror at his blue crystalline eyes, which had a slight gold band ringing the pupils. They were unusual because he was unusual.

He focused back on the woman who worked to unbuckle his trousers. Although her energy wasn't that of an off-world threlphax, the resonance was compatible enough. He stopped her hands and asked, "Do you know what you are?"

"A free spirit?" she quipped as she pressed against him.

Mroniea cupped his hand around her neck. The cramped bathroom of an airplane was no place for violent action. Besides, she was unaware she was a threlphax host. Her threlphax was not aware, or even awakened, enough to offer her healing and longevity. Mroniea wasn't even sure if her Earthborn threlphax could patch his off-world energy signature.

"You are beautiful, and therefore to be wooed; you are woman, and therefore to be won," he said, paraphrasing Shakespeare. Leaning in, he gave her a long, lingering kiss, the kind that women liked and remembered. She wrapped her arms around his neck, confirming her interest.

"You should be more careful," he whispered as he drew his lips along her neck. "Predators sense the weaknesses of their prey."

At the base of her neck, his palm glowed, drawing an exhalation from her lips. Mroniea leaned away as tendrils extended from his palm and penetrated her to explore her energy signature. She moaned and tilted her head back in pleasure. In his long life, he had bedded both threlphax hosts and pure humans, and he had learned to find their pleasure points while exploring their energy signatures.

Though this woman's threlphax energy signature was unlike his, it was compatible enough for his purpose. When he withdrew his tendrils and released her, she fell back against the sink, exhausted and disoriented. Mroniea repositioned her more comfortably before exiting the cubicle and returning to his seat. Moments later, the woman exited the room and stumbled to her seat, unsettled after the touch of the threlphax Mroniea.

After they disembarked at the airport, he would follow her. If she remained unaccompanied, he would approach her and sweep her off her feet.

While he waited for that opportunity, he developed a compassionate plan to remove a part of her threlphax energy signature to patch his own.

35
ANOTHER

(SEPTEMBER 2, 2019)

Students' return to their academic pursuits marked the waning days of summer. Naeem started middle school, Jong lectured at Sempiternity University, and Renuka welcomed enthusiastic youngsters into her classroom. Sameer Khan's sabbatical continued, so he invited Seung-do and Emily on an outing to fulfill a KSH House order from a restaurant chain.

They followed a man across the grassy field to the stable. KSH House received an order for decor for a ranch-themed restaurant, so Sameer Khan brought Emily Scott and Seung-do to a local farm and stable auction. Seung-do arranged for horseback riding afterward at the nearby equestrian ranch.

Seung-do grinned his enthusiasm as they brought out a large mare already saddled.

"She understands 'walk,' 'trot,' 'whoa,' and 'quit,'" explained the stableman. "She may be feisty with an unfamiliar rider."

Seung-do nodded, took the reins, and walked the mare around the pen, talking to her and petting her head and neck.

"He's a natural," said the stableman. "He said he had experience, and it shows. Some folks try to ride the horse right away. He's getting to know her first. Those two will get along just fine."

After several turns around the pen, Seung-do stopped and climbed into the saddle. With a few subtle kicks and clicks of his tongue, the horse circled the pen in a gentle trot. The stableman opened the gate.

"If you're up to it, you can untack when you're done. The halter is hanging just inside the stable. While you're riding, don't jump any fences. Our neighbors will be upset."

Seung-do acknowledged the directive with a nod and a raised hand. He walked the horse out of the pen, then kicked the horse into a trot. After taking a turn around the stable, the horse galloped across the field, kicking up grass and dirt. The stableman closed the gate and headed to the barn.

"He looks so handsome on a horse," Emily said. Sameer remained silent as he watched the horse and rider. "Does what I said bother you?" she asked.

In his usual straightforward manner, Sameer replied, "I understand that part of you was once married to that handsome rider."

More than a month ago, when Lee Seung-do's arrival provoked a mental breakdown, Sameer encouraged Emily to accept the merge with the threlphax Tamar. When she awoke from the merge, Emily experienced a newfound delight in the color of her auburn hair and the shade of her green eyes. Lee Eun-sol, the Joseon woman she had been in a previous life, thought herself plain. It was Park Bong-soo who made her feel special. Even now, her heart felt full as she watched the man, who had once been her husband, race across the field.

Despite her connection to Seung-do, Emily felt closer to Sameer after the threlphax merge. Before that, culture, gender, and religion separated them. But now they shared something in common.

Tilting her head back, she took a deep breath. A month ago, her new life had begun. Tamar's energy felt familiar, as if Emily were meant to be a threlphax host. Yet the familiarity of Tamar's energy didn't transform her into the demure Joseon woman from her previous life. She brushed a strand of hair from her face as she watched Sameer watching Seung-do.

"Park Bong-soo will remain in Lee Eun-sol's heart," she said. "But, now he is Seung-do, and I am Emily Scott. Regardless of whatever past I have access to, it was someone else's life."

"What about Tae-hee and her brother?"

She could not deny that the memories of her past life created a new obstacle in her relationships. It was strange to think her previous incarnation had given birth to Tae-hee, the woman she had only known as a friend. Even stranger was her connection to Kit. Although she hadn't spoken to Kit about Tae-soo's transmigration, Tae-hee had explained it. Kit carried the energy signature of Tae-soo, but he was not the physical form her son would have been.

"Lee Eun-sol gave birth to Tae-hee and Tae-soo," she said, "but she died before she knew them. They lived long enough to find me and become my friends. Their threlphax energy resonates with my threlphax, Tamar, but that's it. I am glad to know Tae-hee. It would have been nice to know Tae-soo before he became part of Kit."

Under Seung-do's direction, the horse slowed to a trot and circled the stable, before emerging on the other side and speeding up into a canter. Emily smiled and put her hand to her chest as she felt Seung-do's joy flowing through their artifact connection. Although she knew it was a threlphax thing, she was sure she saw the delight on his face as well.

Park Bong-soo and Seung-do Lee were two names for the same person, but Emily thought of them as two different people. She leaned against the fence post as she recalled the distant past of her previous life. "Lee Eun-sol remembers that Park Bong-soo's horse loved to eat the bark, leaves, and fruit of the fig tree in her yard," she said in a faraway voice. "His horse brought Park Bong-soo to our courtyard. He had been badly wounded. The village doctor was away, so we removed the arrows and cared for him. He almost died."

She sighed in remembrance before she continued. "Because of the threlphax, Park Bong-soo recovered. Later, when Lee Eun-sol got scarlet fever, he helped Tamar merge with Lee Eun-sol. Even then, Lee Eun-sol loved him. But she was a widow. Her husband had been old and ill, but he was a kind man who married her to protect them both. It would be disloyal to marry again.

"So, when Park Bong-soo confessed to Lee Eun-sol, she rejected him. They parted. It was the right thing to do. But a year later, he returned. He rescued Lee Eun-sol from a flooded stream. Again, he confessed and asked her to marry. This time, she said 'yes.' They were together for less than two years."

She smiled at Sameer, who leaned against the fence, captivated by her narrative.

"I am aware of Lee Eun-sol's feelings. But the passionate love for Park Bong-soo belongs to her alone, not Emily Scott."

She turned to watch Seung-do effortlessly gallop around the field. He was entirely at ease on the mare.

"Seung-do remembers his life as Park Bong-soo," said Sameer. "And the threlphax Taedlum and Tamar were always close companions."

The stableman returned, interrupting their conversation. "So, what do y'all do for a living?" he asked.

"We buy and sell antiques," explained Sameer. "We went to a farm auction down the road."

"McKinley's farm?" asked the stableman.

"Yes. You know it?"

"Yeah. They were city folk who tried their hand at farm life. They weren't good at it. What were you looking for?"

"Items for a ranch-themed restaurant."

"Is that right?" said the stableman. "I got stuff in the barn behind the stable you might like. I never got around to tossin' it. You're free to help yourself."

"Really?" Sameer's eyes brightened.

"Sure! Come, take a look." Sameer followed the stableman, leaving Emily alone to watch Seung-do, who trotted a wide path around the field. Circling the stable, he disappeared from view. When he reappeared, he galloped to the far end of the field, the horse's hooves pounding a powerful rhythm that faded into the distance. Emily could see the faraway fence marking the property line and worried Seung-do might jump it. Instead, he slowed to a trot, circled the field, and headed back toward the stable.

Lee Seung-do slowed into a walk as he approached the stable. "Do you want to try it?" he called.

"No, thank you," replied Emily, emphasizing each word.

"Are you sure?" Seung-do guided the mare to walk alongside the fence.

"I'm sure." Emily smiled and matched his pace inside the fence. "You always looked good on a horse," she added.

"Is that why Lee Eun-sol married me? Because I looked good on a horse?"

"That was one of Park Bong-soo's charms."

"Whoa," said Seung-do, stopping the horse. Emily stood still, nervous, realizing her playful words were flirtatious. She didn't want to lead him on. With Seung-do, walking the line between her past and present could be difficult.

"Well?" he said. "Are you going to open it, or do you want me to try jumping it?"

Emily realized she stood in front of the corral gate. She opened the gate, and Seung-do walked the mare into the pen. He dismounted and led the horse into the stable. Emily closed the gate and followed Seung-do.

"Where's Sameer?" asked Seung-do when Emily entered the stable. He placed the halter around the horse's head.

"Sameer is looking at more antiques." She sauntered over to Seung-do. Her bright smile turned into a look of distaste. "It really smells like horse."

"Horses sweat just as people do. Add horsehair, a blanket, a saddle, and a rider; you've got one sweaty beast. But to get the full effect, try riding a horse bareback."

"What does that mean?"

"No saddle, no blanket, just you and the horse," he said as he undid the leather straps of the saddle. "When you ride, you feel every muscle. The kinship between horse and rider is magical, and the smell is fantastic."

"I didn't know you liked horses so much. I'm seeing a different side of you."

Seung-do moved to the other side of the mare. "You should be with Sameer, shouldn't you?" He pulled the saddle off, slung it over the stall wall, removed the blanket, and hung it beside the saddle.

"Seung-do," Emily said. "We need to talk."

"About what?" he said, removing the bridle and bit.

"About Lee Eun-sol and Park Bong-soo."

"That sounds ominous," murmured Seung-do as he hung up the bridle. The mare moved from between them and walked to the water trough. Emily and Seung-do faced each other in awkward silence.

Emily played with her hands, then clutched them behind her back and said, "Lee Eun-sol never felt she thanked Park Bong-soo enough for marrying her." Using the formal names for their former selves maintained a discrete distance between them. "You were a bright light in her life." She frowned and bit her lip. "And the threlphax, Tamar, regrets not preventing Lee Eun-sol's death."

"We didn't have the medical knowledge we do now." Seung-do stepped closer to Emily and took her hands in his. "Lee Eun-sol was my first and my last love."

"Those two years were enough for Lee Eun-sol. She is happy that you reunited with the twins. She wants you to continue to be happy. But . . ."

Seung-do took a deep breath to prepare for what was to follow.

". . . the love story of Lee Eun-sol and Park Bong-soo has ended," she said. She needed to be clear with him. As difficult as it was, she needed to crush his hope. "Park Bong-soo has moved on to become Seung-do."

"I never moved on from loving Lee Eun-sol."

"Although Lee Eun-sol reincarnated as Emily Scott, I am not the same person. I can't deny that part of me still loves you, but I am not *in love with* you. I understand what Park Bong-soo meant to Lee Eun-sol. Our friendship flows from that. But I am Emily Scott. Even if it's one-sided, my heart belongs to Sameer."

Seung-do nodded. She could tell that her words confirmed what he already knew. "I understand," he said, "yet my feelings cannot so quickly change. However, I will respect your choice. But . . . may I hold Lee Eun-sol once more to say a proper goodbye?"

His heartfelt request was impossible to reject. Emily wrapped her arms around his waist and leaned her head against his chest. He embraced her and kissed the top of her head. "I will let you go, Lee Eun-sol, but I will never stop loving you." Seung-do trembled as he clung to Emily, embracing her as a lover for the last time. Emily rubbed his back, trying to calm and comfort him.

When Seung-do and Emily Scott emerged from the stable, Sameer stood beside the stableman. "I found more items. I've arranged for them to be picked up and delivered to the site. We're good to go."

* * * *

When they returned to KSH House, Sameer showered, shaved, and changed into fresh clothes. He grabbed the pack of cigarettes and small ashtray from his dresser drawer and found Seung-do on the balcony porch. Unwrapping the pack, he strode over to the railing.

"Would you like a cigarette?" Sameer said as he held up the pack.

"Smoking is bad for your health," replied Seung-do.

Sameer tapped the bottom of the pack until the ends of four cigarettes emerged. "Ah, but we are threlphax hosts."

Seung-do took a cigarette, and Sameer held up the lighter for him. He lit the cigarette and inhaled deeply, drawing the smoke into his lungs. Sameer lit one for himself, took a drag, and exhaled slowly. They became enveloped in a cloud of smoke and the sharp scent of burning tobacco.

Sameer asked, "Are you okay?"

"About what?" Seung-do replied, breathing out a cloud of smoke. When Sameer gave him a you-know-what-I'm-talking-about look, he added, "Oh, Emily. I guess it was inevitable."

"I overheard your conversation with Emily at the stable."

"Oh, that's why." He puffed on his cigarette, exhaling the smoke through his teeth. "I said goodbye. I will be okay."

"Tamar still has Taedlum's artifact and vice versa. You still have a connection with her."

"Yes. That can't be helped."

Sameer surveyed the dark landscape as he considered the many repercussions of bringing Seung-do to KSH House. Still, he felt certain it was the right decision.

Seung-do blew out a long plume of smoke. "I was just surprised," he said.

"We haven't . . . you know," said Sameer.

With a raised eyebrow and a tilt of his head, Seung-do frowned at Sameer. He shook his head. "These feelings I have for Lee Eun-sol and, by extension, for the threlphax Tamar won't go away. I've carried her vessel for years. But that is my problem. I know Emily's will is not the same as Lee Eun-sol's. I will adjust to this reality."

Sameer shook his head and chuckled. "What a strange reality it is." He leaned on the railing and blew a series of smoke rings. He tapped the cigarette, releasing the ash into the ashtray.

"I feel that you and Lee Eun-sol had a passionate romance," he said. "My relationship with Emily is like a pot of water coming to a boil. We've been friends for a long time. Somehow, that friendship blossomed into something more." Sameer sighed. "When she was only human, I didn't consider pursuing a romantic relationship. I don't know what to do now that she's a threlphax host."

Seung-do flicked his cigarette into the ashtray. "Are you asking me for relationship advice?"

"Tchah," replied Sameer, before wagging his brow.

"Don't be burdensome," Seung-do groaned, then added more seriously, "I trust you'll no longer hide your feelings. For the sake of both Emily and Tamar."

36
INVESTIGATION

(SEPTEMBER 7, 2019)

Days later, Seung-do leaned against the car as he waited for Sameer and Abhimanyu in the KSH House parking lot. The news reported another incident that, according to Abhimanyu, bore the earmarks of a threlphax host dissipation. And it was within an hour's drive of Springfield.

Overhearing their plans to investigate, Seung-do took it upon himself to join them, for several reasons.

The Jackson family returned home after dinner, leaving Emily, Tae-hee, Kit, and Jong at KSH House. Seung-do needed to distance himself from Emily, especially when Sameer wasn't present.

In addition, while Tae-hee accepted Seung-do as her biological father, vestiges of resentment still clung to Kit's interactions with him. Kit would rather spend time with Jong and Tae-hee than with Seung-do.

Sameer and Abhimanyu chatted as they exited the basement, climbed the steps, and walked toward the car. They paused when they saw Seung-do.

"What are you doing here?" asked Sameer.

"I thought I'd come along."

"We can't guarantee your safety."

Seung-do chuckled. "I've survived battles and revolutions. Do you think this little trip will cause me harm?"

Sameer grinned and tossed a drawstring bag to him. When Seung-do caught it, he felt the distinct shapes of multiple threlphax vessels within.

"What is this?" he asked.

"The tribe will help us," said Sameer as he and Abhimanyu climbed into the car. After Seung-do settled in the backseat, Sameer backed up and drove out of the parking lot and down the tree-lined, winding road.

When they reached the highway, Seung-do leaned forward and asked, "Why do you think this was another threlphax dissipation?"

"I'm hoping it's not," said Abhimanyu. "The name of the victim is Idris Massi. He was identified as a young man, and his cause of death is still under investigation. If he wasn't a threlphax host, we could just say we are visiting as fellow Indians."

"That may work for you. Not for me."

"It was your decision to come along," grinned Sameer. "But as a doctor, you can view the scene through a medical lens."

Seung-do smiled and sat back in his seat, watching the late-day sunlight filter through the trees as they continued to their destination. Spending time with Sameer and Abhimanyu was a freeing experience.

They took the highway exit and followed a winding road leading to a stoplight.

"Seung-do, please pass me the bag," said Sameer.

Seung-do handed the bag to Sameer, who opened it and pulled out two threlphax vessels. He gave them to Abhimanyu and pulled out several more.

Abhimanyu placed the threlphax vessels at the bottom and top corners of the windshield. Sameer placed four more vessels at the corners and the center of the glass. Translucent, glittering tendrils extended from the vessels across the windshield, creating a film. The tendrils turned transparent, except for a faint glittering stream of energy trailing down the left side of the windshield.

When the light turned green, Sameer turned left and proceeded down the narrow road. The faint, glittering threlphax energy moved from the left to run along the top of the windshield.

Seung-do knew that threlphax could sense the energy of other members of the tribe. Unfortunately, this was not a skill Seung-do had cultivated as a threlphax host.

"This is a unique use of threlphax abilities," said Seung-do.

Abhimanyu turned to look at him. "Over the years, we've depended on such abilities to locate other tribe members."

"Today," said Sameer, "we're trusting that they can sense the remnants of threlphax energy left behind after a dissipation. Assuming, of course, that the victim was a threlphax host."

Seung-do sat back in his seat. That explained why so many threlphax vessels were at KSH House. Even his coming to KSH House resulted from Abhimanyu and Kiran sensing the threlphax in him and introducing him to Sameer.

In contrast, longevity and rapid healing were manifestations of his threlphax self that he took for granted and tried to hide. Seung-do had also disregarded his threlphax thoughts throughout his long life as a threlphax host. Sameer and Abhimanyu embraced their threlphax selves—and the tribe—in ways Seung-do had never considered.

In the past, he thought of searching for other threlphax hosts, but experience made him wary of pursuing such a goal. Apart from Lee Eun-sol, he had met only one other threlphax host. Their friendship had ended decades ago—and badly.

Seung-do watched the faint threlphax energy flow to the right side of the windshield. At the next intersection, Sameer turned right, taking him into a neighborhood of single-family homes, all similar in design.

As Sameer drove down the street, the stream of threlphax energy moved to the center. It continued to the left of the windshield, then grew brighter. According to the threlphax, their destination was a house on the left. Sameer pulled to the side of the road and stopped the car.

Across the street, the house was colored by the last rays of the sun against the soft shadows of dusk. A large picture window revealed a woman walking across the room and turning on a lamp.

"Someone is there," said Seung-do.

"The victim was married," said Abhimanyu.

"She looks as if she is alone," Seung-do replied. "Shouldn't she be surrounded by family members?"

"If the victim was an off-world threlphax host, he could have outlived his family. The same might apply to his spouse."

Sameer grunted. "Although the tribe senses threlphax energy, we shouldn't assume his spouse knows about the threlphax." He opened the car door and said, "Let's go."

They stepped out of the car and approached the house. Just as they reached the porch, the front door opened. A young Indian woman looked at Sameer.

"Trax?" she asked.

Sameer glanced at Abhimanyu and Seung-do. Calling out the name of the threlphax tribe leader identified her as a threlphax host or, at least, someone who knew details about the threlphax. Because of his years of ignoring his threlphax self, Seung-do could not read this woman's energy signature.

"No, Mrs. Massi," said Abhimanyu. "We have not found Trax yet. My name is Abhimanyu Khatri. These are my colleagues Sameer Khan and Seung-do Lee."

She sniffed and dabbed at her eyes with a tissue. "Call me Dalia. Please come. We can talk inside."

The three men followed her inside the modestly decorated living room, which featured a sofa, a wing chair, and a lamp. Boxes were stacked along the walls, and the only personalized item of decor was a framed wedding photo of the woman and her husband. The scent of spices and baked bread filled the air.

"Have a seat," she said. As they settled on the sofa, she asked, "May I get you something to drink?"

"Please don't trouble yourself," replied Abhimanyu. "We know you've been through an ordeal. We won't stay long."

Dalia nodded and sat in the wing chair. "Thank you for coming. I felt so alone after Idris . . ." She pursed her lips together as she forced back her emotions.

"Can you tell us what happened?" asked Abhimanyu.

"Idris and I were together for less than a year," she said. "When we found each other, we thought we'd be together forever."

"He was of another tribe," said Sameer.

"Yes," Dalia said, surprised by his statement. "How did you know?"

"We know another tribe exists."

"Does Detective Smith know about the threlphax?" Dalia asked as she clasped her hands tightly together.

Abhimanyu shook his head. "I don't believe so."

"I know that only tribe leaders can dissipate threlphax," said Dalia. "But I sensed no other energy."

"May we see where you found your husband?" asked Seung-do.

"Yes, of course," said Dalia.

They followed her through the back of the house to the sliding glass doors that opened onto a patio. "I went out that evening to run some errands. When I returned, I found Idris lying on the ground over there," she said, turning on a patio light and pointing to the grass beyond the flagstones. Her voice became tight as she explained, "When his threlphax dissipated, so did his will to live."

"We are sorry for your loss," said Sameer.

Holding back her tears, Dalia wobbled her head and forced a weak smile. "In the days leading up to his dissipation, Idris had been acting strangely."

"How do you mean?" asked Abhimanyu.

"He was more affectionate than usual. He took days off from work to spend time with me. After the funeral, I learned he had quit his job. He also left an envelope with his passwords and account information in his desk drawer. He even had life insurance. A threlphax host doesn't need life insurance. He knew this was going to happen."

That the threlphax host knew of his impending dissipation was troubling. They examined the area for other clues about Idris Massi's demise. But the recent rains had washed potential clues away or buried them in the soil. Seung-do could discern no physical evidence of the threlphax host's death. He hoped his threlphax self, Taedlum, would sense something. But silence met his pleas for aid. Seung-do could only rely on his experience as a human doctor.

"Was he drinking anything?" Seung-do asked.

"Occasionally, he drank gin and tonic. It was strange, though. In the past, Idris would have a gin and tonic to celebrate some major event. He had a glass that night. The investigators took it."

A dose of Chymzafyde in the gin and tonic might have caused Idris' dissipation. "Did he meet anyone?" Seung-do asked. "Did he meet Mroniea?"

"Mroniea?" echoed Dalia. "No. I didn't sense his energy at all."

"What did the police say?" asked Sameer.

"I'm worried that Detective Smith thinks I did something to Idris."

"Don't worry about Detective Smith," said Abhimanyu. "He is a good man."

Sameer knelt and exposed the tendrils in his palm, running them over the grass.

"What are you doing?" asked Seung-do.

"Trying your trick." He stood and wiped his damp hands on his pant legs. "There is not enough here," Sameer said. "I cannot sense any remnants of your husband's energy."

"So, his energy is really gone." Tears welled in Dalia's eyes. "I hoped that somehow . . . maybe his energy was still here . . . maybe if Trax came—"

"—Mrs. Massi," said Sameer, "when we arrived, why did you think I was Trax?"

"Because I felt the resonance of Trax's artifact. It was only for a few seconds, but there is no mistaking that feeling."

"When was the last time you felt Trax's resonance?"

"A few months ago. Around the middle of May. The eighteenth. I remember because we were at the zoo that day."

"That is good to hear," said Abhimanyu. "Unfortunately, we don't know where Trax is."

"I am sorry we could not be of more help," said Sameer. He pulled out his wallet and handed her his KSH House business card. "If you need anything, please contact me."

Dalia looked at the card, running her thumb over the imprint. "Mr. Khan, Idris and I just moved into this house. But after what happened to Idris, I don't plan to stay here long."

Seung-do understood her sentiments. Threlphax remembered everything, and the physical manifestations of a tragedy gave those memories a sharper, more tangible weight. Over his long life, Seung-do had tried to escape his grief by changing physical locations.

The three men bid Dalia Massi goodbye and walked around the house to return to the car, where a stranger was taking a keen interest in their vehicle.

The man crossed the street to meet them. Standing between Sameer and Seung-do, Abhimanyu said in a jovial tone, "Detective Smith, let me introduce you to my colleagues. This is Sameer Khan, co-owner of KSH House, and Dr. Seung-do Lee, a colleague and doctor visiting from South Korea."

The detective regarded Seung-do with a raised eyebrow as he shook his hand. When he took Sameer's handshake, his brows drew together, and he squeezed his eyes shut. Sameer put his other hand on his shoulder to steady him as the detective leaned forward and shook his head.

"What is this?" Smith muttered as he opened his eyes and stared at the ground.

"What do you feel?" asked Sameer.

"I don't know. I just . . ." He raised his head and looked at the three men. Regaining his balance, he released the handshake to draw his hand along his forehead and temple.

"Are you okay?" asked Abhimanyu.

"Yes, I'm just tired I guess," replied Smith. He exhaled and straightened, shrugging off the episode. "I am surprised to run into you here, of all places."

"The Indian community is a tight-knit one," said Sameer. "We came to offer our condolences to Mrs. Massi."

"Really?" said Detective Smith, glancing at Seung-do.

"Well, we'll be on our way," said Abhimanyu. With a touch of his palms against their backs, he encouraged Sameer and Seung-do to continue toward the car.

Aware that the detective watched their every move, Seung-do barely glanced back as Sameer started the car and pulled away.

"Abhi," said Sameer. "You were right. Detective Smith is an Earthborn threlphax host. Your presence must have awakened it. Our presence made it aware. Explain it to him soon."

"I will."

"Also, don't mention this to Kit or Tae-hee, but the day Dalia Massi felt Trax's artifact was the day Kit arrived at KSH House."

37
CELEBRATION

(SEPTEMBER 13, 2019)

"Happy birthday!" shouted Tae-hee as the waiter placed the birthday cake, topped with thirty-three candles, in front of Jong. Tae-hee arranged for outdoor seating at Jong's favorite restaurant. She said the cake should hold the correct number of burning candles without setting off the smoke alarm.

Waitstaff gathered around the large table and sang their rendition of a birthday song. Jong smiled and clapped for the performance. When they finished, he closed his eyes, made a wish, and blew out the candles. Tae-hee handed him a cake knife, and he cut the first slice before passing the task to Tae-hee, who distributed the rest of the birthday confection.

"Any words of wisdom to impart?" asked Sameer.

"Asks the erudite Sameer," laughed Jong. "Okay, okay," he said as he held up his hands. "There is a Japanese proverb that says, 'Even a sea bream loses its flavor when eaten alone.' On my birthday, I celebrate another year of meals shared with old friends." He turned to Kit. "And new friends." He raised his glass and everyone followed suit. "Thank you, everyone."

The group clinked glasses with one another, which took a long time with ten people. Naeem was adamant that he needed to clink everyone's glass.

"I always feel bad that your birthday falls on the thirteenth," said Jackson.

"I was born on a Saturday, not a Friday," said Jong.

"Saturday is an auspicious day ruled by two gods," said Renuka. "Lord Shani and Lord Hanuman. Lord Shani is the god of justice and karma, while courage, power, and selfless service are the traits of Lord Hanuman."

"1986 would make it the year of the Tiger," said Kit. He sat beside Jong and offered a knowing smile as he added, "Independent, outgoing, and optimistic."

Jong chuckled and said, "My mother always reminds me that Saturday births are associated with the element water. When I was a little kid, I thought she meant I was originally a fish."

"Oh, poor Jong," said Tae-hee.

"Saturday's child works hard for a living," recited Emily.

"They say Virgos are loyal and hardworking," Seung-do added. "Although I've only known you for a short time, I see those traits in you."

Jong smiled and took Kit's hand. The temporary move to KSH House had afforded the two men more time together. Although they hadn't taken their relationship to the next level, Kit was by his side. "All I know is that I'm happy with my life. Truly happy."

"Aren't we going to eat the cake?" Naeem's question drew light laughter.

After they devoured the birthday treat and the small talk diminished, Jong said, "Thank you, everyone. Now, I am going to leave to continue my celebration elsewhere." He smiled at Kit and held out his hand. "Kit," he said, drawing out his name.

Kit scratched the back of his head. "Are you sure?"

"You're not talking your way out of this on my birthday!" said Jong. He rose from the table and pulled Kit from his seat.

Half an hour later, Kit and Jong stood in line outside the GMJ Bar on 20th Street. The establishment was hosting K-pop night, and Jong suggested they go. Jong didn't frequent bars, let alone gay bars, but tonight was an exception. It was his birthday, and Kit's presence was his gift.

They stood with their arms folded over their chests, watching the line of men queued in front of them. They exchanged apprehensive glances and nervous smiles each time the line moved forward.

"First time?"

Kit and Jong turned to the man standing behind them and nodded. Recognizing the tension in their posture, they uncrossed their arms and tried to appear more at ease.

"GMJ is one of the better bars in the area," the man said. "When you go in, you'll get your choice of wristbands: Red for don't touch me, orange for ask, and green for touch with consent."

Kit and Jong nodded, acknowledging his guidance.

"You two together?" he asked, chaining his index fingers.

They nodded again.

The man smiled and nodded. "Okay," he said.

A group entered the bar, and Jong and Kit moved to the front of the line. The bouncer asked for their IDs. Jong pulled out his wallet and showed his license, and Kit showed his passport.

"You're from Thailand?" asked the bouncer.

"Sort of," said Kit. Jong couldn't help but chuckle at the subtle nod to Kit's dual identity.

"Sort of?" said the bouncer as he arched his brow.

"Sorry. It's a private joke. I'm from Thailand."

"What's your name?" the bouncer asked as he examined Kit's passport.

"Chanchai Thanadorn Noratpattanasai."

"Thanadorn Norat—" The bouncer struggled under the size of Kit's name.

"—Noratpattanasai," replied Kit.

The bouncer smiled. "That's a mouthful."

The man behind them snickered as the bouncer handed Kit his passport.

As the bouncer opened the door, the pounding rhythm of pop music spilled into the air.

"Red, orange or green?" asked the greeter.

Kit reached for two wristbands. "Red for both of us," he said. He wrapped one around Jong's wrist before putting the other on himself.

The dimly lit, cavernous room was full of people clustered together—laughing, dancing, exchanging knowing glances or warm embraces. It felt like more than nightlife; it was sanctuary, celebration, and connection. The DJ stood at the far end of the dance floor. Behind him, three large screens featured a mix of abstract motion graphics and music videos. Tables, sofas, and booths spread out around the large room—something for everyone.

Jong and Kit adjusted to the welcoming ambiance with broad smiles. The pounding beat forced their bodies into action, and Jong pulled Kit to the dance floor. Slowly, at first, they moved in sync with the music and each other. Jong grinned at Kit, who moved with effortless confidence, as if the music had unshackled him from his worries. There was no self-consciousness, no hesitation—just pure, uninhibited motion. Something had shifted within Kit.

After the fifth song, they were sweating and tired. Jong led Kit to an empty sofa in a quiet corner. They collapsed together into the cushions.

"I've never danced like that," said Kit.

"Stick with me, and we'll do all kinds of new things."

"I believe you."

"Ah, but it's a shame," said Jong. "Sameer would never let us set up a dance floor in KSH House."

Kit smiled. "The auction hall would be perfect."

"We could hang a disco ball from the stage."

"Floor lights."

"Enormous screens."

"DJ Jong," added Kit, emphasizing each syllable with an outstretched hand.

"Why do I have to be the deejay?"

"What? Do you think DJ Kit works?"

"If we're the deejays, we can't dance together."

"Good point."

"How about DJ Sameer?" said Jong.

Kit burst out laughing. "Don't be ridiculous!" he said.

"That leaves Seung-do, Abhimanyu, Jackson, Renuka, and Tae-hee," said Jong.

"DJ Naeem?"

"Do you think he'd be up for it?"

"Pfft," said Kit. "He'd do it if *you* asked him. He idolizes you."

Kit's assessment felt exaggerated. "You think so?"

"Everyone at KSH House likes you. I'm a little jealous."

"What? Me?"

Kit pulled Jong's hand to his lips and kissed it. "You're just so lovable."

Jong stared at Kit, surprised by his words. He was saying things in ways that Jong didn't expect.

"Can I confess something to you?" asked Kit.

Jong drew in a soft breath. "Of course."

"I don't want you to make a big deal about it, but a few days ago was my birthday."

"Wait, weren't you and Tae-hee born in March?"

Kit nodded once, then continued to gaze at Jong who realized that not only had his dark eyes shifted to a light caramel color, but his aura had changed from pink to indigo. Kit tilted his head slightly, his smile warm.

"Oh," said Jong with a grin. "Happy birthday, Chanchai Thanadorn Noratpattanasai."

"Everyone at KSH House considers me to be Tae-soo only. No one knows the Chanchai part of me."

"So, who am I dating tonight?"

"You're dating Kit. I just thought I'd let Chanchai take the lead for a while. He's not as inhibited as Tae-soo. Does it bother you?"

"No," said Jong. "We can celebrate our birthdays together."

A waiter placed two cocktails in V-shaped glasses on the table in front of them. Jong sat back on the sofa and waited for an explanation.

"Two Manhattans. On the house." The waiter nodded toward a well-dressed Black man at the bar. The man smiled, raised his drink, then stood and crossed the room.

"Well, you boys are cute." He moved with the quiet assurance of someone fully aware of his worth as he took a seat across from them. "This is your first time here, isn't it?"

Jong and Kit nodded.

"Drinks are courtesy of the house for well-behaved newcomers."

"And you are?" asked Kit.

"I'm the house," the man said. His tenor voice was silky smooth, with an underlying husky quality conveying sensuality and undeniable grace. "Most of the guests call me Mama John. Instead of pizza, I offer pizzazz," he said, snapping his fingers. "Fifteen years ago, when I opened GMJ, I dressed in drag," Mama John sighed. "But times have changed."

He placed his drink on the table and picked up the Manhattans, offering them to Kit and Jong. "I give my customers a free drink on their first visit. It's my way of welcoming them."

Kit and Jong hesitated to take the drinks.

"Don't worry. I didn't roofie the drinks. I'm a businessman." When they continued to hesitate, he rolled his eyes. "How would I stay in business if I messed with the drinks of my guests?"

Kit and Jong nodded, then accepted and tasted the proffered beverages.

"This is good," said Jong. He licked his lips before taking another, longer sip. He looked at Kit's glass, which was nearly empty.

"Slow down," he laughed as he put a hand over Kit's glass.

"We make the best Manhattans in the city. Maybe even the state. But they *are* potent," said Mama John, pointing a finger toward Kit. "I noticed that when you arrived, you went to the dance floor before the bar. People usually need a drink before dancing. But I guess you boys are less inhibited."

Kit pulled the drink out of Jong's reach. "I'm inhibited," he murmured.

"He *was* inhibited," said Jong.

"How long have you been together?"

"Does it matter?" said Kit, before he finished his drink. "If you like someone, isn't that what's important?"

Jong smiled. Kit wasn't drunk enough to say something he didn't mean.

"I'm down with that. But let me give you newbies a piece of advice. Everybody is friendly here. Sometimes customers get too friendly. So keep those red wristbands visible. Other patrons are checking you out with interest."

"Checking us out?" repeated Jong.

"With interest." Mama John said. "But I don't think either of you noticed, did you? Have a great evening, you two." With a wink, he rose from the chair and crossed the room to greet customers at a table near the bar.

"What was that?" murmured Jong.

"Mama John was right," said Kit as he grinned at Jong. "I didn't notice anyone but you."

"Dude, are you getting drunk?" He pulled the empty glass out of Kit's hand. "You are. You are drunk."

Kit placed a hand behind his head. "Chanchai's body has a low tolerance for alcohol, so it affects me. But give me some time." He drew his other hand down his body. "My threlphax will flush it out of me," he said. He leaned his head back and grinned at Jong. "Like magic."

Kit's soft glowing eyes beneath dark eyelashes peered at Jong. His smile broadened. "You want to kiss me, don't you?"

Jong leaned back on the sofa. "So much," he said.

Kit shifted on the sofa until he hovered over Jong, his face just inches away. Kit's glowing eyes traced a path from Jong's lips to his eyes, down his cheek, and back to his lips. His wanton exploration ended as he leaned in and kissed Jong full on the mouth, his tongue teasing Jong's. A moment later, Kit ended the kiss and returned to his place on the sofa, leaving Jong wanting more.

The soft glow in Kit's eyes faded as he turned to Jong. "I like you, Jong-hyun Park."

While Jong restrained himself, it was unfair that Kit had abandoned his self-control. If Kit continued this way, Jong's response might embarrass them both.

An energetic hip-hop song began, and Jong pulled Kit onto the dance floor. They pumped their arms and slammed their feet as they sang along to the mix of Korean and English lyrics. Halfway through the song, the DJ riffed off the rhythm, keeping the beat going. The dance floor became even more boisterous, with dancers pounding their feet and clapping their hands. As the song concluded, Jong and Kit collapsed into a joyful embrace.

The dynamic on the dance floor mellowed as a slower song played. Over the intro, the DJ announced, "Time now to relax and find your special someone. PDAs are welcome, but remember the house rules—keep your clothes on and the restrooms available."

Jong and Kit moved together, unaware of the eyes on them. As the music transitioned to the gentle notes of a heartfelt ballad, Kit and Jong rocked back and forth, gazing at each other. They sang along but soon gave way to a silent embrace. When Kit nuzzled Jong's neck, Jong turned his head and brushed his lips against Kit's. When the glow in Kit's eyes brightened, Jong reached into his pocket and retrieved the sunglasses he brought with him. He slipped them on Kit.

"How thoughtful," whispered Kit into Jong's ear.

38
REVELRY

(SEPTEMBER 13, 2019)

Several drinks and songs later, Kit and Jong spilled out of the bar and onto the sidewalk. They grabbed hold of the pole of a sidewalk sign, steadying themselves as they breathed in the crisp, early morning air.

"Jong," said Kit, "I'm too drunk to drive." He slowly slid down the pole until he sat on the sidewalk.

"No," said Jong. "I drove us here, but I'm too drunk to drive. You're too drunk to stand." He leaned over to look in Kit's eyes, which were neither dark brown nor caramel-colored. They were a mixture of both.

Kit smiled and nodded to Jong. "We should call someone." Leaning on his side, Kit struggled to retrieve his phone.

"Okay," said Jong. He reached for his phone in his back pocket, turning around as he struggled to extract the device while standing upright.

Kit laughed and pointed at Jong. "You look like a dog chasing its tail!"

Jong retrieved his phone but was unwilling to let the comment go unchallenged. Seeing Kit curled up on the sidewalk, Jong said the first thing that popped into his head. "You look like a little kitty," he said, pointing at Kit.

"I'm not a kitty," said Kit, dejected.

Jong staggered over to pat Kit's head. He looked apologetic as he said, "But I like my little kitty."

"I'm *not* a kitty," repeated Kit. He pushed Jong's hand away, causing him to lose his balance. As Jong fell onto the sidewalk, Kit did his best to catch him.

"Ouch, my butt!" said Jong.

"I'm sorry," replied Kit. "Do you need me to massage it?" asked Kit, wrapping his arms and legs around Jong as he kissed his shoulder.

"No, I'm okay," said Jong. He held up his phone to scan his contacts. "I'm going to call someone to pick me up."

Kit tightened his arms around Jong. "Pick me up, too, right?"

"You up too," replied Jong, giving Kit a broad smile.

Kit plunged his lips into the side of Jong's cheek and made a loud kissing sound. He tightened his arms around Jong and put his cheek against his. "Good boy," he said. He released the hug to lie back on the sidewalk, his legs still wrapped around Jong. Holding his phone inches from his face, he searched for a number to call.

Jong had already selected a number and held his phone to his ear. Soon after, Kit chose his number and did the same.

Sameer answered the phone. "Hello, Jong. Do you know what time it is? What can I do for you?"

Jong held the phone away from his ear to check the time. He returned the phone to his ear and said, "It's one twenty-seven. Can you pick us up?" He looked back at Kit, who had redialed his phone since the first number he had called was busy. "Kitty and I are too drunk to drive."

"I'm *not* a kitty!" announced Kit.

"Where are you?" asked Sameer.

"We're at a bar," said Jong.

"A gay bar!" corrected Kit.

"We're at a gay bar," corrected Jong.

"Can you tell me the address, Jong?" said Sameer.

Jong couldn't remember the address.

Two men exited the bar together. "Excuse me!" Jong called. He held out the phone to them. "Can you give Sameer the address?"

One man smiled and took the phone. He conveyed the information to Sameer and then returned the phone to Jong. "He says he'll be right over."

"Thank you," said Jong.

"No problem," said the man.

"Take care," said the second man before they left together.

"THANK YOU!" yelled Kit, still trying to get someone to answer his phone call. Just then, someone did.

"What's the matter, Kit? Are you okay?" asked Seung-do on the other end of Kit's call.

"Jong took me to a gay bar and got me drunk, and now I'm sitting on the sidewalk—"

"—laying on the sidewalk—" corrected Jong.

"—laying on the sidewalk. Can you pick us up? Two nice men are here to help us sort out the address." Realizing the two men were gone, he concluded his request with a simple, "Oh."

"Where are you?"

"On the sidewalk outside the bar. Did I tell you it was a gay bar? 'Cause I'm gay. I'm gay with Jong." Kit rested the phone on his chest. "I'm happy being gay with Jong."

"I'm happy being gay with Kit," said Jong.

"Let's be gay together, forever," Kit said with a joyful smile.

Seung-do's voice interrupted their interlude. "Kit!"

Kit raised the phone to his ear. "Hello?" he said.

"Kit, what is your address?" asked Seung-do.

In the background, Kit heard Sameer's voice. "Hey, is that Sameer?" he asked.

"Sameer!" repeated Jong. He maneuvered enough to take Kit's phone. He found the speaker button, pressed it, and held it so Kit could listen. "Sameer, is that you?"

"Yes, Jong," said Sameer. "I'm here with Seung-do. We're coming to pick you two up."

"Good, 'cause Kitty is still lying on the sidewalk."

"I'm a little tiger, *not* a kitty!"

"He hates when I call him a kitty."

"Okay, Jong," said Sameer. "We're coming to collect you. Do you want to stay on the phone or hang up?"

"I think," Jong said before losing his train of thought.

Kit pushed himself into a sitting position and announced, "I want to sing a song for my namchin." Holding a fist to his mouth, he announced. "On K-pop night, I dedicate this song to Jong-hyun Park." Kit wrapped his arms around Jong and sang, "I love you, baby I, I love you, Forever, I love you, baby I, I love you, I do." Hugging Jong, he swayed side to side.

"Hear that, Sameer?" said Jong. "Kitkat says he loves me."

"I like 'Kitkat,'" said Kit. "I don't like 'kitty.'"

"Can I call you Kitkat?" asked Jong. He tried to sound sincere.

"Yes, you can call me Kitkat," said Kit. He was quiet for a moment before he straightened. "I need a nickname for you." He leaned into Jong, hugging him and swaying back and forth as he tested various options for a nickname. "Jong pong song gong prong strong long dong." Kit snorted a laugh. "Jong . . ."

"What?"

"Your rhyming words make me think about you naked."

"Really?" asked Jong, interested in the idea.

Kit snorted again. "I like it." He tightened his arms around Jong and rested his head between his shoulders.

"Jong pong song gong prong strong long dong," repeated Kit.

Sameer's voice interrupted the rhyme. "Okay, Jong. We are nearly there."

Jong located the phone in his hand and said, "Okay, Sameer. We'll stay here while Kitkat thinks about me being naked."

"Naked," murmured Kit with a grin before he sang, "Ring ding dong . . . ring ding dong . . . ringy dingy . . . dingy . . . ding ding ding . . ."

Jong snorted. "No, Kit," he corrected. "It's, 'Ring diggy . . . ding diggy . . . ding ding ding,'" he said, emphasizing each word.

"Diggy, diggy, diggy, diggy, diggy," replied Kit as he rocked with Jong.

As if transported by magical incantation, Sameer and Seung-do appeared and stared down at the two men.

"It's Papa Smurf and Professor Smurf!" Kit said. He tried to stand, even with his legs still wrapped around Jong. "Help me, Papa Smurf," he said as he reached out a hand to Seung-do.

"I guess that makes me Professor Smurf," said Sameer.

Seung-do and Sameer helped Jong to his feet. Sameer steadied him while Seung-do offered a hand to Kit. Tilting his head back to look up at Seung-do, Kit offered a wide-mouthed grin. "I forget what Tae-soo looked like, but if he looked like you, he looked nice," he chortled.

Seung-do raised an eyebrow, then grabbed Kit's wrists. "When I count to three, stand up. Okay?" he directed.

"Okay, Papa Smurf. I will do that."

"One. Two. Three." Seung-do pulled Kit's arms. Kit eased up off the sidewalk a bit before falling back down.

"It didn't work," said Kit, disappointed.

Sameer navigated Jong to a light pole and helped him wrap his arms around it. When he was sure Jong could remain vertical, Sameer went to help Seung-do lift Kit to his feet.

"Okay," said Seung-do. "We're going to try it one more time."

"Okay, Papa Smurf. Let's try again."

"One. Two. Three." Seung-do pulled, while Sameer pushed, and soon Kit was standing. Then he was leaning. Sameer and Seung-do scrambled to keep Kit upright.

"Kitkat," said Jong, pointing at Kit. "You're the leaning tower of pizzazz!"

Kit buckled over in laughter while Seung-do and Sameer prevented him from collapsing to the ground. When his laughter settled, Seung-do pulled Kit's arm over his shoulder and walked him to the car. Sameer followed with Jong. They poured Jong and Kit into the back seat, where they fell into an alcohol-induced slumber. After climbing into the front, Sameer and Seung-do sighed. They glanced at the back seat, then at each other, and chuckled.

"Jong is going to be sorry tomorrow morning," said Seung-do.

"I am not sure about taking these two to KSH House. It feels like letting a bull loose in a china shop."

Seung-do looked at his watch. "It's late. Kit's threlphax should sober him up soon. Jong will be out all night. Nothing should happen tonight."

"You're the doctor," said Sameer, starting the car.

"They went to a gay bar," murmured Seung-do, imitating Kit's announcement.

The two men snickered, and Sameer put the car into gear for the short drive back to KSH House. They helped the inebriated Jong and Kit onto the twin beds in Jong's room and removed the shoes of the intoxicated twosome. Having safely accomplished their mission, Sameer and Seung-do went to their respective rooms to retire for the night.

39
PRELUDE

(SEPTEMBER 14, 2019)

Kit was the first to wake. He sat up in bed and did a series of neck rolls before he noticed Jong sprawled out on the other bed.

"Jong," he called quietly. "Jong, are you awake?"

Jong moaned.

"I'll go get us something to drink."

Kit went downstairs and searched in the refrigerator for something healthy to drink. "Thank you, Tae-hee," he muttered as he grabbed four of her favorite coconut water boxes stored at the back of the top shelf.

He headed back upstairs, happy that he had found something to help Jong feel better. Kit's time at the Full Moon Parties in Phuket had shown that he bounced back far quicker than most people. Now, he realized it was the threlphax that had made him so skilled at shaking off the effects of heavy drinking.

But Jong was a different story. Though he seemed to have a high tolerance, Jong admitted he wasn't a heavy drinker. Kit worried that Jong would suffer a painful hangover, so he needed to hydrate Jong.

As he reached the second-floor landing, the door to Jong's room flung open. Jong stumbled out, holding his hand over his mouth. He staggered down the landing toward the bathroom. Kit caught up to him just as Jong collapsed by the toilet and vomited. As Jong clung to the commode, Kit rubbed his back. He put the coconut water down to pull back Jong's loose hair so it wouldn't become a victim of the cascade of partially digested alcohol and bar snacks. The smell was overpowering, but Kit adjusted by breathing through his mouth.

When the sickness subsided, Jong closed the toilet lid and folded his arms over it, resting his head on the soft flesh of his forearms. Kit flushed the toilet, grabbed a towel, and wiped Jong's face.

"How do you feel?" Kit asked quietly.

"Ugh."

"Do you think you can drink something?"

Jong nodded slowly.

"Let's rinse your mouth out first," Kit said. He stood and found Jong's toothbrush cup on the counter. He rinsed it out and filled it half full of water. "Swish this around and spit it out."

Jong took the cup and did as he was told. Kit opened one of the coconut water packs and held it so Jong could drink. Jong sipped slowly. When he nearly finished the water, some color returned to his face. "Thanks, man."

Kit helped Jong stand and handed him his toothbrush. "It will make you feel better," he said. When Jong finished brushing his teeth, Kit asked. "Do you want to take a bath?"

"I don't think I can."

"I'll help you."

Kit turned on the bathtub faucet and adjusted the water temperature. He helped Jong remove his shirt, then knelt and removed Jong's belt, unzipped his pants, and dropped them to the floor. Jong held onto Kit's shoulder as he stepped out of the jeans. Kit looked up at Jong and silently asked permission to remove his boxer briefs. Jong nodded, and Kit helped Jong step out of them.

With Kit's help, Jong climbed into the bath and sat down. Removing the showerhead, Kit changed the flow of water. He adjusted the showerhead speed to a gentle massage and ran the water over Jong's back. Jong let out a soft moan. "That feels good."

Kit smiled. He noticed Jong's shampoo bottle in the shower caddy. "Shall I shampoo your hair?"

"Sure," said Jong. Kit rinsed Jong's hair, then handed the showerhead to Jong while he squirted shampoo into his hand. It had the fragrance that Kit recognized. Massaging the shampoo into Jong's wet hair, Kit played with the design of his long locks, trying to make them stand up on end, then hand-combing them over to one side.

Jong leaned into the head massage as Kit worked the shampoo to the roots. Satisfied with the job, he took the showerhead from Jong and rinsed his hair. Kit gave the showerhead back to Jong and handed him a towel to remove the excess water from his face and hair.

Kit sat on the toilet lid and dried his hands and forearms on another towel. Jong played with the different showerhead settings. "You're such a child," he chuckled.

"Am I?" Jong gave Kit a sinister grin before breaking into a broad smile. He turned the showerhead and sprayed Kit.

Kit held the towel up in self-defense. "Stop it, Jong!" he yelled.

Jong repositioned the showerhead, so water shot up under the towel. Howling in laughter, Kit grabbed the showerhead from Jong, who kept it pointed at Kit, soaking him. Jong gave up the battle as Kit forced the showerhead into the water.

"You just wanted me to take a bath with you, didn't you?" accused Kit, dripping wet but grinning.

Jong responded with an open-mouthed chuckle from deep in his throat.

Kit quickly placed towels to soak up the sprayed water, then began to peel off his wet clothes. Jong laughed as Kit wrestled against the clinginess of his wet shirt and jeans. After the battle with his attire, Kit stood naked in front of Jong, whose childish smile turned into something more serious. He offered his hand to Kit, who took it and stepped into the tub behind Jong. After he sat down, he wrapped his legs around Jong. Once comfortable, Kit took the showerhead, set it to a gentle massage, and drew the stream over Jong's back.

The addition of Kit to the bathtub displaced more of the bathwater. Despite the overflow drain, water spilled over the edge of the tub. Jong turned off the water and took the showerhead from Kit, letting it hang loose. Water splashed over the sides of the tub as their bodies moved against the porcelain surface.

"I really had fun last night," Jong said as he leaned back into Kit.

Kit wrapped his arms around Jong. "Yeah."

"Kit," said Jong, his voice deep and soft. "I want to make love with you."

Kit moved his lips in tender kisses along Jong's shoulder and neck. "You're still drunk," he said.

Jong turned toward Kit. "No, I'm not."

Jong's gaze traveled to Kit's lips. In response to the unspoken invitation, Kit closed his eyes and tilted his head, offering himself to Jong. The gentle brush of their lips transformed into a hunger for more. Jong leaned into the kiss, inviting a deeper exploration. As they shifted, a wave of water sloshed out of the tub and onto the floor.

Kit pulled away and moved Jong forward so he could step out of the tub. He wrapped a towel around his waist, hiding his slight erection. "I'll go back to the room," he said. He gathered his clothes and left the bathroom, closing the door behind him.

40
SPARKLE

(SEPTEMBER 14, 2019)

Several minutes passed while Jong turned over Kit's parting words in his mind. Unable to fully grasp their meaning, he climbed out of the tub, dried off, and wrapped the towel around his waist.

When he turned off the light and stepped out of the bathroom, he took a moment to let his eyes adjust to the darkness before making his way down the landing to his room. When he entered, he noticed Kit was not lying on the other bed.

"I didn't expect you to take so long."

Kit stood in the corner, his eyes glowing slightly. He stepped forward and ran his hand along the open door to push it shut. Stopping just inches away, Kit studied Jong.

"I wasn't sure what you meant by 'I'll go back to the room,'" Jong said.

Kit chuckled and pushed damp strands of hair away from Jong's face. "Then let me be clearer," he said. After a glance at Jong's lips, Kit leaned in and kissed him. He didn't seek confirmation; instead, he moved with assurance.

It was almost too much for Jong. He wrapped his hands around Kit's waist to maintain his balance as he returned the kiss in equal measure. The stroke of Kit's warm hands along Jong's bare skin drove him crazy, transforming Jong's desire into an urgent need. Kit moved him to the bed, laid him down, and climbed on top. He ran his hands over Jong's chest in an erotic massage that made his skin tingle and his muscles twitch.

Kit's movements suddenly stopped, and his body tensed. Jong opened his eyes to see Kit braced on his hands, staring down at him. Moonlight streamed in through the thin curtains, casting a dull light on his face. His brows drew together above his softly glowing eyes.

"Jong," Kit said. "I've never done this before."

"What? Had sex?"

Kit nodded slightly.

"Are you saying that in your long lifetime, you've never made love with anyone?"

"Well, Chanchai was a monk for a long time, and after Tae-soo merged, we kept to ourselves."

"But Tae-soo had a lover."

"That was a different time, and we never did this."

The glow in Kit's eyes faded, along with the urgency in his desire. Jong ran his hands over Kit's arms and said, "If it makes you feel any better, I've never done this with anyone before, either. I never met anyone I wanted to do this with. Until I met you. And I really, really want to do this with you."

"I really want to do this with you, Jong-hyun Park." Kit sighed, then relaxed into Jong. He moved his lips to Jong's ear, where he breathed, "May I touch you?"

"Yeah."

Kit moved his massage to Jong's arousal. Although a towel separated their flesh, his touch reflected skills that belied his novice status.

Jong didn't want to climax alone. He rolled them over, pinned Kit to the bed, and studied his shape. He exhaled his deep satisfaction before he teased Kit's lips with his mouth, arousing them both further with soft, slow movements.

Jong ran his lips and tongue over Kit's neck, sucking his skin and leaving his mark. He moved to his chest. He teased each nipple—payback for how aroused Kit made him. With each pleasured moan, Kit arched his back, and Jong furthered his fervid expedition.

Kit raised up and rolled them back over, his eyes glowing brightly. "You're making me lose control."

"Is that a bad thing?"

"I'm about to burst," Kit said. His bright eyes remained locked on Jong's as he opened the towels. Kit brushed his fingers along Jong's arousal, causing him to twitch. He licked his palm, wrapped his fingers around both of their shafts, and moved up and down their hard lengths. Jong was hard before, but Kit's touch made him rigid.

Jong's body was on fire, and he felt as if he would explode. It was too much, yet not enough. Kit released his grip and pressed himself against Jong—shaft beside shaft, chest against chest, lips against lips. Pulling him into a tight hug, Kit moved slowly against Jong.

The heat of his body and the throb of their arousals made Jong moan as Kit quickened his movements. Jong's hands found their way around Kit's back and down to his waist and buttocks. He met Kit's movements with equal measure, pressed their hips together as their hard heat moved between soft flesh. Although he had brought himself to climax over the years, touching himself never felt so good.

The rush of blood blocked Jong's senses as his entire being succumbed to pleasure. Just as he worried that his heart might burst into flames, everything turned and streamed toward his pelvis.

"Kit! I'm—I'm—!"

Kit tensed and moaned as he pressed against Jong, who arched into his release in a series of euphoric spasms. When they collapsed together, their ragged breathing drifted into quiet, contented exhalations. They continued to twitch after their shared climax.

"That was amazing," Jong sighed.

Kit pushed up from Jong. His weak laugh confirmed his agreement.

Jong ran his finger over his stomach, tracing a path through the residue of their lovemaking. Kit retrieved a towel, which he used to wipe their stomachs and chests clean. He tossed the towel aside and lay beside Jong, draping an arm and a leg over him.

Jong stared into Kit's luminous eyes. "Are you even aware that your eyes are glowing?" he asked.

Kit shook his head. "No." His eyes dimmed as his focus shifted. "But ever since I learned of the threlphax," he said, "I sense a dichotomy in me that remains hidden. Chanchai and Tae-soo give me a unique duality, but both are human, and neither knew of the threlphax. There were signs, but I never understood."

"You said it's like driving a car, but how does that work?" Jong shifted his body to face Kit. "Doesn't it get confusing?"

"Not when the focus is the same. Like just now. Both Chanchai and Tae-soo focused on how you made us feel."

"What about other times?"

"Chanchai and Tae-soo have been Kit for so long." Kit gazed at the ceiling as he brought his hand up to his forehead. "At first, their thoughts jumbled together, incoherent, random. Tae-soo looked at himself through someone else's eyes." Kit chuckled. "After we merged, when Tae-soo woke up at the hospital, he clung to a metal tray to study Chanchai's reflection."

Kit dropped his hand. "We experience the same things, but how we interpret those experiences is different." He drew loops with his finger on Jong's shoulder. "We're separate but together and in constant communication."

"What are Chanchai and Tae-soo talking about now?"

Kit's eyes glowed softly as he studied Jong's face. "How glad we are that we met you, Jong-hyun Park."

"Me. too."

Kit closed his eyes and remained quiet for a long while. In the silence, Jong's mind bounced from thought to thought until his curiosity forced him to ask another question. "What was your life like as a Buddhist monk?"

Kit took a deep breath as he prepared his response. "Chanchai joined at the request of Siam's royal family. He focused on learning and teaching the Pāli scriptures and practicing Lord Buddha's teachings. It was an important time in Chanchai's life."

"You knew the royal family?" asked Jong.

"The world was smaller. Maybe that's why few leaders followed in the footsteps of the sons of Mongkut."

"Leaders don't always live up to our expectations," said Jong.

Kit closed his eyes. In a quiet voice, he said, "Those who can't dance blame it on the flute and the drum."

"What did Chanchai do before then?" asked Jong.

"Siam was a country that sought strength through international ties. Chanchai spent half his life in England. When I returned to Siam, I became a monk. Then soldier, then teacher, then statesman. When I returned to soldiering during the Korean War, Tae-soo transmigrated. I became who I am now. I avoided anything that could make me stand out. I never revealed my true self to anyone."

"Maybe you needed permission to reveal yourself."

"Perhaps," Kit said. He clicked his tongue and asked, "How did Sameer explain the threlphax to you?"

"He sliced open his hand," said Jong as he dragged a finger across his open hand.

"Didn't that frighten you?"

"I was more worried than frightened," said Jong. "But Sameer has a calm stoicism that made everything okay. He healed in less than a minute."

"Sameer continues to amaze me."

"Yeah."

"Jong," said Kit. "I want to tell you something."

Kit's tone had become more serious. "Go ahead," said Jong.

"In 1919, when Tae-hee and I moved to Hanseong . . . Seoul . . . I met Lee Seung-gi." Kit paused, then took a deep breath and released it, as if to cleanse his mind. "We were college classmates who became friends, then fell in love," he said. "We were together less than two months. Lee Seung-gi had an older brother named Lee Seung-do."

"Lee Seung-do? Our Lee Seung-do?"

Kit shook his head. "At the time, the Lee Seung-do we know was called Park Bong-soo. He was staying with his friend Lee Seung-do. Park Bong-soo looked so much like Lee Seung-do that they were often mistaken for each other. On his deathbed, Lee Seung-do asked Park Bong-soo to take his name and identity to protect the Lee family."

"So, Tae-soo met his father before."

"Yes. But we didn't recognize each other. Tae-soo and Tae-hee were only four years old when our father disappeared. Our foster parents didn't speak of our birth father. We never celebrated his death anniversary. My only memory of him was that he was tall with dark hair. Fifty years had passed when we met. He had a Western haircut, not the long hair and top-knot of our father, and I had no reason to say I was older than I looked."

"Lee Seung-gi left an impression on you."

"I saw him die at the hands of a Japanese soldier—the same soldier who shot the original Lee Seung-do. They both died around the time of the March First Independence Movement."

"Does it bother Tae-soo that I'm half-Japanese?"

Kit sighed and rolled on his side to face Jong. "Of course not. You had nothing to do with those events. Although the memories of that time are still clear in my mind, I feel being here—at KSH House—has helped me mitigate the pain."

Jong gently drew a path along Kit's arm. Kit shifted so their hands met and fingers intertwined.

"Jong," Kit said. "You're the only one who ever made my eyes sparkle."

"Sparkle? Why sparkle instead of glow?"

"It seems more appropriate, given what we've just done."

"I'm glad I'm the only one that makes your eyes sparkle and glow."

Kit chuckled and played with their interlocked fingers. "I regret that I rushed our first intimate experience."

"There's nothing to regret."

"I want to take it slow, to take our time. I want to experience the warmth of what it feels like to be connected with you."

Jong knew there were many ways to pleasure each other, and he wanted to try everything. But whether giving or receiving, he was human—not a threlphax host. "I'd like that, too," said Jong. "What you're asking requires a bit of preparation. I don't have any lub—"

Before Jong could finish, Kit stepped off the bed and crossed the room. Moonlight peeked through the break in the curtains and cast patterns across his bare skin.

"Stop," said Jong.

"What's wrong?"

"The moonlight is shining on you. You're a work of art. You're beautiful."

The shadows across Kit's face shifted as he smiled. He returned to Jong and gave him three slow, deep kisses. Resting his forehead against Jong's, he said, "You're beautiful."

He turned and headed to the walk-in closet and pulled out his backpack.

"What are you doing?"

"I left before you because I wanted to check whether it was still here. I was glad that I hadn't unpacked everything." He put down his backpack and held up a small paper bag.

"What is that?" Jong asked.

"Lubricant and condoms."

"When did you get those?"

"Tae-hee gave them to me on the camping trip."

"Seriously?"

"She's a nurse. She thinks like that."

Jong chuckled and stepped off the bed. "This is the best birthday ever," he said.

41
MORNING

(SEPTEMBER 14, 2019)

When morning came, Seung-do flung open his door, shuffled out of his room, and grimaced. Next door, Jong and Kit had not slept as he had predicted. He frowned, then plodded down the staircase. Bracing himself on the handrail, Seung-do stopped to close his eyes and yawn. When he opened his eyes, Sameer gave him a hard stare from the doorway of his room.

"You said nothing would happen," Sameer said in a low, sleep-deprived groan.

"I said I *thought* nothing else would happen. Kit's threlphax burned off the alcohol. I couldn't have predicted Jong would."

The smell of breakfast wafted from the kitchen toward them. They closed their eyes and inhaled the delicious aromas. Sameer waved his hand, and the two men lumbered toward the kitchen.

Emily, Tae-hee, and Jackson prepared the meal while Renuka and Naeem hovered around the table, laying out the plates and silverware. Despite the bustling activity, a subdued hush hung in the air. The two men exchanged haggard glances, then turned to retreat from the room.

"Oh, no, you don't!" said Tae-hee in her happy sing-song voice. "You need to come in and eat."

Tae-hee grabbed Seung-do and pulled him into the kitchen. Emily walked behind Sameer and guided him to a seat at the table.

"I'm more tired than hungry," said Seung-do.

"And whose fault is that?" asked Emily.

Jackson, busy at the stove, chuckled and became more animated.

"It's not ours," said Sameer.

Emily exhaled. "Nevertheless, none of us slept last night. *None of us.*"

"It sounded like a porno video," whispered Tae-hee, hoping that Naeem didn't hear.

"They were still going at it when I arrived," muttered Jackson. "I thought a wild animal snuck into the house."

Emily put her hand on Sameer's and faked a smile. "Have you seen the upstairs bathroom?"

Sameer raised an eyebrow and looked at Seung-do, who shrugged.

Naeem looked around the room. "Where's Jong and Kit?"

"Jong and Kit are still sleeping, baby," replied Renuka.

Naeem jumped up from his seat. "I'll go get them."

"NO!"

The communal reaction stopped Naeem. He frowned and returned to his seat. "Okay, I get it. I'm not stupid." With a smirk, he muttered, "I guess they're in trouble."

"Doesn't he have school?" asked Seung-do.

"It's Saturday," explained Renuka.

Sameer stood and announced, "I'll go wake them." He went to the stove and reached around Jackson to grab two large metal pot lids from a shelf. Seeing Sameer so armed, Seung-do took a metal pot and ladle from the shelf and followed Sameer out of the kitchen.

"What are they going to do?" Naeem asked.

"Nothing good," said Renuka.

Sameer and Seung-do positioned themselves in front of Jong's room like officers prepared to raid a criminal lair. Using the bowl of the ladle, Seung-do tapped on the door. Both men listened intently but heard no response. With the pot lids tucked under his arms, Sameer made a series of indecipherable hand gestures at Seung-do before unlatching the door.

When he pushed the door open, the aromas of sweat, alcohol, and chestnut flowers wafted out of the room.

Sameer swung the pot lids back and forth before entering. Inside, Kit and Jong were asleep, naked, and wrapped around the bedsheets and each other. They lay along the seam of the twin beds, now pushed together.

"They look so comfortable," whispered Sameer. "I feel a little sorry for doing this. But only a little."

Seung-do smiled, and the two men lifted their kitchenware. Sameer mouthed, "One, two, three," and the two men beat and banged their instruments of torture. Jong and Kit yelled and struggled to sit up, but their entanglement made it difficult. Their tussle caused the beds to shift apart, and they dropped to the floor, still wrapped together in the sheets.

"AH, SAMEER!" yelled Jong, holding his head.

Kit held his head and moaned.

Seung-do said, "Papa Smurf, Professor Smurf, and the other smurfs didn't sleep last night because of you two. Get dressed and come downstairs for brunch."

Sameer pointed two fingers at his eyes, then at Kit and Jong, before he and Seung-do left the room.

Jong raised an eyebrow. "Papa Smurf?" he asked, confused.

Ten minutes later, after a quick shower, Kit and Jong appeared in the kitchen entryway. The room became silent as everyone looked at them. The two men wandered in and took the two empty seats side-by-side. Tae-hee poured tomato juice for each of them and placed a banana on their plates.

Without a word, they grabbed the bananas with their left hands and peeled them with their right. Aware that they were being watched, they rethought their approach and broke off a piece of banana with their fingers. They picked up the tomato juice glasses with their right hands and searched the faces of everyone in the room for any potential juice-related issues. Finding none, they drank a bit and sighed.

Naeem, who sat on the other side of the table, said, "Jeez. You guys are acting weird!" Renuka chuckled, half-embarrassed, half-glad someone raised the issue.

"Sorry," said Kit and Jong. They both broke off another piece of banana and ate it.

"What's wrong with your necks?" asked Naeem, pointing at his own. "It looks like a rash or insect bites."

Kit and Jong each reached up to touch their necks. Their eyes widened when they saw the love bites on each other. They adjusted their collars to cover the marks.

Ignoring the stares directed at them, the duo stacked three pancakes on their plates. They each added three sausage links arranged in a curve around the pancakes. Since there was only one bottle of syrup, Jong poured first. He lifted each pancake to pour syrup between the layers, then poured more on his sausage links. He handed the syrup to Kit, who did the same.

The others snickered at the twosome, synchronized in word, action, and reaction.

Tae-hee held the butter dish out to them. "Butter?"

"No, thank you," they both replied.

Jackson shook his head. "I can't take this anymore."

"What?" replied Kit and Jong.

"Can't you see it?"

"See what?" they said.

"You two are doing the exact same thing."

Confused, Jong and Kit exchanged nervous glances with the group.

"It's weird," added Jackson.

Kit and Jong shrugged, drank their juice, and smiled at each other.

"Ugh," said Naeem. "Are you guys in love or something?"

Kit and Jong looked at their plates and grinned.

Tae-hee leaned forward. "So, Kit, which of the pancakes tastes the best? The top one or the bottom one?"

The adults froze, surprised by Tae-hee's inappropriate question. Nevertheless, they remained silent, awaiting a response.

Jong took his fork and cut into Kit's pancakes. He stuffed a forkful of all three layers in his mouth. With a satisfied smile, Jong chewed and swallowed. "Delicious," he said.

With a grin, Kit helped himself to a forkful of Jong's pancakes.

42
EMERGENCE

(SEPTEMBER 14, 2019)

KSH House members spent the rest of brunch in mild amusement as the adults gently teased Jong and Kit while Naeem raised issues with deeper meanings unknown to him. After everyone had finished and cleanup began, Sameer pulled Kit and Jong aside. "I need you two to clean up the bathroom upstairs," he said. "And Jong's room. Remember, I intended it for Airbnb."

"You won't kick me out, will you?" asked a worried Jong.

"No. But I suggest you pursue private activities together at the loft apartment." Sameer looked at Kit and raised a brow. "After we resolve the Chymzafyde issue, of course."

Embarrassed by the reprimand, Kit followed Jong upstairs. In his long life, Kit had never behaved so irresponsibly. Still, he couldn't ignore the sense of liberation that came with being around Jong. What he hadn't anticipated was the physical evidence of that freedom. The bathroom floor shimmered in places, and clothes and towels were crammed behind the toilet or draped carelessly over the towel bars.

"How did I not notice this?" said Kit. "This is the first time I've been this messy."

"It seems we're encountering many firsts," said Jong.

While it wasn't the catastrophic mess Emily had suggested, it was unpleasant. Kit and Jong shrugged out of their shirts and went to work.

They sopped up the dampness, wiped the tiles, and gathered the towels. Sameer appeared in the bathroom doorway to check the cleaning progress.

"Jong, get dressed. A large shipment arrived three days early. We need to go to the airport to pick it up."

Jong frowned and clicked his tongue. "Sorry," he said. He handed Kit his sponge and slipped on his shirt.

"This isn't just a tactic to separate Jong from me, is it?" Kit asked.

"Well, this is a big shipment. Besides, we have to pick up Jong's car."

"Oh, right," said Jong, "I guess it's still parked near the bar." He followed Sameer out of the room. A moment later, he strode back in, quickly kissed Kit, and hurried away.

Now that Jong had left, Kit lost his enthusiasm for cleaning. He ran to the landing just as Jong emerged from the office. "Are you sure I'm not needed?" he asked.

Jong turned and smiled at him. "Are you feeling left out?"

"A bit."

"Is that why you're standing there half-naked, trying to tempt me?"

Kit leaned over the railing. "Is it working?"

"A bit," Jong said, holding his thumb and index finger close together.. He chuckled and headed toward the door. "Sameer will fill the SUV so full of boxes that they'll need my car for the overflow."

"Still . . ."

Jong waved a hand over his head as he passed through the entryway.

Kit finished cleaning the bathroom. Then he collected the dirty towels and sheets from the bedroom and took them downstairs to the laundry room. After starting the wash, he grabbed clean bedsheets from a shelf. He returned upstairs and made the beds, carefully tucking in the corners of the sheets. Finished with his work, Kit made his way downstairs.

KSH House was unusually quiet. While he was used to spending time alone, the previous night's events made him energetic. He went to the office, where Jackson was busy at the computer.

"Oh, hey, Kit," Jackson said, focused on his laptop. He rolled his chair backward to grab several pages from the printer.

"Where is everybody?

"Tae-hee and Emily went grocery shopping. Renuka dropped Naeem off at soccer practice and then went to a meeting at school. Abhimanyu is doing who knows what, and Sameer, Seung-do, and Jong are picking up stuff from customs."

"Yeah," murmured Kit, "Jong went with them."

Jackson's glance was rife with amusement. Turning his attention back to the paper, he ran his finger down the list of items before looking at his watch. "Hey, Kit," he said as he stood. "Can you do me a favor? Renuka will kill me if I don't pick up Naeem on time."

"Sure, what?"

Jackson stapled the pages together and handed the document to Kit. "Can you go downstairs and pull the boxes labeled with these IDs? They'll be on the box lid or the box end. Once you pull them, you can leave them in the auction hall. I'll weigh them for shipping when I get back. Track your time." He pulled a keyring with several keys from the desk drawer. Handing it to Kit, he said, "It's the key with the green cap on it."

Sameer and Jackson explained how the KSH House business operated, so Kit was confident he could fulfill the request. He had never been down to the basement storage, so Kit welcomed the chance to explore and spend his time doing something useful.

"Should I lock the front door while you're gone?" Kit asked. He would be the only one at KSH House.

"I'll take care of it," said Jackson as he left the office. "Thanks, man. I owe you one."

Kit studied the list of inventory codes as he descended the stairs. Each entry featured a brief description followed by a string of letters and numbers. When he reached the turn in the steps, he flipped on the basement light.

The basement was cooler than upstairs, but not uncomfortably so. A narrow hallway ran from the stairs to the back door. Two doors stood on opposite sides of the hallway. Kit decided to check the door on the right since it most likely was the larger of the storerooms. He put the green-capped key into the keyhole and turned it.

The door unlocked. Kit pulled open the heavy door and reached around the corner, searching for a light switch. When he flipped it, the room revealed dozens of well-organized shelves full of cardboard shipping boxes of varying sizes and shapes.

Kit put the keys in his pocket and looked at the list of IDs. Scratching his head, he surveyed the shelves again. He turned to find a map of the storeroom hanging on the inside wall.

"Impressive," he murmured. Comparing the listed entry numbers against the map, he identified the pattern and navigated to a shelf containing dozens of small boxes. Kit collected the first three boxes on his list and placed them on the table next to the door. A pen lay on a small shelf inside the door, and Kit used it to place a checkmark beside the corresponding IDs of the items he collected. Then, he went to collect the next group of boxes from another shelf.

Within half an hour, he had found all but one item. Rather than waste more time, he would take the collected items upstairs while double-checking them against the list.

Kit searched for the dumbwaiter to transport the boxes up to the auction hall. He found it just outside the room, in a passage on the far side of the basement. Sliding open the door, he estimated that the car was large enough for a single person to fit inside. He loaded boxes into the car, closed the door, and pushed the button to send it to the auction room.

The sound of the dumbwaiter mechanism led Kit to a corner of the stage in the auction hall. He unloaded the boxes and sent the car back to the basement. The exercise took the balance of the hour and the multiple trips—up and down the stairs—tired Kit. He went to the kitchen to fill a water bottle with ice and water, then headed back downstairs to enjoy the cooler air of the basement. As he drank from the water bottle, he studied the map on the wall. He reconfirmed that there was no identified location for the last item.

He leaned against the door jamb and looked at the door on the other side, which was offset a few feet further down. After he took another gulp of water, Kit tucked the water bottle under his arm. Stepping up to the door, he tested whether one of the remaining keys would unlock it.

He scanned the basement to identify the cause of the annoying vibration. Unable to locate the source, he assumed he had overexerted his muscles by traipsing up and down the staircase following his active night with Jong.

Jong.

Kit grinned as he shook provocative thoughts of last night out of his head, then selected a key and slid it into the keyhole. When he turned it, he heard a click. He turned the knob and swung the door open. Stepping inside the dark room, he felt for the light switch and flipped it on.

A shocking vibration shot through him. He dropped the water bottle and collapsed, holding his head in his hands. A piercing pain ran from his forehead, down the back of his neck, and along his spine.

He moaned and writhed as he tried to shake off the pain that pulsed through him.

A moment later, the pain eased to a dull ache. He examined his trembling hands for signs of electrocution. Apart from their trembling, his fingers looked normal. He closed his eyes and took several slow breaths to calm his racing heart.

When he composed himself, Kit opened his eyes and got to his feet. He scanned the small, nearly empty room. At one end, a series of padded wooden shelves contained small, elongated stones, each the length of a small egg. There were hundreds, maybe thousands.

Curious, Kit stepped up to the shelves to examine the stones. They were the same size and shape, each featuring a faint but ornate design.

I saw one when I was a child.

Chanchai's earliest memory was gleaning in a sugarcane field at night. Across the field, a falling star exploded and a glittering translucent cloud blanketed him. The next day, he found a small stone like this in a hole in the ground. At his touch, it fell apart to reveal itself as a shell.

Vessels.

Vessels for what?

Not what. Who?

A shiver ran up Kit's spine.

These aren't stones.

These are threlphax vessels.

One by one, the vessels glowed as if controlled by a series of switches. Kit backed away from the shelves as glittering translucent tendrils rose from them and circled above him, transforming into a shimmering whirlwind. A pulse rippled through him and resolved into a soft vibration. The glittering, spinning cloud enveloped him and grew brighter, causing every nerve in his body to tingle.

What is happening to us?

Something is wrong.

"Stop!" he yelled.

He gasped for breath as the attack continued. Unable to support himself, he knelt on the floor, wrapping his arms around himself for fear that he might explode.

Something is shifting.

Pulling, seeking, exposing.

On the verge of blacking out, the disparate thoughts that reverberated through in Kit's mind merged into one word:

TRAX.

A loud crack burst through Kit's core. He sat back on his heels, compelled to release something inside him. Glittering translucent tendrils burst from his body. Startled but feeling no pain, he ran his fingers through the tendril shoots. They vibrated with warm, comforting energy.

Whatever this was, it didn't mean to harm him. As he relaxed into the quiet, the tendrils flowed back into him. He brought his hands to his chest as the whirlwind became silent. A bright warmth bathed him as if liquid joy flowed through his being.

The buzzing of whispered thoughts returned, forcing a fissure in the partition between his being and an intense energy. The whirlwind closed in around Kit, forcing something new to emerge.

Above him, flickering lights like sparklers danced across a dark expanse, releasing shimmering particles of energy that floated away. They appeared like sparklers, releasing energy particles that floated away. An unbearable sadness overtook him when he understood these remnants signified the dissipations of thousands of threlphax.

Accept it.

"No!" a voice, not his, bellowed from his lips. The word ended in a desperate cry as he forced himself to stand. A low growl from deep within welled up, and he brought his arms up in front of him, hands raised. He pushed against the cyclone that surrounded him.

"Stop!" the voice cried out. A surge of energy broke through the tempest, slowing the whirlwind into a sluggish, spiraling cloud.

In the momentary stillness, Kit sensed a formidable presence. Multitudes of tendrils wafted out of him, moving together in perfect unison, forming a glittering translucent apparition. Though the being was imposing, it didn't threaten him. As he touched the apparition with his fingertips, tiny sparks of energy danced across his skin, sending tingling sensations through his body. "Beautiful," he whispered.

Accept.

It was a question that seemed irrelevant, for he sensed an unmistakable familiarity with this being of energy. "Haven't you always been a part of me?" he murmured. He lifted his arms, seeking to embrace the being. "Yes. I accept you."

Tendrils wrapped around Kit, pulling the entity back into its vessel. Tendrils wrapped around his arms, forcing them upward and outward as the cloud of threlphax increased its rotation. Energy poured through him like starlight in liquid form, warm and radiant, flooding every corner of his being with otherworldly light. The whirlwind slowed, the tendrils receded, and the threlphax returned to their vessels.

Silence.

Dazed, Kit dropped his arms and stood for a moment longer, wobbling back and forth, before he slumped to the floor.

43
SUSPICION

(SEPTEMBER 14, 2019)

Sameer backed up his SUV to the basement entrance. Packed full of packages picked up from customs, the vehicle required Sameer to use the backup camera instead of the rearview mirror.

When he stopped the SUV and turned off the ignition, he sat still and stared straight ahead.

"Seung-do," he said.

"I feel it," Seung-do replied.

They exchanged a glance before stepping out of the SUV.

"Stay here," Sameer said. He took the stairs to the basement and found both storage room doors open. He peered inside the small storage room. In the middle of the floor lay Kit, crumpled in a heap, facing the threlphax vessels.

"Kit?" called Sameer. When he received no response, he ran over and shook Kit's shoulder as he called his name. Although Kit remained unresponsive, his pulse was steady, and he was breathing normally. Sameer turned his attention to the threlphax vessels, which glowed just as they had on the first day Kit came to KSH House. Kit had triggered a reaction in the tribe. Sameer ran to the back door and shouted for Seung-do.

Jong, who had just arrived after parking his car, followed Seung-do into the basement and the small storage room. Sameer and Seung-do hovered over something on the floor. It was Kit.

"No, no, no," Jong said as he knelt beside Kit. "What's wrong with him?" he asked in a voice strained with fear.

"He's alive," said Seung-do, addressing the heart of Jong's question. "He's just passed out." Seung-do put his hand on Jong's shoulder. "Let's get him upstairs."

Jong nodded. "I'll carry him," he said. Sameer and Seung-do helped lift Kit onto Jong's back. Seung-do followed Jong upstairs to his room. After they laid Kit on the bed, Seung-do left the room to get his medical bag. Jong sat on the bed beside Kit, holding his hand.

"What happened, Kit?" he murmured.

In the basement, Sameer picked up the water bottle near where they found Kit. He walked over to the threlphax and ran his hand over the shelves. The soft glow made him confident that Kit and the threlphax interacted. What had the threlphax done to cause Kit to pass out?

He examined the water bottle for signs of Chymzafyde. Unscrewing the lid, he sniffed it but didn't sense anything unusual. He closed his eyes to allow his threlphax self Mussick to check their energies. Everything seemed normal. Maybe the bottle just contained water.

Sameer locked the storage room doors. He hurried upstairs to Jong's room, where Seung-do finished checking Kit's vital signs.

"I'll have Abhimanyu test Kit's water bottle," Sameer said.

Seung-do nodded. "Can you get a bag of saline from the refrigerator?" he asked as he prepped Kit's arm for a saline drip. "There should be a few bags on the bottom shelf." Sameer gave an affirmative grunt and left the room.

"You keep saline in the house?" Jong asked.

"It's a habit I've adopted. We can save lives with a simple saline drip. Even threlphax can use help sometimes."

"Do you think the water bottle contained something bad?"

"We don't know. Sameer is just trying to be thorough." Seung-do examined the veins in Kit's arms.

"Should we take him to the hospital?" Jong asked.

"Not unless we have no choice. His threlphax physiology might raise questions," Seung-do told Jong. "We should see what we can do."

Even though the tension made his body rigid, Jong managed to nod.

Sameer returned with the saline and a rolling stand. He hung the bag while Seung-do placed the cannula and taped it into place. He connected Kit's line to the bag and began the drip.

The three men remained silent for several minutes as they watched Kit.

"I shouldn't have left him," Jong said.

"Nonsense," said Sameer. "We don't know what happened."

"As a doctor, I have to ask," said Seung-do. "Did you drink anything, or do anything dangerous last night?"

"No. Admittedly we got drunk, but Kit woke up in better shape than me. As far as the rest of the night, well, we're both newbies at this. But we were careful. Besides, if I did something to him, his threlphax should heal him, right?"

"It's okay, Jong," Seung-do said. "I'm sure you did nothing wrong. I just had to ask."

"If I did hurt him, I'll never forgive myself."

Sameer crossed his arms. "Let's let Kit rest. We'll find out what happened when he wakes."

"I'm staying here," said Jong.

Sameer patted Jong's shoulder. "We'll be available if you need us," he said.

Seung-do rose from the bed and joined Sameer at the door. "I'll check on Kit in an hour," he said.

They closed the door behind them.

Jong rubbed his hand up and down Kit's forearm.

"Please," he said. It was the only thing he could say before worry stole his words.

Sameer and Seung-do returned to the vessel room. Sameer sat on the floor, his legs crossed, his hands resting on his knees, palms up, middle fingers and thumbs connected. The energy in the room had changed since

Kit's incident. He was sure the threlphax hid something. Sameer focused on connecting with the threlphax and learning what they knew.

Seung-do sat just inside the doorway and watched Sameer. After twenty minutes, Sameer relaxed and lay back on the floor.

Seung-do stepped over to crouch beside Sameer. "Are you alright?"

Sameer frowned. "I know something is different. Mussick feels Trax's energy artifact."

"Taedlum feels it, too."

"The threlphax are not sharing."

Seung-do shifted from his crouching position to sit on the floor. "Do you suspect Kit?"

"I do." Sameer sat up. "It's like the feeling I had when I first met Mroniea. It's a power behind the threlphax energy signature that I don't feel with anyone else. And Tae-soo jumping into Chanchai has always bothered me. I've never heard of such an ability."

"I was so focused on Tae-soo that I never asked about Chanchai's past. Tae-soo's Earthborn threlphax may be powerful under duress, but could it transmigrate both a threlphax and a human energy signature? His Earthborn threlphax was unaware of itself," Seung-do said. "What are you going to do?"

"What I always do."

Seung-do chuckled. Sameer would confront Kit, just as he confronted Seung-do when they first met.

"You might scare him away."

"Ah, but I've got you, my friend. You're the good threlphax to my bad threlphax."

Seung-do stood up and offered a hand to Sameer. "Mussick was never a bad threlphax. Just an impulsive one." Sameer gripped his hand and stood. "What about Jong?" Seung-do asked.

"He may be the one most helpful and most hurt." Sameer stepped up to the shelves of threlphax vessels. As he moved his hand back and forth above them, he felt the change in the resonance of their energies. "Do you think Jong can be useful?"

44
AWARE

(SEPTEMBER 17, 2019)

Jong spent the next several days too focused on Kit to eat, sleep, or leave his side except for a few hours to fulfill his lecturing responsibilities at Sempiternity University. Though he said he wasn't hungry, Tae-hee brought Jong food and ensured he ate.

After another fitful night during which Jong drifted in and out of sleep, Kit stirred. Jong checked the clock on the nightstand—5:47 a.m.

Kit opened his eyes. He focused on the ceiling, then on Jong.

"How are you feeling?" Jong asked.

"I have to pee."

Jong chuckled. "Well, at least your body is functioning."

Kit sat up and noticed the tube sticking out of his arm. "What's this?" he asked.

"You passed out in the basement three days ago. Seung-do has been treating you with saline. Do you remember what happened?"

Kit held up his free hand and shook his head. "Can you help me down the hall?"

Jong helped Kit stand and hold on to the IV pole. They walked down the landing together toward the bathroom. After Kit went into the bathroom, Jong took out his phone and called Seung-do. The phone rang four times before Seung-do responded.

"Is he awake?" Seung-do asked, his voice deep with sleep.

"Yes. He's in the bathroom."

"Okay." Jong heard Seung-do yawn and stretch. "Keep him there. I'll come and remove the saline bag."

Jong ended the call and knocked on the bathroom door. "Are you okay in there?" He heard the toilet flush and the faucet turn on.

He didn't wait for a response to open the door. Kit's hands wrapped around the edge of the sink. Jong reached over to turn off the water.

"Seung-do will take out the IV."

Kit nodded.

"Do you feel better?"

"I feel strangely weak."

"Do you remember anything?"

Kit's face scrunched up in thought. "I don't think I can talk about it now. My mind is muddled."

Seung-do appeared in the doorway.

"How is the patient?"

Kit held up his hand with the IV.

"Let me take care of that for you." Seung-do removed the cannula, letting it fall into the sink. Kit rubbed the wound until it disappeared. "Tae-hee is at the hospital," Seung-do said. "I'll call her to let her know you are okay." He left the room.

"Thank you." Kit turned on the faucet and washed his hands. "I'm okay," he assured Jong.

Jong's eyes moistened as he took a deep breath and nodded.

"What time is it?"

"Around six o'clock, Tuesday morning. You should eat something."

Kit nodded, and the two men headed to the kitchen.

Sameer leaned against the counter, his arms folded across his chest, his attitude pensive. Across the room, Seung-do closed a biohazard bag containing the saline, hose, and cannula. He took the bag outside.

Kit sat at the far end of the table.

"You should sleep, Jong," Seung-do said when he returned. Jong forced a smile and nodded. He ran his hand over Kit's shoulder before turning to leave. Seung-do followed him out of the kitchen.

"Do we have any juice?" Kit asked.

Sameer pulled a carafe of orange juice from the refrigerator. He swished it around as he closed the door and opened the cupboard to retrieve a glass. Still swishing the carafe, he placed the glass in front of Kit. After pouring the juice, he put the carafe down, stepped back, and crossed his arms over his chest. He raised an eyebrow as he watched Kit.

"Thank you," said Kit. Between sips of the juice, he glanced at Sameer, who continued to scrutinize him.

"Jong was worried," Sameer said. "He only left your room for a few hours yesterday."

"I'm sorry."

Sameer narrowed his eyes and said, "I have a doubt."

"What?" replied Kit, putting the glass down.

"Who are you?"

"You know who I am."

Sameer shook his head. "No. You are more than Chanchai and Tae-soo and an Earthborn threlphax. I feel it."

"I don't know what you're talking about."

"Let me put it another way. How long will you masquerade as Kit?"

"I seriously think you are—"

"—you seriously think Sameer is what?" asked Seung-do as he stepped into the kitchen.

"Do you think I'm not Kit?"

Seung-do leaned on the table. "Should I?" he asked.

Sameer stepped forward. "Why were you in that room?"

"Jackson asked me to collect the packages for him while he went and picked up Naeem. I couldn't find one of the packages, so I checked that room."

"Then what happened?"

"I passed out!" Kit was losing his patience.

"Why?"

"I don't know!"

"You do know!"

"Why are you doing this?"

"Why are you lying?"

Kit's grip tightened on the juice glass. He was relieved when Jackson entered the kitchen behind the men, interrupting their impasse.

"Oh, hey. Good to see you're awake, Kit," said Jackson.

Sameer straightened and turned toward Jackson, shooting him an unfavorable glance.

"Everything alright?" Jackson asked.

"What are you doing here?" said Sameer.

"I had to drop Naeem off for a field trip. So, I came early. What's the problem?"

Sameer raised an eyebrow and frowned. "Why did you leave Kit alone on Saturday?"

Jackson raised his hands. "Whoa, I told you—I had to pick up Naeem from soccer practice."

Sameer shook his head.

"Hey," Jackson added, "I'd rather have you guys mad at me than deal with Renuka's wrath. She'd go full Durga on me."

While Jackson might act tough, he always respected Renuka's requests.

"I'm watching you," said Sameer as he left the room.

Kit leaned over and watched Sameer until he entered the office. Then he shifted back in his seat. He drew a hand over his stomach. "Are there any leftovers?"

Seung-do nodded at Jackson, then gave Kit an indiscernible glance as he left the kitchen.

The confrontational atmosphere he had walked into clearly confused Jackson. He shook his head and muttered, "What did I miss?"

Kit felt the pull of a smile, but the rumble of his empty stomach kept it at bay. "If you're busy," he said, "I can find something myself."

"No worries." Jackson opened the refrigerator door. Rooting around, he pulled out several small, covered bowls filled with leftovers and set them on the table. "You are in luck, my man. It looks like I can make you your favorite." Jackson held up a carton of eggs. "How about a rice omelet?"

Kit's eyes brightened. "Yes, please!" he said.

After a satisfying breakfast, Kit kept to himself for the rest of the day. Sameer's early morning confrontation irritated him.

Jong was still asleep when Kit ventured out of KSH House, across the field, and into the woods. A light breeze blew over him, and he watched the branches sway as sunlight filtered down on him in a playful dance. The woodland was alive with the energy of rustling leaves, the birdsong, and the movement of small creatures in the undergrowth.

Then, like a lightning strike, a single word flashed through his mind and disturbed his tranquility:

TRAX.

His breath hitched, and his pulse pounded in his ears. It was just a name, a thought—but it carried weight.

Kit clenched his jaw and pressed his hands against his temples as if he could bury the thought deep into the recesses of his mind.

Change is inevitable.

Kit let out a sharp breath, his chest tightening. He slammed his foot against the damp earth. "We are not ready," he said.

His heartbeat slowed, his breath evened out, and the storm inside him settled into an uneasy quiet. Kit exhaled and walked deeper into the forest. The scent of decaying leaves and damp earth wrapped around him, an invitation to escape. His deliberate steps sought refuge in the wild embrace of nature before the future could find him again.

Kit knelt and tied Naeem's undone shoelace. "I thought you liked pranks."

Naeem shoved Kit away and strode deeper into the woods.

"Naeem!" called Kit. The boy stopped. "KSH House is this way," Kit said as he pointed in the opposite direction.

Naeem glared at Kit, then marched in the direction Kit indicated. As he passed, Kit stopped him with an outstretched hand. "I'm sorry," he said. "I didn't mean to upset you."

Naeem turned to Kit, his lips pursed, brow furrowed, eyes narrowed. Suddenly, he broke into a wide grin. "Okay. I forgive you," he said.

Kit smiled and patted Naeem's shoulder. He paused when he discovered a unique shift in Naeem's energy flows he hadn't noticed before.

An Earthborn threlphax.

Sameer must have awakened it.

"I'm used to Jong pranking me," said Naeem. "You just surprised me."

Kit nodded, but his mind was elsewhere. As they walked back to KSH House together, Kit cast confused glances at Naeem.

Naeem stopped and glared at Kit. "What's wrong with you?"

Kit hesitated, unsure of what to reveal. "What do you know of your parents? Your birth parents, I mean."

"I told you already. Nothing. Why?" Naeem turned and trudged forward as if to distance himself from the topic.

Kit fell behind Naeem as he organized his thoughts. That Naeem was an Earthborn threlphax host had ramifications for Naeem's parents, who were mere humans. "There are things—characteristics—that we might share," he said, "like some unique attribute."

Naeem continued walking, unaware of the weight of the statement.

Kit held his hand up behind the boy, palm out. Tiny glittering translucent tendrils emerged, creating a shimmer across his palm. "Naeem.," he said. "Be still."

Naeem's shoulders slumped as he came to a halt in obedience to the command. Kit dropped his arm and moved around to face Naeem, now in a stupor. Naeem's vacant and unfocused eyes waited for instruction as his mouth hung slightly open and his body swayed back and forth.

Kit placed his palm against Naeem's chest, sensing the energy he felt a moment before. When he found it, he said, "Come forward."

The teen inhaled a deep breath, straightened, and met Kit's gaze. A faint glow filled his amber eyes.

"Who are you?" Naeem asked.

"I am a friend." As an Earthborn threlphax, Naeem would not understand who he was. It was best to keep things simple.

Naeem nodded, drew his brows together, and asked, "Who am I?"

"You are part of this vessel called Naeem," replied Trax. "You are an observer and companion. You are an Earthborn threlphax, a being of energy who helps maintain this vessel."

"How did I come to be?"

"You existed in this vessel as an awakened being. As an infant, you existed without knowing, nourished by the energy of this vessel. I have made you aware."

Nodding again, Naeem smiled. "Yes. The energy of Naeem's thoughts nourishes me."

"Now, Naeem's experience will become yours as your energies merge."

"What about Jackson and Renuka?"

"They are merely human and know nothing of the threlphax."

Naeem frowned. "That saddens me."

Kit wondered whether he did the right thing in making Naeem's Earthborn threlphax aware. He acted without calculating the implications. More importantly, Naeem's threlphax expressed sadness at having parents who were not like him. Both Chanchai and Tae-soo understood the pain of that lonely existence.

For now, he would keep Naeem's Earthborn threlphax a secret. Taking a step back, Kit raised his palm to Naeem's eye level and said, "Forget."

The glow in Naeem's eyes faded as he closed them for a moment. When he opened them, he recoiled when he saw Kit standing in front of him. He spun around to where Kit was moments ago. "How did you . . . ?" he asked, pointing in both directions.

"I'm sorry," said Kit as he realized his blunder in not returning to his original position while Naeem was in his stupor. "I didn't mean to leap out at you. It must appear strange."

"Yeah, well, you are a strange person," said Naeem as he pushed past Kit to continue on to KSH House. Naeem was agitated, even as he brushed off the inconsistency.

Hoping that playful repartee might ease the tension, Kit said, "No, you're the strange one."

"No, you are," replied Naeem, latching onto Kit's good-natured taunt. "No, you are."

They continued their lighthearted banter as they walked through the forest, across the field, and back to KSH House.

46
MANIFESTATION

(SEPTEMBER 20, 2019)

Kit wasn't sure whether it was a surreal dream or the energy fluctuations that woke him up. He rolled on his side and checked his cell phone: 1:23 a.m. Behind the window curtain, moonlight illuminated the floor and wall. Kit sat on the edge of the bed and drew his hands through his hair.

"Are you okay?" Jong's sleep-drenched voice broke the silence.

"I just need to use the bathroom."

"Okay," exhaled Jong. He rolled over and pulled an extra pillow into a hug.

Once in the bathroom, Kit's eyes adjusted to the light. After emptying his bladder, he washed his hands and splashed warm water on his face. He stared at his features, so familiar yet somehow altered.

Most notably, his eyes were no longer the dark brown that belonged to Tae-soo, nor were they the crystalline caramel color associated with Chanchai. Caramel-colored bands ringed the pupils and transitioned into dark brown. The edge of his irises were ringed with a gold border.

This was new. What questions would Jong ask when he saw these eyes? Would he casually comment about them or seek an explanation?

Jong.

His eyes glowed slightly as his thoughts turned to his lover, but this no longer frightened him. The change related to who he was now, yet he needed time to adjust to the shift of energy signatures and flows. Taking a deep breath, he closed his eyes and relaxed. When he opened his eyes, his irises reflected the familiar dark brown shade associated with Tae-soo.

For how long?

Before he returned to his room, he stopped on the landing. Someone moved through KSH House below him. Kit leaned on the railing and watched for activity in the main foyer.

Sameer emerged from his room and disappeared into the office. Moments later, he took the stairs to the basement.

Sameer suspects.

Sameer's connection with the threlphax tribe already proved a challenge, and his descent to the basement worried Kit. He didn't need the threlphax tribe to reveal his secret.

Curiosity turned into an insatiable desire to know Sameer's intent. Kit quietly descended the staircase, crossed through the main foyer, and took the stairs to the basement. The door to the small storage room hung open.

Invitation?

Trap?

Kit peeked around the corner of the doorway. Sameer sat on the floor in a pose of meditation. On the shelves at the far end of the room, the faint glow of the threlphax vessels intensified. Did the threlphax sense Kit's presence?

Sameer turned and looked towards the doorway. Kit pulled back and froze. Pinpricks of energy circulated through him as he sought to gain control of his energy flows. Already suspicious of him, what reason could Kit give for being there? He should have never followed Sameer to the basement.

What to do?

Sameer knew too much, and the threlphax reaction to Kit's presence reinforced that knowledge. Kit hurried toward the staircase.

Before he reached the first step, Sameer asked, "Why are you hiding?"

Kit stopped and turned to face Sameer, who stood outside the vessel room. Candor was the best choice. "I saw you come downstairs," Kit said.

"I was curious. I wondered what you were doing in the middle of the night. I see you were meditating. Now, I'm going back upstairs."

"The threlphax have waited for you for too long," said Sameer. "Mussick, Taedlum, and even Denyal feel the resonance of your energy artifact. So do the threlphax vessels."

"I'm going back to bed," said Kit.

As Kit put a foot on the step, Sameer called out, "Trax."

Kit paused as the name of the threlphax tribe leader reverberated through him.

No.

Not yet.

But soon.

"Goodnight, Sameer," Kit said. He continued up the staircase, seeking sanctuary with Jong.

47
FLOW

(SEPTEMBER 25, 2019)

Kit dribbled the soccer ball several yards before kicking it back up the field. Jong took control of the ball before Naeem could reach it. After a brief skirmish, Jong relinquished control. to the more determined teen. Naeem raised his arms and laughed triumphantly before dribbling the soccer ball across the field.

Kit felt Naeem's Earthborn threlphax energy even at this distance.

What to do about Naeem?

Sameer did nothing.

Naeem kicked the soccer ball high in the air. Kit backed up and waited for the ball to hit the ground before capturing it beneath the press of his foot. He smirked, then turned toward Jong. When he kicked the ball to Naeem's right, Naeem grunted as he ran and twisted his body to kick the ball toward Jong.

Does Tae-hee know?

Tae-hee had spent the past week introducing Seung-do to the medical staff at Community Care Hospital. As an accredited South Korean medical professional, Tae-hee had convinced the administrators that he would be a welcome addition to the hospital, even as a short-term advisor.

Kit returned his focus to Naeem, a happy middle-schooler with friends on the soccer team and an extended family at KSH House.

Naeem doesn't know.

Tae-hee is an Earthborn threlphax.

Jackson, Renuka, and Jong are mere humans.

The incident in the threlphax room had faded from Jong's focus. With the fall session now in full swing, he spent a good portion of the workweek at Sempiternity University, returning each evening with a bright smile on his face.

What are we planning to do?

Jong kicked the ball toward Naeem, who caught it and dribbled it in a circle. He kicked it toward Kit, who passed it to Jong.

Jong.

After the incident, Jong gave Kit space to recuperate. But last night, Jong confronted him. Kit sat on the end of the bed while Jong leaned against the dresser, his arms crossed over his chest.

"I told you I'm an expert judge of people, right?" Jong said.

"Yes."

"I can tell that the experience changed you."

Kit had prepared a response for this moment. "I didn't tell you, but after I came to KSH House, I suffered headaches. I told Tae-hee, but there was nothing I could do. After I lost consciousness in the basement, my headaches disappeared. That's a good thing, right?"

Jong relaxed enough to unfold his arms. "Yes. That's good," he said. But it was clear the explanation didn't allay Jong's concerns. "You're not hiding something else from me, right?"

Kit had stood and cupped his hand along Jong's cheek. He ran his thumb over Jong's lips, then leaned in and kissed him. It was the only assurance he could offer. When he withdrew, he stared into Jong's eyes. "I can't tell you what happened to me in that room. But I need you to know that whatever happened doesn't change my feelings for you."

"I don't question that. I just worry that you aren't telling me everything."

Nothing Kit said could sway Jong from his suspicion.

"Jong, I'm okay. I just need time. Please be patient." Kit continued the masquerade even though he hated to hide the truth from Jong. It might have been a mistake for Kit to fall in love with a human. Chanchai and Tae-soo could suffer because of it.

48
TURNING

(OCTOBER 1, 2019)

As the days passed, Kit unobtrusively tried to connect with Naeem's Earthborn threlphax, but getting time alone with him was difficult. Naeem had a hectic schedule with school and soccer practice. His loving but human parents would not understand how to guide the host of an Earthborn threlphax. Without proper guidance, the threlphax within Naeem might never mature enough to understand its potential.

Kit's concern for Naeem became an obsession that required action. Apart from Tae-soo and Tae-hee, Naeem was the only other Earthborn threlphax host he had encountered. These Earthborn threlphax hosts needed to explore their capabilities. How could Jackson and Renuka, mere humans with no knowledge of the threlphax, offer any help to Naeem?

They are Naeem's parents.

They are not like Naeem. They cannot guide him.

Before arriving at KSH House, Chanchai and Tae-soo experienced life without a threlphax host to guide them. While there was no one to blame for their circumstances, Naeem was different. Threlphax hosts surrounded him, yet they did not act. As mere humans, Jackson and Renuka could become obstacles, limiting his potential. At the same time, it would be wrong for Jackson and Renuka not to benefit from what Naeem derived as a threlphax host.

At the apex of his agitation, Kit decided he could delay no longer. While action might turn KSH House against him, he trusted that his connection with Tae-hee, perhaps even Jong, would afford him some forgiveness. Even Sameer and Seung-do would understand, given their initial encounters with the threlphax.

With those assurances in mind, he resolved to set the Jones family on a unified path forward.

After brunch, Sameer and Jong traveled to the airport to retrieve packages from customs. Abhimanyu met with another contact on his quest for information about Chymzafyde. Tae-hee took Seung-do to the hospital for an orientation, and Emily ran several errands.

The local school district was on some sort of administrative holiday. While Naeem dribbled his soccer ball outside, Renuka sat in the office with Jackson as he reviewed the latest sales inventory.

Kit went to the kitchen and pulled two steak knives from the utensil drawer. He tucked them into the pocket of his hoodie sweatshirt, then wandered out of the kitchen into the office. Renuka stood behind Jackson, arranging his dreadlocks into a neat bun.

Kit asked Jackson for the key to the small storage room.

Concerned, Jackson asked, "Why do you want it?"

"I need to go back," Kit explained. "It's a 'face your fears' thing."

Jackson glanced at Renuka.

"Is that a good idea?" Renuka asked. "Isn't it better to wait for Sameer and Seung-do?"

Kit scratched the back of his head. "Do you think you can come with me? I just want to visit that room for a few minutes."

"Ah, okay. Fine," replied Jackson. Renuka elbowed him, and he shrugged. "It's just for a few minutes," he said.

Jackson grabbed the keyring, and they descended the stairs to the basement. He unlocked the door, and Kit entered the small storage room. Jackson and Renuka remained outside as Kit flipped on the light switch, walked to the center of the room, and closed his eyes.

Stop.

Don't do this.

Heaving a deep sigh, Kit turned around and held out his arms, palms raised upwards. "See? Nothing happened this time." He walked over to the shelves laden with innumerable threlphax vessels. Each elongated vessel—the length of a small egg—bore a unique ornate design and protected a threlphax being of energy. "Have you ever seen one of these up close?"

"No," said Jackson and Renuka in unison.

"Sameer has always been clear about the room. Stay out. I'm nervous just standing here." Jackson said.

Renuka was less apprehensive. She raised a hand toward the threlphax vessels. "What are those?" she asked. "Do they serve a purpose? Or are they just for decoration?"

"Come here and look," Kit said.

"I don't think Sameer would approve," said Jackson.

"A quick look couldn't hurt, could it?" Renuka was more easily swayed.

"Just take a look, then we can leave," Kit said as he picked up a threlphax vessel. "They are stunning."

Don't.

Renuka tugged gently on Jackson's shirt and wobbled her head. Jackson scowled, then rolled his eyes and nodded. The sharp click of Renuka's heels mocked the calm of the room. Sturdier footfalls followed as Jackson joined her.

Kit picked up a second vessel with an ornate design similar to the first. The design reflected their relationship and role in the threlphax tribe. But neither Jackson nor Renuka knew this. Kit handed a vessel to each of them, saying, "Do you see the faint ornate decorations? Ethereal, aren't they?"

"What do these do?" asked Renuka, cradling the vessel in her palm. "I mean, what is their purpose?"

"They're a collector's item," said Jackson. "It's weird that we've never tried to sell them."

"Would you accept these if they were a gift?"

Bewildered, Renuka and Jackson exchanged glances. "These belong to Sameer, don't they?" asked Renuka.

"Those belong to me," replied Kit. "Please accept them."

"Are you sure we can have these?" asked Renuka.

"Say you'll accept them, and they are yours."

"I'll accept this gift," said Renuka. "Thank you."

Renuka elbowed Jackson, prompting him to respond. "Oh, yeah," he said. "I'll accept this. Thanks."

Putting his hands in the pocket of his sweatshirt, Kit wrapped his fingers around the handles of each steak knife. He steeled himself as he watched Renuka and Jackson examine the threlphax vessels. He drew in a deep breath.

"Renuka, Jackson. I am sorry."

Before his apology could even sink in, Kit moved. In one swift, merciless motion, he withdrew the knives and drove them deep into Renuka and Jackson.

Their eyes widened in shock, and their mouths parted in silent, breathless disbelief. The vessels slipped from their hands, crashing to the ground, forgotten. Their fingers trembled as they grasped Kit's hands, still wrapped around the hilts buried in their midsections.

The damage was done.

There was no turning back.

Kit withdrew the blades.

"Why? What have you done?" choked Jackson, his eyes wide in disbelief, his bloodied hand pressing against his wound.

Jackson and Renuka collapsed to the floor.

"It's okay, Jackson, Renuka," said Kit. "Soon, you will understand."

Kit's reassuring words made no difference. "Hold on, babe," Jackson gasped. Reaching a blood-stained hand out to Renuka, he repeated, "Babe, I'm here. I'm here, babe."

Kit surveyed the terrible scene he had created. With one hand, Jackson tried to help stem the flow of blood seeping out of Renuka as he held his other hand against his wound. Ignoring their assailant, they focused on each other.

He picked up the vessels and held each in an open palm. Glittering translucent tendrils snaked out and hovered over Renuka and Jackson.

"These humans accepted you and are your new vessels," murmured Kit. "They are our friends. Merge and heal them."

Glittering translucent tendrils extended from the vessels to blanket Jackson and Renuka. Threlphax flowed through flesh, muscle, and bone to integrate with the human energy signatures and repair the host vessels.

This will work.

No one will ever trust us again.

This must work.

Kit watched the tension drain from their limbs as they drifted into unconsciousness.

We should have told them.

Why didn't we tell them?

They will understand soon.

Kit placed the empty vessels back on the shelf, his movements deliberate and steady. Then, he crouched between Jackson and Renuka and pressed his palms gently over their wounds. A soft glow flickered to life beneath his hands. When it faded, Kit stood.

They no longer bleed.

We were impatient.

"Kit?" Jong stood just inside the door, his eyes wide as he surveyed the scene. "What's happening?"

Seung-do pushed past Jong and rushed into the room, followed by Sameer. He shoved Kit aside as he and Sameer checked Renuka and

Jackson's condition. Although the couple was unconscious, they were both alive. Sameer picked up Renuka in his arms and carried her out of the room.

"Jong," said Seung-do. "Help me carry Jackson."

Jong followed Seung-do's instructions. He lifted Jackson onto Seung-do's back and followed them out of the room.

Kit stood alone. What was done could not be undone. Turning to the shelves of threlphax vessels, he raised his hand and moved it in a slow, deliberate arc.

Trax will not abandon you.

Be silent now.

After he washed the blades and his hands at the utility sink, Kit placed the knives on the counter. He dampened a sponge and returned to the vessel room, where two small pools of blood stained the floor. Crouching down, he squeezed water from the sponge onto the bloodstains. He held his hand over the bloody mess and, when his palm glowed, moved it over the stains until the mixture of water and blood bubbled and evaporated. The glow faded, and Kit stood up and confirmed that the bloodstains were gone. He buried the sponge in a trash bag that he tied shut.

When he emerged from the back entrance to the basement, he saw Naeem kicking the ball across the field. The boy stopped and checked his phone, unaware of events inside KSH House.

They will not forgive us.

But they will soon understand.

Kit deposited the trash bag in the garbage can and pulled out his phone. The Uber would arrive soon. He walked across the gravel parking lot to the trees lining the street. Retrieving his backpack and the duffle bag he had stashed there, he waited for the ride to take him away from KSH House and back to the loft apartment.

49
CHANGED

(OCTOBER 1, 2019)

Nearly two hours ago, he had turned Jackson and Renuka into threlphax hosts. It was a necessary act based on his understanding of the situation. He checked the time on his phone as he waited for the fallout.

You were too rash.

You should have talked to them first.

He sat on the sofa in the loft apartment, trying to calm his energy. Once the merge was complete, they would understand it was the right decision. He was sure of it. Sameer had demonstrated the healing power of the threlphax by slicing the palm of his hand. He used a variant of Sameer's technique on Jackson and Renuka. He knew it would speed the merge and they would heal. Besides, both Chanchai and Tae-soo survived much more devastating wounds and lived.

Despite his reasoning, he knew it was a violent act. Although Tae-soo and Chanchai had experienced the violence of war, what he did was different. While there was a logical reason for injuring his friends, they would characterize it as an unprovoked attack.

Mussick understands.

He will explain everything.

Someone entered the passcode on the door lock. He placed his phone on the coffee table, stood up, and braced himself.

Jong entered, his eyes wide, his face red with rage. He strode over to Kit and punched him hard in the face. Kit fell backward onto the sofa and reached a hand to his bruised cheek.

"What the hell did you do, Kit?" Jong demanded as he towered over him.

"It had to be done," he said.

"Why, Kit?! They are our friends. What about Naeem?"

"It was for Naeem—"

"—That makes no sense, Kit!"

"They needed to know—"

"—What did they need to know, Kit?"

"They needed to understand—"

"—What did they need to understand that required you to stab them?"

Frustrated that Jong wouldn't let him finish a sentence, he jumped up and yelled, "NAEEM IS A THRELPHAX HOST!"

Jong's expression changed from rage to bewilderment. "What do you mean Naeem is a host?"

"We just discovered it."

"Even if he is, what does that have to do with you?"

"We didn't know how to tell his parents."

"So, you thought stabbing them was the best choice?" yelled Jong.

"They need to be hosts to understand how to raise Naeem."

Jong grabbed his collar, shaking him. "But they are our friends, Kit," Jong growled. "How could you hurt them?"

"Sameer demonstrated the healing power of the threlphax to you. Seung-do told you that threlphax merge more rapidly in an injured vessel. What we did to turn them into threlphax hosts was no different."

"Did you even think to ask them?"

"YES!" he yelled. He shrugged out of Jong's grasp. "If they said no, it would hurt Naeem!" Righteous anger overtook any doubts he had. "You can't understand the struggles he'd face without threlphax hosts to guide him. Tae-soo and Chanchai know it. They lived it!"

"You gave them no choice!"

"We gave them a long life together! It was a gift!" He rested his hands on his hips and exhaled his frustration, seeking a calm and steady tone. "Naeem is special," he said. "To raise him, they must understand him. They must be like him."

"I'm not like you. Are you going to stab me and turn me into a host, too?"

"This is what they want. They just don't know it yet."

"Damn you, Kit! What happened to you?" Jong pleaded for the answer that the threlphax host was not ready to give.

He turned away from Jong, leaned on the table, and hung his head. Closing his eyes, he took a deep breath, releasing himself to the powerful energy signature that lay latent for so long. He straightened and faced Jong

"Your eyes . . ." The stunned look on Jong's face confirmed the shift.

Even without a mirror, the threlphax host knew what Jong saw—caramel to dark brown irises ringed by thin gold bands.

The sound of the keypad broke the silence, and Sameer Khan entered the loft apartment.

"Who are you?" Jong asked. "Kit could never do this."

Sameer strode over to them. "That's not Kit," he said.

Jong's attention shot to Sameer. "What do you mean, he's not Kit?"

The threlphax host knew Sameer had waited for this moment, predicated by a violent act only the threlphax understood. The threlphax host could pretend no longer.

It is time.

"When Kit first arrived, the threlphax vessels glowed," said Sameer. "That was because he hosted Trax."

"Trax?" repeated Jong. Confused, he waited for the man he knew as Kit to respond.

Kit-now-Trax sighed. Despite the pain of the moment, a great weight was lifted from his shoulders. It was time to take his place as leader of the

Trax appreciated Sameer's unbiased assessment of the situation. But such an objective analysis had come too late. "How long have you known that Naeem hosts an Earthborn threlphax?" Trax asked.

"Since Jackson and Renuka introduced him as their son."

"Yet, you did nothing."

Sameer should have known that Jackson and Renuka would be unable to guide Naeem. The boy would be lost, disconnected from his parents—or worse, resentful of the unperceived power his threlphax energy wielded—and Sameer chose inaction. Although Trax knew the accusation was unfair to Sameer, the fact remained that action had to be taken for the sake of Naeem and his Earthborn threlphax.

"I did what I could," said Sameer.

"And we did what was needed." The violent act that critically injured Jackson and Renuka made the threlphax merge fast and deep. The threlphax quickly repaired the physical injuries. Even so, Trax failed to fully account for the psychological impact that might extend beyond the moment. Even for Trax, the memory of the deed, now embedded in the human-threlphax merge, caused fluctuations in energy flows. Had he miscalculated his decision?

No one forgets the violence done to them.

Or done to someone they love.

Jong had rejected the threlphax leader for the heinous act. He punched him and called him a snake. The memory of what Trax did—and its repercussions—was now an integral part of his threlphax energy signature and could only be purged by Conveyance.

Trax focused on calming the flow of his energy.

"What do you need me to do?" asked Sameer. Whether it was the loyalty of Sameer's threlphax, Mussick, or the compassion of the human host, Trax was relieved that Sameer approached him with genuine sincerity.

Trax held his hand out to Sameer, palm up. Tiny glittering translucent tendrils emerged and wafted across his palm.

Sameer stepped forward. "What will happen if I take hold of your hand?"

"Your threlphax, Mussick, will remember more."

Sameer frowned. "When Mroniea unsealed Mussick's memories, it was not pleasant."

Trax tried to hide his slight grin. Mroniea and Mussick were threlphax twins, but the cores of their energy signatures were vastly different. Mussick was devoted to Trax, whereas Mroniea's assault on Trax's energy signature was why the threlphax tribe fell.

As observers of the universe, it seemed perversely ironic that both Mroniea and Trax had executed violent acts.

"Mroniea is not yet a recognized threlphax leader," Trax said. "I promise to be gentle. We will only share the memories that will help you assist Jackson and Renuka."

Sameer hesitated before taking Trax's hand and closing his eyes. A soft glow emerged between their clasped hands. Trax watched Sameer's changing expression as memories flowed between them. The glow faded, and Trax pulled his tendrils back into himself. When Sameer opened his eyes, Trax held him steady as he adjusted to the shared visions.

"Thank you," replied Sameer as he unclasped their hands. "You kept your promise."

Trax nodded, then shared the information he had struggled with since he emerged from Kit. "Sameer, we feel the energy fragments of thousands of threlphax. Since you must guide Jackson and Renuka, send Abhimanyu to assist us."

Shaken by Trax's disclosure, Sameer wobbled his head in affirmation.

"And Sameer, we never intended to deceive you," continued Trax. "The injury caused by Mroniea was significant. Rather than risk the life of our host by transforming his energy, we chose to restore our energy through limited dormancy. When we entered the vessel room, the threlphax tribe realigned the energy flow of our pathways. It was sudden and required negotiation." Trax placed a hand on Sameer's shoulder. "We know what we did to Jackson and Renuka wasn't without consequences. We promise to do better. We will protect the tribe."

After Sameer left, Trax wondered if the worst was over. While he was sure of his actions, he had hurt the members of KSH House.

They will never trust us again.

Jong will never trust us again.

Trax grabbed his chest, feeling an ache that spread throughout his body to the tips of his fingers and toes. It was an ache he wasn't unfamiliar with but hadn't experienced often. Trax sank to the floor, unable to control the intense fluctuations of his energy signatures.

By hurting them, we hurt ourself.

* * * *

Five minutes after leaving the loft apartment, Jong stopped on the shoulder of the road. Grief, rage, and confusion made it dangerous to drive. Jong was broken. The man he loved did something reprehensible, then claimed to be someone else.

He pounded the back of his head against the headrest and screamed. A moment later, he exhaled and tried to calm down. "Get a hold of yourself, Jong," he muttered. "You can get through this."

As he put his hand on the key in the ignition, he remembered swinging the key ring on his finger when he took Kit home the day his secrets were revealed. Everything was fine then. Jong accepted everything. Was it all just a sham? Was Trax really that much different from Kit? *When Sameer came in*, thought Jong, *his attitude toward Trax was different than it was with Kit.*

"He's not human," murmured Jong. "He's really not human."

Though he promised himself he would not cry, he could not prevent the tears that mercilessly poured out of him. He gave in and let the torrent of emotions run its course.

It was dark when Jong returned to KSH House. After the assault, Sameer and Seung-do refused to involve the police. With Jackson and

Renuka's wounds healed and the crime scene cleaned, police would find little evidence to arrest Trax. Besides, he was the tribe leader. They needed him.

Jong went to his room to check on Jackson and Renuka. They were asleep. Half-full saline bags hung on hooks above each of them. What would they do when they woke? Would they try to call the police and press charges? Or would they be happy that they were now threlphax hosts? Jong had difficulty visualizing either scenario.

As he approached Lee Seung-do's room, he noticed the door was slightly ajar. He pushed it open and saw Naeem lying on one of the twin beds, his back toward the door. Jong quietly closed it and went downstairs to look for the others. As he crossed the foyer, he sensed a shift in the ambiance of KSH House.

After checking the auction hall and the office, Jong heard voices in the basement. He paused to eavesdrop on the conversation. The only word he could understand was the one he didn't want to hear: "Trax."

He descended the staircase to the basement. Stopping at the turn of the stairs, he saw Sameer, Abhimanyu, Seung-do, Emily, and Tae-hee standing outside the small storage room. Seung-do noticed Jong first, and his gaze drew the attention of the others.

Jong trudged down the stairs and walked over to them. "Kit's gone," he said quietly. "He says his name is Trax, now."

Emily shot a glance at Lee Seung-do and Sameer.

"He said he did it because Naeem is a host. He said Naeem is precious, and Jackson and Renuka needed to become hosts to understand and guide him. He said we couldn't be together anymore because I was a 'mere human.'"

Jong searched the faces of his friends. For the first time, knowing they were threlphax hosts caused him pain. Upstairs lay another three hosts. Everyone he had come to know and love in KSH House was a threlphax host. He was the only "mere human" in this group. If Trax was the leader of the threlphax, would his rejection of Jong influence them?

Do I even belong here anymore? wondered Jong. He shook his head and turned away, heading back to the staircase.

"Where are you going?" asked Tae-hee.

Jong paused and quietly said, "Somewhere where there are other 'mere humans.'"

50
ENKIDU

(OCTOBER 3, 2019)

The shadow of the restaurant awning darkened the window and revealed his reflection. Although he hadn't aged in millennia, Enkidu's long hair had turned gray. If he had never cut his hair in his long life, his tresses might be kilometers long. The thought amused him. Hair that long would make life difficult.

Movement beyond the window glass drew his attention. Mroniea Hadwyn Clarke walked along the sidewalk on the other side of the street. The Anti's only redeeming quality was that he was annoyingly punctual.

Mroniea first captured Enkidu's attention in Shimla after an unfortunate incident with another threlphax host. He pursued Mroniea from India to Italy, England to America, intent on turning the abomination's tribe leader against him.

Enkidu's tribe arrived here long before Mroniea and his tribe. As the leader of a threlphax tribe that would be considered ancient by human standards, he understood the value of maintaining protocol. Enkidu could only dissipate members of his tribe and their Earthborn descendants.

Mroniea required dissipation. The Anti didn't belong in this universe, and it appalled Enkidu that Mroniea's tribe leader had let the abomination exist. Enkidu used the drug Mroniea created to implicate the Anti in the dissipation of threlphax and their hosts. It would be a sure sign the

Anti was a threat to his tribe. The leader of Mroniea's tribe would fulfill his role by eliminating the abomination.

However, Enkidu's interest now flowed in another direction. He felt the echo of a sudden energy shift. The threlphax leader he sought to enrage had finally emerged. Despite Enkidu's repeated provocations, that stubborn being of energy had refused to emerge for over a century and a half.

Before emergence, Trax existed in the vessel of a Thai youth who grew into manhood, unaware of his threlphax self. Although they met several times, Enkidu sealed away memories of their meetings as he waited for the powerful threlphax leader to show itself. When it did, Enkidu planned to unseal the recollections of their many encounters. From there, they would become close friends and allies.

In his quest to force Mroniea's dissipation, he hadn't considered that Trax was Mroniea's tribe leader. This complicated his plans. The compassionate vessel hosting Trax could influence the threlphax leader into altruism toward Mroniea.

Enkidu had followed Mroniea to the Sempiternity University campus, where the Anti had obtained employment as a professor. Surprisingly, the Anti seemed unaware of Enkidu's presence, giving Enkidu time to strengthen his efforts to turn Mroniea into the pariah he needed him to be. To do that, he would meet *her*. Whether by coincidence or fate, *she* held a position of power at NeuBio Research. He would use *her* to accomplish his goal.

Enkidu exited the restaurant and followed the path of residual energy. It led him to the parking garage beneath the corporate offices of NeuBio Research, conveniently located near the university campus. A few years ago, he discovered her familiar threlphax energy trail, but the security on the premises put him off.

A small burst of energy from his fingertips disabled a CCTV camera. Before the guard noticed his approach, Enkidu shot bursts of energy that overwhelmed the human until he lost consciousness. He arranged the guard so incoming traffic wouldn't see him, then followed the ramp down to the elevator lobby.

A few cars arrived and discharged their occupants, who entered the elevator lobby and gave Enkidu a cursory examination as they passed. He ignored them, focusing instead on the latest news that piqued his interest on his smartphone. They had no reason to question him if he ignored them. He occasionally looked up at his reflection in the concave mirror. While Enkidu managed to maintain his vessel's existence, his tribe had forced the dissipation of his vessel's human energy signature. It was a devastating betrayal by his tribe.

A red sedan descended the ramp and parked in a reserved space beside the elevator lobby. A woman wearing a brown suit exited the car. Her dark sunglasses and brown hair arranged in a tight bun gave her a stern appearance that was tempered by the colorful scarf around her neck. After retrieving a briefcase and purse, she came around the back of the car. She halted when she saw Enkidu.

"Oh, my," she said, drawing her hand across her midsection. "You are here. I haven't felt your artifact in so long. It's quite exhilarating."

Enkidu remained silent, uncertain how to respond to her favorable impression of his presence.

"Just a minute," the woman said. She pulled out her phone and placed a call on speakerphone.

"Richard Carver, NeuBio Research," a voice answered.

"Richard. This is Izzy Hale." Holding the phone inches from her face, she stared at Enkidu as she spoke. "I have encountered a wrinkle in my plans. Could we reschedule our meeting for tomorrow?"

"Yes, Dr. Hale. Is there a problem?"

"No. I encountered unexpected personal business. Please email my assistant to say I'll be late today."

"Okay, then."

"Thank you, Richard." Izzy Hale ended the call. Her green eyes sparkled as she said, "Come with me." Correcting herself, she said, "No. I mean, please join me."

The *tap-tap-tap* of her shoes on the cement punctuated her return to the car. After she tossed her belongings into the back seat, she motioned for Enkidu to get in.

Izzy Hale started the car and put on her seatbelt. He stepped into the passenger seat. At the sound of a recurring beep, she raised her eyebrows and wagged her finger at Enkidu. He grunted and put on the seatbelt, which silenced the alarm.

As they reached the top of the garage ramp, she slowed the vehicle as she passed the unconscious guard slumped in the booth. "I suppose he didn't just fall asleep, did he?"

Enkidu stared out the window. There was no need for confirmation.

Pulling onto the roadway, she turned on the local radio station. "Sorry," she said. "Keeping tabs on the latest news is part of my job."

Fifteen minutes later, she pulled into a parking space at a small park. "There's a charming gazebo here. We can visit together without being bothered." She stepped from the car and waited for Enkidu to follow her along the paved path.

When they arrived at the gazebo, she removed her scarf and brushed off the bench. "As you overheard, I now go by the name of Dr. Izabella Hale," she said. "Hale as in 'hale and hearty.' Most colleagues call me 'Izzy.'" She sat and crossed her legs. "So, what do I call you? Father? Daddy? Papa?"

"Enkidu," he replied. Though she was his daughter by birth, they were more like familiar strangers than family. He entered the gazebo and sat on the bench on the opposite side.

"Yes, you gave up your parental rights when you left my mother."

"It could not be helped."

"Mummy loved you until her end, unaware that you were still alive. It would break her heart if she knew you abandoned us. I was twelve years old when they killed her."

Izzy Hale was the seed of a relationship that Enkidu had lost long ago, during one of his torpors. This was the first face-to-face encounter with his daughter in decades. She didn't know he watched over her in secret. Deep within his threlphax signature, Enkidu's energy flows held the promise to protect his hybrid daughter.

She concealed her horrendous childhood memories and acrimony toward him with a smile and simple words. Her mild diatribe sounded more bitter because her hair, face, and figure matched those of the woman who gave birth to her.

"So, Daddy," she said, "are you still feasting on your tribe?"

The provocation sent ripples through Enkidu's energy flows. She never understood what was required to maintain his physical vessel without a human energy signature. The tribe's betrayal caused his host's energy to dissipate. Appropriating the apostates' threlphax energy to maintain his existence was fair retribution. He glared at Izzy Hale.

Izzy Hale rolled her eyes. "Oh, stop," she said. "When your eyes glow like that, you remind me of a snorting bull."

The glow in his eyes reflected a lack of control. Enkidu calmed his energy flows and said, "I need you to do something for me."

"So much for the heartfelt reunion," she replied. With a bemused arch of her brow, she asked. "Did you know they wrote an epic poem about you? It was more about your friend Gilgamesh and your human host. They just rediscovered the work somewhere in the 1850s. Have you ever read it? Did you know that after he buried you, Gilgamesh sought immortality? Isn't it ironic that you were the one with immortality all along? If humans knew you powered the vessel of *the* Enkidu, would they worship you as a god?" Her smirk and the glint in her eye reinforced her amusement.

Enkidu frowned as he waited for his petulant offspring to finish her taunts. He could read her energy and knew she didn't hate him. But she didn't like him much, either. In her eyes, he had abandoned her, and her only weapon against him was to remind him of the tragedies of his ancient past.

"Well, it's nice to be needed, isn't it, Daddy?" Crossing her legs again, Izzy Hale leaned forward and asked, "Why approach me now, after all these years?"

Enkidu pursed his lips together in a frown. "Can NeuBio Research reverse engineer a drug?"

With a sweep of her hand, she said, "Yes. Yes, of course. Is it illegal?"

"It's called Chymzafyde," he said as he held out a vial of the compound. "It affects the merge between threlphax and human energy signatures."

"Isn't this dangerous for you to handle?"

Despite the discomfort Chymzafyde caused, Enkidu believed he endured it thanks to the absence of a human energy signature and the formidable strength of his threlphax energy as the leader of his tribe. Other threlphax would have succumbed to the drug.

Izzy Hale stared at Enkidu, waiting for a response. When he offered none, she crossed the gazebo and took the vial before sitting beside him. Sliding her arm through his, she said, "Do you know that I will be 340 years old on my next birthday? I stopped aging in my late twenties. I have been at NeuBio Research for five years. Soon, people will begin questioning my youthfulness. I shall have to abandon everything I've accomplished. I still have plans to fulfill before I go into hiding again. As a threlphax leader, you could help me achieve something big."

Quid pro quo. The minx wanted to use *him*. Threlphax leader abilities went far beyond granting good health and longevity to their hosts. They could manipulate and transform energy. Thought, matter, and willpower were theirs to control. Izzy Hale knew this. He pulled away from her. "What are you scheming?"

"My little research lab has developed a technology to recognize and sample threlphax energy. We've developed AI models that can decode the resonance of that energy. Recently, our instruments have detected a powerful threlphax source. While you are powerful, it wasn't you. It was much more formidable."

"Trax," muttered Enkidu under his breath.

"Trax?" repeated Izzy Hale. "Is Trax another threlphax leader? Do you know Trax?"

Enkidu glared at her. Yes, he knew Trax—but he refused to share anything that might lead her to him. "You want information I cannot provide." He pulled away from her and crossed to the other side of the gazebo. "I will decide whether to help you after you've fulfilled my request."

"Daddy!" exclaimed Izzy Hale, with a hint of a giggle. "You won't regret it! Together, we will reap the financial benefits of science. Wouldn't that be good for us?"

"There is no *us*."

"There could be, Daddy."

EPILOGUE

"Are you out of your mind?"

Jackson's outburst was to be expected. After all, four days ago, he and Renuka suffered an unprovoked, violent assault by someone they considered a friend.

Sameer Khan's calm disposition in the face of Jackson's rage kept the situation under control. As everyone fell silent, Emily Scott hung her head, letting her long auburn hair curtain her face. She stood in the doorway beside Tae-hee Kim, who hugged herself tightly, pressed down by self-accusation.

"What do you mean we are threlphax hosts?" said Jackson as he ran his hand over his midsection to the place where Trax skewered him with a kitchen knife. His voice bristled with anger, and his expression hardened, giving him a fierce look. "What the hell are you saying? What's a threlphax? Who the hell is Trax?"

"Jackson, you need to calm down," Sameer said.

"Don't tell me what I need to do."

"Jackson," said Renuka. "Let them explain."

Calmed by Renuka's gaze, he exhaled a hard breath, rolled his eyes, then glared at Sameer. "Were you in on it?"

"No, we didn't know."

"Can you remove these threlphax?"

"Removing them could harm the host," said Seung-do.

"You're kidding me." Jackson scowled at the threlphax hosts sitting across from him. "So, we are forced to live with these threlphax, with their alien energy buzzing around inside us?" He spat out the word threlphax through clenched teeth.

Sameer sighed and leaned forward. "Jackson, I apologize for what Trax did to you. But I believe he thought this was necessary."

"Because of me," Naeem muttered as he clenched his fists and stared at the space in front of him. "He did it because I'm different."

"Naeem," said Tae-hee. "Trax just wanted Jackson and Renuka to be like you—like us—so they can better understand you."

"Everything is messed up because of me," Naeem continued. He wrung his hands, his attention locked on their taut movements. "Jong left. Kit turned into Trax. Everyone is upset."

Jackson leaned over and wrapped his large hand around Naeem's. "This is not your fault, Naeem. None of this. It may take a little time, but we will get through this."

Sameer glanced at Seung-do and Abhimanyu, cleared his throat, then said, "There are benefits to being a threlphax host."

"Such as?" asked Jackson.

"Longevity, exceptional health, and—well, you'll stop aging."

Jackson's brows shot up. "That might've been worth mentioning a little sooner."

After a brief pause, Renuka asked, "What will happen to Trax and Jong?"

"Trax and Jong are part of KSH House," said Sameer. "We would like to bring them both back when everyone is ready."